The Blood Archive

by

Minerva Taylor

TELEMACHUS PRESS

Cover Designed by Telemachus Press, LLC

Cover Art:
Copyright © iStockPhoto 136326964
Copyright © iStockPhoto 771714/cold_morning_walk
Copyright © iStockPhoto 11085174 /yuri4u80
Copyright © iStockPhoto 15647142/Antagain

Interior Art:
Copyright © iStockPhoto14872931/Dvougao

Published by Telemachus Press, LLC
http://www.telemachuspress.com

Visit the author website:
http://www.thebloodstiller.com

ISBN: 978-1-940745-93-0 (eBook)
ISBN: 978-1-940745-94-7 (Paperback)

Version 2018.01.15

Printed in the United States of America

10 9 8 7 6 5 4 3 2 1

Also by Minerva Taylor

The Blood Stiller

Blood and Oil; The Devil's Tears

Children's Books

The Mole Brothers' Magnificent Mission

James and the Mini

For John

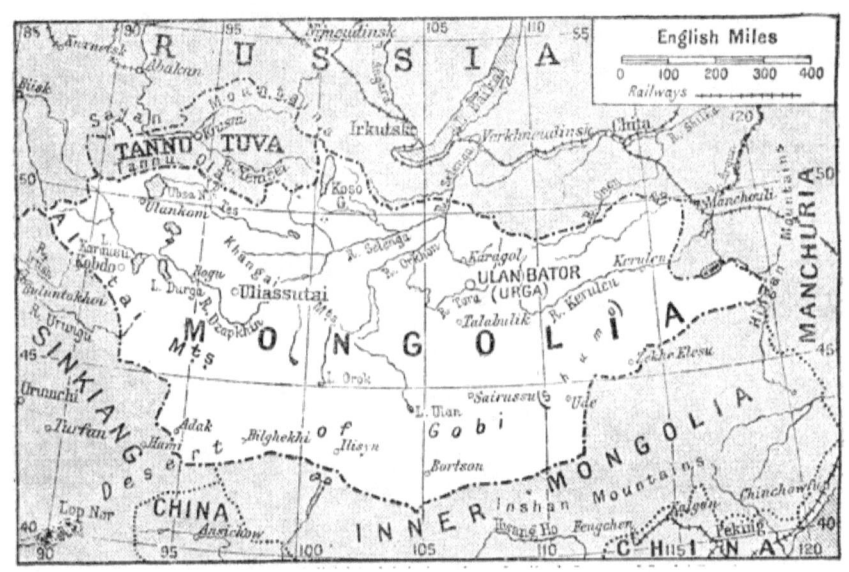

MONGOLIA: CAPITAL URGA;
IRKUTSK AND LAKE BAIKAL,
RUSSIA

MOSCOW CENTRAL: THE KREMLIN

MAGADAN, KOLYMA,
GULAG PRISON CAMPS

Dusha drugovo dremuchy les: 'The soul of another is a dark forest.'

Russian Proverb

The Blood Archive

Prologue

Siberia: 1946
Kolyma Gulag, Arctic Circle
Prison Camp 45 Kilometers
Women's Barracks

IN THE GRAY freezing barracks, a beautiful young woman grips the sides of the bare wooden bunk. She heaves and shudders in pain but does not cry out. Her large shining eyes seem focused elsewhere as though she has separated from her body. She emits a soft sigh, and the rim of the baby's head appears. An emaciated woman with arms like sticks pushes down on the young woman's stomach to force out the newborn and cuts the cord with a piece of rusty metal. She wraps the howling baby in a filthy rough cloth.

The patrol of the Mongolian People's Revolutionary Army had called her the Princess. Like a mystical vision from a past they didn't quite remember, she stood beside her Mongolian pony, straight, unafraid, in her rich fur lined silk quilted robes and soft leather embroidered boots worn against the cold. Her dark shiny hair was braided in an elaborate design that wheeled out above the slim delicate neck. Golden filigree earrings dangled from small perfect ears.

Her tawny soft skin, large dark almond shaped eyes and fine classical features suggested a race apart, a seed of Alexander the Great.

The patrol had discovered her in the Altai Mountains hiding within the ruins of a Buddhist monastery as though she had risen like an ancient deity out of its crumbling stones. The four men escorting her had resisted, but could do nothing against the troops and superior weapons. They were shot instantly and lay like piles of rags in the swirling dust. Body searches revealed that three of the men were Russian, the fourth a Mongolian.

Dorji Djambolon, the Mongol lieutenant in charge of the patrol, was alarmed when the local troops under his command knelt at the young woman's feet. He thought the three dead Russians were maybe important officials on some kind of mission for the great Stalin himself. None of the party possessed identification or the required passes. Gripped by indecision and fear, Dorji looked down at the leather folder one of the escorts had carried under his cloak. Flapping ominously in the strong wind, the folder contained papers he couldn't read but recognized were written in English. Surely this young woman, a magical creature like none they had ever seen, was subversive, one of those Japanese spies they had been hunting.

His questions, first in Russian and then in Mongolian, were short, commanding and hostile, but she did not seem to understand or perhaps was in shock at the death of her companions. Dorji, whose father was a loyal communist, an assistant to Choibalsan, the Mongolian leader, had been educated by the Russians at the Frunze Military Academy in Moscow. He was fully aware of the consequences if the unit killed Russians, maybe important Russians. It was prudent to shoot the woman and bury the entire party on this solitary mountain.

The lieutenant studied the unworldly figure standing motionless like an ancient statue before the firing squad, and on impulse, took out a Minolta camera, stolen during the war from the body of a dead Japanese officer. He snapped her picture and then knew he couldn't kill her. In spite of his privilege, his modern education and his faithful adherence to the communist party line, there were still remnants in his subconscious of a past religion, of spirits and prophecies. What if she were some mystic holy figure? Even though he would regret his actions, he dismissed the firing squad with a violent wave.

The soldiers did not discover she was pregnant until they had thrown her into the truck with forty terrified nomads, also arrested on charges of spying for the Japanese. The open bed truck bumped across the mountains and stopped at Goose Lake. The prisoners were crowded into a freezing cellar for the night in the ruined Buddhist monastery, and then continued across the border to Irkutsk in Russian Transbaikaila. There the suspected spies were herded into a rail cattle car with little water or food. The patrol's name for her, the Princess, was carried along in the unheated boxcar, which tracked slowly across Siberia to Vladivostok. The bewildered nomads, desperate for water, licked the black icicles hanging down in the car. They bowed down to her, pleading with the Princess to save them. She raised her hand in a benediction, and they chanted the Buddhist prayer, *The Jewel in the Lotus,* until the guards banged their rifles on the boxcar and threatened to kill them if they were not silent.

Crowded onto a boat, the prisoners' wretched journey continued across the sea of Okhotsk past Japan. When the boat docked at Magadan, the gateway to Kolyma camps, the nomads protecting the Princess were dead and the captain of the boat had taken her fur-lined coat. At the camp reception waiting criminals fell like vultures on the new arrivals. Screaming and spitting, the *urki* ripped off her jewelry and viciously beat her, leaving her lovely face a mass of bruises. When they finished, the Princess possessed only a thin muslin slip to protect her from a cold that climbed mercilessly like a deadly vine through her limbs.

At Camp 45 the baby moved and kicked furiously to get out as the guards stripped, shaved, and washed her down. Then she was given a *bushlat,* a prison jacket lined with wadding, a rough pair of trousers and felt boots. Their actions failed to dim her luminous beauty. Shivering, her skin turning darker from the biting Arctic cold, she felt her water break, and knew he soon would be free. Her labor pains had already begun when she was dumped at the women's barracks.

Still trembling from her effort, she raises her head and stares at her newborn. Her dark eyes burn and she whispers, "He is the one designated by blood."

Circling the cot, the emaciated women prisoners, many destined to perish, their bodies crumbling into camp dust, do not understand the language. Only one of them who survived the camp later swore it was English and knew the uttered words. The Princess closes her eyes. Her precious blood flows, running swiftly out of her, taking life away.

"The Princess is dead," the woman announces. For a moment she holds the squirming crying baby, a boy with tufts of pale gold hair that glow like fire in the falling darkness.

Rural Ohio: November 2000

It is an idyllic winter landscape, the kind photographed for Christmas cards and calendars. Lush snow-covered trees in the vast forest surround the small cabin like a Baroque frame. It is noon, but snow clouds brood over the isolated farmhouse, obscuring the sun. Two tiny black dots appear in the picture, moving away from the cabin toward the edge of the massive forest. A closer look through a telescopic lens would reveal a slim powerfully built man wearing white camouflage clothes and a balaclava. A sniper rifle is strapped to his shoulder. He stops over the dark bundle he has dragged into the trees and kicks it several times in frustration. There is a slight gushy sound as air escapes from the body.

"*Pizda, Suka,*" he swears, touching his forehead where the balaclava has become soaked with blood. Grazed by the woman's shotgun when he approached the cabin, he had been forced to kill her with his pistol. He had wanted to capture her alive to squeeze the information from her. Through the holes of the white balaclava, his eyes are dull like Bakelite as a brief picture of how he would have accomplished her interrogation passes before him.

He had searched the cabin for any trace of the archive but found nothing of significance, only ashes from burnt rolls of camera film, and on the kitchen table, an open bottle of champagne beside two expensive crystal goblets. The bitch had burned and destroyed everything that could be a clue for his client. After giving up the search, he thoroughly went over every inch of the cabin twice, wiping away all prints, blood and any traces of either him or the dead woman before dragging her into the woods.

The snow is heavy, up to his knees, and he is exhausted from his job begun before sunrise with the hard twenty-mile trek through the forest. He quickly takes the snowshoes from his backpack and fastens them to his boots. The snow has become a blizzard, rapidly blanketing the body. Impatient, he jerks out the hunting knife and viciously rips through the dead woman's clothes, violating the body; blood gushes out on the snow.

He throws down his knife, about to give up when he hears a crackle inside the pocket of the woman's jacket. His groping fingers pick out a crumpled piece of paper. "Fuck your mother," he screams when he discovers it is only a damp wrinkled photograph. He holds it up in the gray light. A young woman poses in ski clothes against a blue sky and mountain peaks. Through the cracks in the photo, her laughing face mocks him, and makes him curse all the more. He examines the back of the picture, but there is nothing, no identification. Placing it in his pocket, he knows this flimsy photograph is not enough, and his life will be in danger even if he does not accept payment. The client demands genuine evidence.

He leans over the body once more, clutching his large knife and grunts with exertion. The dark shadow surprises him, is almost upon him before he senses he is being watched and rises up. Just beyond the trees, a large black wolf stands; its pale grey eyes stare at him. His intention to hide the body vanishes into terror. He has no time to draw his gun and flees into the forest.

Chapter 1

Katya
Courchevel, France: January 2002

KATYA MARSTON, A striking figure in her designer ski suit, posed in the early morning sunlight at the top of Sauliere, the highest peak in the resort of Courchevel 1850, while her fiancé, Philip Thorpe-Lydington, snapped photographs. She smiled and clowned around, slouching, preening, pretending to be a model. But it was a desperate act to keep ever-present sorrow from overwhelming her. Remembering the other times she had stood on this same spot with her guardian Abigail Townsend, she touched the icy rock behind her, and for a moment heard Abigail's voice carried along in the light flakes of snow scattering in the wind.

"Darling Katya, race you!"

Abigail, her only family, the person she had clung to as a mother, was listed as missing, a probable casualty of the World Trade Center disaster. It can't be true; the words repeated like a litany in her mind. She had persuaded Philip to come up the mountain early as soon as the lifts opened, so they could be alone. She loved it up here: cold, clean, silent sweeps of snow in the early morning sun which fired the pure blue sky; a contrast to the inferno which took place in New

York that September day. She only could imagine Abigail's terror, but still, it was real enough for her. Horrifying images from the television screen woke her every night, and she would be grief stricken, crying out for Abigail, unable to sleep.

Philip snapped another picture. Her smile died on her lips as she remembered the call from the New York Police to her London flat. Their deadly message had sent her into numbed shock. This later changed to a stubborn belief that Abigail was still alive. After all, she had reasoned; her guardian's body had not been found. Knowing Abigail, it was possible that she had gone away to some health spa for a few weeks without telling anyone. But after four months without news, she had given way to the terrible possibility Abigail might be gone forever. The police had advised her not to come to New York unless they found some trace of her guardian. But she had pangs of guilt watching the grieving relatives, holding signs, pleading for news of their missing loved ones. She wanted to be there, searching.

"Let's go." Philip put his camera in his pocket and turned toward the slope. He was tall, very fit, almost too thin, with a spare bony face, and light blue eyes, which sometimes seemed only to regard her with desire, but not love or concern. She hurled down Suisse, the black slope, skiing recklessly, challenging the mountain, to erase the pictures of destruction looming in her head. Philip caught up with her on the blue run that trailed past the huge landing mound of the Altiport. Slowing up for a moment, she half expected to see Abigail, smothered in furs, eye stopping, spectacular, stepping off the small plane, waving to her.

"Don't stop here." Philip swerved up beside her, spraying snow, showing his irritation. He had been forced to cut his holiday short because one of his business deals had gone wrong. Katya felt sorry for him and wanted to comfort him, but knew he would shrug her off with contempt.

Back in the hotel room, she sat on the bed still in her ski clothes, worried that Philip was angry at her, idly thinking how he never called her Katya, but always Kate, as though it made her less foreign. She hated the name Kate, but was hesitant to tell him. Philip was undressing and at the same time making phone calls. He impatiently ran a hand through his short dark hair while he shouted into the phone. She called it his daily fix and once had told him his Blackberry seemed permanently attached, like an additional body part.

She never would have returned of her own volition to this scene of so many good times with Abigail. Philip had business meetings in Paris and Geneva and using all his persuasive powers convinced her that the glitzy resort was the most logical place to have a short skiing break. When they first arrived, memories overwhelmed her, and she had felt a terrible pain, like her heart was cracking. She had found herself waiting for Abigail to appear at the hotel desk or at the ski lift. Now she was thinking Philip was really inconsiderate to insist they come here. But then, he always demanded his way. It was bewildering that even though she was going to marry the man sitting next to her on the bed, she felt so alone since Abigail had vanished.

She was the only known figure from Katya's past, her only family. Her guardian had always been there for her, the one stable person in her background. When she was small, living in England, she had believed, really hoped, that Abigail, so far away in America, was her real mother, but later realized it was wishful thinking.

Then during her years at Cambridge they became very close; not, Abigail insisted, like mother and daughter, but more like sisters. She visited often, and at this time suggested Katya drop the Aunt. Katya still always thought of her as mother and hugged this secret to her heart. Their skiing trips had begun then.

Abigail would phone her in London. "Darling Katya," her low voice with the American accent crackling over the line, "Let's take a break. I'm flying into Geneva on business. Then I'll hop on the plane to Courchevel."

Katya would meet her in the restaurant at the Altiport while her bags were being transferred to the Kilimanjaro Hotel, not far from the landing strip. Then it was Katya and Abigail skiing, indulging in spa treatments, and clubbing. Her guardian was amazing fun, like someone her own age. She was a brilliant wild skier, swooping down the most difficult black slopes and skiing off piste with reckless abandon. She loved to party and often shut down Les Caves and the other nightclubs in the resort. Emil, the hotel concierge, told them they made quite a beautiful pair, and always was amused watching men become mesmerized, like idiots, around them.

Katya remembered their final trip last year at this time, and re- morse filled her at how furious she had been at Abigail. It had marred their last days together. For a moment she replayed the scene in those final hours in the sitting room of their hotel suite. There was a breathtaking view of the mountains; the dark green stately pines leaned like giant soft brushes against the windows. They had returned from a massage and facial and were wrapped in white robes and towels, waiting for the hairdresser. 'Coldplay', Abigail's favorite band played in the background. She always liked it loud.

Abigail lounged on the sofa next to her, glamorous, well pre- served. And she confessed, it was "With the help of a few prudent nips and tucks by my expert surgeon." Her dark exotic beauty inher- ited from her Shawnee great great grandmother contrasted with Katya's blond hair and tawny skin.

"I have a new man." Abigail's slim elegant fingers curled around a champagne glass filled with Moet.

"Maxi," she sighed, "unbelievably seductive, almost evil." Her eyes sparkled with humor. "He's very young. Your generation. Men my age can't keep up with me. Everyone in New York is gossiping about my toy boy, but he's an absolute necessity. Oh well, the gossip means more publicity for the gallery."

"How did you meet him?" She felt a twinge of jealousy; saw him as a scheming competitor for Abigail's affection.

"He applied for a job in the gallery, and I hired him immediately. He is utterly charming. Of course, I know his family. White Russian émigrés, nobility, top drawer socially." She took a sip of champagne, celebrating her good fortune.

Katya put down her glass, feeling ill. She had been working up courage to persuade Abigail to let her come to New York and work in the gallery. The Little Swan Gallery, established in the late sixties by her guardian, was extremely successful and influential in the international art world.

"Maxi?" Katya kept her voice even, so as not to betray her disappointment. She pictured a small malevolent dwarf or an evil changeling.

"His full name is Count Maximilian Alexandrovich Suvorov but everyone calls him Maxi. His Maman, the Countess Suvorova, disapproves of me, but pretends not to. She likes the prestige of the gallery and his generous paycheck."

"I don't understand. How can he be a count when he is American?" She thought he had to be a phony.

"It's a Russian title, as you've probably guessed by the name. During the Russian Revolution, Maxi's grandfather and his wife fled from the Bolsheviks through Siberia or Mongolia or someplace like that. I believe they ended up in Harbin in China before getting out. They were penniless when they arrived in New York and lived in reduced circumstances, but would never stoop to an ordinary job. They've always been terrible snobs. Maxi's father died young from a heart attack, so my Maxi is now Count Maxi and head of the family."

Katya took a large gulp of champagne, and choked, filled with hatred for this aristocratic toy boy who had usurped her rightful place at the gallery. It had always been her dream to live in New York and work with Abigail. Nothing else mattered, but now it was obvious she wasn't wanted. She struggled to keep the hostility out of her voice. "Is he an expert on art?"

"Not at all, but he does the most amazing things in bed." Abigail shivered. "Delicious." Then growing more serious, she said, "My Maxi does have important connections in Russia, new business people and a few old associates of his family who managed to survive under the communists. One of them wants to export precious icons to sell in the gallery. You know, darling Katya, there are Russians everywhere with loads of money. Just look around this place. These new mega rich are ready to spend unbelievable amounts. They want antiques, paintings, even bric-a-brac associated with Russian history; anything that recalls the grand Tsarist past." She waved a slim well-toned arm in the air. "I'd like to have a share of that market."

It always amazed Katya that her guardian was not only extremely beautiful, but also possessed a head for business, which she attributed to genes inherited from great great grandfather Jed Townsend.

"And you think Maxi can help you?" Her voice was frosty. She wondered now if Abigail had been aware of her anger. Perhaps she hadn't noticed. She always said Katya was very English and reserved and never showed her feelings.

"At this moment Maxi is on an exploratory trip to Moscow and St. Petersburg, meeting important contacts. I do miss him," She sighed like a lovesick schoolgirl. "I believe he really is in love with me." Her voice trailed off.

"Katya, Come here. You know I have to leave in an hour." Philip's call from the bathroom jolted her into the present.

He peeled off her ski suit and underwear in a sudden swift manner, moving his hands insistently up her legs and then to her breasts. She felt, as she always did, anxious about pleasing him; she was removed from the scene, observing another person. She lost her breath, and before she could catch it again, they were in the shower, water pouring down on them. Pressed against the wall, she felt her body become liquid, dissolving in the water. Grasping her breasts with both hands, he slowly pushed inside her. She saw herself succumbing into desire and gave out a short cry, her legs wrapping around him in sudden capitulation.

They stayed for some moments in the rising steam. As the mist engulfed her, she wondered what was wrong with her; that she could view making love so coldly, and yet enjoy it. A strange feeling of isolation overcame her as she slid to the floor like a morsel of jelly. Philip did have a way of subtly touching her that aroused her, but she had begun to suspect it had nothing to do with love. She waited for some flashpoint, some feeling to ignite her, but it never happened. Was she in love with him? Abigail hadn't thought so.

Her guardian had met Philip once or twice on one of her last trips to London and although it was not her style to pass judgment, she seemed unimpressed. "As you know, I'm not a great judge of men. Very successful I see. Sure of himself. But he does seem cold, and very controlling. Not simpatico." She had wrinkled her nose, a sign of dislike. "Maybe I'm wrong. I don't think you're madly in love with him, but if you are, you should marry him."

In turn, Philip had taken an instant dislike to Abigail, criticizing her flamboyant manners and her dress. "Very loud rather vulgar American voice," he said. "And that suit." His eyebrows rose. "Excellent example of mutton dressed as lamb."

When she had wrapped up in a bathrobe and returned to the bedroom, Philip was buttoning his Turnbull and Asser shirt. He chose a silk tie, and then dressed in his dark Savile Row suit and handmade shoes from Lobbs. She watched him pack, not sorry he was going. He was catching the helicopter to Geneva and then a plane to London. She would be free of anxiety for a couple of days, but what did that mean? Why wouldn't she want to be with him every minute? She supposed it was his intensity, his demand that she be perfect that made her nervous. In contrast, he seemed faultless in every way; Eton then Cambridge and a high profile job in the city. Although he was nearing forty-two and ten years older than she, he was still considered young to be a successful hedge fund manager, a star in the city's financial circles. Recently he had been listed in *Harpers & Queen* as one of London's most eligible bachelors.

"You'd better grab him while you can," Her friend Caroline Squire had said with envy in her voice. It was true that a lot of women were interested in him. Philip never failed to mention this to her when he was angry.

He had been furious this morning after they had come off the slope and reached the lobby of the Carlina Hotel, and she had told him she was staying on since they had the reservation for the week. He had given her a black look. He didn't like any change of plan unless he had initiated it. "What is it with you? I can't understand it. You didn't want to come in the first place, and now you want to stay?"

"Well, actually Philip," she said, nervously clearing her throat, "it has been good. Thank you for bringing me. Most of my memories of Abigail here are happy and that helps." He had turned away from her impatiently, a look of disgust passing over his face.

These few days in the resort had become a kind of memorial, a way to mourn Abigail. She claimed she was collecting material for her magazine assignment, a travel article on the resort's restaurants and boutiques. Mollified after the love making, accepting her excuses, he kissed her goodbye and said he would call her in the morning.

She smiled bleakly to herself when the door closed, reflecting on the strange emptiness in her life. She had no serious career, no direction, and had latched on to writing as a last resort because it came easy to her. She had plenty of assignments, which she often turned down. Her heart wasn't in it. At Cambridge she had discussed her lack of purpose with one of her more sympathetic professors who had said she was too sheltered and advised her to get out there and find out what life was all about.

Several times she had applied for jobs as an aid worker in Africa, but always failed the interviews. The young men who interviewed her were struck by her beauty, but immediately placed her in the category of 'not the right type'. She was trapped by her appearance and couldn't overcome that first impression even though she had a Cambridge degree. She deeply regretted those personnel decisions and her inability to sell herself. Helping in an orphanage would have given her life some meaning and purpose. After the last quick rejection, she gave up, thinking maybe she was just a playgirl.

Since graduating with a degree in English, she had written several articles for Harper's and Vogue with surprising success. These were mostly gossip pieces, and a few interviews, assigned because she traveled with the right crowd, which included the 'it' girls in London who made good newspaper copy. She wasn't exactly an 'it' girl herself. One had to be from a prominent family and have loads of money. She had the money, but no family at all. She realized now that all she ever had wanted was to live in New York with Abigail; not much of a career.

"Don't worry," Abigail had said when she had expressed doubt about her future, hoping her guardian would take the hint and invite her to New York. "You're a party girl and why not? A beauty like you is required to be. It would be a waste. You're a talented writer. It won't be long before something comes up, and your career takes off. You're like me. I just fell into the art business by accident, although some claim I have an eye for paintings that sell."

She thought again of Abigail lying somewhere in a hospital, an unknown victim, and knew she must go to New York against the advice of the police and Philip's angry opposition. But Abigail's past warnings made her hesitant. Over the years when Katya had pressed to visit, her face would darken and she invariably would say, "I would love to have you live with me, but you must stay away until I tell you it is safe. I'll come to visit you. All I ask is that you keep away from New York. I can't say more, but it has to do with your legacy. Promise me." Although puzzled and slightly irritated by the lack of explanation, she had given her word and it now seemed Abigail's warning voice hung over her.

She pulled the robe around her and opened her computer, but instead of typing notes for the skiing article, dropped off to sleep, a recent habit to compensate for insomnia. It was late afternoon when she woke. She threw on the pale brown fur coat Abigail had given her last Christmas and left the hotel. She walked down Bellecote toward the center of the village, passing deceptively rustic looking chalets and hotels, bastions of luxury and comfort, complete with saunas, swimming pools, and private gyms.

Set in the French Tarantaise Alps, Courchevel was a resort frequented by the wealthy and famous. French movie stars, politicians, businessmen, and newly rich Russians skied the slopes and dined on fresh oysters and champagne at Tremplin and Michelin-starred Sauliere.

Her boots crunched on the path leveled between huge mountains of snow, fringed by giant spears of dark green pines, and she stopped halfway down the hill to browse at the food shop which carried gourmet delicacies from Fauchons in Paris. Fashionable policemen in navy blue uniforms directing traffic waved her across the street. She continued past the jewelry and fur shops to the café at the edge of the slopes. It was a beautiful scene, the lowering sun casting a golden light over the mountains.

The St. Honore Café perched at the end of a luxurious shopping complex connected to the Grandes Alpes Hotel. Small and intimate with white chairs curving around small tables, the café's windows looked out onto the slopes leading down to La Croissette and the ski center. The lifts had closed and both the café terrace outside and shops along the street were filling up with skiers, eating crepes, and shopping. She passed a group of stunningly beautiful girls, dressed in furs; some looked as young as fifteen. Any one of them could have graced the cover of Vogue. Hugging phones to their ears, speaking Russian, they made their way laughing and joking to a large table on the snow-covered terrace.

In the past few years, the resort had become a favorite among well-heeled Russians. Bodyguards who drove large SUV's with darkened window accompanied them. These rough looking men, speaking into field phones, followed their employees onto the slopes. Many of the new Russians owned palatial chalets hidden behind huge patrolled gates.

Others, surrounded by small armies of private security men, took over entire luxury hotels. Abigail had remarked that the women in these entourages were always young, at the most in their twenties, and beautiful, while the men, usually 20 to 30 years older, were very rough with barrel shapes. "Too many blini and too much vodka," she said. Their hard battered faces hinted at brutal past histories. It had seemed odd that Abigail had taken up with Maxi since she had been so disparaging of the Russians here. He must have been irresistible.

Tempted by the cozy warmth after her long walk down the hill, she chose a small table by the window inside the café and ordered hot lemon tea. A woman in a fur hat, to the right of her, murmured into her phone, while a young couple in matching ski suits, two tables on the opposite side were ordering coffee and pastry.

Outside, next to the diminutive shaggy ponies waiting to take children on rides, a black Humvee unloaded several men dressed in boots and leather jackets.

A faint uneasiness gripped her as one of them walked in, surveyed the room, and then settled closer than necessary on the curved bench at the table next to her. While removing his jacket he used his cell several times speaking in a guttural low voice. He wore a black turtleneck sweater, sheathed over a muscled torso. A large silver Byzantine cross, studded with huge emeralds dangled from his neck.

He flipped his phone shut and turned on the bench so that she was forced to look at him. A lopsided smile showing gold fillings in his teeth broke over his grizzled face, made fearsome by a very flat nose. He slid off his cap to reveal clipped gray hair and huge diamond studs piercing each earlobe. He seemed of indeterminate age, but she guessed mid forties. Rudely staring at her, he fingered the menu. His large rings gleamed. She noticed a curious tattoo on his hand and wanted to examine it more closely, but feared he would think she was interested in him.

"Hi, let me introduce. I'm Nika. You're beautiful chick. What's your name?" He spoke in a combination of accented American and Russian, using slang he probably picked up from movies.

"There's a large," he emphasized the rrs in large, "awesome party at the boss's chalet tonight." His accent grated on her nerves. "Come on. Keep me company. It will be very, very cool." He coaxed, fingering the cross. "You're most beautiful girl I ever seen." He leaned over and whispered confidentially, "I want to fuck you." He grabbed her hand. She jerked away as though she had been scalded.

She froze in shock. Although she had learned to expect men to react to her, this was like an assault. Hatred, sharp, almost painful, ran through her like a hot electric wire. She flushed, controlling her impulse to slap him or to jump up and leave the restaurant, knowing that like some wild beast he had sensed her fear.

"No thank you," she said in her coldest voice, determined not to be forced out of the tearoom. All kinds of names for him rose in her throat.

Nika's smile faded and his eyes, the color of dirty cement, darkened. She did not look at him again, deliberately shifting away, but was conscious of his hostility, the barely suppressed violence that rocked his body as she forced herself to slowly finish her tea and pay the bill.

She fled outside and across the street to the Hermes shop, determined to wait, hoping he would go away. Her heart thumping, she studied the handbags for at least forty minutes, but when she left the shop, he was leaning against the side of the Humvee, watching her. That creep poisoned the afternoon. In the waning light, she stomped up the hill to the hotel, and packed, intending to arrange a morning flight. But then furious and defiant that a thug could force her to leave, she changed her mind, ordered room service, and began work on her article. The next day she skied from early morning until the lifts closed and did not see the man again.

Early on her last day at the resort, Katya boarded the cable car to Sauliere. As she rode up the mountain, she thought over the incident. Her anger and fear had faded and now seemed out of proportion in the sparkling morning light. Abigail would have punched him in the balls and then laughed it off. Men often said strange things when they met her. She should be used to it. He was just cruder than most with that line.

She began her descent down Suisse, Abigail's favorite run, and thought again of her guardian looking over her shoulder, calling out, "Race you, Katya darling." Two skiers appeared, small dark figures against the snow, zigzagging on the slope in wide arcs, following her trail. They didn't look like experts and were far behind her. It was only when four others joined them that they gained surprising speed. In swift moves, the group split on each side of her and seemed to be chasing her.

Panicked, she raced down the mountain, the wind burning her face, using all her expertise, but they managed to keep near, coming closer, forcing her off into the wooded area separating the two runs. Taking sharp turns through the trees and sliding over rocks, she tried to ski out of the woods to the slope on the other side. For a few seconds she evaded them until her ski hit something hard. She skidded, losing her poles, and then she was looking straight into a tree trunk.

She was lying on her side, her head spinning, underneath the tree, covered in snow from its branches. A hoarse accented voice floated above her. "This is not a wet job, you cunt. I told you not." Then some word in another language. It sounded like *mochit*.

For a moment before darkness came, she saw in the whirling trees above, a pair of black eyes, and scars ranging around a man's hairline like a picket fence.

Chapter 2

Mikhail
Autoroute du Soleil, France: January 2002

MIKHAIL BORISOV HAD memorized the girl's features as though the photograph were engraved on his eyelids. The young woman in the picture, wearing a pale blue ski suit, poses in front of a huge snow bank. She is smiling as though about to speak. Giant icy peaks slash through the pure blue of sky to complete the background. Her free hand reaches out to touch, almost caress the snow. She is very beautiful with large dark eyes and long blond hair pulled off her sensitive face; her classic features resemble those engraved on Greek coins that he once had seen in the Hermitage Museum in St. Petersburg. He must find her, force her to talk.

He sank back on the leather seat of the black armored Mercedes speeding away from his hideout in the hills above Nice toward Lyon and the meeting. Bebe, head of his security unit, who continued to wear the boxy suits and off color shoes of a KGB thug, loomed in the front seat beside the slender Chechen driver, Shamil, fashionably dressed in Hugo Boss. The major accessories for both were Uzi's. A small rocket launcher and grenades were hidden in the trunk, although no trouble was expected.

The bodyguard's real name was Peter Latsis, known in the murky underworld of hit men as Bebe because his face, with barely outlined nose and mouth resembled an unfinished fetus. His miniscule head with barely discernible eyes was incongruously attached to an enormous powerful body. The former Spetznaz operative of Latvian descent was a maestro at wet jobs, a KGB euphemism for murder. Unemployed after the fall of the Soviet Union, Bebe had come to work for Mikhail while he was still a powerful oligarch. Bebe knew all the angles of Russia's security service, recently renamed the FSB.

His driver, Shamil Saidov, slender, lithe, with carefully clipped hair, and small handsome features, claimed he had a poet's soul. Expert with his *kinzhal*, a Chechen knife, Shamil was well-connected to the Chechen underworld. He was comfortable with both men because they went silently about *chernaya robata*, their black work, and discreetly followed his orders without question.

Mikhail had called the *nayekhat*, using the word from *fenya* the criminal vocabulary to give it a more sinister importance than an ordinary meeting. He was suspicious of his personnel in America who claimed they still were searching hard for the girl. There had been no progress, and he had demanded a face to face with their representative.

He opened the small refrigerator and took out a bottle of mineral water, drank it down, then checked his pistol, which lay on the seat within his reach. It was an old rare Mauser, a gift from the Raven. His controller had received it from his friend Lenin, the Bolshevik leader during the early days of the Russian Revolution. Mikhail still remembered his surprise at the Raven's sudden generosity, and after all these years remained puzzled at his uncharacteristic behavior.

The afternoon sunlight pierced the dark windows: he took out a leather case and flipped on his Ray Ban's, immersing him into comfortable darkness. His casual slacks, handmade loafers, and soft Italian cashmere sweater marked him out as a wealthy businessman. But the expensive clothes did not completely hide the powerful contours of his body or the traces at the edges of his shirt cuffs of the vicious scars that tracked up his arms and over his back.

He was balding, and kept his light brown hair, salted with gray in a buzz cut. In contrast to his hair, his skin had a yellow cast; his strong rather fine features, with wide spread eyes, slightly turned up at the corners, firm chin, and generous mouth, were marred by a deep indentation running down the right side of his face. The shattered cheek was related to his return to the Soviet Union in 1970 after his aborted mission in the U.S. and a consequent spell at the hands of his KGB interrogators. The Chief of the First Directorate had spared him, believing he still was a valuable asset. He could pass as an American of German or Irish background as he had done in the U.S. Only someone acquainted with minorities in Russia would notice his trace of mixed blood, discernible in the slight curve of the eyes, and the swarthy skin colour.

'*Chornyi.* Black Shit', the Raven's mocking words floated about the car. Remembering his many humiliations, Mikhail's body tensed, and darkness crept over his face like a shadow reflecting all he had done. His chilling expression betrayed his KGB past, long before he became one of Russia's wealthiest oligarchs. He always affected to be unaware of all around him, but behind the fashionable sunglasses, the cold brown eyes with curious yellow flecks like sparks of fire missed nothing. Now they were hard with anger and frustration.

After the year long investigation, the young woman's identity remained a mystery. His men had checked all Interpol records, and liaised with his contacts in foreign intelligence units, but these efforts had yielded nothing. Someone would pay.

Like the Raven he always hired small squads of hit men who knew nothing of each other. But he was uneasy; he had no word of progress from Stavrogin, his agent, nothing. Lev's contract men from Little Odessa in Brooklyn claimed they had searched the entire area for miles around the cabin where the woman had holed up, but found no significant leads.

The only clue his diverse sources had produced was this measly photograph, sent to him bent and faded from the damp of snow. It had been snapped with an expensive Canon digital camera, but the laboratory could not detect the location in the picture. Even without the memory chip, his technicians were able to scan the photograph, bringing her beauty to life. Little details had emerged, like the thin well-manicured fingers resting on the snow; the way her large brown eyes were lit with fun and a happiness he had never known.

He removed his sunglasses. Darkness had fallen when Shamil turned off the highway into one of the Lyon rest areas, stopping in a deserted section of the parking lot. He switched off the lights, and Mikhail waited in the car, listening to the dim roar of highway traffic while his men checked out the area.

Minutes later Little Lev Siminsky, representative for the Odessa Group who had flown in from the States, pulled up in his new black Jaguar. Lev was slim and dark, with feminine features, his Armani suit slightly too big, his greasy hair flipped in a reverse page boy; his appearance belied that fact that he once had been a member of the Kurgan gang of hired assassins. After the last meeting with Little Lev, Bebe, in a surprising moment of humor, had quipped that the little fuck was getting in touch with his feminine side.

In the faint light from the distant petrol station, Lev jumped out of the car, a strong odor of Chanel No. 5 following in his wake, and opened the trunk. He poured vodka into tiny glasses and with shaking hands presented the offering to Mikhail and his guards on a silver tray. Silently, they all drank with one gulp, and tossed the empty glasses into the bushes.

Then Mikhail asked the question, more than once. There was only one question. Waving his slender ring-covered hands in the air, Lev swore they had found no trace of the girl, and that his Odessa Group was not working for anyone else. No one in his organization would dare to betray Mikhail Borisov, the powerful billionaire.

Little Lev did not change his story even in the darkness of the parking lot with the radio blaring to muffle his screams while Bebe strenuously applied the pliers to what he primly called, Lev's 'private parts'. The stench from Lev's loosened bowels filled Mikhail with disgust, and he returned to the car. When Bebe finished, Mikhail believed the man was telling as much as he knew of the truth.

Before pulling on his clothes and stumbling to his Jag, the sobbing Lev repeated that someone had contacted him claiming to have information leading to the girl in the photograph. They had not been able to trace the unnamed informant, but followed his instructions, left the payment at a drop, and were waiting for his next move.

Bebe jumped in the front seat, a smile floating across his rubbery face, and murmured something to Shamil. His lithe body shook with laughter as he started the ignition. Mikhail flicked on his light and continued to stare intently for a few moments at the photograph as though he would find an answer in her lovely face, then placed it in a small leather folder and turned off the light.

In the past two years, he had spiraled downward from powerful oligarch to an exile in danger of his life; his nadir inexorably leading to a squalid death by poison or a bullet in the back of the head in a dark basement. No longer one of the *siloviki*, the men of power who controlled Russia, he was in desperate straits, his enemies closing in.

Mikhail believed his fate until his exile had been determined by luck. In the late eighties, he returned from his covert assignment in Afghanistan and was promoted to general in the KGB. Because of this position he was appointed director of Siberian Metals, the largest nickel and aluminum factory in the Soviet Union.

In 1992 when the decree on privatization of Russia's factories and natural resources was issued, Mikhail took advantage of the opportunity; eighty percent of the ownership of Siberian Metals was transferred to him, the other twenty percent went to his banking partners, cronies from the secret service. Through powerful connections and bribes to important government officials, he obtained the all important export licenses. These allowed him to appropriate the metals cheaply from his company and sell abroad for great profits.

But even that stroke of luck was not enough for him to feel secure. Perhaps, he thought with a wry grin, there would never be enough money for that. Always very ambitious, he had gone into city property, under the *kyrsha*, roof, or protection of Helos, a Chechen gang. His long alliance with Andrei Vishnuv, a gang leader who had attained the honored title *A Thief Professing the Code* while in prison, had ensured that Mikhail increased his growing empire.

He smiled, thinking of the reality lurking behind those dry words, property investments. The old and infirm were forced by Andrei's thugs to sign contracts with his company to sell their homes after their deaths for a pittance. Soon after signing, the unfortunate homeowners would meet with accidents or come down with fatal illnesses. Their homes were then sold for a fortune in Moscow's booming real estate market. Mikhail had not been present during the brutal visits; he had just provided the capital.

Andrei had arranged everything, but it was an episode in his rise to oligarch that would have to be covered up, like much of his questionable past, to enable his safe return to Russia. He did not feel guilty. His controller had taught him well, always quoting a phrase Lenin often used, *Kto Kovo,* 'Whoever has the power can do as he wishes.' The old Bolshevik's eyes would gleam maliciously as he continued with another maxim, 'There is no room for sentimentality or good works during revolution or upheaval.'

Mikhail became rich beyond his dreams using this philosophy. He rose to be the powerful oligarch, the eminence grise, by far the most influential in the circle around President Yeltsin. He was flattered that many whispered he actually ruled the country. Yet he had been aware that he could lose everything, including his life, if the president, alcoholic and ill, was forced from office. It was down to this.

The privatization of Russia's factories and natural resources had been ordered by a *ukase* from the Russian President, a decree that automatically became law. If Yeltsin lost power, his *ukase* could be overturned and all present ownership of property would switch to new rulers of Russia.

He frowned, thinking of how his luck changed to bad sooner than expected when Putin was elected in 2000. He had supported Putin, but the new ruler turned against him. Their last meeting flashed before him with General Letinov standing in the background. The general, an old enemy, had plotted against Mikhail, ingratiating himself with Putin, and was responsible for his fall and exile.

Two days after that meeting, the government had charged him with fraud, robbery and murder, crimes that could apply to any of the oligarchs. His property was seized, and he fled Russia before they could kill him.

Still, he had one great advantage over his enemies. He thought of the Raven's secret intelligence, gripping the edge of the seat in a spasm of excitement and tension. It held the key to power; it would take him back to Russia, to rule.

He focused again on the young woman in the photograph. He must get his hands on her. He must find her before it was too late.

Chapter 3

Roo
Tecumseh County, Ohio: January 2002

REUBEN YODER, KNOWN to his friends as Roo, woke early Sunday morning lying face down, his nose touching the bottom edge of the toilet bowl. The combined roar of the sports station on television and Alan Jackson's, *It's Five O'clock Somewhere* blasted through his head. He became aware that the putrid smell attacking his nostrils emanated from a yellowish lumpy substance spread around him. Focusing for a moment to his right, he followed a stained brown crack traveling on the lino like a relief map of the Ohio River.

Forcing his body up slowly, he retched violently and threw up in the sink. He turned on the tap, washing everything away and splashed water on his face. Pushing his thick dark blond hair back, he looked in the mirror. Janey's sad beautiful face replaced his, her words coming from the past. "You're wasted. You were so beautiful. Why are you doing this to yourself Roo?"

She was so right. Although his strong muscular body had not yet gone to fat, and he still possessed the square shaped jaw and sturdy even features with broken nose, lines like fine cobwebs spun around his eyes and down his cheeks. They were not yet as deep as the scar on his forehead planted years ago by the cleats of Bobby Clare, linebacker for the Monmouth Tigers, who had deliberately tried to put him away.

He traced the scar and remembered being carried by stretcher to the hospital that evening. His mother had come and gone for the night, and he hadn't expected anyone else to be at his bedside. But Janey hovered over him, anxiety on her sweet face, and in that moment, he fell in love forever. It was his junior year in high school. After her vigil at the hospital, they began going steady, and he couldn't imagine his future without her. He turned off the CD and heard Janey, "You're in a time warp. Still the high school star. Grow up."

"Right again Janey," he said to the mirror. Here he was, alone, another weekend gone, shitfaced, a bum passing out in his own vomit. Low, low, he thought when he had met Ben on Friday at Shorty's Bar. It was the last thing he remembered until he woke up this morning. He tossed a bucket of water over the mess in the bathroom and shed his stinking clothes. The brochure and half completed application form for the Ohio State University extension program still lay on his kitchen table. He heard himself screaming 'Fuck, Fuck' and attacked the papers, ripping them in pieces, scattering them on the floor.

Exhausted after the outburst, he clicked off the TV, still blaring out the score from last night's play-off game. In the ensuing silence he remembered what had brought him down this weekend. The face of Pete Stevens, once his rival at St. Anthony's School, had beamed directly at him from the evening sports program. Pete was retiring from the pros after a spectacular career and had been hired as assistant coach by the Cleveland Browns, expected to take over as head coach in two seasons.

It hurt. He had been miles above Stevens, but his rival had gone on from high school to a brilliant career as a star quarterback at

Notre Dame, continuing into the pros. He had stopped dead at high school. He would soon be thirty-two, and nothing good was ever going to happen to him. There was no one to blame but himself. Searching for his phone, he discovered he had dropped it in the toilet while he was throwing water over everything. He fished it out, rinsed it, and laid it on the table to dry.

He looked around at what symbolized the remnants of his life, and suspected he was going to be living in this one room shack forever. When he first moved here, he had deluded himself into thinking it was only temporary. A table and chair occupied the middle of the room. Against the wall across from the bed was a large high-resolution television, which constantly showed sports. He had subscribed to the complete football package. This was his only luxury except for his books and music, ordered on the computer at the County Sheriff's office. These were piled in stacks along the walls.

He winced as he opened the wheezing ancient refrigerator, realizing that he had hurt his shoulder when he fell unconscious in the bathroom, and located a Coke among the cans of beer. There was nothing else on the shelves. He always ate at Nelson's Diner in town.

He swallowed the Coke down, trying to rid his mouth of the dead mouse taste, and threw the can in the overflowing waste bin, then went over to the line of hooks by the door which held his entire wardrobe of off duty clothes, a couple of pairs of jeans and three plaid flannel shirts. His underwear was stored beneath the bed. His blue deputy sheriff's uniform, provided by the county, was draped on a clothes hanger with his gun and holster on a peg beside it. The shiny badge on the uniform glared as though registering disapproval of his weekend. He dressed and grabbed his hunting gear hanging next to the uniform. The threadbare yellow hunting jacket, boots, and the rifle were the only possessions of his dad's that he had kept after the accident. Dad's angry red face fuelled by alcohol, flitted briefly before him.

The summer after he had graduated from high school his life stopped. He refused the football scholarship and turned into himself. He pulled the plug on his life, disconnected from the present, and retreated into a dream. It was like stepping back into the team photograph he kept in a drawer. They had won the state championship that year.

He withdrew even more from his previous life by moving into this shack after his mom died. He could not go near the family farmhouse, now empty and neglected. The dairy cows had been sold after his dad's death, and he rented the land to his friend Eddie Bascomb who planted corn in the fields and used the hilly parts of the property to graze his own cows. Sometimes he didn't even bother to collect the rent, although Eddie always brought it around. He moaned, leaning down to pull on his boots and decided not to take his rifle and cartridges from under the bed. He staggered out into the yard, blooming with wrecks of cars. Ben Tyler, owner of the shack, his old teammate and drinking buddy, said most of these babies just needed a tune up but he never seemed to get around to all of them before another arrived.

The shack sat on the edge of town, close to the railroad tracks and the old grain mill. A small creek ran beside it, used in the past for transport by the estate once occupying this land. Miss Lindsay, the town librarian, had shown him a very old photograph of the large house and the fenced-in fields. *The Safford Farm, one of the family holdings, 1890* had been written in a quivery hand at the bottom of the faded photo.

He tried to imagine the Safford Farm as he scraped the ice from the windshield of his old Ford pickup. Shivering, he ducked his head from pain. The trees, brittle in the cold, looked about to snap like the membranes in his head. The truck started with a whine, and he drove out into the white landscape, snow squeaking under the tires. Its engine cold, the pickup chortled and jolted in protest like an angry old man. He moved farther away from town and turned off onto a small country road, passing the isolated Granger Farm and headed onto a small track, almost never used, his tires making fresh marks in the snow.

He parked at the edge of the track, and walked into the glistening forest. Just ahead a crow that refused to migrate perched on the limb of a pine tree and seemed to look at him in disdain. *The way a crow shook down on me, the dust of snow.* Frost's simple elegiac words rushed over him. His breath came in clouds in the clean pure air, empty of odors except for those coming from his body. The sun was barely up, and as it pushed farther over the horizon, flooding the snow with light, he felt a sudden exhilaration. He was at his best in the forest. He could slip away far into the past, into the world of the Indians and the pioneer explorers and scouts like Daniel Boone, Colonel Safford, and Simon Kenton.

It was the middle of the hunting season, when the deer were culled to keep their burgeoning population from starvation. Roo was a good shot, but never killed animals, preferring to walk along in his dream of the past.

The alcohol fumes still flowing through his body made him woozy, and he thought he caught a glimpse of something, a black shadow flitting through the trees. A dizzying moment of fear came over him. It could be the ghost of Spybuck, the old Shawnee who had vanished into thin air when cornered and trapped by the settlers. He smiled to himself at his nonsense; not quite sure he wasn't hallucinating.

Then he saw it. He rubbed his eyes, catching moisture from snow falling from a branch and looked again. The wolf stood just ahead, staring back at him. The animal's gray blue eyes were almost the color of his own. Its fur was black and glossy, the luxuriant ruff around its neck sprinkled with gray. The wolf stared at him for a long moment, its large ears pointed, and then turned, heading deeper into the woods. Without thinking, strangely unafraid, Roo began to follow. After a few yards, the wolf stopped and looked back at him, almost as though to make sure he was following the trail, then moved soundlessly on.

Later he remembered thinking that the still, untouched forest, was like a winter landscape painting in a storybook. His recurrent nightmare afterward always began as he entered the forest and became part of the story. First it was the sound of his boots crunching, and then his dark shadow bundled up against the snow, trudging into the bottom of the picture, advancing toward the tiny isolated cabin. He had been amazed that in all of his lonely roaming through the forest he had never known the cabin existed. He coughed, suppressing the need to vomit, as he stepped into the clearing. Only the occasional crack from a branch, heavy with snow, cut the frozen stillness.

The wolf waited past the cabin at the rim of the forest and drew back when Roo walked into the trees and saw the bundle lying in the snow. He became aware of the green of the pine trees, the glistening sky and the pristine snow all in bright garish colors, like a child's primer. Then he let his eyes drop to the scattered bones. Shreds of rotting skin hung on the skeleton like pieces of blackened plastic food wrap. Coarse long white hairs sprouted from the skull. Black torn fragments of clothing lay near the bones. It flashed through his mind. This is a body, a woman's body. A prism of unbearably bright colors wove around him, making him dizzy. He threw up and then forced himself to look again.

The wolf's howl caught at him, pierced his blood stream, racing through his body. He stared down, confused, paralyzed by horror. The woman's jawbone was open wide as though she had been calling him.

Chapter 4

Katya
London

"IT SOUNDED LIKE *mochit.* I think that was the strange word. Of course, I was knocked silly and could have been hearing only nonsense and may have imagined the whole thing."

"True." Claire, Katya's therapist at Skeffington Spa, was giving her a stone massage, gliding the flat warm stones like silk down her legs. Katya winced, anticipating pain.

"Relax. I won't go near your ankle."

"The doctors at the Albertville Hospital said I was lucky to escape with a sprain and a mild concussion." She put her head down, as the hot stones relieved her aching body. There was no better remedy for all one's ills than a beauty session at Skeffington's.

Located in an elegant townhouse between Kensington and Chelsea, the spa was small, very exclusive, and offered the latest and best beauty treatments. But Skeffington's was much more. One of the clients had joked that it was the power center of Kensington and Chelsea.

The names of the best divorce lawyer, builder, psychiatrist, or personal trainer were available through this exclusive network. In addition, customers might hear what the Royals were up to; or receive honest advice on what to wear, or where to buy the little macaroons which were currently the 'in' thing to serve with coffee.

For Katya it was a haven, a warm sheltering place that sparkled with wit and laughter. Claire Skeffington, the spa owner and one of her best friends, listened to all her problems and comforted her, and never betrayed a confidence. She was petite, a sunny blonde with pert features, and a lovely smile. Her blue eyes glimmered with kindness and humor. If Claire couldn't help you, then she would know someone who could.

Katya went on, "I was sure they were after me, but it was silly. The patrol explained they were businessmen from Yugoslavia, inexperienced skiers. Later one of them called the hospital to see how I was and even sent me flowers."

Although the ligaments were torn in her right foot, she was able to walk with a limp, and needed the support of crutches for long distances. She was still dizzy from the concussion, and the episode whirled around in her head. The soft beige walls of the spa treatment room faded, and she was back to the horrifying moments dodging the trees, the dark pine trunk rising up in front of her. The man's face, the jagged scars, the echo of that word *mochit* stayed with her.

It was quiet in the spa. Most clients did not return from vacation until late January so Claire had more time to devote to her. Since the day Abigail had been reported missing, Katya had poured out her heart to her therapist. She told her of the mystery surrounding what Abigail called her legacy; her recent longing to know the identity of her parents and her belief that her guardian knew more about them than she had admitted. With tears in her eyes she confessed how angry she had been with Abigail and Maxi. Their affair meant that Abigail didn't want her in New York. Claire soaked in all of her problems as readily as Katya's skin absorbed the lotions applied.

"Hmm." Claire slid a stone down her back. "But what about the guy you said was so gross; the one who tried to pick you up?"

"Nothing like him. I probably was in a daze, but just before I blacked out, I thought I saw a man with jagged scars around his hairline."

Now Claire was moving the stones down her arms. "What was Philip's reaction?"

She had not discussed her suspicions about the accident with Philip. They were like wisps of cloud that floated away when she examined the hard facts.

"I didn't bother to tell him the details. Just that I had an accident. He would accuse me of exaggerating, just as he does when I talk about Abigail being missing. I just feel there was something strange about the incident, but I suppose I am being dramatic."

"Hmm." Claire was still working on her arms.

She tried to interpret what this 'hmm' meant. Claire was subtle, and Katya always listened when she gave rare advice. Once she had hinted that Philip might not be the right man for her.

"He did send his driver to pick me up at the airport," she said in his defense. Even so, she couldn't hide her unhappiness. Since her guardian's disappearance, she had begun to see a side of Philip that bordered on the abusive. He was contemptuous, even angry at her grief and had told her bluntly to snap out of it or he would end the engagement.

"So where are you off to this evening?"

"Dinner at Caprice with one of Philip's clients. It won't be a late evening." Then she blurted out, "What do you think? Should I go to New York?"

The therapist looked steadily at her. "Everyone is different. I think it's up to you."

But Katya knew that her friend would have been on the plane the day of the disaster. A widow at a young age, she was not afraid of being alone. As she went out the door, Claire said, "Call me when you get home, so I know you're feeling ok." She seemed more worried than Katya by the incident on the slope.

She stepped out of the spa into cold drizzling rain and grabbed a cab up the King's Road to her apartment on Smith Street. As she paid the cabbie and walked toward her door, she noticed a limousine parked at the end of the street. A man in a dark suit stood by the car, his large sinister frame hunched over against the rain. He was staring straight at her. Feeling his eyes follow her, she panicked, fumbling with her keys, and hurriedly unlocked the door.

She threw off her coat, remembering that Mr. Peters two houses down had a car and driver, and hurried into the kitchen to put on the kettle and called Claire to say, not to worry, she was fine. She planned to go over her article again before handing it in. She loved her flat with its pale cream walls, and comfortable furniture covered in flowered chintz. Several small paintings, valuable Impressionists, which Abigail had given her, decorated the walls. Adding to the cozy atmosphere, a large Mary Cassatt oil of a family hung over the fireplace.

She had found the flat, but Abigail had insisted on buying it and helping her decorate. When she had protested, Abigail said, "You need a nest, Darling Katya. Let me do this for you."

She took a comfortable position on the couch, resting her leg on the coffee table, looking through the French doors to the garden, bleak in the rain. She sipped her tea, and began to think again about Philip's attitude. Why couldn't he sympathize with her loss and support her? At the moment it was not going well between them, but she would never be able to face breaking up at this point. She would hate it, alone again, single and without Abigail.

She had gone through several relationships during university and after, including another banker, a poet, a rugby star, and a nightclub manager. Always disappointed she had continued to search for that someone she could love. Perhaps because she was past thirty she had settled for this vague feeling of affection for Philip.

Before she met him she had been frivolous, a party girl like Abigail. She had no ambition except to be as near to her guardian as possible and felt closer to Abigail by imitating her. She had slept around a lot and her reputation as a bad girl grew over the years. She blushed with embarrassment at her wild nights.

She saw herself at a London club, popping pills, stripped to her bikini bottom, pole dancing to wild cheers in the middle of the bar. As always, she was ushered out by friends before the police arrived but not before the photographers. Her impromptu strips and pole dancing became a habit, until she began showing up in the gossip columns, and Abigail put a stop to it. It was the only time she could remember her guardian being angry with her, mainly because she had been photographed. It was a mystery why the photographs had upset her, since Ab seemed to care so little about scandal.

Philip had been attracted by her scandalous reputation. He thought it was sexy. They had met in the Floral Hall at Covent Garden when she was covering a charity event for one of the tabloids. It was an elaborate affair with tiny lights glittering on giant trees brought in for the occasion. They accented the old cast iron structure, once the Victorian flower market.

Philip had appeared at her elbow, charming, handsome with the pick up line. "I caught your act at the Lido. Very original." His thin face stretched into a grin, and she felt this irresistible attraction. Philip had been masterful, taking charge of her, always telling his friends he had saved her. And she had crept into his arms. There was permanence, a certainty to their relationship. It was a safe haven and the right time to be married, to be part of a family, maybe Philip's. Her future seemed marked out when he had invited her to the Thorpe-Lydington Manor for the Christmas holidays to meet his parents.

"What a strange childhood." She still could hear the ringing authoritarian voice of Arabella, Philip's mother. His father, David, looking dubious, stood by the fireplace in his tweed jacket and twill trousers. They were drinking tea in the large sitting room of the manor house facing the manicured garden and the fields.

Arabella's strong almost masculine features crinkled with dismay as she fingered the pearls worn with her blue twin set. "And you really have no idea who your parents are?" She continued in a tone that implied they undoubtedly had been serial killers or spawn of the devil.

His mother's sudden interest in her background could only mean that Philip had told his parents he was going to marry her. She might have imagined it, but thought they had been cool toward her through the many holiday lunches and dinners, and she had been relieved to return to London. She wanted a family, to belong somewhere, but wasn't sure that family was the Thorpe-Lyddington's.

To be fair to them, there wasn't much she could tell them about her background except that she had gone to a posh English boarding school. She had no family pictures, nothing handed down to her. She could be from anywhere. Her lack of background that she always accepted as quite normal, a matter of course, now seemed odd. What did she actually know? Recently she had searched records, traced her name at the U.S. Embassy, but had come up with only the information on her passport. She was registered at the foundling hospital in New York, parents unknown. She believed Abigail had intended to tell her about her parents some day. If only she hadn't met Maxi, and began that torrid affair, Katya might have been with her in New York, might have saved her.

Her chest felt like something heavy was pressed against it. She longed for Abigail to come back, for everything to be the same. Her guardian's last message from September 9th was still on her machine. She could not bear to erase it.

She rose up clumsily from the sofa and pressed the button on her answering machine, playing the message over and over. Abigail sounded out of breath as though she had been jogging or climbing stairs. Her message came in short gasps. "Stay away. It's not safe. Wait, I'll send for you. Your legacy. Hidden in forest."

Chapter 5

Katya
London

KATYA HEARD THE mail flap snap, clicked off the answering machine, and found a thick vellum envelope lying in the hall. Uneasy, she rushed to the drawing room window and looked out at an empty street. There was no sign of the man or the limousine. The envelope contained an engraved invitation to a reception at the Russian Embassy on 10 January, from 6:30 to 8:30 p.m. There was an RSVP and an embassy telephone number.

Mystified, she mentally raced through her list of embassy acquaintances, but no one she knew had any connection to the Russians. The reception was that evening, and she couldn't possibly go. She was about to throw it away when she noticed something at the bottom of the card, which made her stop dead in the hallway. *Abigail* was written with an elegant hand in faint pencil. Someone knew about Abigail, maybe even knew where she had gone.

She quickly phoned and accepted the invitation, even though it meant canceling dinner with Philip and that would be difficult. In a panic she telephoned Claire.

"I am going, even though he'll be furious."

"Stand up to him. It's time," Claire said.

Katya paced the room in a state of torment, rehearsing different excuses, and then decided to tell Philip the truth. Hoping he was out, and she only would have to speak to his answering machine or secretary, she dialed his office and quailed at his sharp businesslike voice. Feeling small and frightened, she lost her nerve. "Hi, it's me." Her voice came out in a squeak and sounded absurd. "I think I'm coming down with the flu, and can't make it tonight."

"Are you sure? You know these are important clients." She could hear the anger in his voice.

"Yes, I'm in bed. I feel rotten."

"I'll talk to you tomorrow." He hung up without asking her what was wrong. She hadn't been convincing. She had never been a good liar.

Even as she rushed in tense excitement to get ready, dressing in an Yves St. Laurent black velvet tuxedo suit, and black leather flats to protect her ankle, she was aware that this was a strange, almost frightening invitation. Someone at the embassy knew she was connected to Abigail. But how could they?

She was apprehensive when she showed her invitation and was driven through the security gates bordering Kensington High Street. But as the cab continued down Embassy Row, she realized she would be safe at a large party.

Then she was inside the embassy, a large unattractive building surrounded by security, presenting her invitation to another set of guards in the vestibule. She walked slowly into the large paneled room hung with Russian pictures. Well dressed men in evening suits and women in brilliant jewels stood in groups, chatting and admiring the paintings. She studied the crowd, but saw no one she recognized and wandered into the next room where tables groaned with appetizers and different vodka drinks. From a gallery high above, a pianist was playing a Prokofiev sonata.

She took a glass of wine from the waiter and studied the painting of Viking looking men in front of her, called *The Bogatyrs* painted in 1898 by Vasnetsov. She moved closer to read that the *Bogatyrs* were a group of mystical warriors from Russian's past. They appear in the *Kiev Cycle of byliny*, Russian poems in oral tradition from the late medieval period.

"A picture of former times when men were true warriors, although I know of one spy during the 1917 Revolution whose nom de revolution was the Bogatyr. He too, like all heroes, is dust." Katya was startled at the low timbered voice; she had not noticed the man who had crept up beside her.

He was elderly, small and thin, with a desiccated look. His narrow wrinkled face, matched by a long nose, was strangely attractive, and became even more pleasant when he smiled. Well groomed, with expertly dyed black hair slicked off his forehead, he was dressed in an expensive evening suit.

"Pardon me for being so forward in approaching you without an introduction. I am Prince Alexander Sergeievich Androvsky, but you must call me Shura, as my friends and family do. I correct myself. I should say former prince. Old titles do not count for much in the West, even though in that legendary period, my family name meant something." He gestured toward the painting.

"And you are the lovely Katya Marston." He bowed and kissed her hand like an old world courtier.

"How do you know who I am?"

He smiled again with a quaint charm. "There are ways."

"Is it through Abigail? Did you write her name on my invitation?" She tried to keep her voice from shaking.

He took a glass of champagne from the waiter's tray. "It is only recently that I have been invited to the embassy. To the communists I was persona non grata. My family fled Russia after the Bolshevik takeover. We were dedicated enemies of the Soviets, but now that our wish came true and the government has changed, I have returned to Russia. I have embraced my homeland, and many of its citizens have embraced me. Their welcome encourages me to think the Russian people may wish for a return to some kind of monarchy, which could result in my reinstatement as a prince." He nervously surveyed the room.

"I have gone into business, acting as an intermediary with new dynamic Russian businessmen, mainly in the art world." He said this in a loud voice for the benefit of two men in ill-fitting suits who had approached the group beside them.

He spoke again about the painting, and when the men moved off, leaned over and whispered, "I must see you alone. Meet me in the vestibule in fifteen minutes. We will go from there. There is something you must know."

"Is this about Abigail?" She found herself whispering.

He nodded slightly. The lines on his face grew deeper.

"Do you know where she is?" Her heart was thumping.

"There is someone in New York who knows everything." He moved away quickly and disappeared into the crowd.

Katya no longer heard the noisy chatter, thinking only that Abigail could be alive. He might lead her to Abigail. In agitation, her ankle hurting, she limped around the room avoiding conversation. She watched a Russian folk dance, and then checking the time, picked up her coat from the cloakroom. She waited for the prince in the vestibule for over thirty minutes and noticed the guards watching her. She smiled, and said her car was late. Then she wandered back into the room where a dignitary was making a speech in Russian. After an hour, she realized the man was not going to show up and left, angry and mystified. She had risked a fight with Philip to come here, and she had no way of contacting this prince. He might not even be a prince. She searched for Androvsky in the telephone directory and on the Internet, but found nothing.

The next afternoon she was returning from a long lunch at the Ivy with Caroline, who had just made partner at Stedman's, a prestigious law firm, when she passed a kiosk and saw the newspaper headline. She bought a paper, hailed a cab and quickly turned to the article.

Prince Falls to his Death at Russian Embassy.
Prince Alexander Sergeievich Androvsky, a Russian émigré and prominent member of the White Russian community in Paris, fell to his death last night from a balcony at the Russian Embassy. The prince, who had attended the reception at the embassy earlier that evening, was found by the cleaning staff in the early hours this morning. Ending his long exile, Androvsky recently returned to Russia for business and political reasons. The prince also resided in Moscow, Paris, and New York. Police believe it was an accidental death but will not make an announcement until further investigation.

His charming face came before her. She remembered the balcony high above the room where the musicians had been playing. Surely it couldn't have happened while she was waiting in the vestibule? She shivered as the thought occurred to her that he could have been pushed from the balcony, even though the police were reporting it as accidental death. She was positive he was going to tell her Abigail was alive. The prince said there was someone in New York who knew everything. As the cab came through Sloane Street and drove down King's Road, she had made up her mind. She was going to New York to find her mentor.

That evening she was nervous, a little scared when Philip picked her up for the NSPCC benefit at the Tate Gallery. Claire had reassured her that surely he would understand and that it was ridiculous to be afraid of someone you loved. She had dressed carefully, in a long Armani gown in blue shimmering silk, which covered her bandaged ankle. Her blond hair was caught up in a loose chignon. But Philip did not hug or compliment her as he usually did. He was silent in the car, and she could feel his anger, like a storm ready to burst upon her.

It was a glittering A-list party at the museum. The tables were decorated to resemble 18th century 'still lifes' with vines and flowers draped over large bowls of fruit like the background of a Caravaggio painting. Elton John and Madonna had performed. But she was jittery, preoccupied with what had happened at the embassy. She had lied to Philip, and now had to tell him that she was going to New York to find Abigail, that there was a chance that she was alive.

Afterward in the car, she lapsed into a fearful silence, waiting for his rush of anger. Without looking at her, Philip said, "I think it's time you stop grieving over that woman. She had no real connection to you."

"I'm sorry you feel that way," she said.

He wouldn't look at her. "You're really a stupid cow. You know she's dead." The car sped along King's Road, dark and deserted, toward her flat.

Tears sprung to her eyes. "No, that's not true."

"Where were you last night? I know you lied to me." His voice was rough, low so that his driver couldn't hear.

Eager to confess and to be forgiven, her words rushed out. "Yes, I'm sorry, I did lie. There is no excuse for it. I went to the Russian Embassy. You see, I received this invitation to a reception. Someone had information about Abigail. I had to meet with this man. I think she might still be alive." She longed for him to understand, to help her.

"You forced me to cancel an important client dinner for that?" His fists were clenched, and she thought he was going to hit her.

"I'm sorry," she said again, her voice breathless. "I'm going to New York to try to find Abigail." She was suddenly inexplicably terrified.

His features were carved in a mask of anger. "If you do, our engagement is over. You'll have to choose between this absurd trip and me."

He meant it, but she sensed he expected her to back down. Waves of emotion swept over her. The scene seemed unreal. Was this happening to her?

Before she realized what she was doing, she heard herself say, "I don't want to be engaged to you any longer." It was as though Abigail were in the background, urging her on.

Philip's sharp features grew incredulous. He was the kind of superior person who never lost a game, or a business deal, had never been turned down on a date, had always been chosen for the right clubs. When they reached her flat and left the car, out of his driver's hearing, she was panicked, realizing that there would be a terrific explosion.

He dragged her to her door, hurting her as he opened it and threw her inside, pushing her up against the wall. His hands gripped her shoulders, and he shook her hard.

She could have borne that, but would never forget his scorn and hatred. His scathing insults still clanged in her head, like the clapper of a bell. Common trash, my mother was right, no good, who knows where you came from, phony career, whore. Then the door to her flat slammed, shaking the pictures, and Philip was gone.

She had never intended to break the engagement so suddenly. She had been still clinging on, afraid she couldn't do without him. In shock, she looked down at her hand, now bereft of his grandmother's antique diamond. She sobbed and stumbled into the bedroom, unzipping her gown as she went. He was right. She was all that he said. She splashed water on her face and lay rigidly in bed, bewildered at what she had done, when her phone rang. She had called the Little Swan Gallery earlier that day after she read of Prince Androvsky's death and had spoken to Maxi, Abigail's lover, telling him she was flying to New York tomorrow. Through the haze of grief she heard him insist on meeting her at Kennedy Airport.

The next afternoon Katya waited in the BA first class lounge at Heathrow wrapped in her light blue pashmina, drinking her second glass of champagne. She didn't usually drink when flying, but she was stricken.

She was groggy when her flight was called and fought to keep back the tears as she limped onto the plane. The stewardess was very sympathetic, took her coat, and led her to the front seat. She was relieved to see that the seat next to her was empty. After the plane took off and was cruising, the stewardess helped her with the flat bed, but she couldn't rest. Not quite believing what had happened to her in the past two days, she listened to the hum of the engine, ignorant of what awaited her in her search for Abigail. She was alone and lost, like a child wandering in a dark forest.

Chapter 6

Mikhail
Autoroute du Soleil, France

LIKE A BLACK predatory bird the Mercedes winged its way to the South of France. Mikhail raised his hands and ran them over his head in a nervous gesture. In spite of his knowledge of the Raven's powerful secret, the scheme for his triumphant return to Russia had not come to him at once.

He went back to the year 2000, to those early black days of his exile in Paris when he met General Mirov and his plan took final form. Sensing he was out of favor and might be forced out of Russia, he planned ahead and deposited most of his cash and stocks in banks in Cyprus and Switzerland. He was granted temporary political asylum in France and lived for several weeks in Paris at the Crillon in a confused state of anger, and despair. The FSB watched his every move, but he felt no urgency then to go into hiding.

The anguish of those first days of exile still tormented him. His anger had been so fierce, so overwhelming that he could not eat or sleep. Even the rare book collection he had brought out of Russia failed to provide a peaceful distraction. His mind worked in overtime, devising plans, dismantling them and starting again. Other than his two bodyguards and housekeeper Anya, there was no one else he trusted. He had no loyal friends; only associates attracted to his wealth and power. Now he was cut off from them. Seedy characters, punks and members of an Albanian gang involved in drug running and prostitution approached him with minor deals, adding to his humiliation.

One Sunday in autumn during his early exile, he was restless, at loose ends and had felt an urgent need to be near Russians, to hear them speaking. With his bodyguards following discreetly by car, he had walked to the Rue Daru to the St-Alexandre-Nevsky Orthodox Cathedral. Standing among the worshippers, Mikhail stared at the beautiful icons and a surge of longing overcame him. Tears ran down his face as the deep rich voices of the choir washed over him. He spoke to no one and left immediately after the service ended.

That evening he received a call. "Mikhail Borisov, my name is General Mirov." The man spoke Russian with a slight German accent. "I have a proposition for you. Will you meet me?"

Intrigued, slightly alarmed that the general had accessed his number, he agreed.

"Do not come to me." The general whispered. "You tell me where."

It was a cool cut glass day, the Paris air clear and fresh. Mikhail sat in the Café Les Deux Magots waiting for Mirov, not sure why he had agreed to meet with a stranger. He had chosen the café because it always was crowded with habitués and hoards of tourists. From his days at the KGB he knew it would be less conspicuous to be among tourists than in a shabby café near the Rue Daru where everyone in the Russian community, émigrés, spies, and modern revolutionaries would be hanging out.

When he arrived at the bustling café, he glanced at the wooden statues of the two Chinese merchants, Les Deux Magots, peering critically down at him from their pillar and then chose an inside table facing St. Germain-des-Prés Church, away from the busy boulevard. He admired the church's ancient stone porch for a few moments, and then looked at his watch. The man was fifteen minutes late. Perhaps he wasn't coming, or more likely his men were checking out the café and surroundings.

He was getting up to leave when an elderly man dressed in a military uniform with a beautiful young woman on his arm burst in and without hesitation came directly to the table. General Mirov was a large vigorous man with strong handsome youthful features. A small white moustache rested on his upper lip like snow on a window ledge. He removed his black beret, setting loose a shock of thick white hair, gave a click with his boot heels and bowed. "I apologize for being late. You are Mikhail Petrovich Borisov. I recognize you from the newspapers. General Dimitri Gregorievich Mirov." His voice with a more pronounced German accent than Mikhail had heard on the phone, was high and fruity. "And this is my lovely secretary, Kyra Andreevna Tikhonova."

Kyra gave him an inviting smile. Mikhail, dazzled, tried not to stare. "Please sit down," he said.

The general wore a Cossack *shuba, a* military cape, and highly polished boots. He stood erect, resembling Tsarist officers in old photographs. His mouth curved up in a merry smile, but his gray eyes were hard and observant. He removed the *shuba*, and with a Russian extravagance of gesture swung it around a chair.

Mikhail felt a stir of impatience. What could this relic from the past want from him? Kyra slid out of her sable coat to reveal a centerfold body with long legs in very tight jeans. Her low cut sweater showed her breasts to advantage. She had a snub-nosed insolent look and liquid slanted dark eyes. Her blond hair, thick and shiny, hung down her back in luxurious waves. She settled in her chair in a languid pose, and the general grabbed her hand as though keeping her prisoner.

"What will you have?" Mikhail spoke in Russian.

"Cognac please," the general said. Faint traces of a traditional German dueling scar marked Mirov's left cheek. Mikhail guessed it was a bungled attempt by a plastic surgeon to erase it after the war.

He looked at Kyra. "The same," she said, pouting.

"You attended Alexander Nevsky last Sunday, not a place one would expect an ex-communist, an ex KGB agent to be seen." Mirov freed Kyra's hand, took a small jeweled box from his dark suit pocket, opened the lid engraved with his initials, delicately pinched some snuff between his fingers and sniffed it up his nose.

"It is common knowledge that you are no longer welcome in your own country. It is an outrage. You are angry, not accustomed to exile, Mikhail Petrovich. I was born in exile, but always felt I am, like my father, a true Russian Cossack. Perhaps together we will return triumphant to Mother Russia." He stopped for a moment, gazing directing at Mikhail. "We know of your background in the security services. My staff has done a bit of research into your past."

His mind raced. What did this stranger know about him? Surely nothing before Afghanistan. The waiter served the drinks, and put the tab on the table. Mirov offered him a cigarette. He refused. He had not smoked since his interrogation at KGB headquarters; cigarettes had become a reminder of pain.

"You are a general?" Mikhail said in a soft voice.

Mirov took a sip before replying. "I suppose it doesn't count for much in leftist circles, but yes, I am a general in our small but dedicated Tsarist army." He petulantly smoothed his moustache.

Mirov's telephone call had prompted him to search his store of Directorate files. In the late nineties planning ahead, he had smuggled the classified documents out of Russia to France. These documents were kept in two places, under guard in a nondescript Paris warehouse and in his house in the South of France. The general's dossier revealed that he had been born in Paris to White Russian émigrés who fled the country during the revolution. His father, the Tsarist General Gregori Alexeievich Mirov had been prominent in émigré circles, a rabid anti-communist, and it seemed from one of his pamphlets, virulently anti-Semitic. His mother the Countess Natasha Feodorovna Zubalova was a great beauty whose family was closely connected to the Tsar's court.

Sifting through the data, Mikhail had been startled to find a black and white photograph dated 1942. A young Mirov in a German officer's uniform posed with Himmler and Hitler in front of the Rauthaus in Munich, scene of Hitler's rise to power. Accompanying the photograph was an anonymous report claiming that Mirov had worked for German intelligence, but there were no official documents to substantiate this.

He had studied the photograph. Mirov was wearing an SS uniform. The general's record after the Germans surrendered was incomplete. He was one of the sinister figures on the fringe of the Nazi high command who escaped punishment from the Allies. Mikhail had closed the file, wondering if Western Intelligence had employed Mirov after the war.

He had placed a French-speaking watcher on the old general, who discovered from Mirov's concierge that he had recently come into money, source unknown. Each month he went to a post office near the Gare Du Nord and returned with an envelope of cash. Since this mysterious rise in fortune the general had moved his office to better quarters and a week ago acquired a new apartment on the Left Bank. He lavished gifts on Kyra, his mistress and secretary. Shamil, the fashion expert, had noted that her fur coat was a recent purchase.

"I am sure your friends in state security know of me. I make no pretense. You have noticed my scar." He stubbed out his cigarette and drew off these last words with a sigh as he delicately caressed the red line on his cheek. "But let me explain my background so there is nothing hidden. My father was a Cossack general in the White Army.

He left Russia shortly before the Bolshevik victory, and settled in Paris. He was a loyal monarchist and dedicated his life to fighting the Bolsheviks. Stalin took him very seriously as a threat. In 1931 my father was kidnapped on a Paris street by the KGB, taken back to Russia, and tortured and shot in the Lubyanka."

Kyra sighed, rolled her eyes in boredom. She leaned forward to give Mikhail a glimpse of her cleavage. Mirov's meaty left hand disappeared under the table, and Mikhail suspected from her expression, gripped his secretary in a vulnerable area between the legs.

He was impressed. The old guy had to be in his eighties and yet, here he was, feeling up this sexpot. He must have undergone the same monkey gland treatment in the Switzerland clinic as those ancient members of the now defunct Soviet Politburo. The treatment proved effective. Some of them were still alive, still defending Stalin. It occurred to him Mirov might have been getting virility shots in an adjoining room to his Russian enemies.

"My father was a great friend of the von Hindenburg family, and as a consequence, I was sent to Heidelberg University and then trained at military college in Prussia. Hence the scar, which I naturally attempted to erase after the war. It was only right that I would fight to liberate my country from Stalin. I escaped from prison before the British repatriated the Cossacks back to Russia and death. But that is the past. We are looking forward to a bright future in the New Russia." He paused to drink his cognac.

The old photograph of Mirov posing with Hitler flashed before him and his guts seized up. He recognized the same neutral inhuman look in the old man's eyes as that of his own torturer long ago. The hum of traffic from the boulevard faded. The smell of tobacco, and coffee was overwhelmed by the odor of blood, of burning flesh. It took him back to the torture room. He heard the general's voice in the distance.

"I sense that my plan may be the only way back for you."

"What plan?" Mikhail said, fighting through his nausea.

"My organization, The Double Eagle is working toward the return of a monarch to rule Russia. Initially it would be a constitutional monarchy. Of course, all could be altered once we have power. We have everything in place. All we need is a like-minded financier." He finished the cognac and leaned forward, lowering his voice.

"We are uniting with monarchist organizations and sympathizers to contest Russia's next election. I have links to most of these organizations, many of them inside Russia. We need financial support. If you are willing to provide it, then you will return as a real power behind the throne. Of course, it is all still in the formative stage and must be kept secret. There is danger in opposing the Russian government. Two of our men in Moscow were recently murdered, although their deaths were reported as accidents. They were found in a curiously mutilated condition, their eyes slashed from the sockets."

Several men in their thirties, lawyers in designer suits, entered the café and took a table near the boulevard. Kyra studied them with interest. Bebe and Shamil also watched at a table nearby, pretending to read newspapers.

"What makes you believe there is any chance to establish a monarchy?" In the pause Mikhail had driven out his images of the torture room, of eye sockets. The old White Russian was unbalanced, a dangerous crank.

Mirov brought his hand from underneath the table. He looked down at both large fleshy appendages, widespread as though he were reading a military map. "You must know, since the fall of the USSR we have been waiting for this opportunity. There are many Russians now, both exiles and those inside the country who respond favorably to the idea of a monarchy."

"How do you know that?" Mikhail watched a group of noisy American students enter the café, crowd up to the bar, and begin taking photographs of each other.

"Last year our organization hired at great expense the Leadenhall PR Firm's marketing department. Their research, polling Russians, revealed strong feelings of nostalgia for the Tsarist past."

Mikhail began to pay close attention. He and others of the prosperous new elite yearned to be part of an intriguing past forcibly blocked from memory until the communists fell. He too, was nostalgic, wanted to go home to live in his Moscow mansion recently confiscated by the government.

"Liebchen, the file please." Kyra brought out a folder and handed it to Mirov. He opened it and removed some papers. "The results of the research and polling are here. Awakening from the drab communistic nightmare to our vivid Tsarist past, the New Russians are restoring old buildings and have rediscovered the Orthodox religion. They are buying period furniture, Faberge eggs, and icons from auction houses all over the world. We have read countless magazines and newspaper articles describing Russia's elite, dressed like members of the Tsarist Court, throwing balls and parties in old renovated palaces. Courses are given to people like you to teach manners from a Chekhovian era; how to hold a teacup with fingers that once smashed empty vodka bottles and pulled triggers." He stopped to laugh scornfully.

"These new rich are ignorant of the arts, but donate huge sums to museums to be appointed to the boards and to gain respectability. I have all the research results here. Everything is here," he repeated, his heavy hand covering the papers.

Mikhail had a sudden absurd picture of Crazy Igor, the hit man with two missing fingers, now president of a bank, traipsing through museums, commenting on the Moscow School. He laughed aloud, causing Bebe to turn around in alarm, and reach for his gun.

The general ignored his outburst. "We are certain it will be possible to win an election using this remarkable nostalgia for the past. The enormous groundswell of support for a tsar will drive out Putin and his government."

He was on the alert, sensing danger. At first he saw only a suit like Bebe's, and then the man turned. Yuri Turvin, a former colleague, now in the FSB, had suddenly appeared at the zinc bar. Two other comrades loitered outside the café. Mirov had also seen the watchers and lowered his voice, changing to English. Mikhail relaxed. He had known they were following him. Turvin had a weakness for women and seemed mesmerized by Kyra.

As if on cue, Kyra said, "Excuse me." She rose and all male eyes in the café followed her provocative walk through the room.

"Who would be the candidate?" Mikhail said.

Mirov smiled, taking another pinch of snuff before answering.

"There are the obvious ones, but I look to an obscure relative of the last Tsar, or perhaps more pliable, an aristocrat who is not a family member. He must, of course, be Russian, young, intelligent, upper class, well bred and presentable. In these days of degeneracy, difficult to find. But we have someone in mind. It is of necessity that his identity remains a secret until we are sure of support."

Kyra had stopped at the bar, chatting up Turvin and then sat down at the table, a seat away from the general, still smiling at the agent.

"It is a very convincing argument, but before I commit to anything, I would have to see your lists of organizations and supporters," Mikhail said, watching Turvin leave the cafe, wondering if he had arranged to meet Kyra later.

Mirov bowed his head in assent, "That is only natural. It will be dangerous, but yes, I will send Kyra to your hotel with the list this evening."

He moved his chair closer and whispered, "Before I go, I must ask you. There is something my father spoke of only to me, a secret that would be of inestimable value to our cause. The information came from an old acquaintance of my father's, someone he knew in Russia during the revolution. It could be lethal for those who knew.

Papa would only give me the man's nom de revolution, the Raven. This man, a Bolshevik agent, swore my father to secrecy before telling him he was searching for this hidden intelligence from the past, instrumental to taking power in Russia. I have heard from reliable sources that this knowledge would give our candidate uncontested legitimacy as the new Tsar."

The café noise muffled as though Mikhail had been plunged underwater, forced to struggle through his shock to the surface. When he recovered, he said, "That sounds very much like fantasy. Something a crank would dream up."

His merry demeanor gone, the general stared hard at him, his grey eyes like clear stone. "My father was a realist. And we do know that Russia's history always seems like a bad fairy tale for those of us living it. My information is totally reliable. Perhaps you have forgotten. We would appreciate anything you might discover."

Still watching the street, Mirov rose to his feet. "Please think about what I have said. It is important for us both." They kissed him a la Russe, like old friends, and left the café, the general tightly gripping his mistress's arm.

Mikhail was charged with excitement when Kyra came to his hotel room that evening. She tossed the folder on the floor and provocatively opened her coat. She wore nothing underneath and stood in front of him, legs apart, breasts jutting out; her expression insolent, challenging. He picked her up and threw her onto the bed, savagely moving over her body, but then his ardor faded. Her noisy lovemaking seemed mechanical and the sounds of ecstasy left him cold and alarmed. She was a trained operative. Mirov had sent Kyra instead of his thugs to search his room for any lead to the Raven's document. The general would not want to risk any undue attention from French authorities.

Afterward, he pretended to sleep and watched her go through his clothes. While she searched the room, he glimpsed the metal handle of a pistol in her coat pocket. He wondered for a moment if she was planning to kill him, but decided that she was armed for protection. He clutched the Mauser he kept under the mattress, then stirred in the bed and sat up in time to assume ignorance of her search. Their parting was cordial. She left him a phone number.

He had carefully examined the members' list for the Double Eagle and other monarchist parties, realizing that the general's plan, even if bogus, fit his objective. But Mirov was dangerous and when no longer useful, would have to be eliminated.

Mikhail came back to the present, reached for another bottle of water from the car's refrigerator and drank it down. The Mercedes turned off the highway and began to climb the hills overlooking Nice to St. Paul de Vence.

Since that fated encounter with Mirov two years ago his ambition had expanded to not only return to his native land, but to rule. He had carefully plotted his return. First, he must be elected to the Duma, the Russian Parliament. As a member he would be immune to prosecution. But getting elected was no longer just a question of distributing bribes and killing opponents. He must win the battle of public opinion. This would be difficult. He had been labeled an unscrupulous murderer and thief in the government controlled Moscow press.

To combat this impression he had hired The Montrose Group, an influential and effective public relations company with branches in Europe and the United States. The firm presented him as an advocate of civil rights, a hero, and martyr for democracy, driven out by Putin's gradual dictatorship. He didn't delude himself.

The Montrose Group's mission, presented to him with glitzy slides and graphics by two smooth men in hand tailored suits, was to associate him with Russia's romantic past. Before Mikhail had become a fugitive, photos of his worshipping at the Orthodox Church in Biarritz and hobnobbing at the races with remnants of

Royalty appeared in *Hello* and *Tatler* magazines. He sponsored charity events attended by important British politicians and bankers. Montrose had placed representatives in both Moscow and St. Petersburg, to promote him and sound out prospects.

He shivered in the darkness of the car. Until his meeting two years ago with General Mirov he had believed that he was the last person alive who knew of the Raven's secret. Mikhail felt sure that Mirov was aware only that the powerful document had once existed, and knew nothing else, but he sensed that someone from out of his dark past in Siberia was tracing the girl.

Chapter 7

Mikhail
St. Paul de Vence, France

MIKHAIL WAS BROODING over the past and his enemies when the Mercedes reached St. Paul de Vence. He must search the Raven's files, a frightening prospect he had avoided for years. They arrived at the ancient hill town in early morning, and although it was January, the sun was breaking warm, flooding the landscape with that beautiful clear light peculiar to the South of France. The oligarch never tired of this view. He pushed a button to lower the car window shade to watch the village men, dark figures against the blue sky, idly chatting, smoking, and playing pétanque in the tiny square.

On the left was the entrance to La Colombe d'Or, the famous inn once frequented by the painters Matisse and Monet, and filled with the works of artists who exchanged paintings with the innkeeper for meals. In earlier times Mikhail had dined there with his two body-guards for company. He would linger over coffee on the mellow stone sunlit terrace, in wonder at this unfamiliar tranquil life, a slow graciousness he had never known.

They drove slowly past the village parking area, an open space before the road narrowed and wound its way through the rocks. The lot was half full of buses carrying day-trippers. Even in winter the village was the haunt of tourists; one reason he had selected it as a hideaway. His enemies would never suspect he would live in such a public place.

Called a village perché, St. Paul was a walled village built on top of rocks in the early Middle Ages to repel invaders. It performed the same function for him and was convenient to Nice Airport where he parked his jet and to the harbor near his yacht berth. His men, posing as parking attendants, waved them on and then barred the next car of sightseers. Only residents were permitted to drive past the parking lot and up through the small cobblestone streets. The Mercedes climbed steeply, nearly scraping the walls of the buildings, until it reached a complex of three charming medieval dwellings and pulled into the house on the left, converted into a garage.

Under guard Mikhail rushed into his living quarters, located in the middle house. His complex was discreet, with nothing on the exterior to distinguish it from other stone buildings on the street. But inside the great oak door of the entrance hall with shuttered windows, his four security guards, armed with assault rifles, patrolled. A sophisticated radar system surrounded the buildings.

He nodded to his men and hurried across the old stone floors, which swept through the living area, and opened the door to the house on the right. This held a communications system, connecting him to his yacht, jet and to news agencies, sources, and contacts throughout the world. The two technicians, Yuri and Anatoly, who manned the computers and radios, handed him the security reports and the latest news from Russia and the United States. There was no news on the girl in the photo, and nothing from Stavrogin, his agent in the States who worked independently from the Odessa Group.

His anger and frustration at sheer incompetence rose to a murderous pitch, and he repeatedly rubbed both hands over his head in a furious motion. This involuntary movement, like a nervous tick he couldn't control when he was disturbed, struck fear in the hearts of his security men. He no longer trusted any of his personnel in the U.S. Stavrogin's silence was unnerving. He thought of placing another agent there, on the ground. He had even considered going himself, but shadowed by his enemies knew it was impossible to get through the heightened security after 9/11. The Russian authorities would send a scurrilous file on him to U.S. Immigration.

Still rubbing his head, he quickly crossed the stone floors covered in antique oriental rugs to his office, an elegantly paneled oak room decorated in French Provincial style, its shelves filled with his collection of rare Russian children's books. He pushed a small lever, hidden in one of the panels of his massive oak desk, and the wall of bookcases opened, revealing a medium sized room lined with large steel filing cabinets.

The files, brought here by his private plane several years before he was forced out of Russia, came from two sources. The most important, which he had never examined, were inherited from the Raven and kept here. The others in the Paris warehouse, had been plundered from the KGB's First Chief Directorate Archive in Yasenevo.

Mikhail had rejected his technician's suggestion that the files be copied and stored digitally. From past experience he knew this method would not be secure. He remained the only person with access and would keep it that way. He opened the combination lock on one of the cabinets and for several hours flipped through folders. Then he stopped, drawn to a thick battered cardboard file, covered with greasy dust. It was stamped *Classified, 1917*. He removed it, locked the cabinet, put the shelves back in place, and returned to the long sitting room.

It was urgent that he read the file before leaving for Courchevel. It meant postponing his trip, even though he had sent half his bodyguard to secure his ski chalet. His mood changed slightly as he thought of what awaited him; his choice of the most beautiful of the young Russian girls brought to the resort by Vlach and Nika. The girls, all virgins, were eager, fun loving and so very young. What gave him the most pleasure was the knowledge that he could do whatever he wished with them. He grew hard with desire at the thought of this complete control. He picked several of the most beautiful girls to try, and would finally choose only one to spend a year with him. It was poor security, very dangerous to have more than one female living in close proximity.

After a year, he would tire of the girl and discard her, but always gave her some reward before choosing a fresh one. He had never married and had no thought of taking one of these whores for a wife. They all were alike to him, indistinguishable, like the Matryoshka stack dolls sold in souvenir shops. He couldn't even remember the face of Irina from last year. He felt nothing, but for a short time could forget he was an exile in danger. It was a pleasurable diversion.

He carried the file as though it would burn his fingers and opened the glass doors to the stone terrace overlooking the valley. Its low stone wall was flanked by tubs of colorful winter plants and herbs. He sat down in one of the brown wicker chairs, part of an elegant set that the decorator had picked for him. Placing the folder on the side table, he poured a glass of Chateau La Tour he had ordered brought from his cellar. It was deep winter, but the warm sun seemed tropical compared to his time near the Arctic Circle.

He poured a second glass of wine and stared at the frayed battered cardboard folder. He knew it held secrets of his controller, General Peter Von Krantz. Mikhail had been ordered always to address him as the Raven, his nom de revolution. A Bolshevik spy during the Russian Revolution, the Raven's past was shrouded in secrecy. The aristocratic old man, tall, groomed to perfection, sophisticated and murderous, materialized in front of him, joking about Lenin's phrase, 'To the Archives'. Lenin, the first Bolshevik ruler of Russia, had believed that his written orders for some unspeakable brutality would be consigned to the archives and would never see the light of day. 'How wrong he was,' the Raven would say with a harsh laugh.

He felt helpless, almost physically sick, terrified of what he would find in the folder. Throughout his life, the old man had complete power over him and taunted him. Once he told Mikhail he had knowledge of his early years and his true identity, but even though he begged, the Raven refused to tell him who he was. He hated it that his obscure past was tied to the old Bolshevik, still controlling him from the grave.

He watched the sun grow more intense, lighting up the terraced valley below. With shaking hands he drained his wine glass, and memories came rushing back. During his last mission in 1970 he learned of the Raven's secret intelligence group, a separate power from the KGB and the Soviet Government. His head had throbbed with fear when he discovered he was not directed by the KGB, but by the renegade spy and his sinister organization. After the mission failed, he was accused of being weak, vulnerable because of the woman.

When he had refused to follow orders, he was bound and gagged and shipped back to the Lubyanka. He rubbed the dent in his cheek. During his most brutal interrogations, a secretive, professorial man, eyeglasses planted on a bureaucratic face, came in often to speak with him. He cooperated willingly with this man. Mikhail's craftiness, his willingness to betray, taught to him by the Raven saved him.

He convinced 'the professor' who showed compassion and stopped the torture, that he would be useful. He answered every question. But he was never asked about the search for the hidden document. The interrogators were interested only in the Raven's secret intelligence force and his planned defection.

After his release, he did not see his benefactor until much later, but felt his influence. He ordered that Mikhail be promoted to the rank of colonel in the KGB as reward for betraying the Raven. Years later, he identified 'the professor' as Yuri Andropov, once Chief of Russian Intelligence before succeeding Brezhnev as head of the Russian state.

Mikhail kept the secret buried; terrified, knowing that it would mean death to reveal the existence of the powerful document. He also had reasoned that it would be of use at some time in the uncertain future. He marveled that it recently had resurfaced when he desperately needed it, his last resort.

He returned to the folder, remembering the strange way he had come into possession of the Raven's files. In the late seventies after his lengthy interrogation in the Lubyanka, and release, he was living in an isolated hut in Siberia near the Mongolian border, waiting to be 'rehabilitated', when he received a message. A man dressed like a shepherd in the old style Mongolian *ger* rode his pony directly to the door of Mikhail's cabin. His lined brown face and broken teeth made him appear ancient, but he jumped off his mount like a young man. He said nothing and nodded his head knowingly as he handed Mikhail the message.

The outside of the note was inscribed **FOR YOU**.

Terror whipped through him when he recognized the Raven's bold handwriting. He would discover later that the Raven was already dead and all had been planned long before. The note contained one sentence, 'You will find the answers in the files.'

There was also a detailed map of the site located a few miles from Perm near the Urals in Siberia.

It wasn't until the eighties when he was an established KGB General that he dared to search the area in Perm for the Raven's files. The map, frighteningly exact in spite of the passage of time, led him to an old abandoned Bolshevik headquarters in a wooded area near Perm. In the dust covered room he found rusting steel boxes. He still recalled his surprise that some of the folders were in both Mongolian and English. He loaded the boxes onto his private plane, and hid them away, thinking he might never open them.

Even now, when his life depended on it, he hesitated, putting down the folder, the old fear returning. He snatched at it as though it was burning hot, and something slipped out onto the floor. He leaned down to pick it up and caught his breath. It was a faded color photograph; he guessed from the forties. The young woman stands straight like a stone statue, a barren hill rising behind her. Dressed in an embroidered robe, she is breathtakingly beautiful and solemnly stares out at him, someone from a lost world. Shaken by its strangeness, he studied the picture, turning it over, but there was no identification. The setting sun exploded into a last red light as he placed the photograph on the table. Shivering in the growing darkness, he noticed the Raven's bold scrawl on the outside rim of the file.

Revised in 1947. The soul of another is a dark forest.

Chapter 8

Roo
Tecumseh County

ROO WAS AWAKE most of the night, picturing the skull with the open jaw lying in the snow. The howl of the wolf echoed through his room. It had been late when he and Sheriff Stumpy Walker, the Coroner Joe Daley and the lab technicians, on loan from Franklin County, had finished their preliminary investigation and removed the body to the morgue. This was partly because, like a fuck off, he had left his phone to dry out on the kitchen table, and had to drive thirty miles back to the sheriff's house in town before the alarm was raised. He was still in a kind of shock over the coroner's words, which spilled out mercilessly over the bones.

Coroner Daley, a thin dry man in his fifties, hunched like a large grasshopper against the cold. He had peered through gold-rimmed glasses, and said there was enough evidence to state that the skeleton was a woman and a homicide, but he couldn't confirm it officially until all the lab work was completed. The crime unit investigators had found two bullets near the bones.

"Rifled," Daly had barked out in his harsh voice. "Probable cause of death. From what I can tell, she's been dead not more than two years."

Roo stared out the window of the shack, the humps of derelict cars looming in the darkness, scarcely believing Stumpy's words yesterday when they finally returned to the office.

"You're in charge of the case." Stumpy had given him a sidelong glance. "I tried to pass it to the State Police but they're swamped. Two of their guys are on extended sick leave," he said.

He jumped out of bed and turned on the shower. As the water coursed down, he wondered who the woman was, and how she had arrived at that deserted place. Her relatives must have searched for her, but maybe they had given up.

He dressed, his fingers nervously fumbling at his uniform buttons, and made a cup of instant coffee, left untouched on the table. He drove in the dark into Paint Creek, the Tecumseh County seat. It was 6 a.m. when he arrived at the sheriff's office. He was the first one in, and he opened the dusty venetian blind of the window overlooking the empty car park. On the other side of the room another window presented a better view of a small snow dusted patch with two evergreens. The office was pleasant, its light walls lined with file cabinets and maps of the county. A steel door next to Stumpy's office led to the jail, a room with four cells, almost always empty.

The table just outside the sheriff's office held the police radios and the coffee maker, still filled with yesterday's brew. He decided against trying to heat it up and sat down at his desk in the big reception area. His desk and Gracie Logan's, the secretary, were side by side. The large space between them symbolized their mutual dislike.

Relieved that the grumpy middle-aged spinster wouldn't be in until nine, he moved to the computer on the table beside his desk and booted it.

Stumpy had said Roo was the legs, would report to him and then he would handle the press. Roo felt he was a phony, an amateur with very little training. He mostly dealt with traffic accidents and violations. Once he had been involved in rounding up a drug ring when the State Police were short of men. His behavior at the crime scene yesterday had been modeled on what he had culled from crime novels and rudimentary training. Tecumseh County seemed in a time warp because of its sparse population of farmers and the Amish, immune to serious crimes that filled the jails of the cities and neighboring counties.

Sheriff Walker bustled through the door, a surprised expression on his wrinkled face, which bore a close resemblance to a fat hound dog.

"You're here early and already working," he said, almost accusingly. Stumpy had a habit of stating the obvious. "Good, it's a big case. Haven't had once since …" He stopped, his small fat hand fussing self-consciously with his sparse comb over.

Roo's dad had been the last and only sensational case to make the newspapers.

"Sorry," Stumpy said, his short squat body poured into his uniform waddled past to his office. "Get a cup of coffee and come in. Let's go over what we have from last night's preliminary report." The sheriff and Roo's dad had been friends. They had both served in Vietnam and after their return, drank together most Friday and Saturday nights, although Stumpy, an elected official, never let his drinking get out of hand.

After his dad's death, Stumpy rescued him by giving him the deputy sheriff's job, in spite of some opposition in the town after what had happened. He had persuaded Roo that his fame as a star high school quarterback on the Paint Creek 1988 State Championship Team would give him 'credibility' in the modern speak that he sometimes affected, with the few teenage delinquents in the area. Roo did have credibility for a while, but now didn't believe even adults his age remembered him.

He hated any mention of his dad and stalled for several minutes, checking the screen for reports he had requested last night, but it was blank and uncooperative. Then he picked up his notebook and knocked on Stumpy's door. "Come in," he boomed. The sheriff had lit one of his cigars, violating all of the no smoking signs he had put up himself, and looked at him through the haze in a sidelong rather sheepish way.

Roo didn't smoke. His weekend binges were enough to kill him without adding additional poison to his system. Stumpy's sly expression always made him squirm. It was a reminder of another reason he had been given the job of deputy when he was virtually unemployable, although he had passed the law enforcement examination. It hadn't been only the friendship with his dad. Once when he was still living with his mom, he'd come home late and passed the sheriff on the porch, his shirt open, zipping his fly, the same sheepish look on his face. He had been too shocked to react at the moment. And afterward, he felt it was too late, that there might even have been other men, and there was no point in talking about it. Besides he and his mom weren't on speaking terms by then.

"I guess it's too early for the coroner to call, so there's no reason to traipse over there," Walker said. The Forensic Department was located in a long low building only a block away, but Stumpy was squeamish and always had an excuse to avoid the morgue.

Roo held up his notebook. "Some of this is not official yet."

"Go on" The puffed bags beneath the sheriff's slit eyes made him look sleepy. But Roo knew better and flipped open his steno notebook and began reading.

"The bones of an unidentified female murder victim, dead approximately two years, found Sunday, January 6th at approximately 9 a.m. in the forest near a cabin off Route 23. Victim had been shot through the window of the cabin at fairly close range. A shotgun was found beside the bed in the cabin. Empty shells near the gun indicate the victim had fired the shotgun twice, probably in self-defense. No fingerprints were found on the shotgun or anywhere in the cabin or on the porch. The body was dragged by the killer into the forest."

Roo looked up. "It's my guess that the killer was interrupted and fled before he could bury or hide the body. Some of the victim's bones were scattered by animals, probably foxes." Stumpy's cigar had gone out, and the deputy sheriff waited while he fiddled around to relight it. Puffs of smoke like a factory chimney again clouded the room.

Roo's eyes welled with tears from the smoke. He went on with his notes trying to couch them in language a trained detective might use "The victim has not yet been identified. Fingerprints, DNA samples from the body, and dental analysis are expected today from forensics. Remnants of the victim's clothing had no identifiable tags, but may be traced through lab analysis of the material. We're still waiting for all the results."

Walker sighed, his eyes disappearing into tiny lines.

"Dammit, I hate this. A murder victim and an election next year. A killer on the loose. How can I run on crime prevention?"

Roo didn't answer the whine. "A gray 1996 Jeep Cherokee was found under a tarp beside the cabin. I am assuming it belonged to the victim. The jeep was clean, no papers, no fingerprints. The fuel gauge and odometer were smashed so there is no way of knowing how far the murder victim might have driven the jeep. I sent the license number to the Bureau of Motor Vehicles to check the registration." He stopped for a moment, wiping sweat drops from his forehead. Christ, he probably sounded like an amateur Miss Marple or worse, like a bumbling Inspector Clouseau.

"I've also requested the Tecumseh County Auditor's Property Registration Bureau to search the title to the cabin and property where the woman was found. Nothing yet from either department." He fidgeted, shaking his knees, restless.

Stumpy leaned back in his chair, as always tempting fate that he wouldn't topple over. "We'll just have to wait."

"One other thing," Roo said, turning round at the door. "I'm checking the state data base for all violent offenders. The sheets should arrive this morning."

When he returned to his desk, there were still no messages. He shut down the computer and returned alone to the forest. Its isolated beauty was marred by tracks from the police vans; the trees bound like prisoners in red and white striped tape marking off the location of the bones.

Inside the cabin, silhouettes were drawn on the floor near the bed where the shotgun had been dropped, and where the woman might have fallen after being shot. On the table, chalk marks replaced the open champagne bottle and goblets, all taken to the lab for analysis. Was she planning a celebration? The bottle, Moet & Chandon, was an expensive brand. Not many locals would buy that. No fingerprints had been found. The killer had wiped the scene, he thought, pacing through the cabin, his steps echoing in the empty bedroom. She must have been desperate, in hiding from her killer, to live in a place like this. It was primitive. The only heat came from a wood stove. She had dragged the bed into the kitchen for warmth and to keep watch for the killer.

Out on the porch he looked toward the woods, his thoughts meandering like one of its many trails. It was possible the killer could be someone local who knew the area. The cabin was isolated, bordered on three sides by forest. Only an overgrown road, more like a trail from the small country lane, led to the cabin. The nearest Amish farm was at least eight miles away. At the far edge of the forest, approximately twenty miles from the cabin was a passable road. The killer could have parked there and walked to the house. Had it been winter and snowing? Roo imagined a dark figure, trekking through the forest on snowshoes.

Before he left, he searched through the trees, going deeper into the woods. He broke through the snow crust; his feet inundated with icy water, and wished he had worn his boots. As he turned to walk back to the car, something shiny, embedded in a frozen patch of earth, caught his eye. He leaned down, pried it loose with his pocket-knife and held it in the palm of his hand. It was a tiny link of gold, broken from a chain. The sun held its gleam. He bent over, using his knife to scrape away the snow, and searched a few feet in each direction from where he had found the link.

An irrational fear slowly crept over him. His hands shook slightly as he took out his pistol and crept even farther into the woods, but there was no sign of anyone, or of the wolf he had seen earlier. He quickly jogged back to his car and drove away toward town.

Still waiting for the Coroner's report, he and Stumpy left Gracie Logan, her sharp features drawn up in a scowl, to type everything up on her antique Smith-Corona, and walked through the picturesque main square of the town to Nelson's Diner. Shawnee Square, named for the tribe who had once lived here, was lined with old New England style buildings painted a crisp white, decorously surrounding a small park with white benches. The two hundred year old Presbyterian Church with its beautiful spire, the school house, county courthouse and library contrasted with the newer part of town built after World War II.

Roo hated these newer buildings of low flat brick, economical square blocks of no distinction. Nelson's at the northern end of Main Street was built onto a gas station and car repair shop. Inside the diner, wooden booths with chrome jukeboxes attached were placed next to the big window with an unspiring view of the parking lot. They sat on stools at the counter, which trailed behind the booths.

Lee Ann Jenkins, her dark hair up in a white cap, came out of the kitchen and took their order of hot roast beef sandwiches and coffee. Her pale green eyes were rimmed with red as though she had been crying. She avoided looking at Roo. He hadn't called her since he'd stayed with her last Saturday night and felt a surge of guilt. It wasn't that he promised her anything. She didn't expect much from men. Her husband had disappeared a year ago, taking all her savings.

Lee Ann had been in his high school class, one of the shadowy figures at the edge of his group of friends who revolved around him like the planets around the sun.

He hadn't even recognized her when he started his job as deputy sheriff and began to eat his meals at the diner. But to Lee Ann he still was the famous quarterback. She worshipped him, remembering all his past glories as though nothing had happened in between, and he had been flattered, feeling important again. When he undressed her slight childish freckly body and enclosed her within his arms, she opened to him and gave herself passionately. Afterward, she would curl up against him, her little arms and legs twined like a frail vine around his sturdy tree trunk body. He wasn't fair to her, substituting her in his mind for Janey. She was not Janey, all glossy and smooth and expensive, but a little country girl from the hills of West Virginia, who had to struggle all her life.

Lee Ann brought their orders, putting down the plates without a word. He wanted to say something to her, but didn't because the sheriff, a terrible gossip, was watching and pretending not to. Roo turned to his plate. His last meal had been at noon yesterday, and he was ravenous, eating quickly, finishing almost before Stumpy picked up his fork.

The sheriff's cell phone rang. He hated all gadgets, but used a cell to seem up to date. He put his cigar down on the edge of the counter and fumbled to answer, dropping it on the floor. "Damn thing," he muttered as he picked it up, dragging his sleeve in his gravy, and answered. "Hi Joe, what have you got? It's the coroner," he whispered. Obviously, Roo thought, taking out his notebook.

"Would you repeat that? What you thought? More than a year? Bullets sent to ballistics in Columbus. We're at Nelson's. We'll be over as soon as we finish eating." Roo stopped writing up his notes, watching Walker's little slits of eyes widen in an unusual expression. "Thanks Joe, nothing to the press as yet until we uncover the woman's identity."

"What is it?" He prodded Stumpy, who sat motionless for a long while, holding out his greasy sleeve; his hot roast beef sandwich congealing on the plate.

"What is it?" Roo struggled to keep impatience out of his voice. The sheriff's words came slowly as though he were measuring them for the truth. "The woman, age late fifties, was shot through the chest and head with a pistol."

Waiting in suspense for him to continue, Roo saw the shattered skull flash in front of him. Stumpy, slack jawed, sat unmoving, almost paralytic, as though his body had yet to take it all in.

Then he took a huge breath, like he was diving into a deep waterhole, and said softly, "Her eyes were slashed out by the killer."

Chapter 9

Roo
Tecumseh County

ON THE WAY back from the morgue, Stumpy said, "This is a sick bastard. I know all kinds of terrible, even worse murders are in the news on TV, but nothing like this has ever happened here." He shook his head. His voice choked up. "A psychopath among us, walking around the streets." The bubble of safety that had surrounded him for years and made his job easy had burst. He stomped into his office, slamming the door.

Gracie looked up from her typewriter.

"What's wrong with him?"

Roo shrugged his shoulders. Wanting to appear on top of the case, he took out one of the official county maps and circled every small town within thirty miles in each direction of the cabin.

"Be back later," he said to Gracie. He drove to every one of the small towns, going into each store, and restaurant, telling concerned merchants that a serious crime had been committed and asking if they had seen any strangers in the last year. It was dumb. He had no description of the killer except that he might be fit, and he knew only that the woman was approximately 5 ft. 7 in. and around fifty-seven years old.

When he dragged himself into the office at nine that night, Stumpy was in the reception room watching out the window for him. "Where the hell you been all day?" he barked, "I ate already."

"Sorry, I should've called. I checked all the towns in a thirty mile radius of the cabin, asking if anyone had seen strangers in the last year, but came up with nothing." Stumpy jerked back looking at him in astonishment. Roo put his stupid behavior down to fear, maybe irrational, that the sheriff would take the case from him.

At the diner he was so tired after his drive he could hardly lift his fork to his favorite order of roast chicken, slaw and mashed potatoes, eating at an uncharacteristically slow pace.

Lee Ann cleaned off his table. He reached out and grabbed her arm.

"Can I see you tonight after work?"

Her small face squeezed into a frown, and she tried to pull away. He held on to her arm tightly, but then stopped, fearing her bones would snap.

"Don't." she said, her voice cold, "Something's happened to you. You're different. I knew you never really cared much, but now I seem to be nothing to you."

Embarrassed at the scene, Roo looked around to see if anyone was watching. Billy, owner of the gas station and garage sat at the counter. His three hundred pounds flopped over the stool like a huge inner tube. He was engrossed in a comic book and a large chocolate sundae.

Roo was secretly relieved that Lee Ann had said no, but was disturbed that his indifference showed. His mind must be as transparent as the large window of the diner. What she had said was true; nothing here mattered to him. It was as though he was not in the diner or even in Paint Creek, but was living in another interior landscape, traveling on an unknown journey, thinking of nothing else but the identity of the murdered woman.

He drove home and dropped, exhausted, on the bed, not even taking off his shoes or turning on the TV to check on the play-off scores. He dreamed about the woman in the forest; her eye sockets wept blood, and her jawbone moved, beseeching him to find her. He woke to her murmurs telling him who she was, but they were indistinct noises in his head.

Then next morning he stared at the computer screen, waiting for more answers to his inquiries before reporting to the sheriff, who regarded the computer with a combined suspicion and hatred usually reserved for Tecumseh County's worst offenders.

Roo was impressed with the new state of the art technology. Thanks to Stumpy, the office always had been behind the rest of the world, but recently the new computers had been updated and linked them to every law enforcement department in the U. S. and even to Interpol, although he doubted there would be an occasion for Tecumseh County Sheriff's Office to contact the international agency.

This step into updated technology, essential for modern law enforcement, was the unwitting result of Stumpy's 1998 campaign for sheriff, when in a mangled speech he had incorporated a few of Bill Clinton's words about being prepared for the 21st century. Promising the voters modern law enforcement, he was horrified that his re-election had brought an even more unfathomable machine into the office. He left all the work on the computer for Roo and would ask, "What does it say?" as though it were a living creature up to no good.

Roo carefully reread the coroner's report, relieved that it confirmed his initial notes, although Daley said it still was not complete.

Then he checked the list of missing persons reported in the state in the last five years. Several of the women, some with carefully arranged hair, others bedraggled, one with a black eye, stared out at him forlornly, but none of their cold statistics fit with the victim's meager description. It struck him as he gazed at the melancholy photos that missing almost always meant dead. He wondered grimly how many on the list were buried somewhere, their fate never known.

Information from the Department of Motor Vehicles arrived, and he quickly opened the attachment. The jeep had been registered in April 2000 to Miss Adelaide Safford. That name jumped out at him, and then he remembered the photograph Miss Lindsay, the librarian, had shown him of the Safford farm in 1890. The murder victim must be a member of that same family who had owned acres of land in Tecumseh County. The Ohio driver's license used to register the car had been issued in 1989 to the same person. He studied the photograph of Adelaide Safford. She wore very thick horn-rimmed glasses, and coarse looking black hair hung down over her face and forehead.

He went to the next page. Miss Safford's first driver's license, used as identification, was issued in 1972 when photos were not required. He clicked back to the current license and immediately checked out the address with the Columbus Police computer. It was now a supermarket.

Deflated, he sat for a moment, musing over the license photograph, and then went on to the property search. There was no website for the auditor's office so he telephoned Mrs. Weeks, the country clerk, who told him most of the records were not yet computerized and that it might take a week or more to find the documents.

Deciding it was easier and quicker to check himself, Roo walked through the snow across Shawnee Square to Tecumseh County Courthouse, reflecting on how much police investigations had changed since the computer and how little leg work he had to do, compared to someone like Sam Spade. He enjoyed the walk; it reminded him of his childhood when he would run along this same path to the small elementary school at the opposite end of the square.

In contrast to the handsome Federal exterior of the county seat, its interior was composed of one main office for each department, and behind each, a warren of squalid little rooms. Roo climbed up the wide staircase to the County Auditor's office and knocked. He removed his stocking cap when he entered, but quickly put it back on. Mrs. Faye Weeks, the clerk, huddled over a desk in the office, wearing a coat and headscarf. It was colder than a barn. The antiquated radiators clanged loudly, giving off a suggestion of warmth as if to justify their existence. The clerk looked at him curiously and said, "Hello Reuben." Only his mother and her friends and his grandfather called him Reuben. He felt red from shame creeping up his neck. She had been one of his mother's friends from the Presbyterian Church before the terrible thing happened.

Mrs. Weeks, with an apologetic look on her pleasant features, led him back to an even colder file room with a musty smell. A dark mold was slowly growing up the walls.

"Mr. Lewis was meticulous about the files, even the very old ones. He was dedicated, but since his death ten years ago, no one has touched the old records." She reached up with a gloved hand and pulled the string on the dim overhead bulb. "The place is a mess. I've tried to keep up but manage only with the current files." She pointed toward the cabinets with the more recent property records. "If you have any questions, I'll be in reception."

Shivering, wishing he'd brought gloves, he spent two hours going through the files searching for the land parcel, but with no success. This was worse than his travels through the towns yesterday. Then he abandoned this method. Mrs. Weeks had said Lewis was meticulous, dedicated, which could mean he had constructed a cross file. Roo went through several of the newer cabinets and found it. He flexed his fingers, dirty and numb with cold, and then dived into the cabinet, furiously leafing through the folders, until he came to S-T, the last in the cabinet. Lewis must have passed away before he got to

Z. He flipped through the S-T folders until he found one labeled
Safford. Quickly pulling it from the drawer, he squinted to read the
faded papers under the dim bulb.

The land parcel, called the Safford Homestead, was listed as part
of the original 1789 Safford land grant. He read on intrigued. The
property had been a repossession sold on April 10, 2000 to Miss
Adelaide Safford by Sensenbrenner Estate Agents in Columbus. He
wanted to shout in triumph; it was like completing a forward pass for
a touchdown. He had identified the mystery woman.

Curious about the repossession and remembering the library's
photograph of the Safford Farm, he walked back to the rows of older
wooden file cabinets untouched since the demise of Mr. Lewis.
Covered in cobwebs, these held early deeds from the 1800's to
1900's. Partially obscured with layers of greasy dirt, the file labels,
printed in a large ornate hand, were fastened by brass clips on each
cabinet drawer.

He searched through them, rubbing away the dirt on the peeling
labels until he came to S. He struggled to slide out the drawer, and it
suddenly flew open, throwing him onto the floor. A cloud of dust,
heavy with dead spiders, flies and wasps enveloped him. He thought
of archaeological sites as he struggled up, brushed off the huge nets
of overhead cobwebs still clinging to his uniform, and dug into the
folder, flipping through ancient land grants until the name Safford
Homestead appeared. A land grant issued to Thomas Safford in 1790
had been sectioned off in the early 1800's. In 1906 it changed ownership and was registered to a Miss Adelaide Safford, obviously a descendant. He stared ahead: a spider was moving slowly across a web
hanging down in front of him. Christ, that was almost a hundred
years ago.

He made copies of the papers in Mrs. Week's office, thanked
her, and promised to come to her house for supper one night soon.

Walking quickly through the square, his mind was fuzzy, in total confusion. Could there be more than one Miss Adelaide Safford?

Rushing back to his desk, he immediately contacted the National Census Bureau. Gracie was typing the latest report and did not look up. She had made coffee and he went over to the small table, poured a cup, then sat down and waited.

The census records with the property owner's name and address astonished him. They listed one Adelaide Safford, born 1890 as the last living member of the family who had settled here long ago. But this Miss Safford had been dead since 1962. Hardly able to contain his excitement, Roo searched for other relatives, but there was only a male second cousin, now deceased.

Clicking back to the original page, he fastened on something even more bizarre and read it twice to make sure he was right. From 1916 until her death in 1962 Miss Safford not only owned the property, but also had lived in the cabin where the mystery woman, also called Miss Safford, was murdered.

Adrenalin pumped through him, like sparklers lit on the Fourth of July. He experienced the same flood of unbearable joy, as when he was on the football field, his hands around the ball, letting it go, in tune with the world. He yelled out, "Impostor." Gracie jumped, her bobbed hair waving in the air, and scowled at him. She ripped out the paper she had been typing from the Corona, muttering that she had to start over.

Oblivious to her anger, Roo was struck by what he had found. The dead woman had stolen Adelaide Safford's identity, and faked her documents. He tried to calm down, to curb his exultation at this discovery and rehearsed how he would tell Stumpy the intriguing news. He didn't want the sheriff to think he was enjoying a murder. He seemed to shrink from the details, hiding behind his newspaper, talking to himself after each report. His behavior was puzzling, and

Roo was beginning to think this murder was beyond his boss, an obscene violence he couldn't handle.

He was dozing in his chair when Roo entered. He woke with a start, embarrassed, moving things around on his desk, shoving a porn magazine into his top desk draw. In a poisonous mood at getting caught, he barked, "What is it?"

"A new development in the case," Roo said, placing the papers on the desk. The sheriff put on his reading glasses and examined the report and the license photograph.

"Hell, I knew Miss Adelaide. You should have asked me instead of fiddling with that machine. The Safford family had holdings out here, but not any more. This sure as hell doesn't look like Miss Adelaide," he snapped.

"The murder victim may have lived in the cabin for a year before her death. She bought the property in Miss Safford's name in April 2000 from a Calvin Sensenbrenner who owns a real estate agency in Columbus."

Realizing he was nearly shouting with excitement, Roo lowered his voice. "I phoned the Giddings law firm. Seymour Giddings, the lawyer who handled the deal, died of a stroke earlier this year. I'm going to pay a visit to Calvin Sensenbrenner." But Stumpy had buried himself in a newspaper and didn't seem to hear him.

Chapter 10

Roo
Tecumseh County

ROO PULLED ONTO Route 3 toward Columbus and stepped
on the gas. The Sensenbrenner Real Estate Agency would not open
officially for at least two hours, but he couldn't contain his eagerness
to interview Calvin Sensenbrenner and had asked the agent to meet
him earlier. Sensenbrenner might be able to describe the victim. She
might not have been not in disguise when she bought the property

On impulse he turned off the main highway and took the winding country road to Henny's to fill up the gas tank. The white frame
buildings of Heinrich Muller's Grain Mill and General Store were
visible as he reached the top of the hill. The two buildings, which included a cheese and sausage factory, stood alone at the crossroads.
They seemed isolated but in the distance on both sides of the road,
white Amish farmhouses scattered across the snowy fields like huge
white birds, their windows, without curtains, like giant blank eyes.

Passing a horse and black buggy, he pulled in and parked at the
petrol pump, used by truck drivers avoiding traffic and the few farmers in the area who did not belong to the community. Several other
buggies arrived, and Roo thought rush hour. The bearded men in

black hats and coats greeted each other while tying up their horses. They nodded to Roo, acknowledging him as Isaac Yoder's grandson. Isaac had been one of the leaders of the small branch of Amish that had left Holmes county and settled here. Unlike the peaceful members of the community, he was fierce, unforgiving.

His first frightened glimpse of his grandfather, with his white long beard and the burning blue eyes of an Old Testament prophet, was a recurring nightmare. Isaac in his large brimmed hat stood at the farmhouse door, shouting through narrow thin lips, "I've come for Reuben," his long bony finger pointing at Roo. "To take him away from sinners. He is my only grandchild. You do not deserve him." Roo running out the back door away from the angry shouts, hid in the hollow of an oak tree until he heard the creak of carriage wheels going away.

After this, he understood that he was different from town kids and that his father, who had grown up in the small Amish community, had been shunned, cast out before he was born. Freaked by this flash into the past, he jumped over some fresh steaming horse dung and hastily filled his gas tank. Heinrich, whom everyone called Henny, came out to collect the money, scratched his beard with a wistful expression, "You must be on a case."

He nodded, thinking how Henny would like his kind of job if he weren't Amish.

On the road again, Roo screeched the tires, skidding on a patch of ice. There was no traffic, and the farmland, its cornstalks poking through snow like stubble on a chin, raced past him. While he was growing up, his tall forbidding grandfather had haunted him. He would appear like a shadow at the edge of the field during football practice. Roo always looked for him, with mixed feelings of fear and anticipation, and once thought he caught a glimpse of the old man at one of his games.

It took a few moments before those childhood pictures faded and his mind turned again to the murder victim and yesterday's reports. The shock of his discovery electrified him, like coming up against a wired cattle fence, charging him with a nervous energy.

He reached the outskirts of Columbus and drove onto High Street into Worthington, the oldest section of the city. Sensenbrenner's Real Estate, a small brick building in period colonial style, was set in a manicured lawn. Checking his watch dismayed that it was only 8 a.m., he parked the car in the gravel lot and waited. Waves of restlessness flowed through him. He worked over what he knew about the case and studied the flecks of snow dusting the evergreen shrubs lining the drive.

He remembered the dead woman's documents on his desk yesterday, the results of his first real detective work. Although ballistics had not yet issued a report, he knew the killer had shot at short range using a pistol. The circumstances surrounding the murder were bizarre. No killer would just show up there. And the champagne and crystal goblets, what did that indicate? That she was waiting for a lover? If so, she might have suspected he intended to kill her, and believed she could talk him out of it. Roo sensed that this case was not just about a lovers' quarrel, but 'big' in some way. He kept this speculation to himself.

It was creepy, like those art house movies everyone pretended to understand. He couldn't ignore Stumpy's point. The psychopath was still out there, and he would kill again. But why cut out her eyes? He tried to blot out the rasp of the knife sawing through flesh and bone. Late yesterday he had put out a bulletin to all law enforcement agencies in the country describing the grisly aspects of the murder and requesting reports on any similarities in other murder cases. He should have done this the moment he learned of the mutilation and wondered if Stumpy noticed his incompetence.

Gracie, resembling an historical figure from the last century in her white high collared blouse and black skirt, hated the computer. Looking over his shoulder she had sniffed contemptuously before returning to the typewriter. He didn't give a shit what she thought. Maybe something would turn up.

Gracie disliked him even more than she did the computer. He often speculated that she resented his closeness to the sheriff. He had heard she had furiously argued with Walker against hiring him. There was a story around town that in the Sixties she had set her cap for the sheriff, that Stumpy had slept with her and then went back on his promise to marry her, remaining a carefree bachelor. Instead of marriage, the sheriff had offered her a job. Gracie became his office wife, straightening his desk, making his coffee and setting out his blood pressure pills every day. He didn't know if Stumpy still went to bed with her. It was a stretch of the imagination.

There was a scrunch of gravel. A new shiny Buick pulled into the drive, and a long faced man stepped out of the car. He wore a tweed sport jacket, gray flannels, shirt with cufflinks, a silk cravat instead of a tie and brown penny loafers. "Friggin' dressed like someone in a Ralph Lauren ad," Roo muttered as the man walked over to the car.

He lowered the window, snow spitting him in the face.

"You must be Deputy Sheriff Reuben Yoder. Calvin Sensenbrenner. Pleased to meet you." Sensenbrenner was tanned a dark orange hue, like he had just stepped off a Florida golf course. He smiled, showing long nicotine-stained teeth.

"Come in, come in." He hurried to unlock the door. Roo caught the scent of Old Spice in his wake.

Feeling out of place, he sat down in a leather-upholstered wing chair, staring at the English hunting prints on the pale striped wallpaper. Sensenbrenner settled in the matching leather chair behind the desk.

"Now, what can I do for you?" He briskly rubbed his hands, like long tentacles, ill at ease in spite of his businesslike manner and luxurious surroundings.

Roo tried to act professional so the man wouldn't guess he had never been involved in a big case. "Mr. Sensenbrenner"

"Call me Calvin," he interrupted.

"All right, Calvin. A woman's body has been discovered in the woods in Tecumseh County. She was murdered." He looked at his notebook.

Sensenbrenner jerked in surprise, and took out a cigarette, offered one to Roo who declined, then lit his with a gold lighter engraved with a large S.

"Records show that the body was found on property purchased in April 2000 by a Miss Adelaide Safford. We believe she is the murder victim. You handled the transaction."

Sensenbrenner stubbed out the fresh cigarette, and quickly moved his chair to his computer at the left of his desk. "Let me check." He clicked through his files. Roo suspected he already knew what property he was talking about.

The agent cleared his throat. "The property had been in litigation, held by the state for arrears in taxes and was on the market for years. When the owner, a Miss Adelaide Safford died, the state wanted to sell it for back taxes. I don't have to tell you folks weren't lining up to even view the property. It was complicated because there was a clause in the owner's will, designating the wooded section a forest in perpetuity. Not great for selling to a developer."

"Didn't you think it was unusual that the buyer had the same name as someone who had been the owner?" Roo said, wondering idly if the agent ordered the hunting prints from England.

"I remember now. The woman said she was a namesake of this distant relative. I did ask about that because, as you say, it was very unusual. Was she using someone else's identity?" A sly look crossed his face as though he might know more about the murder than he was letting on.

"That's what we think," Roo said.

"All the papers, everything was in order. She had proper identification. Giddings was her lawyer." He grabbed for his cigarettes.

There was an uncomfortable silence. Roo was almost afraid to ask.

"Could you identify the woman who bought the property?"

"Is this really necessary?" He lit another cigarette. It occurred to Roo that he hadn't asked how she had died.

"Yes. We need to confirm her identity." Roo gave him his tough cop look, which he sometimes practiced in front of his bathroom mirror, then showed him the driver's license photo and an anonymous one from the missing persons list.

"Could either of these be the woman?"

Sensenbrenner stared for a long moment. "No, nothing like her."

"Can you give me a description?"

"Let me think," he said slowly. His eyes narrowed, and he stared at the door as though seeing her enter that day. "She was refined. A good-looking woman in her fifties, I should think. Well spoken, well brought up. She was slim, well dressed. I can't remember exactly what she was wearing. It wasn't designer, but something conservative, and classic. Believe it was a camel jacket."

"Do you think she was local?" Roo said, barely able to conceal his excitement.

"Hmm. Don't know. It's my guess she was connected to the university."

"Can you remember anything else about her? Did you see the car she was driving?"

"No, I didn't take her out to see the place."

Sensenbrenner stubbed out his cigarette in his gold plated ashtray. He thought for a moment, accordion wrinkles on his brow. "She seemed a little bit old-fashioned. It was her hair, blond, but going gray, and she wore it in braids wound around her head. Attractive, but as I said, old-fashioned. Pretty face," he murmured.

Mentally removing the glasses and the wig from the face in the license photograph. He began to form a picture of the dead woman.

"There was something else, very strange."

Roo sat up straight in the chair.

"It seemed to me she had already identified that property as the one she wanted. Didn't even bother to look at any others. Didn't want to see the property. Never happened to me before. Didn't care about the price. No attempt to bargain. Was in a rush, wanted to sign the papers right away."

He cocked his flat long head in puzzlement, his voice trailing off. "It was as though she knew all about this place. Had been there before."

Chapter 11

Katya
New York

KATYA LIMPED THROUGH customs at Kennedy Airport, her head drumming from the champagne and fitful sleep on the flight. During the last hours before landing, she had worked herself into a state of pure hatred for Philip and Maxi. She had decided that all men were shits. To her dismay, Abigail's obnoxious toy boy had insisted on meeting her at the airport. She didn't feel up to talking to anyone and wanted to make her way to Abigail's alone, but found it difficult without seeming rude to turn down his offer. When she arrived at the meeting point, an eccentric looking young man leaned against the counter, peering through an old fashioned lorgnette. She knew from Abigail's description that he was Maxi.

Good looking in a foppish way, he was medium height with an athletic build. He wore a well-tailored dark charcoal suit, blue shirt and dotted yellow and blue tie. The lorgnette, now held lightly in his right hand, gave him the look of a boulevardier of the 1900's.

His dark hair was combed back slickly from a cheerful oval face with an aquiline nose. As he strolled languidly toward her, she saw that he had pale peachy skin as delicate as a child's and protruding black eyes, lit with curiosity.

"Pardon me, but are you Katya Marston?" His voice was smooth, low, and pleasant as it had been on the phone. He examined her through the lorgnette as though she were some kind of specimen.

"Yes," she said, knowing her tone was bitchy. She really just wanted to be alone.

He seemed not to notice and still couldn't mask his surprise at her appearance.

"Maxi Suvorov." He shook her hand, and then took her baggage cart. "The car's this way. Sorry I didn't get in touch with you earlier. I didn't know Abigail was your guardian, or that you even existed until her lawyer informed me. And I had no idea that you would be so beautiful." His American accent, combined with continental old world manners, was disconcerting. Noticing her limp, he took her arm and helped her to the car.

"What's wrong?" His dark eyes scrutinized her.

"Skiing accident," she said, not volunteering more.

He was good at taking charge. After paying the car park toll, he put her bags in the trunk of his black Porsche, and they zoomed out of the parking lot toward Manhattan. The lorgnette hung around his neck, forgotten, and she wondered if it was an affectation or if he really couldn't see without it.

He glanced over at her warily, and she knew she had not been able to hide her hostility. He had said nothing about Abigail except for mentioning the lawyer. "I know how you must feel. But we won't talk now. Let's get you settled in."

Her picture of him as a threat faded. She understood how Abigail could succumb to his charm and remembered her word 'delicious'. She shifted uncomfortably in her seat. They went through the Battery Tunnel and when they emerged, the skyscrapers rose in front of her, an amazing giant version of the pop up book she'd had as a child. They drove past Ground Zero, at the southern tip of Manhattan, the famous landscape now bereft of the Trade Towers. It was as though the skyline had been pounded by a giant's fist knocking out two gigantic teeth. Dark clouds of smoke still hung over the ruins. She thought of Abigail and the dark horror of being lost in the destruction.

Guessing her thoughts, he said, "The pollution from the debris is bad today. It's the wind's direction. It's getting better, but the clean up will take a long time. The city is recovering, although it's still subdued. People are still in shock."

Maxi had said subdued, but as they went north on West Broadway into the heart of Soho, the city was lively, constantly moving, like a restless teenager, very different from the Victorian dowager pace of London.

He turned right and two blocks later they stopped at the corner of Mercer and Spring. Mercer Street was glitzy, full of luxury shops, gleaming restaurants, and a few of the most notable art galleries. Abigail had said Soho had gone upmarket from when she first opened her gallery in the late sixties. Struggling artists could no longer afford to live here and had moved to Chelsea or Brooklyn. There were more galleries now in Chelsea, but the Little Swan Gallery was so famous, Abigail had preferred to stay in Soho.

Waiting for Maxi to get her bag out of the trunk, Katya caught her breath, gazing up at the giant warehouse buildings, fire escapes zigzagging across their facades. She pulled her coat around her. The wind was raw, the dark sky heavy with snow flurries.

The Little Swan Gallery was exactly as she had imagined and for an illusory moment she expected Abigail to be waiting inside to welcome her. The gallery was in an old ornate iron building in art nouveau style, its huge gleaming windows surrounded by ornate swirls. White screens covered the large windows and a sign announced that the exhibition and sale, *Iconic Russia, from Isba to Palace, Battlefield to Church,* opened in one week.

Maxi came up beside her. "I didn't tell you, but we're going ahead with the exhibition. Abigail would want that." She was surprised. She wasn't so sure of that, and hated the way he spoke of Abigail as though it was an established fact that she was dead.

He took her bags and guided her inside to the wide reception area. Her ankle throbbed, and she was forced to lean on him for support, feeling his surprising strength, a contrast to the dandy appearance. The portrait of Abigail's beautiful great great grandmother Little Swan dominated the entrance hall. It was uncanny. It could have been Abigail in that striking pose, elegant in deerskin leggings and fringed shirt.

When she was at boarding school, Abigail would visit, taking her out for the day. She regaled Katya with tales of her great great grandfather Jed Townsend, a medicine man who fell in love with Little Swan and married her in a Shawnee ceremony. They traveled in a painted wagon around the small farming settlements in the Midwest performing a medicine show with Shawnee dances and selling Townsend's Miraculous Elixir, purported to cure everything from hives to infertility. Abigail always claimed one of the secret ingredients was cow piss. The elixir's popularity eventually led to the Townsend Pharmaceutical Empire.

"Amazing likeness to Ab, isn't it?" Maxi said, ushering her past the entrance to the giant freight elevator. As it climbed to the second floor Katya tried to hold back tears. She was stung with resentment at his calling her Ab as though he had a claim to her. The elevator opened to a large luxurious carpeted hallway leading to Abigail's apartment.

She stopped on the threshold, tears in her eyes. She was finally where she had always dreamed of being, but Abigail was gone.

"You need some rest." Maxi lightly touched her shoulder and led her inside. She thought this a calculated attempt to charm her and yet she couldn't help comparing his warmth and sympathy with Philip's icy contempt.

"Mercedes Ruiz, Ab's housekeeper, will get you whatever you need. Her number is in the kitchen. I think she's fixed you a light supper. Let me know if you want anything. We're working on the opening, so I'll be in and out of the gallery all hours. If you're up to it, we could have lunch tomorrow and talk things over."

Katya hesitated, still struggling to keep from openly weeping. "I have an appointment with the law firm, Collins and Chuter at eleven tomorrow morning."

"I'll take you. Call you in the morning."

After he left, she collapsed on the hall floor. The reality of Abigail's loss struck her hard. She was totally alone in the world. She sobbed wildly, unable to stop. She now knew what people meant by going to pieces. Something inside her had splintered and she couldn't get it back together. After she exhausted her tears, she sprawled on the floor; her breath coming in catches, then wearily struggled to her feet. She did not remove her coat, and walked slowly from room to room, wistfully touching furniture and objects that all seemed to conjure her guardian. Katya felt her spirit, as though she might emerge from her bedroom or be whipping something up in the kitchen. She continued to wander aimlessly, wishing there was something in the apartment that would lead to finding her guardian.

In the hallway leading to the drawing room she paused in front of the Warhol portrait of Abigail. The artist had painted her lips in a curve as though about to break into a laugh. In the sitting room with its large windows overlooking Mercer Street, she rested on one of the modern leather sofas, taking off her shoes and curling her toes into the old faded Oriental rug, longing for Ab to be on the couch across from her making her laugh with an outrageous comment. A

DeKooning hung over the fireplace, just as she had described, and on the opposite walls were two early American primitive portraits, of rugged looking men in broad brimmed hats against a background of log cabin and forest.

Then, as though Abigail was urging her on, she went into the bedroom, catching the faintest scent of her guardian's unique perfume. The bedroom was decorated in early American style with chintz-patterned curtains and a rare worked rug. A framed needlepoint sampler and two paintings from the Hudson River school hung above the bed, covered in an antique star pattern quilt. Ab's clothes, all designer with emphasis on Vivian Westwood, hung neatly in the walk-in closet, waiting for her. Katya felt overcome with sadness and left quickly.

She heard Abigail's whisper, 'For you darling Katya,' as she walked into the guest bedroom, knowing that it had been decorated for her, for when she would have joined her guardian. A primitive painting of a little girl holding a basket graced the mantle piece and above the oak chest on the right of the bed hung four striking Ansel Adams photographs of winter landscapes, in light walnut frames. Abigail's words came back. "I bought them last year. Couldn't resist. Expensive, but beautiful. They will be yours someday."

She wandered through the paneled dining room into the kitchen, filled with folk art. A carved wooden horse and two weather vanes were displayed on an antique chest, and a brilliantly painted old wooden sign that read Townsend's Miraculous Elixir hung over the stone mantelpiece.

She washed her hands in the sink, her mind wandering in a forlorn path back to Philip. Had he really meant those words or was he just angry? She wasn't ready to believe it was over and still waited for his call. She opened the refrigerator, found a seafood salad, and ate it quickly while reading the welcoming note from Mercedes. Not bothering to unpack all her clothes, she took a shower and went to bed.

In spite of her grief, she felt comforted in this room, her room, as though Abigail's arms were around her, sheltering her.

She woke from a deep sleep to a ringing phone and answered quickly, thinking it was Philip calling to apologize.

"Hi, It's Maxi, how are you?" His voice was low and smooth.

"Better," she said, struggling to hide her disappointment.

"Good. I'm downstairs. How about meeting me at eleven? That will give us time to get to the lawyers by eleven thirty."

"Fine, yes." She looked at the clock. It was 9 a.m.

She forced herself out of bed, showered, unpacked and dressed in a black Chanel suit and Jimmy Choo heels, ignoring her ankle. It seemed a suitable outfit for Collins and Chuter. She was pulling her hair back and fastening it with a clip when she heard the front door open and close quietly. There were noises in the kitchen. It was Ab's housekeeper, who had said in her note that she would be in today. In the kitchen, she found a stout middle-aged woman with a pretty face and neat hair drawn back in a bun. She wore an apron over her navy blue skirt and sweater and was cutting up fruit and putting it on a plate.

She smiled shyly. "Hello, I'm Mercedes Ruiz, Abigail's house-keeper." Katya liked her instantly.

"I hope I didn't startle you. I can't tell you how sorry I am. I hope you can find her." Her dark eyes spilled over with tears.

"You must prefer tea. I've brewed some Earl Grey Breakfast."

"Thank you. That is just what I like." While she drank her tea and ate the fruit, Mercedes, whom she had persuaded to sit down opposite her, could not help discussing incoherently, between sobs, what had happened before Abigail disappeared. She constantly wiped her streaming eyes with tissues.

"It was so strange. We were on Long Island at her house in Quogue. That was her favorite. She came to me in the early morning of the ninth and said she had to go into Manhattan to see her lawyer and then downtown to a meeting. She was very upset, almost frightened, hardly ever the case with her."

She knew Mercedes had been with Abigail for years, during many of her escapades.

"I tried to find out what was wrong, but she wouldn't tell me. She hadn't even combed her hair and put on lipstick and was wearing an old sweat suit. I managed to get her to change into something more suitable. It's just not like her. Even Maxi, who was visiting a friend, was surprised that she had gone into New York. She usually told him everything. That was the last time I saw her. Excuse me." She blew her nose, and reached for another tissue.

"I don't understand it either. She called me on that same day and didn't seem herself."

"Miss Marston, I did not know anything about you until the lawyers informed me or I would have notified you. She did confide in me, but never told me you existed. She said her frequent visits to London were business." Mercedes looked at her shyly. "We have been told unofficially that Abigail left everything to you. Maybe this isn't the time to bring this up, but I wanted you to have the choice of whether or not to keep me on. You are under no obligation. I have a flat in the building so would need a few days to move."

"Please call me Katya, and please just go on as you did until I find Abigail." Her voice trembled and trailed off.

"Oh thank you. I will do my best to help you." Mercedes went on in a flood of tears. "It all has been so terrible, so many lost lives. I don't know what she was doing near the Trade Center. Her lawyer is uptown on Park Avenue. When I came here the next day, her safe was open, and papers scattered. I put the papers back, closed the safe, and hung the painting in front of it. I think only she knew the combination. The police came when we reported her missing and found her fingerprints. They assumed she had been in the flat sometime before she disappeared, but nothing came of it. No one saw her in the building."

After Mercedes had gone, it occurred to Katya that Abigail had kept her existence a secret. It was very strange. She limped over to the hall mirror, studied her reflection and said aloud, "What of them?" This question had tormented her since Abigail disappeared. Who were those two mysterious unknowns who had created her? She had been told as soon as she was old enough to understand that her parents had died shortly after she was born, leaving her with a trust fund, which Abigail managed. There were no details about their identity or how they died, and she just accepted it as a fact, like the color of her eyes.

The mirror faded into her first memory, Abigail's beautiful face smiling down at her. She later learned that the glamorous woman was her guardian, and she was to call her Aunt Abigail. Then she saw the plump sweet face of Aunt Clara and thin kindly Uncle Frank peering at her over his glasses. She had lived with the Fletchers in a sunny house with a large back garden in Peapack, New Jersey. She remembered how happy she had been. It did not seem unusual to have the Fletchers, whom she adored, taking care of her instead of regular parents.

She frowned, pouring more tea. Everything changed that day Abigail came unexpectedly. Katya remembered her face had seemed different. Now, she realized her guardian had been frightened. She had hugged Katya tightly, and then had spoken in whispers to Uncle Frank and Aunt Clara.

The next week all four of them were on a plane to London. Abigail had explained that the move was to further her education. She stayed for a year with the Fletchers in Kensington, in a small London house on St. Albans Grove and attended Francis Holland School, then boarded at Cheltenham Ladies College. By that time, the Fletchers returned to the United States. When they left she was inconsolable and cried for days. She was told that Uncle Frank was ill and had gone to the States for treatment. She flinched; the pain of their loss was always there.

She closed her eyes, remembering their kind voices in the weekly phone calls and the letters and gifts they sent. She never saw them again. Two years later, Uncle Frank died of a heart attack and Aunt Clara who lived with her sister in New Jersey survived only another year. She had clung to Abigail, all the family she had. Over time, she recovered from the heartbreak of losing the Fletchers and was content at boarding school, spending her vacations with her guardian, with rarely a thought about her real parents. With the Fletchers gone, Abigail was the only person who knew her true identity.

She would give no hints about her parents or why she was brought up in England. Only once, in all those years, while visiting her at boarding school, she had said, "It's a shame. You are more like me than your mother." She believed Abigail had known her mother and had hung onto this phrase and its possibilities through her teens and university. Now, she might never learn who her parents were.

She wandered back into the sitting room and checked the telephone, but there were no messages. Had Abigail made her last call from here? She clicked on the computer and looked at her email. There was nothing. She knew the police had checked it. Then she walked across the room and lifted the primitive painting, which hid the safe. Mercedes said she found the safe open and papers scattered. Abigail was panicked, in a hurry. Katya wondered if she had removed something valuable from the safe before she disappeared.

Chapter 12

Katya
New York

"YOU'VE HAD A hard time today. I'm sorry for that. It hasn't been easy since we lost Abigail." Maxi leaned toward Katya. He was devilishly handsome, dressed in a tweed jacket, and checked tan shirt.

"Not lost, I can't believe that yet. I'm going to find her." She resented his assumption that her guardian was dead.

The waiter brought them a bottle of white Burgundy, while Maxi studied the menu. After her meeting with the lawyers, he had driven her back to Soho to Balthazar's. She was tired and not very hungry, slightly intimidated by the bustling atmosphere of the bistro, missing the coziness of her favorite restaurants in London. Maxi ordered crab cakes for her and a lobster salad for himself and after the waiter left said, "I hate to bring this up now, but the gallery is a business. I suppose Mr. Chuter informed you that Abigail left specific instructions in the event something happened to her, and that I was to continue running the gallery until further notice. Is that all right with you?" He leaned even closer.

She felt slightly dizzy and thought it probably was jetlag. "Yes, I have the papers here. Yours should arrive tomorrow. It seems right because Abigail left twenty percent of the gallery to you. I hope you'll continue just as before since I have no experience. I didn't know that I was her principal heir, but poor Abigail has no family except for me. I hope that none of this will be necessary."

She was apologetic; Maxi probably resented her now that he knew she would inherit most of Abigail's fortune. But he showed no sign of envy or disappointment.

"They had notified me concerning Abigail's generous gift. I'm glad you have faith in my abilities. Maybe Abigail didn't tell you, but we were lovers. She was wonderful. I loved her very much. But we both know her generous nature. She would want us to go on with our lives."

Katya nodded, recoiling at his honest words. Embarrassed, she stared out the large window fronting Mercer Street, a pain growing in her throat, making it hard to swallow. He reached over and took her hand in a firm grip

"Ab and I had been planning this show for some time. It will be a coup in the art world, and very profitable for the gallery. Many of the icons are for sale, but a number of them, like the Rublev, have been borrowed for the exhibition. Some of these icons have not been seen since the Russian Revolution in 1917."

The waiter opened the wine, and Maxi said, "I'm sure it's ok, just pour." Katya thought how different he was from Philip who would have taken at least five minutes to sniff it and swish it around in his mouth before accepting it.

"Why is that?" She took a drink of the wine.

"The Bolsheviks outlawed religion. They believed what Lenin often quoted: 'Religion is the opium of the masses'. When they began destroying churches and monasteries, the monks and priests hid many of the icons, sometimes burying them, sometimes in caves. It took ages to get this show together, partly because my mother, an icon expert is set against it. She even tried to stop museums from loaning their works of art by making embarrassing phone calls to directors and dealers, claiming the icons for sale are fakes."

"Are they?" She asked over the bustle of the room.

He didn't answer directly, and paused when the waiter came with the food. They ate silently for a few moments, and then he said, "Abigail thought Maman opposed the exhibition because she didn't like her, but it wasn't that. Maman objects to my close association with Alexei, a Russian who is not an émigré. She calls him a crook and a communist."

He paused and glanced around the restaurant, then poured them both another glass of wine. "It makes me furious. I worked hard on this deal, and made a lot of trips with my partner, Alexei Mikhailovich Kayakov, to convince private owners, churches, and museums to send paintings to the exhibition. Alexei has papers for all the icons for sale so there is no problem. It has been a good working relationship so far. I do a favor for him, he does one for me."

He stopped to eat a few bites, and then continued, "Alexei's boss is a billionaire oligarch, connected to powerful people in the Russian government. He has been very generous with the gallery although the money must be loose change to him. Kayakov says if this works out, I can get in on other deals."

"What's his boss's name?" Katya asked.

Maxi looked embarrassed, "I don't know. I've never met him. Alexei calls him the Master, says he is a very private person, almost a recluse. Works behind the scenes. Doesn't like publicity. I may be invited to meet him if the exhibit is successful."

It all seemed mysterious, but she didn't know anything about the art business. "Am I going to meet Mr. Kayakov?"

"He hopes to be in town for the opening. He's eager to meet you. Alexei Mikhailovich is a real character. He is very religious, and belongs to a weird sect. Maman thinks he is a dangerous gangster just because he's eccentric. She could ruin the whole thing for me." He drained his glass and poured another. Katya sensed he was eager to confide in her. He waited while the waiter took away the plates and brought the dessert menu.

He took her hand again, and said, "I thought if it is ok with you, we could dedicate the show to Abigail, perhaps put a discreet memorial in the program, and give part of the proceeds to the families of WTC victims." She let him continue holding her hand for a moment, thinking how kind and sensitive he seemed.

"I believe Abigail would like that. But I haven't given up. I still believe she is alive and I'll find her," she said, removing her hand.

The waiter was standing over them. After they ordered coffee, Maxi said, "You can't imagine my amazement when I discovered your existence. It is strange that Abigail didn't tell me. She was always so open about her life. No secrets with her."

Katya knew that wasn't really true.

"When did she become your guardian?"

"I don't really know. We never discussed my background. My parents died soon after I was born, and she was always there."

He persisted. "You know nothing more of your parents then?"

"My last name in both my English and American passports is Marston, and I was brought up in England. That's the extent of my knowledge." It seemed meager, insufficient.

"Hmm," he laughed, "a mystery woman."

"There's nothing mysterious about me. I'm pretty uncomplicated."

"Tell me more." He implored her, almost comically.

"There isn't much."

"What have you been doing in England since you've grown up?"

She related her school background and her career as a writer, hoping it seemed glamorous, not mentioning how scanty it was. She didn't think it was necessary to include her wild clubbing nights.

"Boyfriend?" He grinned.

"I was engaged, but recently broke it off." She hated herself for telling him. It gave the impression she was making herself available. Thinking of Philip, wondering if he was still angry, she fell into an uncomfortable silence. Maxi was regarding her curiously through the lorgnette, which would have seemed ridiculous if it were anyone else. The waiter brought their coffee, and she was glad of the interruption.

"You probably wonder why I use this." Reading her thoughts, he held the lorgnette in the air. "It's fanciful of me, but I am senti-mental and a bit near-sighted. This was a gift to my grandfather from the last Tsar, Nicholas II."

"Your grandfather knew the Tsar?" She found that hard to believe.

"Yes, he was a young officer attached to the Tsar's *Stavka*, mili-tary staff headquarters at Mogilev in 1917, during the First World War. But he was more than just an officer. He was an advisor and intimate friend of the Tsar's. I know what you're thinking; that I'm not telling the truth, that it was too long ago, but I'm the only child of elderly parents. They regarded my arrival as a happy accident."

The lorgnette was exquisitely made. Thin tortoise shell rimmed each lens; the small handle in the shape of the imperial eagle was en-crusted with diamonds.

"It's beautiful," she said, guilty at doubting his word.

"It was made by Faberge, on direct order from the Tsar and Tsarina. Little did my grandfather dream that it would be one of our few family possessions to survive the revolution." He lovingly turned the luxurious present over in his hands. "It was given to me after my father died. I was only a year old, but still this and all the family photographs keep alive memories of him and my grandfather."

"Abigail told me you were a count."

"Yes, it's true. But that was in the Stone Age. I became fed up with hearing about it every day of my life. There was a lot of plotting and ranting, but nothing effective was ever done to overthrow the communists. It's no good living in the past and doing nothing about it. I like these new Russians, although Maman will have nothing to do with them. I agree, some of them are crude, descended from peasants, but they speak my language, and have the money and energy to make things happen for me." He seemed self-conscious, and stopped to finish his coffee. She noticed that in spite of his laid back air; he did everything quickly, impatiently.

"But I've spoken enough about myself. Let me pick you up for dinner tonight, and I can hear all about you."

A small shudder escaped her as a picture of her legs wrapped around a pole in a nightclub flashed before her. "There isn't much more to tell. I am a blank sheet other than midnight snacks at boarding school."

She hesitated, not wanting to hurt his feelings, and then said, "It's really kind of you. Thank you, but I'd like to rest tonight. I have an appointment tomorrow with the police. I want to know what they're doing to find Abigail."

"You're meeting with the police?" His eyebrows lifted. "That seems a waste of time. I don't want you to be upset, but they don't believe there's much chance that Abigail's still alive. They've had nothing to report since she went missing, but maybe it will make you feel better to talk to them. I'll take you."

"It isn't necessary. A Detective Latham is coming to the gallery to see me. It's possible they might pay more attention to finding her after I speak with them."

"Do you want me to be there with you?"

"That's very kind, but the detective said he wanted to see me alone."

"OK, let's make it tomorrow night then. Abigail wouldn't want you to be in New York alone without going to a good restaurant," he persisted.

While they waited for the check, he said, "I am still mystified by Abigail's strange behavior, like going to see her lawyer. Did Chuter give you any idea what she wanted?"

"She picked up some papers sealed in an envelope. The lawyer was just the recipient."

"Did he know who sent the papers?" He studied the bill and took out his credit card from a dark leather case.

"No, he said they were sent anonymously."

He took the receipt and looking bemused, helped her with her coat. "And they had no idea of the contents?"

"No," she said.

Chuter's words came back to her as he sat in his pinstriped suit at his desk. His eyes were puzzled behind his steel rimmed glasses. "I have been her lawyer for years and have never seen her like that. She was not her usual well-groomed self. She hadn't even combed her hair." He stuttered slightly, "She was nearly hysterical. She demanded the envelope; then literally ran out of the office. But I just don't see any connection between these papers and her trip down to the Trade Center. Her safety deposit boxes were in an uptown branch of Citibank near my office. I told the police there must have been another reason for her traveling down there."

A cold wind blew through the narrow street, suddenly rocked by a huge truck driving by. It had begun to snow while they were inside the restaurant. The sidewalk in front was clean, but the remainder of the street was filled with a deep slush. She looked anxiously down at her ankle and her strappy sandals. Maxi reached around her and picked her up, holding her close, and effortlessly carried her to the gallery door. She was unsteady when he put her down inside the reception room. He smiled and left after pushing the button on the elevator.

Still breathless, still feeling the strength of his body, she looked out the window in the drawing room and watched him walk swiftly up the street.

Chapter 13

Katya
New York

"I KNOW I was advised not to come to New York, but I couldn't wait any longer," Katya said apologetically to Detective Ron Latham, who sat across from her in the sitting room of the apartment. She had been expecting a rough older fat man in a blue uniform with a big cigar and was surprised that Latham was younger than she, very fit and wearing a charcoal suit. He was clean-cut, with stubby features under blond close-cropped hair.

He put down his coffee cup and looked at her with sympathetic blue eyes. "I know how you must feel. I apologize for the delay in seeing you." He was smooth, and she guessed he was from their PR department.

"We're dealing as quickly as we can with the victims of the Trade Center, both living and dead, but we're overstretched. It could take some months before all the bodies are found and identified. There are a lot of relatives like you still waiting and hoping."

She offered him some chocolate chip cookies, freshly baked by Mercedes.

"Thanks," he said, munching one before continuing.

"Miss Marston, We have nothing new on your guardian since we last spoke to you by telephone."

"I am sorry to take your valuable time, but is it really true that you have no proof Abigail is in those ruins? No trace of her?" she said.

His eyes narrowed. "That is correct. There is no absolute proof that Miss Townsend died in the Trade Center. But everything we do know about the investigation points to that." He sounded irritated. "We would have informed you of any progress on the case."

Katya rushed in. "If you knew her you would realize her behavior was out of character that day. She told her lawyer and her housekeeper she was meeting someone downtown. She phoned me, warned me. It was the last time I heard from her."

"Yes, I know. We have all that on record." Now he seemed openly antagonistic, maybe put off by her English accent.

She frantically hurried on, "I also wondered if you had checked out the places I had given you, her favorite retreats. I just remembered another in Mauritius."

He made a note. "We'll check that out. I must go. I have another appointment with bereaved parents." She had begun to dislike him. He seemed insensitive, hardened to his task.

"There is one other thing." She quickly told him about Prince Androvsky sending an invitation to the Russian Embassy, hinting that he had information about Abigail. She described his failure to meet her, and then his fall to death from the embassy balcony.

He stopped, sat down again, and questioned her in detail, writing in his notebook, asking her to spell the prince's name. "And do you think this might be connected to Miss Townsend's disappearance?"

She quailed at his stare. "I think Abigail could have been kidnapped."

"Interesting," he said. "We had considered that possibility, but so far we've found no proof. There was no evidence of foul play in her apartment." He nodded and looked around the room as though to confirm. "No other fingerprints except hers. By this time there should have been a ransom request, either by letter or telephone, although there have been a few cases." His voiced trailed off as he shrugged on his coat. At the door he said, "I see you're going on with the exhibition. Interesting."

She wondered why he kept saying interesting, and what it meant. "Yes, it seemed right to do. Abigail would want that."

He looked skeptical. "We'll check on the new information you've given us. You've been very helpful. We've spoken to everyone here, but will review the case. We may return to search the place again and to question those we've already interviewed."

"Thank you. Thank you for coming." As he closed the door, she sank down on the couch in despair.

Two days later, when they met for lunch, Maxi questioned her about the meeting.

"So what did the cop say?"

"'Interesting' was his catch word. But he was sure no trace of Abigail has been found. And I couldn't help them very much. He asked me a few questions, like when I last saw Abigail. He said they would review the case and that might mean searching the apartment again."

Maxi shrugged contemptuously. "It's a waste of time. Let's hope they stay clear of the gallery until after the opening."

They were eating sandwiches in Maxi's office and sat on brown leather couches, in front of a glass coffee table. The room was large, more masculine than Abigail's, everything in beige and brown. Two large Jackson Pollock paintings hung on opposite walls. It was quiet with only a distant hum of traffic from the street below.

So far, her efforts to find Abigail had been futile, and she was discouraged after checking out restaurants, clubs and spas where

Abigail had hung out. Desperate, sometimes bursting into tears, she questioned the doormen and bartenders and discovered nothing.

As a distraction, she concentrated on learning about the gallery. That afternoon she had watched the workmen finish hanging the icons, and tried to be helpful by answering the telephone. Maxi was supervising the installation and Geoffrey Banks, a new assistant whom she met that morning, was in charge of the catering for the show. A well-known PR firm had been hired, something Abigail would never do.

She was perplexed at other changes at The Little Swan and believed that this was not the way Abigail had run the business. It seemed less personal. Over the years, she had followed each show in newspapers, magazines, and catalogues, basking in Abigail's success.

She took a bite of her chicken club and then risked offending Maxi by asking, "Why icons? It seems a dramatic shift from the usual exhibitions."

He shrugged. "I can't deny it may have been my influence, but Ab was very enthusiastic. Because there are so many rich Russians, there is a real market for them." Katya remembered Abigail echoing these words the last time she saw her.

Maxi said, "I grew up looking at icons. Every devout Russian has an icon corner in their home. Maman is an expert in the field and once worked in the Medieval Department at the Metropolitan Museum. Now that we are allowed to import the antique icons which seem to emerge from hiding places every day, we'll catch these new customers."

She finished half of her chicken club and stared at one of the drips at the edge of the Pollock painting. How did he know when to stop dripping? Abigail had said that's what made him an artist. He was good, but not necessarily better than his contemporaries. "Great publicity is all," Ab had said, her eyes sparkling. "It was the cowboy thing that sold him. Everyone thought he was a cowboy because he was from the West. It set him apart."

She drank her tea; her thoughts returned to the show, "Will I meet your mother at the opening?"

"No. She and my stepfather are in Paris attending a memorial service for a family friend, Prince Androvsky."

Katya was astonished. The Suvorov family knew the prince. It seemed that all these Russians were connected. Not knowing exactly why, she didn't mention her encounter with the prince the evening before his death, although it worried her.

Maxi said, "It was an accident, poor guy. He was an old family friend. My father and he belonged to the same monarchist organization."

He looked at her. "You really are lovely, you know."

She blushed and pretended to examine the other Pollock, wondering what Maxi had in mind. She could not let herself be attracted to Abigail's lover.

His attentiveness made her uncomfortable. He had taken her to Nobu which she had read about in gossip columns, introduced her to important figures in the art world, and had even found her a good spa and hair dressing salon nearby. "I know what beautiful women like you want," he said jokingly. She reminded herself that he was a stranger and that she knew little about him. And she waited for Philip to call, hoping he would forgive her and they would be together again. Miserable, she had telephoned Claire, who said that men were like children and that Philip would come around, she was sure. She longed to talk to him, felt lonely and unprotected without him.

Maxi changed the subject. "The installation is shaping up well. We should be ready. I'll arrange for you to meet Kayakov soon. He's a busy man with important projects in Russia and is in town for only a short time. As I said before, he is eccentric."

His phone rang. "Excuse me," he said. He spoke in Russian, and his face took on an angry look. It was a curt conversation and seemed to be an argument. He snapped his phone closed, and looked up, exasperated.

"I apologize. It was Maman again calling me from Paris, begging me to stay away from Kayakov and his group of men. I told her they were only bodyguards and bound to look a little rough. But that just made it worse. She claims she heard something terrible about him, but won't talk about it on the phone. She says they're all thugs from the secret police, and wants me to sever relations with Kayakov after the show is over."

"Do you have any proof that he's dangerous?"

"No, it's just my mother being unreasonable."

"Why does she hate these people?"

He looked miserable. "It's a long story involving my family and their émigré circle. It's frustrating. I grew up with her neurotic fears. I had a crazy childhood."

"Your life seems pretty conventional to me."

"Only on the surface."

She impulsively reached out and touched his arm. "We have time. Tell me."

"Unlike you who know nothing of your past, I know too much and can't escape. My family's experiences marked them for life and extend to me, although I don't believe all of their horror stories. There is a Russian characteristic called *vranye*. It means creative lying, exaggerating, sometimes even believing it, to make the story better or in some cases, more terrible. My family and their émigré circle use *vranye* as a matter of course. After all, who is left to correct them? It is so tiresome. Hard to know what to believe." He moved closer to her on the couch.

"As I mentioned before, my grandparents on both sides were relatives and great friends of the last Tsar and his family. They knew everyone at the Imperial Court."

"Even Rasputin?" Katya knew the stories about the infamous monk's supposed supernatural powers, and his mysterious ability to stop the hemorrhaging of Alexei, the Tsar's son and heir to the throne.

"Yes, of course, they were part of the inner circle, the mystical group who worshipped him. They called him the Holy One. It was crazy. After his assassination they attended his secret burial service held by Tsarina Alexandra.

"When the Tsar was removed from power, and he and his family were imprisoned, my grandparents followed them to Siberia, first to Tobolsk and then to Ekaterinburg. It was there, in the Ipatiev House, that the Romanovs were murdered by the Cheka, the Bolshevik secret police. But even though it goes against conventional wisdom, my family never would accept the story that they all were murdered."

It was growing dark. Down on the street she saw a few people hurrying along hunched against the cold. Katya shivered and let him put his arm around her.

"But why won't they accept it?"

His heavy lidded eyes closed to narrow slits, "I'm not exactly sure, but I think their refusal is connected to the secret monarchist group my grandparents were part of during the Russian Civil War. They planned to rescue the Romanov family, but someone informed on them and the attempt failed. The Bolsheviks would have shot them if they had not escaped Ekaterinburg by horseback through Mongolia to Harbin."

"My grandfather always claimed that he carried important possessions of the Romanovs out of Russia. Their story after this point gets a little crazy. Actually none of it makes sense. I think that's enough. Let's get back to the gallery."

She held his arm. "No, please. I want to hear more."

Lights flickered on from the street casting a strange half shadow on Maxi's face. He seemed to be something more than a sophisticated playboy.

"This is so fascinating. Please go on."

He frowned and seemed perplexed. "Kayakov said the same thing. He has asked me more than once to tell the story in detail. Unfortunately, I don't have much detail but know that my family began their journey just as the White Siberian Armies under General Kolchak were defeated. The armies broke up into groups of desperate men, some turning into mercenaries and killers who roamed the part of Russia bordering Mongolia. It was very dangerous. It was that time in Mongolia that led to my family's delusions and craziness."

"What happened there?" Katya shivered.

"They ran into Baron von Ungern-Sternberg, a former Tsarist officer who commanded his own army and still was fighting the Bolsheviks. The Baron was a crazy blood thirsty man, who believed he was a reincarnation of *Tzagan Burkhan* the God of War." They were sitting in the dark, but Maxi made no move to turn on the lights.

"Grandfather and everyone in his party were forced to join the Baron's army. Then my grandmother Suvorova was killed in some terrible way. I could never learn the details. Traumatized by her death and the Baron's cruelty, they were desperate to escape, but knew that anyone who tried to desert the Baron was tortured and murdered. For some mysterious reason, the Baron permitted the party to leave unharmed. They joined a caravan through the desert to China."

"It sounds so horrifying," Katya said.

"Yes, if half of it is true." He pulled her closer. "My Papa was only five years old, but claimed he remembered everything about the camp and the terrible journey. Maman, who wasn't even born then, still lives in fear of everyone who remained in Russia, even relatives and old friends. The Baron's cruelty marked them for life."

He shrugged to emphasize his point. "Of course, it all could be *vranye;* to make them seem important when they had lost their wealth and social standing."

"And what about you?"

"I am an only child, the last of the Suvorov's, their Russian hope. Father was in his fifties, and Maman was thirty-five when I was born. They were cousins so everyone hovered over me. When I grew up I discovered that grandfather Suvorov had been a spy for the Whites during the revolution and continued to plot against the Soviets long after he fled Russia. During the Cold War the organization was still sending agents into Russia in the crazy belief that they could sabotage Stalin's Soviet government. What I remember most as a child were the secret meetings in our apartment."

He looked out at the dark street, but seemed far away.

"All the émigrés, like my mother, claim that the KGB, now called the FSB, hunted them down. This is not an exaggeration. Over the years, KGB agents have killed émigrés. Often the murders appear like hit and run accidents or suicides. In 1970 a friend of my father's was run over by them; another was beaten to death with a hammer on the street. Police said he was mugged."

Katya said, "Here in New York? Were you ever afraid?"

"Only once, when two men waited for me outside St. Bernard's School. I heard them speaking Russian. They followed me home. But mostly my childhood was gloomy. I was very lonely and didn't make friends at school."

His smile was closer to a grimace. "They weren't impressed with shabby nobility. We lived in a cold walk up apartment on the edge of Harlem. There were always the meetings with a lot of dispossessed emigrants sitting around, arguing, smoking, and drinking tea from the samovar. There was never any money, but they managed, through connections, to send me away from the city to Choate and then Harvard. I had scholarships and it was easy for me because I majored in Russian. When I graduated, I discovered the family sold most of their valuables years ago, and had mountains of debt. I must repay these debts and recover the family honor."

He was so close to her that she felt his muscles tense. Her impression of him as a spoiled coddled playboy had changed.

"But can't you just forget all this? Their flight from Russia happened years ago. And everything has changed."

"Nothing has changed for my mother." He stood up and paced the floor. "In spite of Maman's objections, I'm going to deal with Kayakov. With his help, I can claim all the property our family lost in Russia. First I must make this show a success."

His intensity was surprising. He had seemed so laid back. She realized that he wasn't satisfied with just running the gallery.

"Did Abigail know all this?"

"Some. She didn't believe I had any ambition beyond the gallery. Maybe she didn't want me to."

He fell silent, but she felt there was more he wasn't telling her.

"I have to get back to work," he said.

"Could associating with these Russians really be dangerous for you?"

He laughed. "Only in Maman's eyes. It wouldn't make any difference to me anyway."

In the middle of the room he stopped. "Katya," he said, leaning his head back, his eyes half-closed, to look at her. "Why are you called Katya?"

"I wish I knew."

He pulled her to him and kissed her roughly, almost violently. "Stay with me," he said.

She didn't answer. It was an impetuous move that went straight to her heart. Forgetting Abigail, everything, she leaned against him, feeling his warm throat against her cheek. "Why did you do that?" she said.

"I don't know," he said.

The next evening she returned to the apartment after her hairdresser's appointment. She was still shaken by Maxi's embrace, agonizing over how wrong it was to be involved. As she went to her bedroom, she reflected on his relationship with Abigail. Maxi hinted that she had opposed his plan of returning to Russia and reclaiming his title and lands. Maybe Ab suspected he was using her as a stepping-stone.

She was deep in thought when she heard footsteps in the drawing room. It could not be Mercedes who always used the intercom. She shrank back in terror as the footsteps came closer.

To her relief, Maxi walked into the hall across from her bedroom. He was reading a paper and hadn't heard her come in. When he looked up and saw her, he seemed startled, slightly embarrassed.

"Oh, I've been waiting for you. You look great." He folded the paper and put it in his pocket.

"How did you get in?" She had begun to breathe normally again.

"I've had a key for a long time."

Of course, how stupid of her. How could she forget that he had lived here with Abigail?

"It slipped my mind. I just forgot to tell you. Do you want it back?"

"No, it's fine." She wanted to ask for it, but couldn't. He would think she didn't trust him.

"Did I frighten you? I'm so sorry." He put his arm around her. It was comforting. She wanted him to kiss her again.

"It's good to know you have a spare key," she said. "You were reading a paper. Did I interrupt?"

"It was just a receipt for some of the icons. Let's go down and see how they're doing." He gave her a hug.

Then he asked, "Did you, by any chance, find anything in the apartment?"

"No," she said, "What should I be looking for?"

"I'm not sure. Did Ab ever say anything to you about important papers?"

"No, not that I remember."

"You know, she behaved so strangely the day before she disappeared. The police told us she left the safe open, and papers were scattered around as though she was looking for something, maybe to take with her. Poor Abigail."

He stared mournfully across the room.

Chapter 14

Katya
New York

KATYA DRESSED FOR the opening, barely looking in the mirror. She was preoccupied with what had happened that morning, wondering if the police had a lead to Abigail and were keeping it quiet.

Detective Devlin, an older man who didn't look like a cop, Detective Latham and three crime scene investigators had swept into the gallery without warning. Maxi had been furious at the interruption even though they had gone directly to the apartment.

Their urgency did seem strange, and they searched the place for almost two hours. She had asked Detective Devlin why they were doing all this. Did it mean they knew something about Abigail? He was sympathetic, but refused to tell her anything. He said the search was a routine part of the ongoing investigation. The police would be in touch.

After they left, Maxi scowling had asked, "Anything else? Did they find something?"

"I don't know. They wouldn't tell me anything."

"Disruptive bastards. We have an opening, and it will be bad for business if the police are hanging around. The press is certain to report it."

At least they were doing something to find Abigail, she thought as she took the elevator down to the gallery. Her ankle was much better and she left the elevator walking normally again. Geoffrey, the new assistant met her in the hall. "You look fantastic. I love the gown." Katya wore a shimmering silver gown draped on one shoulder in classical style. Her hair was coiled up around her face; diamond earrings her only jewelry. Geoffrey stared at her in frank admiration and offered her his arm, escorting her around the gallery. She had grown to like the plump new assistant in the few days she had known him.

Finishing touches had been put on the exhibit that afternoon, and it was like walking into a colorful version of old Russia before the revolution. The rooms were plastered and painted a stark white and the ceilings curved in onion shape, resembled the interior of an Orthodox church. The deep rich colors of the icons were dazzling against the white background.

Rooms labeled for each display of icons divided the exhibit. 'Isba', a peasant home and 'Mansion', showed the Holy Corners where small icons were placed. Next came 'Church' with the iconostasis, tiers of icons in gold frames in front of the altar. 'Monastery' featured a medieval painting studio. 'Battlefield' was filled with icons on tall gilded poles, once carried into battle by the Tsar's armies.

The major attraction of the Church Room was a beautiful Old Testament Trinity Icon by Rublev on loan from the Tretyakov Gallery in Moscow. Katya was impressed that they were able to borrow it for the show. Maxi said one had to pay for everything in Russia, and Kayakov and his boss had provided the influence and the money.

Waiters dressed like Cossacks in baggy trousers and boots, carried silver trays with flutes of champagne and tiny glasses of vodka.

They waited in a line for the guests. Tables groaned with what Maxi called *Zakuskie*, Russian aperitifs, including blini, little pancakes to accompany the mounds of caviar displayed in huge silver and golden bowls.

Geoffrey said, "I'll be back. I have to check on the waiters."

Katya walked past a string quartet warming up and into the gallery reception area to watch the TV cameramen and photographers jostling for the best position on the street. She stared up at the portrait of Little Swan, a poignant reminder of her guardian and how she would have enjoyed this night. Coming to New York hadn't helped. All she had managed to do was get involved with Abigail's lover.

Even though it was too early for guests, a man dressed in a velvet evening suit, and holding an invitation out in front of him hurried through the door toward her. He was dark skinned and rotund, and his large nose, thick lips and enormous dark eyes crowned by a thick black coiffure, seemed overdrawn, like a cartoon character. His small feet, on tiptoe, were encased in velvet evening slippers adorned with diamond buckles.

He handed her the invitation. "Serge Petrosian, I am delighted to meet you. I know you are Miss Katya Marston." He took her hand in his own small plump ones, the fingers covered in large rings. His sweet cloying perfume engulfed her.

"I want to express my great sorrow that Miss Townsend is gone," he said in a strange rough accent. He bowed his head slightly to express his sorrow, then raised it and spoke aggressively in a rush of words. "You probably know from conversations with Maxi that a deal has been struck. I am taking fifty-five percent of the gallery. Miss Townsend and I negotiated this before she disappeared. We are a cultured family. My daughter wants this place. She is a most refined person, very well educated." He took a quick breath. Katya was about to protest, but he raised his hand to stop her.

"You are the new gallery owner. I expect you to honor the deal."

"Mr. Petrosian, I know Abigail's coming back. We'll talk to you then, although I can't imagine that Abigail agreed to sell," she said in her coolest voice. The man's rudeness was breathtaking.

"You come to see me. I'm sure we can settle on a price. No one backs out of a deal with Serge Petrosian." His voice grew even more threatening.

Geoffrey arrived next to her, and greeted the man like an old friend. Grabbing two glasses of champagne from a proffered tray, he handed one to Petrosian and one to her, then reached for another and steered her away.

"Thanks. Why was he invited?" she said.

"Maxi thinks he's harmless, even though he's after the gallery." Geoffrey giggled nervously.

Katya didn't agree. "He's a terrible man. Even the smell of his cologne threatened to asphyxiate me."

Geoffrey smiled. "Well, everyone knows Serge. He gives great parties. Last year he flew a crowd to Cannes for a party on his yacht. We had to invite him. It's good for business."

Limos began to pull up, jamming the street, delivering men in evening suits, and women dressed in long gowns, adorned with glimmering jewels. The gallery doors opened to a flood of wealthy art collectors, museum directors, critics, and socialites. Geoffrey stood beside her with a running commentary on some of the more famous, and notorious guests.

He introduced her to Mrs. Baker-Stoddard, a wealthy collector and valued customer of the gallery. Her tiny face under big hair was stretched from several face-lifts, and her beaded costume was augmented with a large gold necklace and huge carbuncle size rings. More bling than footballers' wives, Katya thought.

"So happy to meet you," she said. "I am sure Abigail would have loved this show." Mrs. Baker-Stoddard moved on toward a group of more famous people.

Geoffrey drew in his breath and hissed, his plump cheeks wob-
bling, "Oh my God, I didn't know he was invited."

He pointed out a tall aristocratic looking man with silver hair
reminiscent of Andy Warhol's wig. "It's Ranulph von Burkhardt and
his partner Magda. He owns the Volk Gallery on Madison Avenue,
which specializes in icons. He was an old friend of Abigail's until they
had a falling out over this exhibition. He came to the gallery in a fury
that she was doing the show without him, and they had a real shouting match. Guess Maxi was trying to make it up to him by the
invitation."

Ranulph advanced toward them through the crowd and introduced his partner, Magda Beck, a tall bony woman wearing a short
leather skirt and top. Her waist, arms and neck were draped with sinister chain jewelry that reminded Katya of dungeons and handcuffs.
Her long hair hung straight with a fringe, and she possessed the same
silver blue eyes and straight features as Ranulph.

"So, you are Miss Marston, the new owner of the gallery,"
Ranulph said, "Abigail never mentioned you, but then the old girl had
a lot to hide."

Magda's burst of laughter sounded like a neighing horse.

Katya said, "It's only temporary. I still believe Abigail is alive."

"You are a dreamer. The woman is dead." Ranulph spat out the
words.

"Please," Katya said, stepping back from him. Her eyes filled
with tears. What horrible people. She couldn't imagine they were
Abigail's friends. He ignored her. "You cannot be such a fool to
think that after four months she is still alive. Even Abigail Townsend
couldn't stay that long in a beauty clinic."

"It's even possible she strangled on her fashion accessories,"
Magda said. They both laughed uproariously.

Katya was turning away, when Maxi, who had seen them from
across the room, hurried over.

"Ranulph, let's talk soon about another exhibit. I'm sure there'll be more demand for icons after this. Get yourself a drink and look around. You know most everyone here." Maxi wiped away her tears with his handkerchief then took her arm and stood with her greeting more guests.

As the gallery filled she noticed a bearded man, oddly dressed in a black robe. Maxi whispered, "That's our grand patron Kayakov, our very own Rasputin."

Kayakov was heaping caviar onto blini and popping them into his mouth, bits dribbling out from his lips and sticking in his beard. He only halted the assembly line of food to mouth when Maxi said, "Alexei, It's great that you could come." They greeted each other, kissing left, right, left. Watching the man, Katya couldn't imagine Abigail liking or trusting him, even though he was generous to the gallery.

Maxi said, "This is Katya Marston who is now running the gallery with me. Miss Townsend was her guardian."

Kayakov didn't wait for Maxi to continue, "Alexei Mikhailovich Kayakov. It is a pleasure to meet you," he said, staring at her with cold intelligent eyes. He was in his fifties with long dark hair and angular features. His long thin nose poked out above his small beard. A large hammered aluminum cross embedded with precious stones hung around his neck. She shivered, hardly believing it. The cross was similar to the one worn by that Russian who tried to pick her up in Courchevel.

"Ah, you are Katya. And not Russian? How did you get such a name?" Resembling an insect, with his sharp nose and moist eyes, he formed his lips in semblance of a smile.

"I don't know. Many people ask me that." She changed the subject, uneasy at his intense scrutiny, his comment about her name. Word of her existence obviously had circulated in the art world. "It is a very beautiful exhibition and a great honor for the gallery. I hear you are responsible for much of it."

Kayakov bowed his head in acknowledgement, "It is my belief that the power of these icons will bring many back to the old religion of Russia. It is why we sponsored the exhibition."

"You mean the Orthodox Church," she said, trying to avoid staring at his cross.

"No, this is much older, deeper, and more primitive. One must be totally committed. I know what you're thinking; I sound crazy. But this religion is very powerful." His voice was low and intense with a strange timbre; his dark eyes held her. "We are True Believers, the only true religion." Hoping to escape, she looked around for Maxi, but he had moved to the other side of the room greeting late arrivals.

Kayakov inclined his head. "It is a terrible tragedy that Miss Abigail Townsend is missing. Has there been any news of her?"

"Not as yet," she said, "but the police have begun a more intensive search."

"I have said many prayers for her."

Katya was despondent. Everyone seemed to think Abigail's death was a foregone conclusion. "I am sure we will find her. She would have enjoyed this evening."

He nodded slyly and images of the man conducting medieval tortures loomed in her head.

"Let us enjoy, and have some champagne and *Zakuskie,* as Miss Townsend would wish, I am sure. We will meet again later," he promised as he turned into the crush of guests.

Later in the evening, a group of guests who were not the usual art patrons swaggered in; men with designer stubble dressed in black suits, menacing in dark glasses; women in high boots, net tights and short mini skirts. They spoke in Russian and sauntered around as though they owned the place. They were just not Abigail's type. "What are they doing here?" she whispered to Maxi.

"New clients," he said. The crowd was thinning. Kayakov had gone, after thanking her and raising his hands over her giving his strange mumbled blessing.

Maxi excused himself and went upstairs to his office with several clients interested in purchasing paintings. She wandered alone through the rooms for some time, staring at the icons, thinking any one of the guests could be suspect in Abigail's disappearance.

The deep pain in the eyes of the martyred saints seemed to reflect her sorrow. She began to feel sick, slightly dizzy, her head aching. At the close of the party, the icons began to spin in front of her, slowly becoming a mass of fuzz, as though she were looking through a woolly sweater. In the midst of shouting from afar, she heard someone say they were going to continue the party. Disembodied voices, speaking in Russian, surrounded her as she found herself ushered into the street and felt the cold air hitting her, making her shiver. Then too weak and dizzy to protest, she was shoved into a car by a man who pulled her close in a painful embrace.

The next afternoon she woke in her bed with a violent headache. Pain shot through her body. She was naked; her gown lay in shreds on the floor, beside her shoes. The evening rushed back in a series of disjointed scenes, like flash snapshots.

The letters RUS light up garishly in the sky. A voice speaks into her ear in a Russian accent, "We're in Little Odessa, bitch, as close to Russia as you can get."

Katya thinks she had seen it all in London clubs, but is shocked at the sight of twisting bodies and naked girls dancing on the bar. A man leans over, his face a bright blob, his voice harsh above the heavy metal music. "We like it rough," he says. The word 'rough, rough' echoes over and over. She slides away.

A sharp point of light wakes her, and she is alone, walking down a highway, merciless lights stabbing her eyes. She feels herself losing consciousness. Jerking awake, she is standing at the edge of a dance floor with people ripping off their clothes; a whip flies and cracks in the air. Terrible head banging music breaks into her skull.

There is a flash, and she is standing in front of cubicles, stretching along like small garages. Then she is inside the cubicle and hears the lock click. Unearthly howls come through the wall. Wild fear overcomes her, and she struggles toward the door, but a man stops her. "I am Vasily." He smiles and waggles his tongue at her. "You are mine. But I am easy, little princess." He shrugs his shoulders. Three men stand by the door; they wear bandannas, and army clothes. Tattoos on their arms and necks squirm as though alive. They move toward her, pick her up, and carry her away.

She is on the floor, cold cement on her cheek; a loud buzz fills her head. Sharp pains in the lower part of her body, pain everywhere, surprises her. Thirst overcomes her. She hears her voice babbling, crying, and is slowly sinking again into the blackness. But there is a cold line of reasoning inside her that has not yet been erased. They have not done the worst. The worst is to come. Heavy weights slow her arms and hands as she struggles to rise. She hears shouting, and the door crashes open. Maxi's face floats before her. She feels his strong arms around her carrying her away.

Out of the nightmare, she stared at the blank ceiling of the bedroom. She began to heave and gag, staggered to the bathroom, and threw up. As she stumbled back to her bed, she caught a glimpse of herself in the mirror. Screaming, she dropped to her knees in horror. A huge bite mark, blood caked around it, was gored into her right buttock. Sobbing, dragging herself toward the bed, she knew this was her fault. But why couldn't she remember? What had she done? She must have been drunk, like a slag, as Philip had called her. She was torn between trying desperately to recall the evening and not wanting to know what happened. Hearing her screams, Mercedes had come in quietly. Sobbing, unable to stop shaking, she told the housekeeper all she could remember before she had passed out.

"I think you were poisoned. Someone spiked your drink. You did nothing wrong." Mercedes bathed her fevered body and then handed her a cup. "Don't worry. This will not harm you. It's an herbal sedative." She kept watch over Katya, once giving her more of the sedative when she woke crying.

She slept through that day until late the next morning, waking to find the housekeeper sitting in a chair by the bed. Mercedes said Maxi had called to find out how she was. "Thank God, he arrived in time." She crossed herself and looked toward heaven.

She said Maxi had come downstairs, just as the last guests were leaving and couldn't find her. One of the waiters had seen her get into a car with four men, and heard that the crowd was going to RUS. Maxi had followed and rescued her. Mercedes said he was insisting they get a doctor and report the incident to the police but Katya, filled with deep shame, refused, unable to face anyone. She knew Maxi had saved her from a violent gang rape. Her sense of self, her confidence that she was a good person, always flickering like a small weak flame, spluttered and died. She wanted to hide forever.

Chapter 15

Roo
Tecumseh County

"YOU CAN'T BE going to New York City. It's fuckin' danger-ous, a hellhole," Ben said in a voice that registered shocked disbelief at Roo's plan to enter that pit of evil. They were in Shorty's Bar, a brick building slightly bigger than an outhouse, containing one room with walls stained brown from nicotine, a few crooked tables and chairs and a long bar lined with twelve stools. Roo and his friends had been coming here before they were old enough to drink. The place made no pretense to atmosphere. A neon beer ad flashing in the windows provided the only decoration. Shorty, six feet, five, was wiping the bar with a grimy towel, and nodding in agreement with Ben. Even as a child Roo had puzzled over the Paint Creek nick-names which had no rhyme or reason. Here was Shorty tall: Stumpy, short and stocky.

The other two at the bar, old team members, John Shaw, an end and Ed Cosby, a linebacker agreed with Ben's assessment of New York.

"Why would you do a thing like that? There might be more of those bastards running around there, planning another attack." Ben ranted on. Toby Keith's *Courtesy of the Red, White and Blue* roared in the background reflecting the feelings of the guys in the bar.

On September 11, like everyone else, Roo had watched the TV with horror as people jumped from the Trade Towers to their deaths. In early morning the day after the terrorist attack he tracked deep into the forest until time for work. He had found the old Shawnee trail that led from their woods near to Ben's farm. He didn't think anyone else remembered it was there. The trees, not yet turning color, bent down as though caressing him, and the small animals and insects rustled in a reassuring way. The hijacked plane that had crash-landed in Pennsylvania had flown over Ohio. This unreal occurrence had stunned and terrified everyone in Tecumseh County. That week he and Stumpy patrolled the entire county trying to calm people, tell them they were safe.

He realized his friends were still waiting for an answer. "The NYPD asked for me. I'm on loan. That's all I can tell you."

"Haven't seen much of you lately. Guess you've been busy on the murder," John said. They all looked at him, wanting inside information.

"The newspapers have pretty well covered what we know so far," Roo said.

Shifting his large bulk on the bar stool, Ben Tyler, his best friend and current landlord gave him a skeptical look. Ben had been the star linebacker on the football team, and his shape curiously had stayed the same all these years; a total block of hard flesh from wide shoulders on down, miraculous in light of all the beer he consumed. He had been the protector, the enforcer on the team, always looking out for Roo, and still did.

He couldn't tell them why he was being sent to New York. The press release from the sheriff's office stated only that an unidentified body of a murdered woman had been found in the forest near Paint Creek and asked for citizens to come forward if they had any information pertaining to the victim. So far, there had been no re-sponse. Because he was in charge of the case, Detective Devlin from New York Homicide, Stumpy's old buddy from Vietnam, had re-quested his assistance. The sheriff was surprised at the coincidence. After the first few years back from 'Nam, he had lost track of Devlin and discovered he worked for Homicide in New York.

Roo, who had always laughed at superstition, felt this coinci-dence meant he was fated to go to New York, that somehow he was tied to the bones of the dead woman.

Ben was still looking at him like he'd lost it. His buddy had worked since high school as a mechanic, and thought he was crazy, always wanting something more from life. Ben was content with things as they were; working at a job he liked, hunting and fishing, having an occasional love affair. He even owned a couple of horses.

"She's never coming back. Grow up man. Stop living in a dream world," he would say when Roo became very depressed about the long ago break up with Janey. "You've got to get your shit together. If you don't like your life, why don't you go back to the farm or maybe sell it and do something with the money." His friend's sug-gestions sent a perceptible shudder through him.

"Not now," he would say, "Not just yet." He couldn't deal with the memories. There were whole successful periods recently when he was able to forget ever living at the farmhouse, the wretchedness of it.

Ben was slow moving, deliberately ungrammatical and uncouth, but underneath this façade, he was upright, trustworthy, and a gen-tleman. And he had common sense, something that Roo felt he lacked. His friend looked like Paul Bunyan with his long bushy dark hair; high cheekbones sticking out from where the beard began, well-formed thin nose, and very large dark eyes. They joked about it now, but once he had been forced to arrest Ben for punching a man who'd insulted the girl he was escorting. He was locked up for the night in the county jail. Roo had embarrassed the guy, who had suffered a broken nose, into dropping the charges.

Later Ben said, "The bastard might have had a point about the girl, but it ain't right to hurt a person's feelings, no matter what."

Roo left the bar early, slapping everyone on the back, saying he'd be back in a couple of weeks. Then he went over to Lee Ann's trailer to say goodbye even though she had stopped speaking to him. She had not been in the diner for the past two days, and he thought it was because he had not made love to her since he found the woman's remains. It seemed a cut off point with him, as though the murder had wakened him from a dreamlike state. The last time he saw Lee Ann at the diner, she had looked at him with her sad faded eyes and said, "I hope it works out for you." She knew he was never coming back to her.

He walked through the small clearing at the edge of town and knocked at her door several times, surprised to find that her trailer was empty. Her neighbor, an elderly man, poked his grizzled face out his door like a startled chipmunk, and said that her husband Jerry had come for her. They had moved to Detroit where he had a job in the Ford plant. So, Roo thought with a wry grin, she had been marking time with me all along, waiting for her ex, just as he waited for Janey. At least Jerry had returned for her.

At home, he puzzled over what to pack, an inexplicable panic rising in him. His life so slow and uneventful was suddenly on fast-forward, whizzing by, and he still had to catch up. It all had happened so quickly, within a few days, finding the body, the call from the NYPD; Stumpy's look of respect that he had made the inquiry and was requested for this special assignment. It seemed incredible that a brutal murder and mutilation could happen here and be related to an incident in New York.

He pulled out an old suitcase from under the bed and stood in confusion. No uniform; that would be ridiculous. He wondered if detectives in New York wore dark suits and if all the girls looked like those in *Sex in the City*. Then he remembered the suit he'd worn to both parents' funerals, but knew it was wrong, even before he dived under the bed again for the box, taking out the suit and examining it with disgust. It was light blue, the shoulders too wide and the pants too short. What could he have been thinking? In desperation, he opened the suitcase and threw in two pairs of jeans, flannel shirts, underwear, socks, and shaving kit. He would wear his boots, heavy plaid lumber jacket, and Cleveland Brown's ball cap. He wouldn't be cold.

He tried to sleep, but the image of Janey smiling at him, seemed engraved in the darkness of the window facing the junkyard. Maybe someone in town would speak or write to her about his new assignment. 'Guess what Roo is up too. He's on a big case. Called to New York by their police department.' And she would be so impressed, so full of love that she would come back to him.

He stared wide-eyed into the dark slats of the wall and said aloud,

She walks in beauty, like the night of, cloudless climes and starry skies. / And all that's best of dark and bright, / Meet in her aspect and her eyes. He had discovered Lord Byron's poem when he and Janey started dating, and always thought of it as hers, although he had never recited it to her. He slept little that night, alternating between the poem and its other two verses and worrying over what awaited him in New York.

Ben, a stocking cap pulled low over his eyes giving him the look of a desperado, saw him off before daybreak, handing him a bag with a thermos of coffee and some sandwiches. Stumpy had issued an expense account which covered everything including air fare, but Roo had decided to drive his pick-up; felt that he had more freedom with it. Parking had been reserved for him at One Police Plaza, where he was to meet Bureau Chief Seamus Devlin. Roo had looked up the address on the web; it was located at the southern tip of Manhattan.

He began the trip listening to Toby Keith's *How Do You Like Me Now?*, thinking of Janey. It was freezing, the air clear and still. Driving out of Tecumseh County through the rolling countryside, he passed fields and barns, static in the cold, as though forever etched in stone along the highway.

Speeding along Route 40 East, his mind turned to Stumpy and his weird behavior. Why didn't he go to New York himself? It was a chance to see his friend. He had begun to understand that Stumpy was not a cop but a politician and sensed that his boss wanted nothing to do with this murder. He had refused to listen to Roo's theories about the woman, based on good evidence. Roo believed that was what policemen were supposed to do. It was part of the job.

Instinctively, he had kept his most recent evidence from Stumpy for a few days, and even then the sheriff had taken it as a personal affront. Roo had reported the real estate agent's description of the victim, and his view that she had known of Miss Safford and the property. Although the sheriff conceded that the victim had been using a false identity, he refused to believe she could be local. The idea was too outlandish, beyond his imagination. To placate him, Roo agreed that maybe the dead woman had been a friend who had once visited Miss Safford.

It was dark somewhere in the middle of Pennsylvania. He pulled into the Green Tree Motel with the sign, 'Truckers Welcome'. As soon as he paid for the room and went into the diner, he regretted his choice. It was empty of customers and had that air of neglect and enterprise gone wrong. Behind the counter, a thin man in a dirty apron, a cigarette between his teeth, nodded to him. He chose a table, the top sticky with jelly that might have been there since WWII, and ordered from the menu, smudged with greasy thumbprints.

Waiting for his order, he looked out the window, his eyes staring back at him from the darkness. His steak, chips and beer didn't look too bad, and his mood lightened. He was hungry, but after a few quick large bites, he put down his fork, his mind going over events of the past few days.

He had gone to the library and asked Miss Fiona Lindsay, the librarian to do some research for him. Ben, who seldom read anything but the sports page of the Paint Gazette, had offered to come with him, which seemed strange. Miss Lindsay, tall and slim, her curly red hair drawn back in a bun, blushed and stared at Ben with wide green eyes behind her horned rimmed glasses while Roo explained that the sheriff's office was trying to identify the dead woman, who was about his mother's age. He asked her to check town records, high school yearbooks, and old newspapers for the five years before and after 1970, for any unusual event, and for anyone who had moved into the town during that period.

It was difficult because he couldn't tell them anything that wasn't in the press release. And besides, neither of them seemed to be listening. He noticed with surprise that Ben seemed to be looking into Miss Lindsay's eyes, and then realized how pretty the librarian was, even with those clunky glasses. He mentioned this to Ben before he left this morning; his friend smiled mysteriously.

The steak and fries had gone cold. He finished his beer and paid his check, and went down the hall to his room. His bed was damp, the limp blankets smelled of urine, and the portable heater in the corner was broken. He lay down without taking off his jacket or boots, and stared at the torn curtain and the peeling plaster, worrying about Detective Devlin. What would he think of him, an inexperienced redneck from the country?

Depression settled over him like the moldy blankets, and he considered returning home, to the anonymity and safety of his desk. At some point, he must have dozed, and then the dream was upon him.

He watches the bundled up man enter the forest and then realizes he is the figure. Just ahead the wolf stands, and he follows it, searching frantically for the murdered woman. He walks through the clearing, and reaches the cabin. It abruptly changes to his family's farmhouse. Everything spins in front of him. The floor seems to be moving, and he steps cautiously into the kitchen. A woman sits in a chair in the corner by the door. There is a shotgun in her lap. She is saying something, but he can't hear. A thrill of excitement fills him; he has discovered the identity of the murder victim. He steps closer. His mother looks up at him in the terrifying way she did that night.

His shrieks brought him upright in the bed. Shudders like giant waves poured through his body. He jumped up, and went into the bathroom to piss and caught a glimpse in the mirror of his thick uncombed hair, his unshaven face, and his wild eyes like the chipmunk old man in the trailer park.

Rushing outside, he shivered uncontrollably as he unlocked the pickup, warmed it up, and raced onto the highway, wondering if he ever would sleep again. His truck motor hummed, like the murmur of the woman's voice. The darkness flew by. He could see nothing out there, and tried to concentrate on the line in the road. The motor's noise turned into Stumpy's choked disjointed voice.

'Call from New York, from Detective Devlin. Woman's body found in World Trade Center ruins. Full report follows. The woman, in late fifties, was tortured and murdered they believe one day before the planes hit the towers. Terrible, terrible, eyeballs slashed out with a hunting knife. Like a Jack O' Lantern.'

Chapter 16

Katya
New York

EARLY AFTERNOON THREE days after the gallery opening, Geoffrey Banks phoned Katya from reception. A policeman
named Reuben Yoder was waiting in the gallery to speak with her.
She cringed; even the sound of Geoffrey's voice was embarrassing
after her disgraceful behavior at RUS.

She had been hiding in her flat, unable to overcome her trauma
and burning humiliation. Maxi had been kind and tactful. Since that
disastrous evening, he was the only person she had spoken to other
than Mercedes and even that had been painful. She avoided the gallery, not yet able to face Geoffrey, and fearing that she might encounter one of the men who would recognize her from the nightclub.

But knowing the police could have news of Abigail, she threw
on some clothes and, took the lift down to the gallery.

Geoffrey was waiting at the elevator and examined her curiously
for a moment, then leaned his plump body toward her and
whispered.

"I'm not sure he's for real, though he does have a badge. And his name." He rolled his eyes. "I thought he was interviewing for the job as maintenance man."

The man had his back to her, studying the Rublev, his sturdy broad shoulders slightly hunched in concentration. His dark blond hair was thick and shaggy, in need of a cut. He held a cap in his hand and was wearing a faded plaid jacket, jeans and scuffed cowboy boots.

"You asked to see me," she said.

He turned quickly and smiled at her with obvious pleasure. He was good looking in a rugged sort of way. His gray eyes stared straight into hers. "Are you Katya Marston?" His voice was low and nasal.

"Yes." She was suddenly aware of her appearance. Her hair was tied back from her face, and she wore no make up. She was wearing an old pair of jeans, a pale blue sweater, and the high-heeled sandals, which had been lying where they had been dropped that terrible night. She winced, conscious of the bite mark; it burned through her jeans.

"Reuben Yoder, Tecumseh County Deputy Sheriff." His handshake was firm. His rough calluses scraped against her palm. A gun tucked in his belt was visible underneath his shabby lumber jacket. "I was looking at your icon exhibition while I waited. That's beautiful."

"The Russian artist Rublev painted it in the 15th century." Her voice sounded small, like a child's. "It's on loan from the Tretyakov Gallery in Moscow."

He stared for a moment and asked, "Did Miss Townsend have many connections with Russians?"

"I've already told the police what I know," she said. "Detective Latham said he would check on the Russian Prince Androvsky who seemed to know something about Ab's disappearance. It was strange. He fell to his death the same night we met at the embassy. I think you also know that Maxi Suvorov is from a White Russian émigré family. The exhibition may have been his idea. He speaks Russian and made the necessary contacts. But he and Abigail organized it together." Her voice faded on a hopeless note. She sensed he had bad news.

"I'm assisting New York Homicide with your guardian's case." He handed her a small plastic bound ID card with his picture and a second one issued by Bureau Chief Detective Seamus Devlin, giving him the title of Detective Investigator on special assignment. "Reuben's my official name, but everyone calls me Roo."

Detective Latham had come into the room and stood by the door.

"I think you've met," Roo said. They nodded a greeting. He still seemed hostile to her.

"I'll be outside," Latham said, closing the door, leaving them alone.

The deputy sheriff stood awkwardly in front of her, hands in his pockets, while she examined the cards. They blurred before her eyes. She dropped them on the floor, panic coming suddenly.

"What case? What do you mean?" She was shrill with emotion, on the edge of tears.

He picked up the cards and then looked around at Geoffrey, still in the doorway, transfixed with curiosity.

"Is there some place private I can speak with you?"

She led him to Abigail's plush office at the rear of the gallery, offered him a chair, and then sat behind the desk facing him.

"Miss Townsend's body has been found."

The Hudson River landscape on the wall behind him weaved back and forth, blurring the autumn colors. Air rushed from her chest as though she had been punched hard, and she fell back into the chair.

"Are you ok?" Concern filled his pale gray eyes.

She nodded, and then said, "In the Trade Center?"

"Yes."

"But how do you know?"

"The remains were identified with DNA samples and dental records."

She hated the word 'remains', knowing it could only mean there was nothing left of

Abigail. "Can I go now?"

"Not yet," he said gently, and she knew there was more. She experienced the same feeling she once had as a child before a terrifying fall down a flight of stairs.

The cop tried to hide his nervousness by reading in an official voice from his notebook. "Miss Abigail Townsend was murdered. Approximate date, September 10th. Time of death not determined. The forensic report indicates her body was moved from the murder scene and placed in the ruins of the Trade Center sometime after the attack."

"What, what?" She jumped up to run from the office, but he was beside her, holding her close, murmuring something almost as though talking to himself. She shook uncontrollably, and heard only the last sentence clearly. *"We will grieve not, rather find strength in what remains behind."*

She wiped her eyes, leaning against him until she stopped shaking.

"Abigail," she said in a choked voice.

"I need to ask you some questions, but if you're not up to it, I can come back." He still held her for a few moments,

"No, it's all right." She walked back to her chair in a trance, thinking how strange everything looked, as though she were seeing the chair, the desk for the first time.

"Murdered," she repeated. "But how can that be?" Her face was wet with tears. Abigail's fate was much worse than she ever could have imagined. "But who would do such a thing?"

"We're working on that. We have some leads."

"You mean the killer's still out there?"

"Yes," he said, looking over his notebook. She turned on him, hating everything in her grief and fear.

"How could you know anything about it? Where is Tecumseh County? Why would they send you?" She wanted him to go. She wanted to hide forever; return to the past when Ab was still alive.

"It must seem strange that I'm involved. Tecumseh County is located in the state of Ohio, but I don't suppose you would know the geography, being English. A week ago, we found the remains of a woman in an isolated forest in our jurisdiction. She had been murdered."

"But what could this possibly have to do with Abigail?" Distraught, she covered her face with her hands for a few moments, then removed them, and looked at him.

"We're looking into it. The victim has not yet been identified." He stopped a moment to consider his words. "There is some evidence that links the victim to Miss Townsend."

"What evidence?" She sounded cold, and very English.

"I'm afraid I can't tell you just yet." His brow furrowed as though he had been presented with a great puzzle.

"Why not?" Again she felt a momentary overpowering anger at everything, and everyone, particularly this bumbling cop.

"It's an on-going investigation."

"I see." She sank back into the chair.

"Did Miss Townsend have connections to anyone in Ohio? Could she have a friend there or a business acquaintance?"

"I don't know," she said, her breaths coming in jerks.

He seemed hesitant, almost as though he were making it up as he went along. Was he really a policeman? Was any of this true?

But he persisted. "Did she ever travel to the Midwest?"

"I only know about her trips to Europe on business and to see me." Her grief, compounded by a throbbing head, threatened to boil over again.

"We know that Miss Townsend had a high profile lifestyle and that she was having an affair with her assistant, Maxi Suvorov." He blushed and went on. "Could she have enemies, for this or any other reason?"

Katya struggled to steady herself, to think, and then said slowly, "She had a relationship with Maxi, but no enemies because of that. Yes, she did have enemies. I met them on the night of the opening." She told him about Petrosian's threat, spelling his name for the detective swiftly writing in his notebook. "And there was another man, von Burkhardt, who owns the Volk Gallery, specializing in icons. Geoffrey Banks, our assistant told me he was furious at Abigail, claiming she had promised he could co-host the show and then cut him out. I could see that he and his girlfriend hated Abigail. They made mean remarks about her and said it was certain she was dead. And that they were happy about it." She began to weep again.

"What can you tell me about Miss Townsend's past? Her friends, relatives. Can you go on?" She nodded, wiping her eyes with a tissue.

"She was an only child and lost her parents several years ago. She had an Aunt Beatrice who died in the sixties. That's all I know." It came to her with a shock how little she knew about Abigail's past.

The office door crashed open, and Maxi barreled through. "Katya, what's wrong?"

He swept behind the desk and put his arms around her. "I heard you crying. Is it this man? Did he do something to you?" He turned to Roo. "Get out or I'll call the police."

"I am the police," Roo said. "Tecumseh County Deputy Sheriff Reuben Yoder on loan to New York City Homicide." His words sounded comical as he showed Maxi the two badges.

Katya said, "Maxi, it's Abigail."

"Miss Abigail Townsend, your employer, was murdered. Her body was dumped in the ruins of the Trade Center. It was the work of a psychopath, someone seriously disturbed," Roo said.

"Murdered," Maxi said slowly. After a long pause he said, "And you haven't found the killer?"

"That's right."

"Do you have any leads?" he asked, "I want the monster behind bars."

"We're working on it," Yoder said.

"I see." Maxi took out his silver card case and handed the cop his business card. "Maxi Suvorov," he said.

Roo studied it for a moment, looking up at his face. "Yes, I know," he said, unimpressed. "You're next on the list to be interviewed."

Katya thought the deputy sheriff seemed out of place, although she had no idea where he belonged, maybe on a farm or in the woods. "I have no more questions for you, Miss Marston. We searched the premises two days ago, but may want to return. Is that all right or do I need to get a warrant?"

"Please, do whatever you have to. You don't think she was murdered here?" Her voice went up an octave.

"No, I don't. But we might have overlooked an important clue. Is there someone who can stay with you?"

"I'll ring Mercedes." Maxi took out his phone.

"No thank you, I just want to be alone for a while," she said. She had exhausted her tears.

"Someone will be around tomorrow to make sure you're all right," he said. "Don't leave the city."

She wondered what he meant as Maxi led her out the door. Was she in danger? But why? It didn't make sense. As the elevator climbed to her apartment, she began to quake, realizing that she had been swept into a frightening evil world. She nervously paced the apartment, her own pain and humiliation trifling. Abigail's terror now seemed real; something palpable that hung in the air, staining the atmosphere.

Katya forced herself to lie on the bed, but still could not find any peace. She began to reflect on how kind Deputy Sheriff Yoder had been, holding her tenderly. His comforting words had seemed vaguely familiar. Restless, she went to her computer, googled the words she remembered, and was astonished. They were lines from Wordsworth. She wondered, through the haze of her grief, what sort of cop quoted poetry?

Chapter 17

Roo
New York

AFTER KATYA LEFT, Roo kept his head down, pretending to read his notes while he tried to control his impulse to punch the scumbag holding the ridiculous lorgnette. He was buried in a deep swamp of rage and fought to climb out, to get clear. He could recollect only one other time when he had instantly hated someone. Years ago at his high school class reunion, he had beaten up Janey's fiancée, Hal Pritchard, a successful corporate lawyer, and would surely have gone to prison if Stumpy and Janey hadn't intervened. Roo felt an unreasonable fury at Suvorov's proprietary interest in Katya. He must be screwing her. But why should he care what complete strangers did? He struggled to be rational, to keep his temper under control.

He was unimpressed with Suvorov's foppishness and suspicious of the expression of grief he affected.

When he glanced up, the man was standing over him.

"Sit down, Mr. Suvorov. The information I have here states that you were Miss Townsend's assistant for three years. We have some reason to think you had an intimate relationship with Miss Townsend. Is that true?" He failed to keep the anger out of his voice.

"Yes, we lived together." He didn't offer more about the relationship, but he had lost some of his assurance and reluctantly sat down opposite Roo.

"And is that why Miss Townsend included you in her will?" He phrased his question to humiliate the dandy.

"I don't know." Maxi was tense, upright in the chair.

"When did you find out that you would inherit part of the gallery?"

"Abigail's lawyer told me after she had disappeared. They put me in charge of the gallery until she was found or declared dead."

"You have formed a partnership with a Russian citizen named Alexei Kayakov. Is that right?" Roo glared at him.

"Yes, he provided half the money and most of the contacts for the exhibition."

"And did Miss Townsend object to that? Did you have a falling out?"

"No, never, she was in complete agreement. I still can't believe this. That she's been murdered." He put his hands over his eyes for a few moments.

"Mr. Suvorov, do you know where your friend Kayakov is now? I'd like to talk to him."

"He's back in Moscow. I spoke with him yesterday. By the way, it's Count Suvorov."

"Whatever. My notes say that you've made eight trips to Russia in the past two years. Was there a specific reason for these trips?"

"That shouldn't be hard for even someone like you to figure out. I traveled there to set up the exhibition, find sponsors, and negotiate to borrow icons from churches, museums, and private owners. Are you finished?" He made a move to get up from the chair. "I must make arrangements for Abigail's funeral. Can you tell me when her body will be released?"

"We'll let you know. The Chief Medical Examiner is still conducting tests. Just a few more questions. Can you tell me where you were on the ninth, tenth and eleventh of September?" Roo persisted.

"I told you people all this before. It's insulting. Yes, I have an alibi. I was visiting a friend, Yuri Kutusov in Sagaponeck. That's Long Island," he said, in an irritated voice. "By the way, what authority do you have over this case? It seems to me the FBI should be handling this."

Roo ignored his question. "And where are you living now? Just want to check that address again."

"This is a waste of time. I'm staying at Yuri's place on East 87th Street."

Roo folded his notebook, "That's it for now. Detective Latham will be around to interview the other employees again."

He walked toward the door, conscious that the heels of his worn boots clicked like loud castanets on the smooth floor. Then he felt a rush of blood and turned, unable to control his anger. "So tell me, are you fucking the new owner or are you still in mourning?"

"Go to hell," Maxi growled.

"We'll be in touch. Don't leave town. I'll let myself out."

Some say the world will end in fire, / Some in ice. / From what I've tasted of desire, / I hold with those who favor fire. Lines from the Frost poem came to Roo, as he stood outside the gallery in the freezing wind whipping around the tall industrial buildings. It was growing dark, and lights had flashed on inside the shops, restaurants, and galleries. In the shiny gallery window, his shabby reflection merged with the colorful icon inside, his face superimposed on that of the angel's head.

Oblivious to the well-dressed crowds hurrying past him, he absently studied the strange pastiche, disgusted with his amateur way of breaking the news to Miss Marston. He looked up at her apartment and thought he saw the shadow of her slim figure through the drawn curtains. He had made a total ass of himself by reciting poetry to a complete stranger, wanting her to like him, like a dog rolling over on his back. He didn't know what had possessed him. Maybe it was the fear in her eyes. Poetry always had calmed his own helpless fear when his dad went on the rampage.

He stared back in the gallery window at his face, a ghostly shadow over the icon. He was ten years old, back in his bedroom, looking into the mirror over the chest, his sturdy face flushed, the straight features distorted, eyes wide with fear. He would sit on the bed then, unable to move, nowhere to go, his head hurting, going over in his mind how he had been very good, and if he were very good, the old man would let him alone. If he said anything at all, it incensed the old man. If he remained silent, it could be even worse. His dad would take that as an insult. What was it to be, he would ask in panic, hearing the door slam and the stumbling footsteps come near. He chose silence. Poetry was his only barrier against the unpredictable violence. The verses would rattle through his head as the door opened.

He quickly moved away from the gallery window and hurried along the street toward the subway, thinking of Katya Marston. She was beautiful, privileged and spoiled, but he detected vulnerability and sweetness in her dark eyes. He felt a strange, inexplicable burning where his arms briefly had enfolded her.

Suddenly realizing that he might be lost, he stepped into a doorway near a street lamp to get his bearings. A scratching noise and a growl startled him, and he reeled back. He faced a vagrant who looked like a furry beast, with tangled hair down past his shoulders, the lower half of his face covered in red virulent scabs. The poor man was wearing only a plastic garbage bag with holes torn for head and arms, and his feet were wrapped in rags. He stared at Roo in rage at being disturbed. For a moment, Roo looked into his eyes, bloodshot like small poisoned streams and the strong smell of piss and shit closed over him. He let out an involuntary yell and moved quickly on, appalled at the encounter. Then filled with guilt, he went back and dropped some money in the doorway.

The vagrant haunted him, a reflection of what he might become, but he would face that future back in Paint Creek. The town had its down and outs, but everyone had a place to live. Even Old Joe would be taken back to his shack and put to bed for the night.

The city's damp greasy streets repelled him. Its outsized buildings made people look like ants. The crowds pushed past him, their eyes focused inwardly, intent on their own business, contrary to the news reports of outbreaks of compassion and brotherly love after the 9/11 tragedy.

Running in the street, he found the subway stop, hurried down the steps and caught the train to Bensonhurst. The car jerked and he swayed, standing in the middle holding onto a strap, smashed in with the rush hour crowd.

Three women speaking Spanish, chewing gum, and gripping overflowing shopping bags surrounded him. His feet pressed against those of a well-dressed executive engrossed in his newspaper. Two young guys in hooded sweatshirts, headphones clamped to their ears, swayed to their music. At the next stop five teenagers with baggy trousers jumped on, yelling to each other with ear splitting brash Brooklyn accents. Tired looking laborers sat with heads down, going home for the day. Sweat broke over him. He hated the subway. It was like being inside a huge mechanical diseased worm, shaking and noisy.

The subway rocketed on, and he tried to slow his heartbeat by thinking that Devlin was waiting with new information on the case. His anxiety about working for him had disappeared as soon as they met. He immediately liked this somber experienced detective; wiry, dark with deep wrinkles down his long cheeks and sad intelligent eyes. He spoke with a lilting accent, which Roo guessed was Irish.

Unlike the cops he'd seen on TV or those he'd met at homicide, Devlin was quiet and deliberate, seldom swore and seemed almost too kindly to be a policeman.

Roo had phoned as soon as he arrived at the Manhattan South Murder Task Force Division at One Police Plaza. Devlin had been waiting for him, taking him down one of the long busy halls into a shabby small office, explaining as they walked that the department was swamped dealing with victims of 9/11. On his way downtown to headquarters, Roo had gaped with disbelief at the smoldering ruins: his imagination and the pictures on TV had not lived up to the vast horror of it.

After asking him to sit down, Devlin went right to the point. "Since you have been the chief investigator of the case in Ohio, I have asked Stumpy to spare you for this. I am grateful for your help. I'll fill you in briefly now." As the man spoke, he had felt increasingly ill at ease, thinking he was deceiving the detective. "The victim Miss Abigail Townsend, a prominent socialite, and art dealer, was last seen two days before the attack on the Trade Center, and it was assumed that she was among the missing. When her body was found in the wreckage, it was initially thought she was a casualty of the attack. The crime lab investigators discovered that she was murdered at another location, and her body dumped here." He pointed to a map of the Trade Center buildings, and a circled spot near the South Tower where her remains were found.

Then they reviewed the autopsy report. There were photographs of Miss Townsend's body under a pile of debris. Later, at the crime lab, Roo stared at the corpse, cleaned and only partly decomposed, and fought desperately to keep from passing out, wondering if he really was cut out to do this kind of police work, thinking he should have stuck to traffic violations.

Devlin had said, "Do you want to go out for a moment. It's always difficult to get used to this. After all these years, I still have trouble with bad cases."

"I'm ok," he said in a thick voice. His mouth felt like it was growing fur. As he read the dry descriptions, Roo visualized pain and terror flickering over the woman's face.

"The victim's death was caused by a pistol shot to the head," Devlin said quietly.

"You mean after she was tortured?" Roo said.

Devlin nodded.

The subway wheels shrieked against the track, and in the dirty windows he saw again the green decomposed corpse, face partially gone. There were puncture wounds and stabs all over the body. Burn marks covered her breasts, and there were sunken places in her flesh from a club or a man's fist.

The cold print stating that the woman had been sexually violated many times seemed mild compared to the sight of the enormous hole where her vagina had been. Every orifice had been turned into a large cave of pain. Sweat broke over him, soaking his clothes. The subway ground to a stop.

Chapter 18

Roo
New York

ROO EMERGED FROM the subway station around 6:30 p.m., sucking in the cold air, hurrying down the street, grateful that he had some place to stay. The night he arrived, Devlin had invited him home for a drink, much needed after the visit to the morgue. His boss lived alone in a clean spare flat, almost military in its neatness. The walls in each room, even the bedroom, were lined with books, most of them on the subjects of history and military intelligence.

In the living room with two large windows overlooking the parking lot and the street, they relaxed on plain beige chairs with tumblers of Chivas Regal. One corner of the room had been made into an office with a computer on a plain desk, stacked with more books. The only wall not lined with books was filled with photographs of two little girls, progressing from their first communion to high school, then college graduation and more recently, weddings. Devlin had noticed Roo glancing at the pictures and said he was divorced and had two grown daughters, but didn't see much of them. "My fault," he said.

There seemed to be something lost about his new boss, as though maybe, like his own dad, he had left part of himself in Vietnam. He didn't know what background Stumpy had provided on him, and hoped Devlin wouldn't mention his dad or ask about his family.

That first night they had dinner at Katz's, a Jewish deli two blocks from the apartment. Devlin said the neighborhood was mainly Italian, but there were also new enclaves of Orthodox Jews.

The deli was new, with shining counters exhibiting dishes of food that Roo had never seen before. They took a table next to the counter and ordered quickly. He had eaten only a roll and coffee since the meal at the Pennsylvania motel and devoured an enormous pastrami sandwich and the most delicious fries he'd ever tasted.

After dinner they had walked back to the apartment, and when they reached the lot where Roo had parked his truck, Devlin said, "Where are you staying?"

"I don't know yet, but probably a hotel near the police station. It's no problem." He tried to shake off a feeling of desolation.

"Why don't you stay here? I have a spare room no one uses, and you can keep your truck in the lot," his new boss said, a faint smile lighting up his sad features.

Roo tried not to sound too eager, or to show the relief that he felt. "Thanks, but I don't want to put you out."

"It would make it easier to discuss the case. You can come and go as you please." He sounded like he meant it.

The apartment complex, composed of four large drab brick units, brightly lit against robberies and muggings, was set in what Roo considered a concrete wasteland. It occurred to him that just one of those buildings would hold the entire population of Paint. It was frightening. He thought of hamsters in a cage. And yet tonight when he turned the key and entered the flat, he felt a surge of gratitude for this sanctuary.

Devlin wasn't home yet, so he went to his room and sank down for a moment on the bed, his eyes shut, exhausted, overwhelmed by the strangeness of everything, worrying if he was good enough to do this job. Washing up, he searched the bathroom mirror for resemblances to that poor creature he had disturbed in the doorway. He would ask Devlin where to get a haircut.

He arrived fifteen minutes later, and after a drink of good scotch, they walked to a small Italian place for dinner. They slid into a large booth, one of three that lined the front window. Dino, the owner greeted the detective like an old friend and took their order. Roo was shocked at the prices, twice as much as Nelson's Diner, but he had regained his appetite and ordered spaghetti and meatballs and a large salad. His boss had the same. They drank the Italian house red, which to his surprise, he enjoyed. His usual drink was beer.

Devlin said he didn't believe in discussing cases over dinner. Instead they talked about the Browns and the Jets and their chances for next season. Then after a silence he said "It was a real surprise to find Stumpy involved in one of my cases. An amazing coincidence. I'd completely lost track of him after the war. He was a very close friend. I don't suppose you know how bad it was for him there."

"No," Roo said, surprised.

"He was captured and then escaped the Viet Cong. He was tortured." He stared out at the street, empty in the darkness.

Roo choked up, trying not to think of what Stumpy must have suffered. He seldom mentioned his time there, and Roo now understood the sheriff's motives in avoiding the morgue, and neglecting the murder case.

"Anyway, nice to know that he's prospered." He watched Devlin as he spoke, thinking he was sober, kindly, and intellectual and wished he'd had a father like him.

At the end of the meal, he said, "You don't need to keep calling me sir. Just call me Devlin like all my friends and colleagues do. My first name is Seamus, but only the priest and my mother use it."

"Everyone calls me Roo back home," he said, finishing the last of his wine.

They walked back to the apartment in comfortable silence. Roo sat at the pine kitchen table while Devlin ground the coffee beans, put them in the filter, and then heated the water and milk. The kitchen was very neat, self-contained, like its owner, with white cabinets, brown lino floor and an old fashioned upright stove.

"How did it go today?" Devlin's dark eyes glimmered with curiosity.

"All right, I guess. Miss Marston was pretty hysterical. She didn't seem to think I was for real because I couldn't tell her much, or explain the connection between the murders. She did give me some leads, the names of two men who were enemies of Miss Townsend." He told his boss about Serge Petrosian and Ranulph von Burkhardt and said he planned to interview them tomorrow. Devlin nodded agreement.

"And the elegant Count Suvorov?" Devlin retrieved mugs from the cupboard as the delicious smell of coffee permeated the room.

Embarrassed at his unprofessional behavior with Suvorov, he said, "He seemed grief stricken. Wanted to know if we had caught the murderer. Suvorov and Miss Marston seem to be involved. He isn't wasting time after the death of his lover."

Devlin's thin lips curved in a smile. He held up a cup. "Milk?"

Roo nodded, and he served the coffee with biscotti, brought back from the restaurant. While Roo helped himself, the detective picked up a file from the stack on the counter, and began laying out papers on the table. "I thought we should do this tonight because tomorrow you will be in charge of these cases." His low voice was almost apologetic. "I have a technique that I've used over the years and although it might seem pedantic, I suggest that we try it."

Roo, his mouth full of biscuit, nodded agreement. Devlin's face was serious; almost haunting in its gauntness while he reviewed everything they knew.

"Two women about the same age were murdered approximately a year apart. In 2000, one woman, still unidentified, was killed near an isolated forest in Ohio. The other, glamorous, wealthy, with a high profile lifestyle was found in the rubble of the Trade Center."

He pointed to another folder on the counter, "That's the background check on Miss Townsend. Very spicy reading. I thought you might want to go over it later."

He went on, "Both women were mutilated in a similar way, and as far as records show, there are no other murder cases of this type recorded in this country. It seems highly likely that the women knew their killer. From your excellent detective work we know that the first victim was in hiding in a cabin and had stolen the identity of a Miss Safford who previously had owned that property. She defended herself with a shotgun, making it impossible for the killer to capture her; otherwise she might have suffered the same agonizing death as Miss Townsend.

"Witnesses reported that Miss Townsend seemed frightened, harried in the hours before her death. She behaved erratically, demanding papers kept by her lawyers, telling them that she was meeting someone downtown. Her safe was left open, but it is not known if anything was removed. Those are the facts so far."

He placed another large official looking folder on the table. Roo recoiled, thinking it might contain the lab photographs of Miss Townsend. He put down the biscuit he had been eating. "The ballistic and weapons report." Relieved, he opened the folder, and Devlin interpreted for him. "Ballistics took some time to analyze the bullets because no one thought that the weapon would be foreign." His boss stood up and stretched his long wiry body.

Roo recovered his appetite, and crunched on two more biscuits while Devlin began to read again.

"The bullets found on the site in Tecumseh County indicate that the unidentified victim was shot twice with a Russian pistol, a 9mm Makarov, used by Russian police forces in Chechnya, and Warsaw Pact countries. After she was tortured, Miss Townsend was murdered with the same type of pistol." He hesitated. "The use of Russian weapons could be just coincidental, but I think not."

Roo turned the page to photographs of large hunting knives with brand names, *Kizlyar, Zlatoust, and RosArms*, and close-ups of the chipped and grooved eye sockets of the two victims. He tried to keep his hands from shaking as Devlin continued. "The identical grooves in the eye sockets indicate that the same type of Russian made hunting knife was used to slash out the eyes of both victims. Furthermore, the pressure exerted on the bone indicates it was the same killer. The lab thinks it was this knife."

He pointed to a *Kizlyar*, a Russian hunting knife made to cut through bone. Roo let out his breath as he read the description, *Total length 215 =10 mm. Blade length 100-+10 mm.* He had been right. It had to be the same killer, even though it didn't make sense.

"There is something else, something curious about Miss Townsend's death. Her torture resembled a brutal interrogation, the work of professionals."

He wondered how his boss knew this, but had noticed many of his books were on intelligence and the techniques of interrogation.

"But cutting out the victim's eyes is more like the work of a psychopath with a particular hang up. A pro doing something like that could make sense only if it was a warning for someone," Devlin said,

"But why put Miss Townsend's body in the Trade Center?" Roo said.

"That's an important question. It could be that she was tortured nearby and the killers didn't have time to get rid of the body. They also might have thought burying it under a pile of ruins would further disfigure the corpse, leading investigators to believe the victim was killed in the disaster. It is a possibility that Miss Townsend reported missing rather than dead would force someone out of hiding. Why, I don't know. Even more important is motive, and we have no idea in either case."

Devlin continued, "Unfortunately, crime scene investigators found no fingerprints or DNA of the killer in the ashes or on the body. It seems farfetched but from the evidence, the killer could be from the former Eastern bloc, or from Russia, someone who once worked for their intelligence agency. The KGB, now called the FSB, has a history of using brutal torture, more recently in Chechnya. It also has government permission to conduct assassinations outside their country."

The idea of Russians in rural Tecumseh County struck him as totally crazy, equal to aliens from another galaxy showing up in Nelson's Diner, but he didn't express his doubts.

"It's a stretch, but the killer could have arrived legally, blending in with other Russian émigrés in Little Odessa. Some bad characters hang out there."

"Where is that?" Roo said.

"Brighton Beach, not far from here, a section of Brooklyn. So many Russians have settled there, that it has been named after the Black Sea port. That isn't much to go on, but I am intrigued by the Russian connection to Miss Townsend. It's one line to pursue."

He drank the last of his coffee, his eyes reflective, sad, reminding Roo of the martyred saints depicted in the icons at the gallery.

"It is curious that Miss Marston turned up, looking for her guardian. And it seems that no one connected with Miss Townsend knew this young woman existed. And there is no record of her identity other than her passport. Miss Townsend had no close relatives, and this young woman is her heir. That could be a motive."

Roo was incredulous at this suggestion. "That can't be."

Devlin studied him for a moment, surprised. "It is highly unlikely. The killer almost certainly is a male with strength to wield that knife and cut through bone. Miss Marston doesn't seem the type to hire an assassin. But more will become clear when we know the identity of the first victim. If there is a connection between her and Miss Townsend, it could be a vital clue to the murders." Roo had been thinking that himself.

"One possible motive for Miss Townsend's death may be linked to the gallery. Miss Marston might be in danger. Keep an eye on her." He wound up the discussion by putting the remaining biscotti in a glass container and the coffee cups in the sink.

Roo felt a sudden leap of joy. His hatred of the city faded. Before going to his room he turned and asked, "Do you know where I can get a haircut?"

Chapter 19

Mikhail
Courchevel, France

THE LATE AFTERNOON light broke in splinters through the dark green pines, as Mikhail strode outside his chalet in Courchevel and surveyed his property, which abutted the Vanoise National Park. His chalet, the only one facing the mountain wilderness, was a virtual fortress, strategically close to the Altiport where small planes, private jets and helicopters flew in wealthy skiers.

He stared at the blue sky past the tree line, and for a moment, forgot his anxieties, briefly sustaining the illusion that he was deep in the Russian forest that had surrounded his dacha. But there were no beautiful white birches that he longed to see again. He despised his exile, a limbo filled with sudden violence, death in wait behind every tree.

The Interpol arrest warrant issued two days earlier by the Russian Government meant that they were closing in on him. If he left France, FSB goons would pick him up. He recognized the hand of his old enemy and rival General Letinov, a favorite of Putin's, behind this move. Letinov's fat face always beamed with a friendly smile, jovial and harmless until one looked into the feral eyes of a conspirator, capable of brutal torture and murder.

Mikhail walked to the door of the enclosed terrace of bulletproof glass and waved a salute to the two guards facing the forest. Acknowledging the greeting with nods and thumbs up, they looked frozen and tired, waiting to be relieved. Both had been officers in his paramilitary covert group and were loyal because he paid well and promised they would return to power with him. They believed in him and would guard him with their lives.

Back in his sitting room, he shed his outdoor clothes, and sat in front of the large glass window, watching the winter sun fade across the peaks. He put a spoon of jam into his hot tea from the samovar and took a bite of dark bread that Anya, his Russian housekeeper, had learned to make to his taste.

Anya Sergeievna Egorova, born in the outer reaches of Siberia, had nursed him during his rehabilitation. She was his only constant domestic arrangement unless one counted his detachment of security. He stirred nervously in his chair, wary, vaguely sensing imminent danger, but knew this feeling had possessed him since he had begun the search through the Raven's files.

His eyes fell on the thick cardboard folder on the low table in front of him. He had searched all the files recovered from the old Bolshevik headquarters in Siberia, and this one, stamped classified and dated 1917-1970, examined only briefly, was most important. He had removed it from the secret room at St. Paul de Vence.

Mikhail knew that for years after the revolution, his controller continued to hide his secret records in the abandoned Siberian shack. Aware that death awaited him, he had returned to the shack one last time to deposit these records before he was quietly murdered in a psychiatric hospital in the late seventies. He could not fathom the Raven's complicated mind. The old Bolshevik spy had meant this file for him? A chill, like the cold breath of the powerful old man looking over his shoulder, made him shiver as he put on his reading glasses and again opened the folder. He had been progressing slowly through it and had barely made a dent in its contents.

It contained in no chronological order, a jumble of photographs, newspaper clippings, dossiers, telegrams, and random reports. He continued on leafing through several receipts and newspaper clippings, and then stopped, breaking into a sweat. The official document was soaked in blood, a smear of human tissue dried across the words rambling all over the page and into his memory.

It was 1970, and the long aristocratic hand of the Raven was thrusting this same paper out to him. He had lounged behind his Louis XIV desk in his luxurious Moscow office, and watched Mikhail's horror stricken face with amusement.

The old agent lit a cigarette in his long ebony holder, sending wisps of smoke into the room and walked over to the window, gazing down on Red Square. "As you can see by telltale marks on the paper, this confession was extremely difficult to obtain. I personally interrogated this former friend, a member of the Brotherhood. This ill-fated organization was formed to rescue the Tsar and his family. The fool never suspected until his last painful moments that I had been an agent for the Bolsheviks and had infiltrated his group.

"Like many others, my friend escaped during the revolution and was repatriated, or should I say forced, with his Cossack troops, back to Russia after World War II. He was imprisoned for life in the bowels of the Lubyanka. I had forgotten about his existence until I recently discovered that he had knowledge of a secret I have been seeking since 1918. It became necessary to resurrect him if only briefly. He informed me, not without discomfort and impending death, that the document still exists."

He moved with quick steps back to his desk, his voice betraying his excitement. "I have located this document, a direct route to power."

Mikhail had been summoned to the Kremlin office, eager to
begin his mission to the U.S. Still holding the confession in his hands,
he had stood quaking before the Raven, an old man, but frightening,
full of power. He was in thrall to him. Looking into his blue luminous eyes always carried Mikhail to a sinister dark place.

The story etched in blood on the confession, came back to him,
and he stared through a long lens, drawn back in time, an old strip of
film running through his head.

It is 1918: Tsar Nicholas II sits with military bearing at his desk
in a cold room in Tobolsk, Siberia. He looks straight ahead, waiting,
expecting death to arrive at the hands of the Bolsheviks. From the
desk drawer, the Tsar takes out a piece of stationary engraved with
the Double Eagle. The captive ruler's pen scratches across the page
as he writes his last *ukase*, his only hope for the survival of the
Romanov Dynasty. He lays the pen aside and places his final edict in
a precious carved ivory casket, The Box of the Harpuiai, and quickly
thrusts it into the hands of his waiting aide Prince Dolgorukov who
carries it away in a suitcase. Mikhail sees the prince lying dead in a
field; the suitcase holding the casket and its powerful contents had
vanished in the chaos of the Russian Civil War.

Shaken by this precise vision, Mikhail remembered the Raven
casually placing the bloody confession in his desk drawer, his cold
voice explaining the mission. He had listened with a sinking feeling of
impending disaster. It was not what he had expected. He was being
sent to New York. His cover would be Jack Reilly, Vietnam veteran,
a detective in the New York Police Department. His mission was to
find the Tsar's *Ukase* hidden in an ivory casket. It had seemed crazy,
totally unbelievable, that a law issued by a long dead Tsar would have
any importance. But he knew the reputation of the Raven. He was
never wrong.

It had been painful for the old Bolshevik spy to give up any
information even if it was needed to successfully carry out this

assignment. The Raven's perfect features, once described as those of an angel, had contorted into a frightening mask as he searched his armory for exact words, warning that in the past he had eliminated anyone who had knowledge of the powerful document. He had been forced to reveal that the Tsar's edict would give its possessor the power to overthrow Russia's government. The image faded and Mikhail slumped in his chair. His mission had failed and the *ukase* had vanished again.

Then in 2000, a communication with an old colleague put him back on the hunt. This former KGB officer, who had stolen files from headquarters and sold the secrets to select clients, contacted Mikhail. The officer had received anonymous puzzling requests for information about him. To his astonishment, the details requested inadvertently revealed that the *ukase* still existed and was within his grasp.

He had been sitting for some time, still holding the old blood-stained document, its gore disappearing into the growing darkness. Then he got up and switched on the lights. Two days ago he had abandoned the hunt for anything more significant in this file and in frustration and anger planned to burn the useless documents. But then it had occurred to him the contents could have been deliberately arranged to appear random and disorderly. That would mean the information would be comprehensible only to those who could fit together the disparate pieces of the puzzle.

He read through several more papers until his eyes fell on a KGB dossier on Gregori Petrovich Suslov who defected from the Soviet Union in 1951 with classified government documents. Suslov had been a dedicated administrator for the MVD, the branch of the KGB in charge of the GULAG, the Russian prison system.

Earlier that year, on the recommendation of Beria, head of state security, Suslov was promoted and posted as a KGB operative to the Russian diplomatic mission in Paris. It was unprecedented that a prison officer in the MVD would be assigned a post on the diplomatic side. Shortly after Suslov arrived at his Paris posting, he was ordered to return to Moscow. It was obvious. Someone close to Stalin discovered the prison officer had stolen classified files. Apparently aware of what happened to colleagues when swiftly recalled, Suslov defected to the U.S. Embassy in Paris. Mikhail stirred his tea and watched a chamois with majestic antlers cross the snow directly in front of the window. Its big eyes regarded him with curiosity.

Attached to Suslov's dossier was a note from Stalin, commanding Beria to find the defector and bring him back alive. Mikhail read on, intrigued. Another official report stated that shortly after defecting, Suslov had disappeared somewhere in the United States and was believed to be dead. It was signed by the Raven. He could not yet attach any significance to what he had read.

With growing impatience, he picked out another bunch of papers, held together by a rusting paper clip. Removing the clip, he found among receipts for office stationary, a short handwritten note from Beria. 'Suslov problem resolved.'

He also discovered a series of Stalin's commands to Beria issued from 1947–1948 handwritten on cheap lined notebook paper. His repeated orders, in raving, ranting language were to locate those criminals, 'who had escaped from Mongolia.' He described them as 'deviants, usurpers, wreckers of the people's government.' Mikhail looked out at the trees, transfixed and saw the tips of the chamois' antlers as it retreated into the forest. No names were given; that must mean both Stalin and Beria knew the identity of these people who had somehow escaped the KGB.

He opened a typed report from Mongolia. It was dated 1947, signed by A. Rogovin, station chief.

*Lieutenant Dorji Djambolon and his patrol of thirty men were ar-
rested on the charge of aiding the escape of enemy usurpers and spies.
The Lieutenant and his men were interrogated and confessed to the
crime. They were found guilty of counter-revolutionary Trotskyite activ-
ity and executed by firing squad.*

Beria's note, 'case closed' and signature ended the report.

Mystified by the set of old documents, he studied Beria's signature for a moment. It was genuine. He had seen it many times in the
Raven's papers. Why would Beria, the powerful head of Russia's state
security, personally handle a small incident in Mongolia, with a special
report to Stalin? From Stalin's barrage of notes, it was clear that he
was furious, had threatened Beria, and personally ordered the executions. This trial and the subsequent executions in far off Mongolia
ordinarily would be insignificant to Comrades Stalin and Beria, who
with a casual lift of a pen had sent so many millions to death. What
was so different about these deaths? He could not grasp the meaning.

A large shadow loomed above him. He pulled off his reading
glasses, his eyes blurring for a moment, dropped the papers, and
grabbed for his pistol.

Bebe's tiny head leaned toward him. "Time to dress for dinner,
Boss," he said, bending over to pick up the papers.

"No, leave them. I'll do it." Mikhail's command was sharp. After
the bodyguard left the room, he picked up the scattered papers and
locked the file in the safe in his bedroom. He sighed as he dressed in
a cashmere sweater and jeans for the dinner. It would be a bore, but
it was a formality Vlach Reshkov, head of Red Star Entertainment
Corporation, insisted upon. In this past year he had avoided public
places, but he couldn't let Vlach believe he didn't have proper security and was vulnerable.

Shamil parked the Humvee down the street and kept watch after Mikhail entered the restaurant, his Uzi concealed under the seat. The dinner at the Italian restaurant La Cendree at the far end of the resort began well. The party consisted of himself, Bebe, Vlach, Nika and their two bodyguards he recognized from the Helos group.

The food looked and smelled delicious. It was an irony that after starving at different times in his life, he now could afford any delicacy he wished, but was terrified to eat. He was aware from his own past KGB experiences that there were ingenious ways to poison him.. He forced himself to take a sip of wine from a bottle opened and poured in front of them.

Vlach leaned over his food, pressing his face against the plate and gobbled the pasta, a habit developed in prison that marked him as a former *zek*. Wiping his mouth on his sleeve, he began his pitch, swearing that all the girls were clean.

The discussion of the girls brought up unwanted visions of Beria, and Mikhail recalled again the reports on Stalin's head of secret police, which the Raven had once shown him.

"My life insurance. In case they turn on me," the old man had said removing them from his private safe, handling them as though they were precious jewels. He explained that he also kept copies of Beria's dossier outside the USSR and could always exchange it for his life. It was a mystery how the Raven had acquired them since the FSB still refused to release Beria's file, even though he had been executed on 23 December 1953.

Vlach droned on, but Mikhail couldn't stop thinking about those reports on Beria, how he'd read them with shock. He shuddered at the image of the fat man with the cold eyes behind rimless glasses roaming the Moscow streets. The black Zel would glide up beside a 12-year-old schoolgirl, and Beria would wait while his Mingrelian henchmen forced her into the car. He tried to block out the words in the file describing Beria's vicious rape and torture, and the secret burial of the child in his garden.

Vlach's voice broke Mikhail's hellish vision and brought him back to the present. A sinister air seemed to hang about their table in spite of the friendly atmosphere of the restaurant. He tried to dispel this threatening cloud by smiling congenially and speaking to the owner whose photographs posing with French celebrities were posted on the walls. It was safer to be discreet, to be thought of as respectable.

Vlach Reshkov did not care about respectability. Without his sunglasses his red eyes resembled a rabbit's. The greasy ponytail and balding head did not flatter his weak ineffectual face with pointed nose, but the harmless look was deceptive. In a previous life, he had been called the Shovel and had taken pride in using one as his only weapon. He would hit the victim in a death blow, and then like cutting roots of plants, dismember the body with the shovel's sharp blade, often throwing the head into a convenient water reservoir or river. Pimping could be said to be a step up for him.

Nika Trofimov looked like the tough *zek* he was, with short gray hair, diamond earrings, and an elaborate cross hanging from his neck. He leaned over his pasta bowl and sucked it in, making pig like noises. Nika had been employed as a hit man by the KGB before branching out into crime. After his release from prison in the early 90's, Vlach had hired him to keep the girls in line, and he was good at it. He bought them presents, took them on trips and beat them up if they got out of line; whatever was required.

Most of the girls came from remote areas in Siberia. The towns were abandoned by the government, their rusty factories and collective farms closed. Inhabitants who could afford it moved to a better climate and job. The girls had been left behind and had no future outside of one Vlach offered them. The pimp managed two trips a year flying into desolate areas in an old Sikorsky helicopter and then switching to a four wheel drive which took him over disintegrating potholed roads looking for beauties. 'His treasure hunt', he called it, snorting with laughter through his long nose.

They finished dinner and moved on to dessert which Mikhail, in a state of restless boredom, declined. They did not speak of anything but the girls. Vlach gave him the bill for the party and related expenses, and they left the restaurant.

Chapter 20

Mikhail
Courchevel, France

LATER THAT EVENING, Vlach arrived at Mikhail's chalet, his car leading a string of SUVs carrying the girls and wealthy Russian businessmen vetted for the party. Bebe waited outside, checking ID's, and then handed Vlach his envelope of cash.

It was snowing hard, and the huge fire in the party room seemed all the more inviting. In the corner of the room, fresh lobster, caviar and other delicacies were placed on a large table along with vodka and champagne. Vlach gravitated toward another table offering copious piles of cocaine and helped himself. Rock music blasted, and the girls, wearing bras and thongs, danced as though in a stage show. The music grew louder; men chose partners and as the dancing continued, some moved onto large couches or into smaller private rooms.

Mikhail did not dance, but sat like a pasha, watching, stirred by the action. He preferred having the parties at his isolated chalet, with his own security, rather than at one of the hotels, where the French police would have subjected him to scrutiny. There could be no danger of deportation for him. He had to maintain the patina of respectability.

"You see," Vlach said, expansive after a few lines of coke. He extended his hand toward those girls still dancing, most of them now topless. "All beautiful and virgins. But, there is one special girl. I keep back for you, just for you, Boss."

He opened the door from the hallway, and a slim beauty in high-heeled sandals wearing a magnificent sable fur walked in. Her blond hair was plaited in thick braids wound like a coronet around her head.

Enormous slanted green eyes accented her slender nose and beautifully formed mouth. She smiled at him showing gleaming even white teeth, and he no longer heard the music or noticed anything in the room. She was perfect for him.

"Perfect, magical, no?" Vlach echoed his thoughts. "Let me introduce Marousia Nicholaevna Solovieva."

Then he brought the girl over to Mikhail. "Do you know this man?" Not giving her a chance to answer. "He is the famous billionaire Mikhail Borisov." Marousia stood before him, smiling anxiously until he nodded. She sat down, taking a drink from him. Her face screwed up in distaste, and he wondered if this was her first drink of alcohol. Close up, with her coat open, she was surprisingly slim and fragile, not quite mature.

He asked her some routine questions. She was from a collective farm, a *kolkhoz*, a long distance from Irkutsk. Yes, he knew Irkutsk, he said, his vivid memory of that city's railway station returning. The *kolkhoz* was nearly abandoned, she said, only rusting tractors and machinery, and little food. The remaining men were drunks. It seemed alarmingly similar to what he had read of the early days of the 1917 Revolution. Then the peasants had taken over the large estates and did not know how to run them.

Marousia said she hoped to learn English and wanted to continue her studies in the West. She smiled tremulously, knowing her big chance rested in that smile.

They sat for a while with his arm lightly around her, and a slight depression settled over him. He did not ask her age. The shadow of Beria, eyes glinting, seemed to lurk in the dark corners of the room.

When Vlach handed him Marousia's passport and medical certificate, Mikhail noticed he was wearing a cross, like Nika's.

"Don't tell me you've got religion."

The pimp smiled, adopting a prayerful pose. "We are involved with a religious organization."

Mikhail abandoned the party, leading her by the hand as though she were a child through the long hall to his room. Bebe would see to it that his guests all left quietly.

He pulled her onto the bed, his hands shaking with eagerness, awaiting this escape from everything. He could see she was scared and did not seem to know what to do.

She was completely silent, submissive when he entered her. Then he saw her surprise and pain. Tears leapt to her eyes. She was too soft; her legs and arms so tender they could break under him. Her fragility made him angry and brutal. She gave out a hoarse cry that made him think of an injured bird, but she seemed not to have thought of struggling. There was blood on the sheet. She watched him, dull-eyed, her bright innocence gone.

Aghast at what he had done, he had removed the sheet, gone to the cupboard and found others. With trembling hands, he made up the bed around her, moving her light body effortlessly, and then left her to sleep.

He tried to lessen his guilt with the knowledge that she considered herself lucky. If she had not been chosen, she would have been used by the men at the party and transported back to St. Petersburg or Moscow to work the hotels from taxis.

Leaving the bedroom, he stopped in the hall in front of the huge curved mirror. Did she think he was cruel and gross, just a wealthy

old man with power? Was she repulsed at the thought of making love
to him and terrified that he would kill her? He studied himself, surprised, as always, that he looked normal. At times, he still believed he
was ugly with sores covering his face.

His strange coloring, sallow skin, brown slightly curved eyes, indicated he had Asiatic blood, a *chornyi*, the demeaning term used indiscriminately for either Asians, black Africans or anyone of mixed
race.

He ran his hands across his head, an unconscious nervous gesture from childhood, and looked down, expecting to see blood.
Choking sobbing sounds erupted from his throat. Angry for being
unable to control his memories he turned away from the mirror. But
he was forced back to the past.

His first memory, pain. The razor, sharp across his head cuts
through scabs. He moans, and runs his hands over and over his head
to wipe away blood and hair. Smells of vomit, feces, and rotten food
surround him. He watches through the bars of his crib, not able to
get out and walk. Slaps. He dirtied his crib. The women, thin, like
sticks, in ragged clothes, do not clean him. They laugh at him, tell
him he is dirty, ugly, *a chornyi*.

He is hungry, waits for food. They shake him; pull him up by his
arms and stuff something hot, into his burning mouth, gagging him.
He cries and screams, but there are only more blows. He stops, never
cries.

Sasha stares through the bars of his crib at him. Sasha is his mirror. He hears the women say, 'They look alike, could be twins except
for the eyes.' He has dark sallow skin, straight nose; very light hair,
and slightly curved white gray eyes. The women call him possessed
because of his eyes.

Sasha is silent when they scrape the razor over his head. His
white hair falls around him; tears of great sadness roll like rivers
down his face. He reaches out to Sasha. They never speak, but say

things with their eyes, their own sign language. They become brothers, signaling when danger approaches.

When the visitors come, he is older and understands most of the stick women's words, but cannot speak. He hears them say that he is about five and fears he is growing too big and will disappear like the others. He folds his small hands, vigilant, silent, trusting only Sasha.

A tall fair man in uniform with gleaming boots stands in front of the crib. The man stares for a long time. His dark blue eyes burn through him. He seems angry. He shouts, "Mistake. Take them out."

Another visitor, also wearing high shiny boots, stands by the cribs with the Lockup, the boss all the women fear. The Lockup calls the visitor Kosloff. They sit very still in their cribs, watching this man Kosloff who has a flat face and slanted eyes like them.

"My God," Kosloff shouts; his face is pale. "What a hell hole." The visitor is afraid to touch them because of the sores on their bodies.

Kosloff leans over the crib and looks closely at him. "What is your name?" he asks.

He shakes his head and shrinks back, to avoid the slap. He has no name.

"Don't be afraid. I will take care of both of you."

He does not know how to answer.

Kosloff takes him and Sasha away.

Chapter 21

Mikhail
Courchevel, France

UNABLE TO SLEEP, Mikhail sat half dozing in the chair facing the forest. At first light he drank some tea brought by Anya and watched the sky above the mountains open to a wide expanse of blue drawing him into its dazzling brightness. He opened the glass door and took a great breath of air, and he is back in the past, a child again.

He and Sasha are hiding under blankets. Kosloff says they are going in a boat on the sea and must be quiet. It sways and bumps for a long time until he falls asleep. Kosloff says, "We are travelling by truck farther south." They have no idea what he means. He lifts them high up onto the seat.

Then they are in the truck with Kosloff watching the sunrise going into an endless brilliant blue. He looks down at his *valenki*, the felt boots that are too big and dangle on his feet. Before Kosloff took them away, he bathed and dressed them in warm clothes. All his life he would remember the gentleness of the big man and the feeling of warm water flowing over his body.

They huddle together beside him, watching the wide bare land-scape dart by in the window. Kosloff's light brown face, with a big nose, has no expression while he drives. His bald round head is attached to a very thick neck. He studies the man's face with its slanted lively eyes until it becomes part of his memory like the landscape they are passing. Kosloff steers the truck with massive hands: his body, like a large block of wood, seems even larger because of the fur coat he is wearing. He feels the man's warmth and wants to go closer, to touch him, to be against him, but does not.

The speed of the truck scares him, but he is more afraid of the unknown. He has always been in his crib behind barbed wire in the barracks, in the hands of the stick women, never out of the Zona. What did it mean to be out here in the frightening blue sky without fences, without towers? In spite of his fear, the wide sky and the freedom make him happy.

Sasha rocks back and forth and cries silently. Since they left the Zona, his eyes have grown even lighter, the same clear color as his tears, so they look like the huge dripping beacons on the Zona towers. He reaches over and holds his brother's hand, still and cold in his warm one.

Kosloff's eyes dart in all directions, and sometimes he touches a big gun on the seat beside him. Once he said as they approached the rim of something vast limitless blue, like part of the sky had dropped, "That is Lake Baikal."

He does not know how to count, but they are in the big truck for many days and nights. Sometimes the road or pathway disappears, and then they are jerked back and forth, the truck wheels screaming. Sometimes Kosloff stops and stands with his gun while he and Sasha pee and slowly walk beside the road. Sasha's leg is withered so he helps him. They are both very weak and only go a short way. He breathes in the cold air. It overwhelms and destroys the smells from dirtying his crib, which he had carried with him.

During the stops, Kosloff gives them milk and a little bread. Nothing has ever tasted so good, nor ever will. He puts the food away even when they make grunting noises, and cry out for more. "You will get sick," he says. Once he takes out a square box and points. "Camera," he says, his face cracking into a smile. He lines them up beside the truck and clicks the box many times.

They move on through the frozen waste, and become accustomed to the bumping truck, now their sanctuary, and sleep for hours at a time. He waits for the Zona with barracks to appear any moment but it has vanished. Only land, a frozen flat grey, passes by in the window before them. Then the window changes and trees appear. The truck has stopped at the edge of a large forest. Kosloff carefully lifts them out of the truck and carries them through the trees to a hut.

They sit on the floor inside the bare hut. Kosloff looks at him, and again asks his name. He does not have a name except *Chornyi*. He does not answer because he is not sure of making the right sounds even though he has practiced speaking, mimicking the women, and murmuring to himself. Others in the cribs could only make noises, except for Sasha who could say his name, but nothing else.

A bearded man covered in a fur coat and hat creeps up to the opening with his gun. He looks afraid, but when he sees Kosloff, cries out and puts his arms around him. The man in fur kneels down and stares into their faces. He has black savage eyes, and his dark beard is flecked with snow. He and Kosloff carry them to a sledge, pulled by small sturdy horses. Then the bearded man is gone.

It is a long time gliding in the cold under a clear sky among the trees that are alive to him. He thinks he is dreaming in that silent still way he often did in the barracks, as they move deeper into a forest of great birches and pines.

The snow hits his face; something with dark fur stands at a distance. Kosloff says it is a wolf. It watches them for a moment, and then slips away into the trees. Sasha doesn't see the wolf. He no longer rocks back and forth, but his eyes are shut. A clearing in the trees appears ahead. They stop, and Kosloff whistles a sharp clear sound.

An old man, dressed in heavy fur robes with long hair past his shoulders and a beard covering the lower part of his face, comes out of the forest to meet them. A woman in black robes follows him. He hears Kosloff speaking to the man and woman, but doesn't understand what they are saying. Then Kosloff is gone.

"I am the Elder." The old man smiles at them. His face is a blur, as though they are passing him quickly in the truck. "Welcome children, to the Ark, our community." The Elder looks at him. "You have darkness in you. You are like the night. You will be called *Noch*. And you," he turns to Sasha, "have the light of the Holy Spirit in your eyes. You are like the day so we will call you *Den*."

The woman in robes, who tells them she is the Mother of Christ gently takes them by the hand, and leads them on the path into this dream place of warmth, and food, and safety. There are now two places in the world, the one with the barracks and the guards, then a long journey to this place of peace and beauty. The Mother who takes care of them calls Sasha, *Solnyshko*, Little Sun. He does not resist, but in his strong willed way repeats the only words he is able to speak.

"I am Sasha."

His mind went blank, empty after that. Even though he remembers his name is *Noch* and he is happy, he waits every day for Kosloff's return.

The past faded, leaving Mikhail still in his chair looking at the mountains. He picked up the leather bound book on the table beside him. It was disturbing that he could not recall his time at the Ark, and yet remembered everything about Kosloff. Closing his eyes he still could see his broad back retreating into the forest, disappearing forever.

All his adult life he struggled furiously to bring back concrete pictures of living at the Ark, but he succeeded in only short flashes of recognition. The memories were like undeveloped film coiled in some recess of his mind.

Even the few images he did possess had slowly faded over the brutal years. He had sometimes wondered if it had all been just a dream. He wanted desperately to revive his memories of home, that one time he had felt safe, wanting most of all to find Kosloff.

Miraculously, he had recaptured some of the sketchy memories while he was a KGB general and in Paris for a conference at the Russian Embassy. Browsing in a store in the Louvre des Antiquaires, he had found an old Russian children's book most likely brought out of the country by émigrés. Bound in a leather medieval style cover, it was called *Tales of the Heroes*. The tales describing the epic deeds of the *Bogatyrs*, ancient heroes of Russia, were based on the *Byliny*, old epic poems recited and handed down orally to each generation of minstrels.

He experienced a thrill of recognition when he opened the book. The illustrations were in colorful iconic style and took him back to the Ark, with its carved onion shaped domes of the church; the wooden and stone houses set against the snow and birches; the bearded men dressed in long fur cloaks and fantastical hats. He had bought it, the first of his collection of rare illustrated pre-revolutionary Russian children's books, a strange hobby for a KGB general.

Tales of the Heroes remained the one book he turned to for comfort. It was printed on thin expensive paper, like parchment, with lettering resembling a medieval manuscript. Now he caressed the hand tooled cover, and as he opened it, flashes of memory came to him. He turned the pages carefully as though looking at a photo album. There he was, in the church, praying before icons. He lingered on one page, remembering he and Sasha playing in the snow. Next, he saw the Elder wearing a high fur hat in a circle of light, stopping the flow of blood from a man's severed hand. And there, in front of the church with its onion dome, Sasha, shouting in ecstasy, saw the light and was possessed of the Holy Spirit; his stiff little body trembling and falling to the ground. Mikhail closed the book, the cries still ringing in his ears.

After the discovery of the book he had begun to search in earnest for the location of the Ark, wanting desperately to return, if only to fill in the puzzling blanks in his memory. Even as a KGB general he had to be discreet in combing secret archives not in his domain. On pretext of researching for a book on Lenin, he had gone first to the State Archive of the October Revolution, which contained dossiers and information relating to the revolution and famous Bolsheviks. But he was at a loss. He did not know where to look and found nothing that could help him.

And Kosloff, who was Kosloff? Once he had asked the Raven. The old Bolshevik's eyes had congealed to a hard midnight blue and several times he repeated, "Who is Kosloff?" and threw back his head laughing loudly. "He no longer exists."

After his futile search in the October Revolution Archives, he poured over old maps and flew by plane and helicopter over isolated wilderness areas where the Ark might have been, but the place had vanished, like his dream, without a trace.

Mikhail locked the book in his bedroom safe. Then he put on his white camouflage clothes, strapped on his assault rifle, and summoned Oleg, a former member of the Special Forces ski patrol who always accompanied him. Ignoring the rule that it was off limits to skiers, they headed toward the Vanoise National Park adjoining the ski resort. Rules never applied to him. He took a deep breath and raced through the opening between the trees, Oleg going slightly ahead.

Mikhail glided along on his skies, vague memories of the Ark, hidden in the wilderness of Siberia still with him.

Suddenly awake to danger, he swerved to avoid two dark shadows in front of him at the rim of the forest. His ski caught the edge of the ice and sent him sprawling. He rolled over and pulled his rifle from the straps. His first instinct told him the dark men waited for him. He lay there, gripping his rifle, shuddering at the nightmare vision.

He is back at the Ark in the White Nights when the dark stick men come out of the bushes. They say they are from the Zona, the place of the towers. They have curious pictures and writing on their bodies. The elders and the women welcome them. But the men are evil and do bad things to everyone, including the Mother of Christ. He hides his eyes from them.

Sasha saves him. Sasha has a power he believes in, and had pictures in his head that the newcomers are going to kill them all.

While the stick men are drinking spirits from the storeroom, they take the horse and cart and set off. Sasha, his light eyes burning, sees the way, and directs them through the wilderness. *Noch* has grown, but still has to strain to reach the reins. The wild fear inside him makes him gasp for breath. They travel south to find Kosloff.

Mikhail came back from the nightmare, aware that he was in the French Alps, and Oleg was helping him out of the snow. The dark shapes were merely bushes sheltered from the snow by overhanging branches of huge pines. He told Oleg that he was all right and for him to go on ahead to survey the area. Brushing off the snow, breathing in gasps, nauseated with the fear, which always came to him in blinding white light, he started back toward the chalet. This particular nightmare flashback had occurred only once before while he was fighting in Afghanistan, after he and his troops had killed off the inhabitants of a small village.

It was late evening when he shed his ski clothes and took a long shower, and unable to shake this depression and anxiety, went into the bedroom. Marousia was sleeping, her frail limbs sticking out of her nightgown like a child's. He looked at her meager possessions, a lipstick and comb, a pair of jeans and a sweater with holes. The precious sable coat had not belonged to her. Vlach had retrieved it, to be worn by another of his girls to entice customers. The sable was a relic from the tsarist past. It had once belonged to the Tsarina Alexandra and had been confiscated by the Bolsheviks before her death at their hands.

Later Bulganin, a member of the Central Committee, stole the fur and gave it to his mistress, a famous ballerina. He was following Lenin's order, 'rob the robbers' perhaps too earnestly. After Bulganin's indiscretion had been discovered, the precious fur was returned to the Expropriations Department until Vlach had acquired it through some bribe. Nothing had changed, even though there was a new order in Russia.

A pain rose in his chest as he watched her stir and roll over like a child, tired this afternoon from her long walk in the snow exploring the resort. She was nothing more than that, like him and Sasha, at everyone's mercy. The Raven's voice came back to him. "I picked you up from nowhere. You were a street kid. Black worthless shit."

Unwilling to disturb her, Mikhail returned to his chair by the window, watching the sun dip in a glorious red over the mountain, the birds circle overhead before sleep, until the sky turned dark. Oleg returned sometime later with his patrol. They had discovered faint tracks in the mountain above his chalet. His men searched the area, but found nothing else.

There was a knock, and Bebe tiptoed in and handed him a note. It was a message from Lev. He hurried downstairs to communications, waves of exhilaration sweeping over him. His men had located the girl in the photograph.

Chapter 22

Roo
New York

THE WOMAN CAME to Roo again in his sleep. Sensenbrenner's flat nasal voice is describing her. The skeleton, like a computer simulation following the voice, rises and stands before him. The jaw chatters, bone on bone. He must have shouted because Devlin knocked on his door to ask if anything was wrong.

"No. Sorry for waking you."

Still haunted by the nightmare, he studied a crack in the ceiling for what seemed like hours. Tomorrow was his first day in complete charge of the murder cases, and he worried that in the morning the detective would say he didn't think he was up to the job. After all, he had no experience and no record of doing anything remotely successful since his high school quarterback days.

He crept out into the living room and browsed through Devlin's bookshelves, finally picking out *The Russian Revolution* by W.H. Chamberlin. He figured it might be handy to know something about the subject if there actually were Russians involved in his case. He read frantically for several hours, devouring pages to dispel his anxieties.

The next morning at breakfast, he said, "I'm sorry I woke you. I couldn't get back to sleep and borrowed one of your books. Hope you don't mind. It's a history of the Russian Revolution."

Devlin put down his coffee cup and said, "I'm glad you have an interest. I've studied Russian history for many years, and now find the knowledge is very useful in my work." He methodically buttered his toast, took a bite, and continued, "You know, the Bolsheviks used terror to take power after the fall of the Tsar in 1917, and operated in similar ways to today's terrorists. They were organized in cells, independent of each other, same as terrorists now." He looked at his watch.

"I'm late for a meeting."

Devlin told him to take his time, and meet him later at his office. He gave Roo a card with the address of the Sunshine Barber Shop.

The Sunshine Shop was a small hole in the wall three blocks from the office. Lionel, an elderly wizened man with little bald spaces between bunches of short dark black hair, waved his scissors while he talked about politics. As his hair fell in clumps around the chair, Roo worried he would walk out looking like Lionel. When the barber finished, he was pleasantly surprised. The haircut was up to date, short all over, and stood up nicely in front.

When he arrived at the office, Devlin turned off his phone. "Great haircut," he said. "I have a series of meetings today. Meet you back here, around seven. Dinner if you have nothing else on. You have my number if you can't make it. By the way, there'll be a press release announcing Miss Townsend's death. Don't worry, we didn't give them anything. It's an ongoing investigation."

Before he left, he gave Roo the codes for getting into the computer files he might need, explaining that his computer could access not only police, but FBI and national intelligence files. Devlin also left him the keys to his black Chevy Impala parked in the lot across the street.

He thought it was odd that Devlin's office was not in the large busy police station, but down the street in this small room on the second floor of a quiet nondescript building. Walking through the long halls, Roo had noted that the other offices on the floor, a brokerage firm, an insurance company and a cleaning service, did not seem connected to the police. The office was spare with two plain desks, a computer terminal, two chairs, and a place to hang coats. A sink and a counter with a coffee maker, a can of coffee and long-life milk were the only amenities except for the toilet in a cubbyhole near the counter.

His new boss was more than a bureau chief in the homicide department. He had not tried to hide this, but had said only that he was a liaison officer to a Federal government agency. Roo guessed he was a member of the Joint Terrorism Task Force.

He also suspected that Devlin had been in intelligence during the early years of the Vietnam War, because of the numerous books on that country's guerrilla fighting and intelligence that filled the shelves of his apartment and the office. For a few moments he browsed through the books and noticed an entire section on Russian history. Reading about the Russian Revolution had distracted him when he couldn't sleep, and he had nearly finished the book he had borrowed.

Curious, he pulled out an old book entitled *The Cheka*. From his reading last night he knew this was the Bolshevik secret police organization set up by Lenin in 1917 with Dzerzhinsky as its head. He opened to the first chapter.

Interrogation Techniques:
The interrogator must strip the subject of clothing. The subject is humiliated and vulnerable, more open to cooperating.

Devlin's comments about Miss Townsend's torture, 'like a secret police interrogation,' flitted into his consciousness. He slapped shut the book and put it on the shelf. He wasn't in the mood to read about tearing out fingernails.

He was stalling, his mind in a turmoil. There were so many leads and possibilities, he didn't know where to begin. It was like being on the football field, the target of a rush defense dodging tackles from all directions. First he went over the list of suspects questioned and eliminated those with solid alibis.

Next he phoned the sheriff's office.

"Nothing new since we found the bullets," Stumpy said.

"Did Ben get in touch with you yet?" Roo said.

Stumpy had authorized Ben and Miss Lindsay to do some library research for the case.

"Yeah, but so far, they haven't found anything. And there were no results from Sensenbrenner's description of the murder victim, which we put out everywhere. Are you ok there in New York?" Stumpy's gruff voice had a wistful note and seemed far away.

"Fine," he said, swallowing hard. "Thanks for everything." He wanted to say I won't let you down, but didn't.

"Stay on as long as Devlin needs you."

The phone clicked off, and he thought of the poor woman's bones still lying in a steel drawer in the morgue. She would be been better off slumbering in the snow. *Rolled round in earth's diurnal course, / With rocks, and stones, and trees.* He said Wordsworth's lines aloud. He would certainly prefer that for himself.

Shaking off these thoughts, Roo picked up the thick folder on Miss Townsend. It was filled with newspaper articles and photographs from the sixties and seventies. Headlines screamed notoriety. One read *Heiress at Warhol Factory Party* and was accompanied by a photograph of a very young looking Abigail sitting on a couch with someone named Ultraviolet. *Party Life* featured several photos of her with Andy Warhol's film crew at Max's Kansas City restaurant. He browsed through piles of clippings, and stopped when he found a picture of Abigail posing as a Playboy Bunny. He smiled at the head-line, *Heiress Hops to Hefner's. Harvard Graduate, Class of '66 Opts for Bunny Career.*

Another account described the opening of the Little Swan Gallery in 1968. Abigail holds a glass of champagne and stands below a large portrait of a beautiful Native American woman dressed in buckskin. The headlines underneath the photo read *Soho Gallery Opens. Heiress Names Gallery after her Shawnee great, great grandmother, Little Swan.*

Roo leafed through the rest of the material and found one gossip item suggesting Abigail was part of a ménage a trois. Devlin was un-derstating it when he said her file made spicy reading.

Miss Townsend's every move was reported and analyzed in de-tail, but he found no clues to her murder and nothing to link her to the victim in Ohio. It was possible she had a boyfriend there and had been cheating on Suvorov. Then she might have become acquainted with the other victim. He closed the folder, placing it on Devlin's desk along with the others, deciding to concentrate on the Russian connection and phoned Latham.

When the detective heard his voice there was a long silence, which Roo interpreted as hostile. "Could you get a guest list and check out the Russians who attended the opening?"

After another long pause Latham said, "All right. We'll get back to you." Roo could hear acid in his voice and knew he resented taking orders from a country hick, and that he made fun of him at headquarters.

He typed in the code opening the computer to police files, and checked on the two major suspects, Petrosian and von Burkhardt. There was nothing on von Burkhardt, but some interesting infor-mation on Petrosian. A Russian of Armenian descent from Baku, he had made millions in the oil business. He immigrated to the U.S. in 1998 and now ran Petrosian Enterprises, a metal recycling firm. Last year, he was investigated for money laundering by the New York

Attorney General Eliot Spitzer, but there was not sufficient evidence to charge him.

Next, he contacted immigration for information on Alexei Kayakov. The Russian had left New York for Moscow the day after the opening. At least Suvorov was telling the truth about that. Interpol's records showed only that Kayakov was CEO of the Brotherhood Security Service and had connections to several powerful officials in the Russian government, among them General Letinov, a military advisor to the Soviet cabinet. During Kayakov's recent visit to the U.S. on a legal visa, he had been seen in Little Odessa, but stayed at the Westbury Hotel on Madison Avenue in Manhattan. Roo requested a more thorough background check and a trace on his current movements in Russia.

He went over to the counter and made some coffee, then read Maxi Suvorov's file but failed to find anything incriminating. Roo was closing the dossier when he noticed something intriguing attached to the last page. It was a missing person's report on Maxi's father Count Suvorov, dated March 10, 1970. Countess Suvorova, his wife stated that he had been missing for two days. On March 12, the count's body was found at the bottom of an airshaft in the Chrysler Building. The verdict was accidental death caused by a fall from a fourteenth floor window.

He closed the file; disappointed that Maxi was clean, still suspicious of his expensive lifestyle. It seemed unlikely that he could afford that Porsche on his salary as assistant director at the Little Swan. It may have been a gift from Miss Townsend.

Katya was the only person left to investigate, and she was innocent, he knew. It was curious how she had sprung out of nowhere into the case. There was no file of any significance on her. They had checked on the leads she had given them, including the Russian Prince who fell to his death at the embassy, but had not yet received the verdict on the cause from British authorities.

He checked his pistol before leaving the office. The day he arrived Devlin had issued him with a Glock 19, and he had immediately inserted a loaded magazine, and racked the slide back to put a bullet in the chamber. Seeing it was still loaded, he tucked it into his belt.

While he waited at the parking lot for Devlin's car, he took out his notebook and read over the information Katya had given him about Petrosian. Despite her guardian's murder and Petrosian's threat, Katya wouldn't believe that she might be in danger. She was suspicious of everything he said, mainly because he couldn't tell her any details about the case.

He signed for the car and drove out of the parking lot, turning the heat on high. It was below zero. Traffic whizzed by him on the Pulaski Highway. Hunching in his plaid jacket, he couldn't help thinking of Katya, of her golden softness, the way wheat fields looked from the distance.

Planes roared overhead, diving out of the huge gray cloudbanks and landing at Newark Airport. This was alien, hardly recognizable as land where once trees and grass might have grown; a wilderness of wrecked machinery, abandoned warehouses, spawning puddles of greenish oil and dark grease. Spilled garbage and refuse blew in the wind.

He drove slowly, staring at the satnav with Petrosian's address, irate drivers honking at him as he turned off the highway, and the road disappeared from the screen. He stopped and checked the address and directions. It seemed wrong, an unlikely place for a millionaire's corporate office. He bumped along on the dirt road passing lines of junk cars, and then saw the sign, Petrosian's Car Dismantling, Car Parts. Turning down the smaller road, he was surrounded on both sides with huge machines crushing the skeletons of cars, and bulldozers scraping and moving the corpses of machinery into piles. The noise mingled with the deafening sound of airplanes.

Noxious fumes rose out of the ground, seeping into the car as he arrived at a rundown two-story building, its front cluttered with trash from wrecks of cars. Two burly men with short haircuts and brown suits stood at the bottom of stairs rising to a second floor. Roo pulled off his cap and got out of the car. His pistol inside his jacket felt reassuring as he walked over to them and showed his badges. Unimpressed, they waved him on, raising their stubby faces to watch as he gripped the shaky rail and climbed the rusty iron steps swaying with his weight. This did not seem like the office of an art connoisseur.

The hallway and office door with half glass windows and old fashioned lettering advertising a button factory reminded him of a set from an old detective movie. He pushed a large round bell and a buzzer opened the door. A sweet cloying scent of cologne pervaded the room. Petrosian sat at an old oak desk ignoring Roo's entrance. He wore a dark suit and a red fez and clutched a set of worry beads that he clicked through his fingers like an eastern potentate.

He cleared his throat and said, "Mr. Petrosian."

"Yes." He looked up; his thick accented voice hostile as though Roo had no right to disturb him. "And who are you?"

"Deputy Sheriff Yoder." Roo handed him the badges. Frowning, he held them in his small pudgy hands, the fingers gleaming with rings.

"And why are you here?" He handed them back as though they were radioactive.

"You are acquainted with Miss Abigail Townsend?"

He nodded.

"Miss Townsend's body has been found in the Trade Center."

"So, just as I thought." He swiveled back in his chair and lit up a cigar, but didn't offer Roo one. "Take a seat."

Roo sat down in a rickety chair that threatened to collapse under his weight.

"She was murdered. Her body was dumped in the Trade Center after the attack. It will be in the late news today. I want to ask you some questions."

Petrosian's rotund body shook. "Well, well, this is unexpected." He placed his cigar in an old tin can.

"Can you account for your whereabouts on the eight, ninth and tenth of September?"

"You mean do I have an alibi?"

Roo nodded. He knew he sounded stupid. An engine started up outside and the protesting sound of cars being crushed invaded the room.

"I was here, at my office. Check with the boys downstairs."

Roo raised his voice over the din. "Is it true you had a deal with the deceased to buy an interest in The Little Swan Gallery? Miss Marston said you mentioned it to her the night of the gallery opening. You don't seem like the type. I guess Miss Townsend might have wondered where your money was coming from."

"It is true. She and Suvorov were coming around to it. I do not have anything to hide. You ask Maxi. The Petrosian's are a very artistic cultured family."

"When did you last speak to Miss Townsend?"

"I telephoned on the 9th early in the morning. She was at her Long Island house."

"That was the last day she was seen by anyone. You didn't have a deal, did you? She had refused you outright."

Petrosian's dark eyes shot forward out of his plump face like cold little bullets.

"Not exactly. I was using my persuasive powers. They never fail me." He clicked his worry beads.

"Did you meet Miss Townsend that day?" Roo persisted.

"No, she refused." He admitted. "Now, you are finished."

"Not yet. Are you acquainted with Ranulph von Burkhardt and Alexei Kayakov?"

His eyes flickered, "Yes, you could say I'm acquainted with them, but they are not intimate friends."

"Have you been in touch with either of them since Miss Townsend's disappearance?"

"I saw them at the icon opening. That is all," he said.

Roo rose and opened the door. "Don't leave town. We may need you as a witness."

With surprisingly nimble feet the Armenian led the way down the stairs. They stood in the yard, while Roo took the statements from the hoods verifying their boss's alibi. Overhead the machines grated in protest. "Quite a business you have here," Roo shouted, getting into the car.

Petrosian leaned over, motioning him to open the window, the fringes on his fez grazing Roo's cheek. His voice was low and menacing. "This is an honest business, but very dangerous for those who poke their noses in places they don't belong. I hope you won't interrupt my work day again unless you have a legitimate reason."

"I'll be back," Roo said. He took the small road back to the highway, the sound of crushing machines following him. The man remained a suspect, although there was only circumstantial evidence. He had tried to buy the gallery and Abigail had refused his deal. She might have discovered he was a crook, maybe a money launderer. The Armenian had the machines to transport a body to the Trade Center. Slowing to a chorus of horns from impatient drivers, he checked directions, going through Brooklyn Battersea Tunnel, past the dark ruins of ground zero; screams and cries of the lost ones seemed to rise in the air with the smoke.

Chapter 23

Roo
New York

AS HE DROVE to midtown to interview von Burkhardt, his thoughts turned to Katya. She could be at the mercy of Petrosian and his thugs. It frustrated him that she doubted his word. On impulse, he telephoned the Little Swan Gallery as he went under the bridge to Manhattan and asked for her. Geoffrey said she had just left the gallery for the Metropolitan Museum to view one of the icons in their collection. Then she had an appointment to meet a Russian collector and would return early this evening. Roo stepped on the accelerator, racing up Madison Avenue.

He parked on 80th Street near the museum, ran to Fifth Avenue, and spotted her near the entrance to Central Park. He kept his distance, intending to catch up with her in the museum, until he saw the black car crawling slowly toward her. The car turned suddenly, and a man walked beside its open back door. Roo couldn't believe it. This only happened in movies. They were going to grab Katya, throw her in the car and turn up the road through Central Park. His heart knocking, he raced through the park, sliding on slush, burst through the 82nd Street park entrance, and reached her seconds before the car. He pulled her to him, and she shrieked with fright before she turned and saw him. He took her along with him, making her run to the museum entrance.

"What are you doing? Are you following me?" Her anger made her only more beautiful, and she struggled furiously, but he refused to let go and hurried to join a crowd of tourists.

He was still breathing hard. "I thought you were in danger, but they're gone now."

"Are you trying to scare me?" Her eyes narrowed with suspicion.

"No, I wanted to check that you're ok."

Her anger cooled at these words, and she let him walk with her. When they sat down on a bench in the main hall, she was still trembling. "How could you do that?"

"A car was following you," he said rather lamely, "And I needed to talk with you, to explain that the murders may have some connection to the gallery."

She glanced around in a nervous gesture. "Are you sure?" The main hall, filling up with museum visitors, seemed perfectly safe.

"Just tell me something. Why you? Why would they put you on this case? Can you tell me now what connection there could be between Abigail and the body you found?"

"The two victims were both murdered with Russian manufactured weapons. Forensics examined both sets of bullets, and believe it is the same Makarov pistol."

Her voice was a whisper. "So you think it was the same murderer."

"It's a good possibility," he said.

She was quiet for moment and then said, "How did you find me?"

"Geoffrey said you were coming here and then meeting a collector."

"Yes, von Burkhardt."

"He's Russian?"

"Yes, his family like Maxi's came here to escape the Bolsheviks. He's that former friend of Abigail's, the gallery owner I spoke to you about. He phoned yesterday to apologize for his rude comments about Abigail, and suggested we meet to discuss collaborating in a new show of icons."

"You're going to meet with him, a suspect?" Roo said.

"He sounded nice, very apologetic. I don't think he's really a suspect. I can't see what's wrong with having a meeting with him." She was angry again, moving farther away from him.

"I guess not," Roo said, "I was on my way to the Volk Gallery to interview him."

"I don't think you'll find him there. I'm to meet him at his apartment in the Waldorf Towers."

"You're going alone to his apartment?" Roo said, his tone implying that was a bad idea.

She stared at him, her dark eyes glinting with golden sparks. "Sheriff Yoder, I appreciate your concern, but don't understand why you seem to enjoy scaring me. I have enough to worry about without creeping around in fear. I don't believe poor Abigail's death has anything to do with me. I'm not sure you haven't made this last incident up, just to make yourself important. Could it be you have an overworked imagination?" Her voice was haughty, very English.

He was silent. What could he say that would make her believe him? She hadn't seen the car with the open door following her. It was so unreal maybe he had imagined it.

"I'm going with you to meet von Burkhardt. We'll drive there," he said firmly. She sighed in exasperation, but didn't argue with him.

Roo was impressed as they caught the ornate bronze elevator to the Waldorf Tower's luxury suites and apartments. It certainly was different from the Homestead Inn, which he once had regarded as the height of luxury.

Katya said, "Isn't it beautiful? It's a landmark, one of the city's famous Art Deco buildings." The elevator stopped at the 44th floor, and they rang von Burkhardt's bell.

The door opened to the odors of pot and incense floating out along with loud strains of heavy metal music. Ranulph von Burkhardt stared at them in shock. His skin peeked through the loosely belted velvet robe. He was wearing black leather gloves. Clearly the man was not expecting a cop.

Before von Burkhardt could close the door, Roo caught a glimpse of the room, dimly lit with candles. A table held a bottle of wine and glasses and what appeared to be syringes. Beyond that, it looked like a chair with leather straps. He squinted, incredulous.

Von Burkhardt managed to half close the door.

"Miss Marston, I am sorry I'm running late. I just finished my exercises. I was expecting our business meeting to be confidential. Who is this man?" Katya seemed to have lost her voice from shock and had stepped back as though to run. Roo showed him his credentials. He struggled to examine them while holding his robe closed and blocking the scene inside his apartment.

"I have some questions for you. Miss Townsend's body has been found. She was murdered and placed in the ruins of the Trade Center," Roo said.

"So she is dead." His eyes bulged out like the carp Roo caught in Hunter's Creek. "I suppose you want an alibi." He tightened the belt on his robe. "Magda and I were in Southampton until the end of September. Check if you wish with our housekeeper."

"You had a falling out with Miss Townsend," Roo said.

"It's no secret. We had been friends for years. I never thought the bitch would try to ruin my business." His light blue eyes were glacial with malice. "She agreed to include me in the show. I had done many favors for her. But then she shut me out, gave the excuse that she had trouble with her other business partners. She was a liar."

"Maybe you had a separate agreement with Suvorov," Roo suggested, unable to hide his disgust. He wanted to punch the sack of shit.

"No, nothing of the kind. She was the one who betrayed our friendship." Von Burkhardt was restless, stranded in his doorway. He was reluctant to shut the door and stand in the hall, and obviously didn't want them in the apartment.

"How well do you know Suvorov?"

"He is the son of a good friend. Our families are émigrés. We stick together."

"So you must know Kayakov," Roo said.

"No, only met him at the icon opening. Look, can we do this another time?" The door swung open, revealing again the chair with the leather straps attached to its arms before he managed to close it.

Roo ignored him. "And Petrosian?"

"I know him, but he's not a friend." He nodded. "Miss Marston, I will be in touch."

Katya did not answer.

When they were out on the street, she said, with a shudder, "I'm glad you were with me. What a creep."

"Yeah" he said, feeling vindicated, wondering if she saw the chair. It was enough to generate a search warrant. In the car she was silent, looking crushed, and humiliated as though the whole scene was somehow her fault.

When they came into the gallery, Geoffrey looked up from his desk. "Everything all right?" he asked. They didn't answer, and he watched them curiously as Roo escorted her to the elevator.

She turned to him, "Was there really someone after me?"

"Yeah," he said, "Two men were going to grab you near the entrance to the museum and take you away in a car. The car pulled off after I got to you first."

"I just can't believe it," she said.

"You need police protection."

She looked at him, her eyes filled with misery. "Thank you. Let me think about it. I know I won't be going to any man's apartment, so I'm probably safe."

"If either Petrosian or von Burkhardt comes near, call me right away." He realized he was clenching his fists.

On his way out, he stopped at Geoffrey's desk.

"Did you know Miss Marston was meeting with von Burkhardt?"

"No, I had no idea." A horrified look passed over his chubby face. "Alone?" he asked.

Roo said. "She would have been if I hadn't run into her."

"Oh my God," he said, raising his eyes to the ceiling. "The man's a pervert."

Roo saw him standing in the doorway, with the barely closed robe, the leather gloves.

Geoffrey lowered his voice even though they were alone.

"He's a scary guy. He likes the rough stuff. You know chains, whips, and nails, whatever. He runs private sex shows in the Volk Gallery, with lots of coke and other stuff. I went once and was scared to death. Magda too. They are a frightening pair. Sometimes after the shows Magda and others have been taken to the emergency room. She never presses charges."

That night, he and Devlin passed a newsstand on the way to the Italian restaurant. Headlines screamed. *Wealthy Gallery Owner Murdered. Body Found in Trade Center Ruins.* Roo was startled at seeing the case he was working on in the papers.

Devlin said, "I released the information we previously discussed to the press late this afternoon." They sat down in their usual booth and ordered quickly. Then he said, "The papers will be hot on this for a few days, but it will die down, especially when there is no information coming from us and bigger stories come along. I don't think it will impede your investigation."

He took a drink of wine and looked so intently at Roo that he thought he'd done something wrong. "I have some other news. I've been called out of town for a series of meetings so you will be on your own. Don't know how long I'll be away. I'll leave a secure phone number and email so you can contact me. I'm sure you can handle it without me."

Sudden panic gripped him, and he looked away from Devlin, out the window, watching a ragged man search through a trash bin at the corner of the street.

"I'll find a hotel tomorrow," he said.

Devlin's voice was edgy. "Nonsense. You'll stay where you are. That's an order."

They discussed the case over dinner, not the usual routine, his boss wanted an early night. Roo reported the interviews with the two suspects, and they agreed on round the clock surveillance. Devlin said he would get search warrants for both men's residences and businesses. Then Roo told him about the kidnap attempt on Katya.

"Are you sure?"

"No, but it seemed as though that's what they were doing. I got to her first. They drove off. I think the guy was foreign, but it was a quick impression. He had scars around his forehead."

Devlin asked him to describe the incident again and nodded when he finished. "You did the right thing," he said.

Chapter 24

Katya
New York

KATYA WATCHED ROO walk away, and took the elevator to the apartment, shuddering at the image of von Burkhardt's sinister presence at his door. He had expected her to be alone. She had met the man only once at the gallery opening, but he assumed from her appearance that she would welcome his disgusting perversions.

The music and smell of pot brought it all back; the bite mark. Von Burkhardt could have been at RUS that night. The thought sickened her.

She fumbled with the key to her apartment, glancing over her shoulder at the empty hall. The sheriff claimed that she was in danger, but she really didn't believe that someone had tried to kidnap her. He was a stranger, and she couldn't trust him. It was hard for her to trust anyone.

Yoder was attractive in a rough way with those intent gray eyes that certainly must see her in a bad light. His face was tanned as though he spent a lot of time out in fields or hunting or whatever else they did in the Midwest somewhere. Although he was strong and athletic looking, she guessed that he had never seen the inside of a spa or gym like most of the men she knew.

She noticed that his hair had been freshly cut which made him seem vulnerable, like a young boy and in a weak moment, she had felt an unreasonable urge to reach up and touch the white exposed areas around his ears and the back of his neck.

She walked into the sitting room, pulled back the curtain and looked down on the street alive with TV cameras and reporters stationed there early this afternoon after the police department had released the news of Abigail's death. She couldn't face the publicity, just couldn't. Maxi had told her to use the old warehouse door to avoid the press.

Desperate for a distraction, she looked again at her article on Courchevel, long overdue, then closed it, and checked her email. There was a message from Claire who had tried to telephone and said she understood why Katya wasn't answering and that she would be in touch. She read the next from Caroline, and let out a strangled sob, almost a scream. Philip was engaged to Lady Arabella Huntington-Drake. They planned to be married next month. How could he do this so soon after they broke up? She obviously had meant nothing to him. Staggering to the kitchen, she opened a bottle of wine and poured a glass, drinking it down, and then, still not quite believing it, went back to look again at the email. Lady Arabella Huntington-Drake was beautiful, her picture splashed across every fashion magazine. He must have been seeing her while they were engaged.

She jerked up from the desk as though she had been stabbed. In her hurt, she did not know what to do. He had cast her off like a piece of trash, had never even called her. She finished the bottle of wine as she stumbled through the apartment, weeping, feeling that she never could stop. She longed for Abigail to be here to comfort her.

She did not remember when she fell onto the bed in a stupor; but came to in darkness. The bedside clock registered 3 a.m. It was puzzling how much it hurt, even though she had broken the engagement. It was his deception, the fact that he obviously had planned this, had been sleeping with Arabella, while she scurried around trying to please him.

This thought fuelled a sudden burning anger; she marched to the bathroom, wet a towel with cold water and returned to bed. Placing the towel over her eyes, she leaned back on the pillows, refusing to be mired in self-pity. She could hear Abigail. 'It's only your pride, you didn't love him, forget it. What happened to your stiff upper lip, your English reserve?'

She must pull herself together before Abigail's burial. It would be hard to face, even though her guardian had planned everything well in advance and there had been nothing for her to do except sign papers. Abigail's explicit instructions surprised her. But then Katya knew Ab who appeared frivolous, was practical and always planned ahead.

It seemed odd that Abigail, who was so thorough, had left no information about Katya's parents. She had assumed there would be some details in the will or other papers, but the lawyers had nothing to this effect. The envelope her guardian had withdrawn from their custody two days before her death might have been for her. The only clue that supported this was her last phone message. She heard it all again, Abigail breathing hard, distressed. Her words, 'Legacy. Hidden in the forest.' Then, a final silence. Wondering what her legacy meant, she removed the towel from her eyes and absently stared at the three Ansel Adams photographs that her guardian had promised would be hers someday. In shades of black and white, they recorded winter scenes from the majestic far West. The first was entitled *Clouds, Mt. McKinley Range, 1948*, the second, *Monolith Face of Half Dome Yosemite National Park 1948*.

The third captured her attention. Suddenly alert, she jumped out of bed and studied the photograph, *Pine Forest in Snow, Yosemite National Park, 1932*. Perhaps it was the wine and her exhaustion that caused her to repeat Abigail's phrase, 'Hidden in the forest'. On impulse she removed the photograph from the wall. It seemed a chance thing, but she knew how Abigail thought. She could have hidden something here in a panic, knowing the murderer was coming for her.

Katya turned the print over. Taped clumsily to the back was a manila envelope. Trembling, she gently pried away the tape, laid the package on the bed and quickly hung the photograph back on the wall, making sure it was straight.

With fingers that seemed frozen, she struggled to tear open the envelope. Inside there was a note and a smaller heavier envelope. The shock of seeing Abigail's handwriting made her go blank for a moment. Her message seemed to shout at Katya.

For you Katya. Your legacy. Trust no one. Do not open this until after I am buried.

She stared at the envelope, the panic in Ab's shaky handwriting. Overcome with grief, she lay back on the bed, unable to continue. Sometime during these early hours she again dropped off to sleep, waking late the next morning with a pounding head, and finding the envelope beside her, realized it was not a hallucination. She was reading the note when she heard the key turn in the lock, then footsteps, and knew it was Maxi.

Remembering Abigail's warning to 'trust no one', she quickly threw the bedroom door lock, looked wildly around for a place to hide the envelope, put it in her Kelly bag and locked it.

Chapter 25

Roo
New York

WHEN ROO ARRIVED at the Little Swan Gallery, a sign, *Closed until Further Notice,* was posted in the window. The show had been scheduled to run through February. A mob of reporters and TV cameramen were gathered on the sidewalk. They rushed toward him, but he pushed through without comment and rang the bell to the gallery. Katya buzzed him in, and asked him to wait for her in her office.

Conscious of her cool upper crust English accent, he nervously paced through the downstairs exhibition. The rooms with closed blinds were in semi-darkness and the icons stood out even more vividly in the dim light. Ancient saints stared down from the walls, their ghostly eyes following him. He wandered away from the main gallery into a well-lit small room, furnished with leather couch and coffee table, and stopped, amazed at the portrait in front of him. His dreams of the past when he had spent his days tramping in the forest came alive. The great Shawnee Chief Tecumseh looked ready to step out of the dark wooden frame.

There were other early portraits in the room, but the oil of Tecumseh took center stage. The chief wore a red turban decorated with an eagle feather and a necklace of bear claws over a colorful blanket. His chiseled noble features were set in a fierce expression and he stared out with great dignity, in defiance at a hostile world. A vast forest formed the painting's background, its shades of green foliage rendering the portrait even more vivid. Looking closely at the background, Roo noticed a small figure dressed in buckskin, entering a trail.

The picture was labeled: *Anonymous painter, approximate date 1799. Purchased in 1981 from The Digby Estate.* The name Digby nagged at him for a few moments until he recalled the sign for Digby Downs, the upmarket housing development near I71 that he passed on the few occasions he drove to Columbus.

His head buzzed with a tense excitement as he turned tangential facts over in his mind, knowing they were connected in some relevant way. Miss Townsend had named her gallery after Little Swan, her great great grandmother. The newspaper article describing the gallery opening had mentioned that the pharmaceutical business had begun with Little Swan and her husband Jed Townsend touring the Midwest selling Townsend's Elixir. Abigail was born in New York, but her family was originally from one of the Midwestern states. None of his musing proved Abigail Townsend had any connection to Ohio or ever visited there. She may have only wanted to add to her collection.

"Priceless," Katya said, startling him. "They are my favorites. They were Abigail's too."

"Yes," he said, "I don't suppose there are many other portraits of the great Tecumseh. Only a few artists were painting Indians, I mean Native Americans, at that time." He put his hands in his pockets, ill at ease.

"Actually, this is a private room, not open to the public." Her cool English voice seemed a rebuke.

"I'm sorry. I wandered in by mistake."

"Oh, that's quite all right. I didn't mean." She broke off. He noticed her eyes were red and guessed she had been crying. She was dressed in jeans and a sweater and evening sandals again, even though it was the middle of winter.

Distracted, he found himself searching for some flaw in her beauty besides her red eyes. Expensive, he thought. Ben would call her high maintenance, with smooth shining hair, perfect skin, toned body, and manicured nails.

"Why did you want to see me? I've told you all I know. And the newspapers have found out everything about Abigail. It's all over cable television. They run videos and pictures of her over and over. And of course, a lot of it is just untrue, just slander." Her voice broke. "Poor Abigail, no dignity or privacy. The reporters have been camped outside since her death was announced."

"I'm sorry to bother you again, but sometimes people recall things they didn't remember when they were first interviewed," he said, thinking he should stop apologizing.

She didn't answer.

"Look, I'm only trying to find your guardian's killers." He decided it wasn't the time to ask about the Tecumseh painting, but it preyed on his mind.

"I know," she said. Her voice was sad and low. "Come into the office."

They sat down, and she pushed a button on her desk. Geoffrey popped his head around the door, and she asked for tea and coffee.

They waited in uncomfortable silence. She eyed him with suspicion, and he could hardly blame her. He felt bare, his ears sticking out. He was sure that she had noticed his haircut. He must look to her like one of the Dukes of Hazzard, a complete contrast to that elegant fop Maxi.

Geoffrey brought in a tray with tea, coffee and cookies. Thanking her, Roo quickly ate two and restrained from gobbling down a third. He always was ravenous when nervous. She poured his coffee, her delicate hands trembling.

"Can we go on? I'd like to get this over with." She rubbed her temples and a golden tendril of hair escaped from her ponytail. He stifled the crazy urge to brush it from her cheek.

He quickly finished his coffee. "Did Maxi ever tell you anything about his business arrangements with the Russian?"

"No, but he did go over the gallery books with me. They seem fine. I see no reason to question his dealings with Kayakov. He told me the man works for someone quite powerful in Russia. Maxi says his mother, the countess, hates Kayakov. She thinks he's dangerous, but Maxi says it isn't true and dealing with him is the way to get back the family property lost in the Russian Revolution. It all seems terribly strange and irrelevant to me." She sighed, an expression of sorrow on her face.

"I have to ask you about some of your associates in London. You were engaged to a Mr. Philip Thorpe-Lydington?"

"Yes, but it didn't work out."

He wanted to know more, but she wasn't volunteering. "Was he aware of your guardian's disappearance?"

"Yes, but he wasn't interested. I am sure he doesn't know anything about Abigail's murder."

"And did your other friends know about the disappearance?"

She turned red, and snapped, "My social life is none of your business."

He wondered what had angered her, and quickly changed the subject to the painting of Tecumseh. "I apologize again for trespassing into your private gallery."

"It was Abigail's family gallery. Ab collected many of the paintings and hung those she cherished."

"I'm curious about the picture of Tecumseh. I know it's private, but can we look at it again."

She nodded and led him back to the gallery. On the way, she said, "Tecumseh County is obviously named for the chief. Is that why you want to see the painting again?"

"There is something to that," he said, as they entered the room and both stared at Tecumseh.

"It would be helpful to know the details of Miss Townsend's purchase of the painting," Roo said.

"I can check the gallery records." She disappeared down a hallway near her office and a few minutes later came back with several files labeled Townsend Collection.

She placed them on a low glass coffee table in the middle of the room. They sat down on the leather couch and leaned over the folders, heads almost touching. He was conscious of her slim body, the delicate curve of her neck; the faint scent of her perfume made him light-headed.

The receipt showed the portrait had been purchased by Miss Townsend in 1981, one of an entire collection of early artists from the Digby Estate Farm, Tecumseh County, Ohio. The auction was held at Sotheby's, New York.

"This could be the link," he said, trying to keep his voice level.

She looked at him coolly. "What link?"

"That your guardian may have known the woman whose body was found in the forest."

"I can't think how Ab would know that poor woman. According to this record, she attended the auction, but I can't imagine her ever going to Tecumseh County."

They heard footsteps, and Maxi opened the door.

"Hello darling." He glared at Roo. "What are you doing here? Haven't you guys caused us enough trouble?"

"We've been assigned to protect Miss Marston until we catch the killer," Roo said, glaring back.

"That could be many years the way your department works."

Roo smoldered, but said nothing.

"No need for you to hang around since I'm with her," Maxi said, dismissing him as though he were a servant.

Katya said, "That's true. If Maxi's here with me, I probably don't need the extra protection."

"Thanks to New York's finest, the press coverage is terrible. Those animals are camped out there on the street." Maxi looked at Katya, ignoring Roo, "I've managed to keep your name out of the papers, and mine is only mentioned briefly, but poor Abigail is being slandered. They have no respect for the dead. After the burial tomorrow, they won't have anything else to write about."

Katya's eyes overflowed with tears. Maxi put his arm around her and looked at Roo. "Hadn't you better go?"

"Yes, but not before I call Detective Latham. He will be first on duty outside the gallery. You've met him, I believe."

"That isn't necessary. I'll phone tomorrow and get you guys called off," Maxi said.

Roo ignored him, phoning for Latham.

Maxi left the room to make a call, and she walked to the door with Roo. "I want to thank you for comforting me after you told me about Abigail's death. But I've been wondering something. How do you know Wordsworth?"

Turning a deep red, he looked past her at the portrait. "I like poetry. Poets say things more eloquently than I ever could. I have no imagination," His voice was stiff with embarrassment as he closed the door.

He rushed back to the office and not bothering to take off his jacket and cap, hurried to the computer, and brought up Digby Estates, Digby Corporation. The firm was started by the Digby's in the early 1800's and became very prosperous, manufacturing canned goods during the American Civil War. Over the years, the business expanded into a huge conglomerate. Lawrence Digby, the last family member to run the company, sold it to the Braybrook Company in 1981.

There was another entry under Digby Land Development. Lawrence Digby also sold a huge plot of land to Pioneer Estates Company who built Digby Downs. It was possible Abigail knew the Digby's. They could have traveled in the same social circle. He took out his phone and called Ben at the garage. There was no answer, but he felt certain Ben and Miss Lindsay would have found something for him by now. A second after he hung up, the phone rang.

It was Ben. "Sorry I didn't answer your call, but I've been busy. Two semis broke down. Anyway, it took us a long time to find the information. None of it's computerized."

"Anything important?"

He could hear clanging in the background and an engine starting up. Ben shouted over the noise. "Yes. Wedding in 1968. A Miss Christina Gartner, from Tecumseh County married Lawrence Digby of the Digby Corporation at the Digby Estate, but it didn't last long. The Gazette reported a divorce in 1969. I'll send it all down to Stumpy, and he can forward it."

He absently thanked Ben and hung up. "Christina Gartner," he said aloud as though addressing her. This had to be the woman whose bones he had found. He burrowed through the New York Times archives and found the clippings of Christina Gartner's wedding. There also were several articles about the divorce proceedings. He laughed aloud, hardly believing the words in front of him. Lawrence Digby had run off with a man named Pinky.

With shaking hands he opened Abigail Townsend's file, rifling through the clippings and photographs until he found her, Christina Gartner Digby sitting next to Abigail Townsend at a society ball. She looked just as he had imagined.

Chapter 26

Katya
New York

AFTER ABIGAIL'S FUNERAL, Katya sat across from Maxi at the kitchen table of her apartment, eating the supper Mercedes had prepared for them.

"I'm glad it's all over," Maxi dug into his second plate of pasta.

"What do you mean?" She studied the Townsend Elixir sign over the mantelpiece.

"I mean the funeral and all the hassle with the press."

She couldn't eat and found it difficult to speak, thinking how final this was, that she never would see Abigail again. Her guardian had been buried in a private ceremony at the exclusive Marble Cemetery with only Katya, Maxi, and the Episcopalian minister at the grave. The cop Reuben Yoder had watched from the cemetery gates.

The casket was closed, and she realized that Abigail must have been disfigured, but she had been given no details. She had not wanted to know. The horror of it without details would never leave her. It disturbed her that Maxi originally had opposed the burial, insisting that Abigail had told him she wanted to be cremated. But there was no proof of another will, and Abigail's explicit instructions were followed.

Everything attached to her murder had been terrible, including the headlines and television reports revealing lurid details of her guardian's past. There was no mention of her kindness and generosity and charitable works.

Thanks to Maxi, Katya was kept out of the headlines, even though the gallery remained notorious. Rumors were circulating that some of the icons were fakes and that prominent customers had been swindled. Maxi suspected von Burkhardt was responsible for the gossip but couldn't prove it. Sales were affected, and they had been forced to close the current show. Workers had begun dismantling the exhibition that morning, loading the paintings on trucks to be taken to the airport.

"Excuse me." Maxi's phone was ringing. He went into the next room, but she could hear him speaking loudly in Russian. He stomped back, and threw his phone on the table.

"Closing the exhibition will cost us a lot. The unsold icons going back to Russia will be a great expense to Kayakov." His face was drained of color. "He'll let me know how we'll arrange things tomorrow. Kayakov wasn't happy about the publicity either. His boss is furious at the notoriety. He insists on complete privacy."

He reached over and squeezed her hand. "Sorry, I wasn't thinking about how you feel. Losing Abigail is hard for both of us to deal with. Don't worry so much about the bad publicity. In a few days, there will be other stories to replace this. I know you talked to that cop at the cemetery. He didn't get it that he wasn't welcome. What did he want?"

"He can't help being assigned to the case. You heard him say I'm in danger," she said.

"It's ok. I've managed to call him off. Police skulking around here would just excite the press," Maxi said.

"He thinks Ab's murder is connected in some way to the gallery." She didn't know why she was defending the cop.

"That's really stupid." His voice dripped with contempt. "But you don't have to worry. I'll take care of you."

"I know you will," she said, in a conciliatory tone.

"What else did he tell you?"

"As I mentioned before, he said that both Abigail and this woman were killed with a Russian gun. But there seems to be something else."

Maxi stirred in his seat, restless when Katya told him about the Tecumseh portrait and how it might connect Abigail to Tecumseh County.

"He says there has been a break in the case, that Abigail and the murdered woman found in the forest knew each other. He also has identified the victim as a Christina Gartner and told me they are getting closer to the killer. I am so relieved."

He paused, dropping his lorgnette onto his chest.

"Absurd, that's not enough evidence to connect the murders. He's just trying to impress you."

"I am not sure that it's absurd and can't imagine why he would want to impress me. He's working hard on the case."

"I see." He pushed back his plate.

"This does seem to be a very tenuous connection, I know. At least the only one he's told me about." She believed he had a point.

"I wonder if there is something else he hasn't told you. He must be assuming it's the same killer."

"He didn't say that exactly, but I know that's what he's investigating." She shivered.

Maxi jumped to his feet and picked up the bottle of wine from the counter. His hand shook as he poured, and he spilled some on the table.

Wiping it with his napkin, he said, "This is depressing you." He leaned over and rubbed her shoulders.

"You look so sad. Let me take you away for a week."

"But we're not supposed to leave New York," she said.

"Nonsense. Poor Ab is buried. They have no legal right to detain us. There won't be any danger. I'll take care of you." He came around the table and held her tightly in his arms. "Listen, one of my old Harvard classmates has a place in Vermont. It's not far from Stockbridge, so we can go there for dinner if we get tired of being alone."

"Oh, I would love that. Besides it won't be hard to reach us. We can leave numbers." She felt suddenly more cheerful.

"And that cop won't be able to pester you."

Something in his tone made Katya suspect he was jealous. She didn't know if she loved Maxi, but she was very attracted to him, felt safe with him. He had rescued her that night at Rus and had never spoken of it, treating her with kindness. Maybe it was Philip's tossing her off like a candy wrapper that made her susceptible to Maxi's charms.

Later that week, Maxi steered her into the bedroom. She did not resist when he gently picked her up and laid her on the bed. He was very sensuous, slowly removing her clothes, drawing her, enfolding her, bringing her totally under his spell. There was a sharpness, almost a pain and then she gave way, defenseless. She felt him, like a creek flooding its banks, flowing over her, turning inside her, drowning her in a rush of passion. She knew it was wrong, so soon after Abigail was buried, but some part of her was still the bad girl, and she desired him. She rationalized that it brought both of them closer to Abigail.

Afterward, he pulled her to him and said, "I'll take care of you. Stay with me." His heavy eyelids were like half drawn shutters, giving him a secretive look.

She lay awake, mulling over Abigail's admonition to 'trust no one'. She was beginning to believe she was in love with Maxi. Why couldn't she tell him about the envelope? Abigail's words made her cautious, but something else stopped her, some vague recollection. It was Maxi on the phone this evening, speaking in Russian. The words were incomprehensible, nothing but background noise, but then, clear sharp out of this background, she heard a word she recognized. She had heard it once before, after her skiing accident when she lay injured among the trees and a voice floated overhead. It was the word *mochit*.

Chapter 27

Roo
New York

ROO DROVE TO the office refreshed after a night of uninter-
rupted sleep. It was strange that his nightmare had vanished once
Christina Gartner was identified as the dead woman. It was as though
she no longer needed to keep calling to him. After he parked he
stopped at Dan's coffee shop and bought a bagel with cream cheese,
and when he arrived at the office Stumpy's files had been delivered.

The sheriff had phoned him last night, his voice crisp, and interested. "It's definite. The murder victim is Christina Gartner."

Like everyone in Paint, Christina had been a patient of dentist
Dr. Ian Stratton. Stratton's son, called Dr. Junior, had continued the
practice, and kept all dental records from 1925 to the present.
Christina Gartner's were a perfect match to the murder victim. Roo
made some coffee and read quickly over the files.

Stumpy had attended high school with Christina, and interviewed everyone in town who had known her. He said she had been
an open book, leading an uneventful life until her marriage to Digby
and her move to New York. Roo poured his coffee and sat down at
the desk, finishing the file. There was no trace of her in Paint after

her wedding. It was just like Stumpy said, "She never came back here after her marriage to Digby or even after her divorce. Everyone felt sorry for her dad, the salt of the earth. She didn't even attend his funeral."

Jubilant at the break in the case, he phoned Devlin on his secure number. He sounded impersonal, far away, "Good development. I have to go now. Keep at it." Roo had expected enthusiastic praise, but his boss seemed lukewarm, uninterested. Deflated, he munched dispiritedly on his bagel, gazing out the dirty office window, the sill caked with black stained snow. The gray building opposite was coated in pigeon shit.

His former life in Tecumseh County seemed to be slowly fading into this hostile city landscape. He missed the tranquility, the woods and countryside, and the sinking into an undemanding life.

He was stung by Devlin's abruptness. His original triumph at identifying the murder victim now seemed a small insignificant break in the case, and the possibility of failure loomed. He desperately wanted to solve the murders before Devlin returned. His boss had not even told him where he was going, but he supposed the meetings were in DC.

He missed their evening talks and now felt even more isolated, adrift. He'd had a few drinks with two of Devlin's colleagues last night, Chief Detective Joe Burns, and Latham. They had been friendly enough on the surface, and politely curious about life outside New York. But they were totally unlike him, reminding him of the cops in CSI. He suspected they copied the macho characters on the show.

He opened Abigail's file, searching through newspaper clippings until he found the photograph of the two murdered women, snapped in 1969 at the Four Seasons Restaurant. Abigail Townsend and her friend Christina Digby, nee Gartner, both young and beautiful then, laugh at the camera, with not a glimmer in their eyes of the horror that awaited them. He wondered if they could have been in touch over the years.

He had two suspects, Petrosian and von Burkhardt, but at this point it was stretching it to think either was involved in Christina's death. Search warrants had been issued and police were combing the premises of the two men. So far, nothing had been found to incriminate them. And there was no real proof, only strong circumstantial evidence, that the murders were linked.

Earlier, he had run a check on all of Abigail's known boyfriends who proved to be clean. Lawrence Digby, Christina's former husband, the last Digby to head the multi-million dollar Digby Corporation, was ruled out. Digby, who lived in retirement in Morocco with two young men, had suffered a stroke and was confined to a wheelchair in his Marrakech villa.

Thinking again of Christina, he sensed her disappearance was connected to the murders. Obsessed with tracing her, he was unable to find any record of her in the city or anywhere in the country after 1970. He knew divorce was bad but surely wouldn't cause someone to vanish for thirty years.

He went back to the wedding announcement in Stumpy's file. A clipping from the Paint Creek Gazette gave Mr. and Mrs. Lawrence Digby's Manhattan address as 1180 Fifth Avenue.

He fought his way through uptown traffic, crossing Madison to Fifth to Christina's last known address, parking in front of the elegant building shaded with a green awning, facing Central Park.

A uniformed doorman led him to the manager, Dave Mahoney, an elderly gentleman wearing a dark suit. His yellow wrinkled face was topped with white hair swirled like a dairy whip. "Yes, I remember the couple. Wait here." Dave retreated into a back office and returned with several cards dark on the edges with age.

"She was very beautiful. Can't say I liked the mister much. They divorced you know. And she moved. Yes, here it is. December 1969.

I remember the day she left. She was pretty broken up. She said she was staying in New York, moving somewhere near Second Avenue." He searched the cards again, and then looked up. "Sorry, no forwarding address here."

Thinking this was a nice part of town, Roo walked over to a deli on Madison Avenue and bought a pastrami sandwich. He ate quickly in the car, gazing absently at traffic whizzing by. For a moment, he imagined Christina among the shoppers, a sad figure leaving the apartment, vanishing into the streets.

It occurred to him that when Christina moved to 2nd Avenue, she would have changed her address and telephone number. That meant her name and address could be listed in an old phone book. He telephoned the public library, and by the time he ran up the steps between the two lions, four heavy telephone books were waiting on a trolley. He signed a slip at the desk and sat down in the reading room, going through 1969 first, checking both the D's and G's. Lawrence Digby was listed at the 5th Avenue address, but there was nothing under Gartner. Discouraged, thinking she had an unlisted number; he picked up the book for 1970. Miraculously, there it was, under Gartner C.; he rushed uptown.

The apartment building at 302 East 82nd Street had been renovated, but the vegetable stand on the corner and a laundromat across the street indicated it was down-market in comparison to the grand building on 5th Avenue. He wondered why Christina would move here when she had plenty of money. The newspapers had stated she had received an unusually large divorce settlement.

At the rental office two doors down the street, a pretty girl in jeans momentarily stopped chewing her gum and frowned when he asked to see records from 1969-70. "That long ago? I doubt it, but just a minute." She disappeared through a door to the back office and was gone for some time, returning with a smudge of dirt on her button nose. "Yes, we do have them. Don't know why. Do you want to come with me?"

She led him back to a windowless room with fluorescent lights, stacked with old metal file cabinets, explaining that the tenants were filed alphabetically by year. Roo eagerly flipped to Christina's file. She had signed a lease for Apartment No. 1 on December 28, 1969. He quickly reviewed the quaint looking typewritten notes.

Previous address. 1018 5th Avenue. Insurance payment for damage during break-in, April 15, 1970, Amt. $1000. Tenant left same date, leaving possessions. Forfeiture of deposit. No forwarding address.

Going through the list of other tenants, he saw that a Mme. Feodosia Petrovna Antonova and daughter Anna had lived in Apartment 2 across the hall from Christina. The girl came back into the room and stood by the cabinet, fidgeting. "Are you going to be long? It's time for my break."

"No, only a few more minutes." Roo couldn't believe her rudeness, especially to a law enforcement officer. He noticed her look of disdain at his plaid jacket before stomping back to the front office.

A thick bundle of cards held by a rubber band noted each year the Antonovas occupied the apartment. He stared in surprise at the oldest card. They had moved into Apartment 2 in 1922. Previous addresses listed were St. Petersburg and Omsk, Russia and Harbin, China. Underneath was an explanation that the Antonovas were Russian refugees. The last card noted:

Vacated apartment April 2, 1970. No notice given. Forfeiture of deposit.

The girl was standing over him now, loudly cracking her gum, and blowing huge bubbles.

He ignored her, struck by the coincidence of the departure dates. Within two weeks of each other, Mme. Antonova and Christina had vacated their apartments without notice, losing their deposits. Christina and her neighbor must have been acquainted, if only to say hello in the hall. What had happened to them? He left in a fog, forgetting to thank the girl. Every aspect of this investigation led to a Russian connection and then came to a halt. Christina still eluded him, like a phantom flitting just ahead of him on the streets of New York.

Back in the office, he dived into New York City Police archives for April 1970, and found the report for a break in at Christina Gartner's apartment. The case had not been solved.

It was now late afternoon and dark clouds crept around the tall buildings, threatening rain. He flicked on the lights, his mind returning to Mme. Antonova suddenly leaving her apartment. Going back to the archives, he quickly tapped into all police files under the name and discovered something startling and very weird. Feodosia had been reported missing five days after she left her apartment. Christina had filed the report.

Stunned by the discovery, he stared out at the dirty courtyard. But what did this mean? Christina was not just a neighbor, but a friend of the Russian woman. Intrigued, he read the follow up. Mme. Antonova was never found. He did not know how any of this fit into the case, but filed it away in the back of his mind.

Outside, the clouds had spread like spilled ink staining the sky a deep black. Rain blew sideways crashing against the window. Pigeons flew past helter-skelter, confused in the wind, like his scattered thoughts.

All of his research today lost him in a maze of coincidence and unrelated facts. Staring up at the buildings shrouded in gloom like outsized tombstones, he thought of calling Katya Marston to make sure she was ok, picked up his phone and then decided against it.

Latham was on duty at the gallery today so he had no excuse for speaking to her.

Roo had gone to Abigail Townsend's burial in the vague hope that a mystery person might turn up, like in the movies. It was a society death, but only Katya, Suvorov and the minister were at graveside. Katya leaned against Suvorov, resting her head on his shoulder. They were both elegant and glossy thoroughbreds, and he had to concede they looked good together, like a society picture from *Vanity Fair*. After the short ceremony, he stopped her outside the cemetery. "I'm sorry," he said.

Pale and withdrawn, her grief making her even more beautiful, ethereal, she looked gravely at him and said, "Are you any closer to finding Abigail's killer?"

He had been a total jerk, bursting out that he had identified the woman. "We are close to solving the case," he had said, barely finishing his sentence before Maxi came up and took her away.

He picked up his phone again, changed his mind, and went back to the computer. A report from Interpol was flashing at him from the screen.

Biography: Alexei Kayakov, born in 1957 in Irkutsk, parents unknown, spent his teen years at Norilsk prison. He was released in 1977, but on July 10 1989 was convicted of robbery and murder and returned to prison.

Roo read on eagerly, wondering how Katya would feel if she knew the gallery's partner had been convicted of murder.

Kayakov was pardoned by the government and released in 1998, and is currently chief executive of the Brotherhood, a security firm. He is a wealthy art collector and financier, but his source of income other than his salary at the firm is not traceable.

He knew money laundering was not unusual in Russia.

Kayakov is connected to a mysterious figure called the Shaman whose real identity and background are unknown. There is no photograph of the Shaman and no physical description.

The Shaman's source of wealth is also unknown. He is believed to be extremely powerful and well connected to influential officials in the Russian government. He controls a large private army, consisting of commandos, ex-Spetznaz forces, and veterans from Chechnya.

Devlin had described the murderers as professional hitmen.

The Shaman owns a vast territory near the Mongolian Border. There is strict border enforcement, and it is impossible for outsiders to enter without his permission. This rule is enforced by the Russian Government.

He read the next paragraph twice.

It is rumored that his organization is a mystical, semi-religious cult, but few details are available. There have been some accounts, not proven, of ritualistic murders within the compound.

Roo forgot his loneliness, fear of failure, everything as he stared at the photograph on the screen.

Unaware that the Interpol investigator was photographing them, Maxi Suvorov and Alexei Kayakov were speaking with a man be-lieved to be the Shaman. He could be anybody. The Shaman wore a long robe with a huge cowl that totally hid his face. Roo studied the small bit of background of barren hills at the top edge of the photograph, the Shaman's camp. When Maxi checked out of his

Moscow hotel room and wasn't seen for a week, he must have visited the Shaman's headquarters.

He disliked Suvorov for a lot of reasons, but it seemed incredible that Maxi, a well-groomed city guy who affected a lorgnette, would be involved with a sinister group. The report ended with a note from the investigator.

They are gathering the followers in from the settlements. The rejoicings have begun.

Interpol stated that the investigator had not yet returned, or filed a final report.

Roo wanted to call Katya, to tell her about Maxi's connection to this dangerous group, but she might already know this. What could he say? Watch out for Maxi didn't sound credible even to him. There was no evidence that Suvorov was involved in any crime, but the photo made him jumpy. He had to move, to do something.

Chapter 28

Roo
New York

HE DROVE UPTOWN in the cold rain to Kutusov's apartment, a third floor walk up in an old brick building on 87th Street and 2nd Avenue. Avoiding the garbage cans by the door, he pushed the buzzer to Apartment 3A, heard the unintelligible crackle of the speaker, and announced that he was the police. The outside door buzzed, he walked up to the third floor, the narrow stairs creaking under his weight.

He knocked, announcing again that he was police, and the door flew open. Startled, Roo stepped back. "You are Professor Kutusov?" He had expected a flash Harvard classmate, not this elderly portly émigré staring at him with crazed eyes.

Kutusov's wild gray hair stood up like exclamation points, punctuated by black eyes peeking out of bushy eyebrows. A short beard framed his broad face. He was dressed in a white shirt, with red braces holding up his black baggy trousers. A gray cardigan stretched over his paunch.

"Yes, I am he, the famous professor of Russian history at Columbia." His thick accent was flavored with New York slang.

His eyes darted, targeting Roo's old boots and plaid jacket. "Are you some kind of cowboy?"

Roo grinned, and said no.

He examined the police badges closely, sniffed and handed them back. "You seem a cowboy. Cowboys to me are west of New York."

"Has Maxi Suvorov been living here? He gave this address as his home." Roo went to the point of his visit.

"Yes, yes, come in. For sure, I have not seen Maxi for weeks. I do not live here all the time. I told this to cops who questioned me about the poor Miss Abigail. I have a house on Long Island, and until recently spent a lot of time in Russia on business. I only came in from the island yesterday because I am giving a lecture at Columbia."

He wheezed like an accordion box, his words rushing out, "For sure, I was an old friend of Maxi's deceased father and have known the boy since his birth. After the disappearance of the unfortunate Miss Abigail, the dear boy was looking for an apartment and didn't have much money, so I gave him a place to stay. He isn't good about money. None of his family is. They spend like they are nobility with great estates." Kutusov shook his mane back and forth ruefully and motioned Roo to follow him down a long hall.

The flat was large, but cluttered, with books and papers on shelves that ranged from floor to ceiling. It smelled of dust and cigarette smoke. The huge drawing room was crammed with ornately carved furniture. Worn oriental carpets from the Caucasus covered the floors and large oil paintings of Russian peasants and fierce Cossacks stared at Roo from yellow cracked walls. Several icons in one corner lent a heavy mysterious air to the room. Roo had seen old photographs of 19th century Russia in one of Devlin's books and thought the place was like a broken fragment from that time.

The professor led him to the kitchen, its counters piled indiscriminately with unwashed dishes and papers. Kutusov had been sitting at the kitchen table, drinking tea from an ornate samovar, and reading from a pile of the Russian émigré newspaper *Novoe Russkoe Slovo.*

"Please sit down. Please; I beg you, have one of my pirozhki and some tea."

He was wary of the small pockets of pastry. "What's inside?"

"I buy them at the White Guard Café. They are the best, filled with cabbage and curd cheese. Breakfast and lunch, so efficient. Take, take." He vigorously pushed the pastries toward Roo, who sat down across from him in the one spot clear of stacks of papers.

Roo bit into one. "Very good." Kutusov beamed. "I'll try some tea, please." He was intrigued by the samovar. Kutusov poured the hot water from the samovar and served the tea in a glass, stirring in a large spoonful of strawberry jam before he could protest. It wasn't bad and perked him up.

Kutusov laced his with a shot of vodka from a silver flask and offered it to Roo who declined. "This is my morning ritual now that I'm semi-retired. Now that my country is no longer communist, it has only billionaires and a lot of poor people. I have adjusted. Émigrés always do. I take notes, lecture at universities, and write newspaper columns, but also I act as a consultant to these new Russian entrepreneurs. But I am retiring for good. It is too dangerous."

Roo said, "You said you were a friend of Suvorov's father."

"Ah yes, for sure, a great friend of Maxi's father even though we disagreed politically. His father was a very well respected monarchist and worked every minute of his life toward restoring the Romanov Dynasty to the throne." His plump cheeks wobbled in disapproval. "I'm afraid he was somewhat deluded, out of date. On the other hand, I was a realist and knew this never could happen, but now with the turmoil, what do I know?" He raised his hands in the air. "It seems there are many who would wish to have a tsar again. We Russians always need a strong leader. More tea?" he interrupted his monologue.

Roo shook his head.

"These new Russians are intrigued with a past they knew nothing about until the end of communist rule." The old man cocked his head to one side. "It does not seem a fairy tale that one of the powerful oligarchs could become a new kind of tsar. With a little public relations this could be accomplished. It might be good for business." He chomped down on his pastry and chewed, reflecting on this thought for a moment, then continued.

"But some of these businessmen are crazy. On my last trip, I was forced to fly over frozen wastes of Siberia in an old Soviet military plane while my clients slide open the chute and shoot at reindeer below. Then we fly lower, and I am told to jump out. Me, an old man. In chest deep snow. To retrieve the poor dead animal. Then we go south and land near Mongolia. There I am dragged off to a nightclub with ferocious women of the night. Everyone gets raving drunk on vodka. They fight; bottles crash over heads. There is blood everywhere." His eyes rolled toward the ceiling. "These businessmen are too threatening, and they play by different rules than the West. It is too dangerous for me. I could have a heart attack." He shrugged his shoulders and took another drink.

Roo went back to the subject. "Maxi Suvorov stayed with you the nights of September ninth, tenth and eleventh. Is that right? I need to confirm his alibi."

The old man didn't answer directly. "Maybe yes, I think so, but my memory is not so good these days. Let's stick with what I told the police. I hope that the boy is not in trouble. I don't interfere. Live on Long Island, so let him have the place. He is always a nice boy, very clever, but a little concerned with money. What's not to like?"

"Did he tell you anything about his business dealings?" Roo persisted.

"No, I have no idea what he's up to." He frowned; his furry eyebrows crawled together like caterpillars. "But I did notice a change in him when he began going to Russia. I confess I did introduce him to some of the businessmen who had hired me as a consultant. He asked me to, said he wanted Russian business for the gallery. The boy moved fast, out of my orbit, doing business with people I didn't know."

"Like Kayakov?"

"Maybe, I don't know. He doesn't confide in me. I only heard of Kayakov, have never met him. I do know Maxi recently decided he wanted to be a real count, and recover his inheritance."

"What do you mean?"

"He believed that these new contacts would make it possible to return to Russia and recover the family lands lost in the revolution. I am like an uncle to him. He's not in trouble, is he? These men think nothing of eliminating someone who disagrees with them." He took a large swig from the flask, not bothering with tea. "I even discovered my phone was tapped here in New York. They are all ex KGB." He was whispering. Roo thought he might be crazy.

"Can I see his room?"

"Of course, of course." He hurried out of his chair.

"I never go into his room," he said as he led the deputy sheriff to the end of the long hall, his carpet slippers flapping.

In contrast to the rest of the flat, Maxi's room was like a monk's cell, containing only a bed with a plain white cover, a bare table, and a chest. Roo, who had put on gloves for the search, was disappointed. It looked like Suvorov had moved out. He went through the closet, the dresser drawers, and found nothing. Then in the top drawer of the chest, he noticed some papers had slipped between two drawers and pulled them out. There was a photograph of Katya and a computer printout of a blank paper with a strange letterhead. *The Ark* was printed at the top of the page, with a swastika below it.

"What does this mean?" He showed Kutusov the page. "Is Suvorov a neo-Nazi?"

Kutusov sank down on the bed in a trembling heap. "It has nothing to do with Nazis. The swastika is an old Tibetan good luck symbol used by the last Tsarina Alexandra of Russia. It was adopted as a secret sign by the Brotherhood, an organization formed to rescue the Tsar. I have heard there are those, murderers, who have taken the Brotherhood name. They will come for me if they discover I know anything about them."

"What about this Ark?"

"The Ark was the meeting place for Khlysts, a religious group forced underground by the Tsarist regime. Rasputin was reputed to be one of them. I don't know anything else. I don't understand why Maxi would have this paper."

Roo did not know whether the old émigré was telling the truth or just crazy. He was standing now, still trembling, and rubbing his arms and hands. "They are dangerous. Arrest me," he said, his eyebrows again crawling up and down his forehead. He impulsively thrust out his wrists to be handcuffed. "I will be safer in prison. They kill anyone who gets in the way. You know, Turbatov, Maxi's stepfather, has always done business with the Russian police. He thinks it's a secret, but I know."

Roo wasn't listening, didn't care. He wanted to find Katya, make sure she was all right. He had an overwhelming sense that she was in danger.

Devlin's words came back to him. "Many of these oligarch types have their own security forces who think nothing of whacking people. They're experts at it."

Chapter 29

Roo-Katya
New York

ROO'S PHONE RANG as he was running from Kutusov's to the car. It was Latham. He had been ordered off surveillance after Suvorov had filed a complaint threatening legal action. How stupid was that, he thought, as scenes of Katya being manhandled, taken from the street by force, passed before him. Freezing rain pelted him while he fumbled with the phone, dropped it, and dived for it before it slid into a drain. Shivering, he started the engine and tried her number twice. Finally she answered.

"Katya, Katya Marston? It's Deputy Sheriff Reuben Yoder." He was still breathless from his run and sounded ridiculous.

"Oh, it's you" she said.

"Where are you? Are you alone?"

"I'm shopping at Saks. Yes, I'm alone."

"Where is that?" He had not included shops in his study of the city.

"At 49th and 5th." She seemed impatient.

"Where are you exactly?"

"At the cosmetic department. Why are you calling me?"

"Stay there. I'm coming for you. I'll find you."

"But why?" she protested. There was silence at her end when he said, "Listen to me. You're in danger."

He came to a halt, serenaded by the din of horns, in a traffic jam on 5th Avenue. Tempted to use the siren, he thought better of it. Doubt crept over him. What was he doing? He had to be certain she was all right.

The minutes ticked by, and he was trying to call her again, when the traffic began to move. He pulled the car in next to St. Patrick's Cathedral and burst through the 49th Street doors of Saks. Dazzled by the shining floors, the glitzy dark mahogany showcases, the well dressed clerks and customers, he stopped for a moment, breathing hard, to get his bearings, then asked a woman in a black suit where the cosmetic department was located. She stared dubiously at his wet clothes and muddy boots as though she was going to call a security guard, then said 'this floor' and pointed him to the right aisles. Sweet cloying smells of perfumes, crèmes, and lotions wafted over him as he squished across the gleaming floor, astounded at the multitude of beauty products on counters that seemed to stretch for miles.

He spotted her across the room and wove his way past women sitting on stools applying face creams, testing perfume and putting on eye make up. They didn't notice that he was soaked, and the front of his plaid lumber jacket was smeared with dirt from his dive for the phone.

Making his way toward Katya, he saw a man moving in the same parallel direction. Looking as out of place as Roo, he wore a tight shiny gray suit, his enormous arms threatening to burst the jacket seams. He turned his thick neck slowly, like a giant tortoise, revealing a tough scarred face and crooked nose. There was a bulge in his suit from the gun tucked in at his waist. The thug was tailing Katya, was going to harm her. The hood was watching her, moving closer, his thick hands outstretched. Roo had to ask himself if this was really happening. Sweat broke out over him as he felt himself moving sideways in the aisle as though in slow motion. He stuck out his foot, sending the thug sprawling, crashing headfirst into a glass counter, shattering it into splinters, knocking an entire display of cosmetics from the shelf. The hood was unconscious, pieces of glass sticking from his head. His jacket was open, revealing the gun in his belt. A crowd gathered, and one of the clerks was applying first aid while they waited for the ambulance.

He rushed toward Katya, standing at the Crème de la Mer counter watching in fascinated horror. Unaware of the gun and that she had been in danger she said, "What a terrible accident. The poor man may have had a heart attack." The girl behind the counter nodded, her heavily made up eyes staring at his wet clothes as she handed Katya her purchase. Even in the circumstances, Roo couldn't help noticing the shocking price.

He took Katya's arm. "We've got to get out of here."

She flushed red. "What's happened? Is it serious?" Store security carried the thug out on a stretcher.

"What did you tell Suvorov?" He steered her with the shopping bags out of the store, into the darkness and cold rain toward the car.

"Just what you told me. That the killers were after me; that I was in danger."

"The man who fell into the counter was tailing you and waiting to pick you up when you left the store. He may have partners. I have to take you into protective custody."

Her eyes were wide, startled at his comment, as he opened the door and helped her into the car. She was silent as he pulled onto 5th Avenue and into the traffic jam.

"Do you know where Suvorov is?" His voice was hard.

"Not at this moment, but I did speak to him when you were late. He was waiting for me. We are going away for the week and wanted an early start." She was apologetic.

"I know we were not to leave the city, but everything has been so horrible, I wanted to escape and Maxi suggested it."

"Where are you going for the weekend?" Roo didn't say that she wouldn't be going with Maxi.

"Vermont," she said.

"By car?" He swerved to avoid a jaywalker running to get out of the rain.

"Yes." She turned away, looking out of the window.

"You'll have to change your plans. We're bringing your boyfriend in for questioning." He could not disguise the satisfaction in his voice.

"Questioning for what? The killer could be that creep von Burkhardt or that horrible Petrosian. Why don't you pick them up?"

"We have only circumstantial evidence, not enough to press charges," he said, taken aback at her vehemence. "We're just questioning your boyfriend, not arresting him."

"It seems to me there is more evidence on them than on Maxi. Both of them threatened me. You think he would have anything to do with the murders or would want to harm me? It's totally ridiculous."

There was a small opening in the traffic, and he zigzagged between lanes. In the wake of protesting horns, he couldn't resist saying something he later regretted. "You haven't known Suvorov that long. Do you think your judgment could be faulty because you're sleeping with him?"

She wildly reached out to slap him.

The car swerved toward a row of expensive shops as he caught her hand. "Do you want to cause an accident?"

She sat back still angry, biting her lip. "You have no right to keep me in custody. Either let me out here or take me to my apartment."

They drove downtown in hostile silence. Checking in the rear-view mirror for anyone following, he caught a glimpse of his face splattered with mud, a huge glob resting on his nose. Embarrassed, cursing for looking ridiculous, he cleaned up with a towel he found in the glove compartment. He was a fucking incompetent amateur. The hood in Saks was tailing her, was going to kidnap her, and he had no idea who he was, and no real proof that Maxi Suvorov or Kayakov were involved in the murders. What did he have? A photograph of Suvorov's alleged visit to a cult center in Siberia and the strange letterhead found in his room at Kutusov's. Maybe she was right. Maybe he wanted Suvorov to be guilty.

Mercer Street was in a state of chaos. A crowd surrounded two police cars parked outside the gallery.

They rushed over to the policeman standing beside one of the cars. "What's wrong?" Katya said. "I own the gallery." He took her name. Roo showed his badge. The cop nodded, wrote something in his notebook, and looked up. "It was a break in, probably a burglary, but no sign of the perps. Must have had the key. It's a fucking mess in there."

Another cop was speaking to a large plump young woman dressed in a fake fur coat, her big legs teetering on very high heels. As he and Katya approached, Roo noticed a large line on the side of her neck where heavy makeup ended. A dangling earring sparkled, moving back and forth as the woman spoke. Her dark hair was long and glossy, falling over one eye. The visible eye fluttered with an abnormally long eyelash. The policeman's broad face was slit by a huge grin. The young woman turned to face them. It was Geoffrey Banks in drag.

Katya said in a choked voice, "Geoffrey, is it you? I can't believe this."

Geoffrey's face seemed to break into little pieces of distress when he saw Katya, but he continued talking, nervously flicking his hair. "After closing the gallery at four, I went out with friends. You see, in the evenings I am Jennifer Banks." His voice was breathy, catching at each syllable.

"After a drink, we were walking to Kinks and passed the gallery. I saw lights on upstairs and a car parked below. Men were moving around in the apartment. It was all very quiet, but I felt something was wrong and was worried about Katya. Thought she might be in there. I called you fellows immediately."

The cop glanced at Roo, suppressed a laugh, and bent over his notebook.

"Just before you arrived, I had second thoughts about my call because I saw Maxi escorted out by five men in dark suits. They got in a car and drove off."

"Did you recognize any of them?" Roo broke in, trying not to stare at Geoffrey's startling transformation.

"They were complete strangers. I couldn't begin to describe any of them. They moved so quickly, right by me. Maxi didn't recognize me." He giggled nervously.

"Can you describe the car?" The cop asked.

"Well, it was large and black. I'm not good at things like knowing makes of cars. Ask me about a painting or a fashion item, I'd know instantly."

Geoffrey opened his large mock croc handbag and took out a lace handkerchief, then snapped it shut. He blew his nose, turning then to Katya, his eyes full of tears, mascara running down his cheeks.

"Oh Katya, I am so glad you weren't inside. I suppose you'll fire me, now that you know I lead a double life. I should have told you. It will be in the newspapers because of the publicity surrounding Abigail's death."

She put her arm around him. "Of course not. You're essential to the gallery and me. Thanks for calling the police. I could have been there alone. But you said they took Maxi? He must have been here waiting for me. Was he all right?"

Geoffrey hesitated, thinking, "It's hard to know if he went with them voluntarily or was forced. He was surrounded by the men. I couldn't see."

Katya glared at Roo. "You're wrong. Maxi is innocent. It's obvious he's been kidnapped."

The patrolman said, "There was no sign of a break in." The rain was coming down even harder, but Katya didn't seem to notice.

Roo said, "Maxi could have let them into the gallery, but how did they get into your apartment?"

Her face flushed. "Maxi had the keys. They must have forced him to open my door."

So, that scheming bastard had access to her apartment. "Let's get out of the rain," Roo said.

A wave of fear hit Katya when she saw the damage to her apartment. All the drawers and closets had been disgorged, and her belongings lay in piles on the floor. Pictures were torn from the walls, the frames pried off. Her computer was smashed; the safe was empty. But even worse, they had ripped and urinated on her clothes. The violence terrified her. It seemed so vindictive.

"They were looking for something. This was not a robbery," the deputy sheriff said, looking down at her. They stood dripping from rain, pools of water around them. "Look, you can't stay here. They might come back."

She was shivering in her wet clothes. "I'll go to a hotel."

"No way," he said, "They could follow you. I want you to come with me. It's the only safe thing to do."

"Is that really necessary?" Then she realized it might be. They had kidnapped Maxi.

There was a horrible feeling in her stomach as she picked through the ruins of her wardrobe and salvaged a few things from the bathroom. What if the murderers were out there on the street waiting? She gripped her Kelly bag, a present from her guardian. The key was in her pocket. Abigail had instructed her that she should always carry her passport and credit cards and money locked in the capacious bag.

The crime scene investigators, still searching for fingerprints and DNA samples, took a statement from her and said she could go.

Downstairs in the gallery, Geoffrey, looking harassed, his long wig hanging crooked, was still with the police. The major exhibition space had been empty since the close of the icon show and seemed untouched. Geoffrey came over. "Nothing seems missing here. I'll fill out the insurance reports on both the gallery and your apartment when I come in tomorrow."

"Thank you Geoffrey. Will you be in charge until I can return?"

"Yes, don't you worry about a thing? It might be dangerous here for you." He hugged her. "I want to say how really sweet you have been to me."

On the way to Bensonhurst, Roo looked over at Katya, curled up under her coat, her eyes tightly shut. They were both soaked and cold so he turned up the heat. She opened her eyes once to ask where they were going, and when he said Bensonhurst to Detective Devlin's apartment, her look implied that it could be another planet.

She was quiet for a moment, and then said, "So what are you going to do about Maxi? You know he's been kidnapped."

He didn't give a shit about that slimeball's safety, but he tried to look concerned. "We don't know that, but it could be true. When you phoned him earlier, did he sound different, nervous?"

"No, he was the same, but furious that you ruined our plans."

"Yeah, I imagine he was," he said, again not able to disguise his satisfaction.

He suspected she was not as innocent as he had first thought and that she was keeping important information from him. He could no longer protect her, and decided to shock her into cooperating by reciting the grisly details surrounding her guardian's death.

The rain had turned from sleet to heavy snow forcing him to drive slowly into the neighborhood. He parked Devlin's car three blocks away from his apartment, hoping it wouldn't be vandalized on the street. He couldn't take the risk that they had been followed.

"We're here," he said, gathering her shopping bags and quickly looking around before they started toward the apartment. The wind was nearing gale force, hurling huge flakes of snow past them as they struggled to the building.

Katya was shaking from the cold and fear when they arrived at the flat. He forced her to drink a shot of whiskey, gave her some towels to dry off, and led her to his room to change. He took some clothes from the room and dressed in the bathroom.

Then he phoned Devlin, and gave him a detailed update. A missing person's report had been filed on Suvorov and a statewide search had already begun. Devlin sounded far away. Roo heard clicks and movements, but nothing to indicate his location.

After he hung up, he went into the kitchen and found two cans of vegetable soup in the cupboard, poured the contents into a pan and heated it. Then he opened a bottle of wine and placed two glasses on the table.

When he turned she was standing there, watching him. Her hair was tangled, and she was deathly pale.

"I heard you on the phone. Is there any news of Maxi?"

"Not yet. I was reporting to my boss, Detective Devlin. A statewide alert has gone out for your boyfriend. Sit down. Have some soup."

She obeyed, took two bites of soup, dropped her spoon, and began to cry. "I know Maxi has been kidnapped. What will they do to him? They could kill him?"

He waited until she stopped crying, then he poured two glasses of wine and led her to the living room. She was shivering violently. He wrapped her in blankets on the couch, and sat beside her. He told her about Abigail's torture and the mutilation that connected the two murders. She was very still.

When he finished, she didn't cry, but seemed unable to take it all in. "But why would anyone want to do that to someone as beautiful as Abigail? The eyes. Why would anyone do such a horrible thing? And why would they search the apartment now that she's gone?"

"Are you sure there isn't something you haven't told me that might help. You owe it to Abigail. You have to trust me." She had moved closer to him, and he became acutely aware of the curve of her breasts under her sweater.

"There is something I found. It's marked personal, addressed to me from Abigail. Her lawyers mentioned that she went to their office and asked for it just before." She couldn't finish the sentence. "I found it quite by accident, behind an Ansel Adams photograph."

"That could have been what they were after tonight. Did you leave it in the apartment?"

"Oh no, I have it with me. I didn't know what to do. I thought it was personal, but Abigail gave me orders not to read it until she was buried. I was afraid. I just couldn't think about it. I still can't. It's too painful." She hunched over on the couch.

"Does anyone else know you found this?" He said, thinking that she must have told Suvorov.

"No, Abigail wrote that I was to tell no one."

"So Suvorov doesn't know about this?" He wasn't sure she would tell him the truth.

"No," she flared up in anger. "Sheriff Yoder, you are the first person I've told. I hope I can trust you."

Even though she still refused to use his first name and insisted on calling him sheriff, Roo felt elated that she had kept this from Maxi.

She rose unsteadily, went to the bedroom, and returned with her handbag. She took the key from its leather case, and unlocked it, gingerly removing a large envelope as though it contained explosives, and carefully placed it on the coffee table between them.

He poured more wine. Katya took a gulp from her glass and leaned back on the couch, in shock, anesthetized.

He pondered the last phrase of Abigail's note. *Do not open this until after I am buried.* Katya pointed to the envelope.

"Would you look at it?"

Roo carefully pried it open; a set of keys clattered out on the coffee table. Folded inside were a torn fragment of very old crumbling paper and two documents of several pages written in another language. "Another message from Abigail," Katya said, catching her breath.

Dear Katya, I knew you would find this message. If you are reading this, I am no longer alive. I am sorry I couldn't protect you from them. They know you exist. You must find the Blood Archive.

"What the hell is this?" The hairs rose on the back of his neck.

The clock ticked in the hallway. It sounded muffled, far-off, marking time in another, more treacherous world.

Roo continued to read.

It may save you. It is your legacy and will tell you everything you yearned to know. But I must warn you dear Katya. The Blood Archive holds powerful secrets from Russia's past. Dangerous men are hunting for it, willing to kill for it. It is hidden in Tecumseh's Forest. Love for all time, Abigail

"This is so scary. But it is Abigail's handwriting," she said.

They examined the other documents. One, resembling a piece of waste paper, was undecipherable. Both of them recognized that the other two were in Cyrillic. Katya said, "Who would have written these documents? I don't think Abigail knew Russian."

"We'll have to find a translator. I'll contact Devlin."

Looking shattered, she said, "Do you really think Abigail was murdered for this? Nobody would believe it. I wouldn't know it was true if Abigail hadn't written it. She was a very down to earth person, always exact about everything."

"All the evidence points to this archive as the motive and we have no idea what it is." Roo said.

Chapter 30

Roo-Katya
New York: February 2002

IT WAS CLEAR to Roo; the killers believed Katya knew where the Blood Archive was hidden. They could have tracked them here. In the muffled silence of the apartment, he tried to plan their escape.

Katya had fallen into a deep sleep on the couch. In spite of all her traumas, she looked peaceful, untroubled, and didn't wake, clinging tightly to him when he carried her to the bedroom. It was 2 a.m.; he gazed out the living room window at a blank wall of white. The storm cut them off from everything; they could be at the end of the world.

The spotlights, dimmed in the storm, showed vague shapes of cars covered in snow. Suddenly, he jerked forward, a spasm of fear holding him rigid, stopping his flow of blood. Barely visible through the falling snow, a dark figure appeared like an apparition at the parking lot gate. Thinking he imagined the phantom, he squinted, blinked, and it was gone. He scanned the entire parking lot but saw nothing. He waited, rigid, listening for footsteps in the hall, and then tucked his Glock into his belt, put on his jacket and cap and crept down the stairs.

Wind and snow whooshed toward him and his heart racing, his gut curling into knots, he fought his way to his truck at the edge of the lot.

He unlocked the truck, opened his toolbox, and found his screwdriver. His fingers were stiff with cold, and he fumbled to remove the Ohio plates, working in a deadly quiet except for the gusts of wind banging the entrance gate. Looking back at the gate, he raced farther into the parking lot, crouching between cars. Near the last row, he slipped and fell, raised himself up and crawled over to a van. Gasping, his hands trembling, he removed its New York plates. It was difficult in the driving snow; his hands were scraped from the plates' sharp edges.

Slipping and sliding, he hurried back to the truck, and working in a panic, attached the van's plates. The phantom figure at the gate and the puzzling words, Blood Archive, blew like the blizzard through his mind. He remembered snow chains and dug them out of the toolbox. They clanked against his hands as he stretched them out in front of the back tires. He started the engine several times before it coughed into life and slowly drove the truck forward onto the chains, jumping out to fasten each one with the large rubber bands. Before he leaned down over each wheel, he would turn and gaze at the white blankets of snow, in sudden horror that he could be shot in the back.

The snow was falling in straight hard sheets, and his stomach felt better when he saw his tracks were covered even as he ran, buffeted by the wind, to the safety of the apartment. But these guys were pros. He had to get her out, hide her or both of them could end up in a steel drawer wearing toe tags. They would leave early tomorrow, but there was one visit he had to risk before they could escape.

The warmth of the apartment penetrated his frozen limbs. He pulled off his wet clothes, dried off and dressed again. He washed the scratches on his hands, and feeling guilty found Devlin's bottle of

Chivas Regal and poured a drink. The alcohol wound its way through his body, releasing the tightness.

He sat for a moment on the sofa, his heart pumping wildly like an overworked engine and then went to the window, seeing nothing but white. He might have imagined the black figure.

He pondered Abigail's strange message. The Blood Archive hid something powerful from Russia's past. He envisioned this archive as an ornate Russian box, dripping with blood. Then he pictured enormous rows of files, containing top secret documents stacked on shelves over twelve feet high, something like he had once seen in the State Historical Library, but in this case, guarded by steely Russian troops. It could be hidden in a library, although Abigail did write that it was in a forest, Tecumseh's Forest, whatever that meant.

He put in the secure email code and sent the report. Blood Archive typed on the screen seemed unreal. Devlin would struggle to believe such a hokey story. Roo requested authorization for his next move. Although it was probably too soon, he asked for news of Suvorov before signing off. He closed his eyes, listening for noises in the hall.

He had fallen asleep at the desk and when he woke at 6 a.m. there was a message giving him the sanction to go ahead with his plan, and confirming that a translator had been arranged. Devlin's last words remained with him. "Don't let them find you." The lengthy message struck him as being in a different style, as though a stranger had written it. It seemed odd that Devlin had changed the secure number and told him to report no matter where he was.

He leaned over to shut down the computer, and discovered that the cord led into a small cupboard at the bottom of the desk. He opened it and found the switch behind a stack of books. He stopped in surprise. The books were in Russian.

Katya woke to fear gripping her, like strong bony fingers. Images of Abigail's torture hovered over the room. She heard the sound of running water, a shower, and then remembered she was somewhere outside of Manhattan with this sheriff she barely knew.

Her apartment had been ransacked, and Maxi had been kidnapped, she was sure, in spite of this cop's accusations against him. She regretted giving him Abigail's secret message and wished she had gone directly to the police station. She just didn't believe everything he said. It couldn't get much worse for her.

He knocked, appearing at the door, his face serious. "Can you be ready in a half hour? Do you want some coffee? I'm sorry but Devlin doesn't have any tea."

"Yes, I'll be ready. Coffee will be fine, thank you," she said. It was a struggle to dislike him. He had folded her clothes neatly in the chair, and next to it, stacked her packages, sport clothes for the canceled trip to Vermont. She forced herself out of bed, showered quickly, and washed her hair, brushing it and pulling it back off her face. Then she opened her shopping bags and dressed in tan cords, and a cream turtleneck sweater, pulled on socks and went out to the kitchen.

He was putting breakfast on the table, and stopped to pour her coffee, looking her over with approval. "I'm glad you have some outdoor clothes. You'll need them." He pointed to the window. The blizzard obscured everything, the street and parking lot a white blur.

"I have to get you out of here, into another hiding place."

"But what about Maxi? I want to find him. And shouldn't I tell Geoffrey where we're going?"

"That wouldn't be safe. I told you we've put out an alert for your boyfriend. There's nothing you can do but wait. Sit down and eat something. It might be a while before we have another chance."

"No thank you. I'm not hungry." Tears sparkled in her eyes. This was so sudden. Where was he taking her?

He handed her one of Devlin's messages. "I think you should read this."

She sniffled, and blew her nose, while she read. "So he thinks I'm in danger from more than one gang of killers. So where is Detective Devlin? Why can't they do something?" Her questions tailed off into a wail.

He concentrated on dipping toast into his eggs.

"Who are they?" she said, "I suppose all Russians."

"We think so, but we don't know how many are out there hunting this archive." Even as he said this, it seemed a wild story.

"You don't really know anything, do you?"

"Look." His voice was quiet. "There are dangerous men out there who want this archive. And somehow they've discovered you have information leading to it. They're professional hit men, and won't hesitate to do the same things to you that they did to Abigail and Christina Gartner. Do I have to show you the pictures from the forensic report to remind you?"

"No." She started to cry again, turning her head away from him.

"You can't return to your old life. Even with police protection, they'll find you. You have to come with me. It's the only way you'll be safe." He took the bread and butter from the table, and loaded more dishes in the sink.

"But where?"

He didn't answer her. He had left the kitchen and was watching out the living room window. Then he picked up his bags and opened the door.

"Get your things together. I want to make one stop before we head off. Don't worry," he relented, "Devlin will contact me if there is news of Suvorov."

Katya pulled on her new snow boots, threw her clothes in the shopping bag, and waited while Roo went to the parking lot. She put on a dark blue ski jacket and left her fur coat, Jimmy Choo shoes and Prada suit in the closet, but took her locked Kelly handbag with her, a reminder of Abigail.

He returned in fifteen minutes holding his gun in front of him, and led her down the stairs to the fire exit. She backed away in disbelief when she saw the battered snow covered truck parked by the fire door.

"Are we going in that?"

"This is safer. I'm sure they spotted Devlin's car and are closing in. They'll never suspect we're in my pick-up. Get in," he ordered.

She scrambled in, and he took off to the edge of the street, stopping to put his gun in his belt. The battered old truck, painted a faded green, was clean inside, but retained the slight odor of manure.

He said, "Sorry it stinks in here. A few months ago my friend borrowed my truck to haul some cow manure. I scrubbed it out, but the smell just seems to linger."

"That's ok." She said, not meaning it, and fastened her seatbelt.

The truck had hard straight benches and as they jerked forward, rattled and vibrated as though coming apart. Hunched over the windshield, Roo drove slowly around three blocks until he came to the street where he had parked Devlin's car.

"It's gone," Katya cried out. The empty space where the car had been was filled with snow.

Chapter 31

Roo
New York

ALARMED AT THE missing car, Roo stomped on the accelerator, jerking Katya forward. The truck slid on the ice and bumped over ruts, as they crossed Houston and headed uptown.

Accustomed to being driven in a limo by a chauffeur or in Maxi's Porsche, Katya bounced on the torn leather seat, as though she was inside a blender. "Where are we going?" she said, hanging onto the door handle.

"To see your boyfriend's mother." He couldn't keep sarcasm from creeping into his voice, even though he knew it would only make her hostile. He had discovered from Maxi's file that the countess had married Sergei Alexandrovich Turbatov in 1978, and was known as Countess Suvorova-Turbatov. The couple owned an antiques shop called Imperial Treasures on 82nd and Madison.

Roo slid the truck into a parking place and put money in the meter. He tried to take Katya's arm to help her across the icy street, but she pulled away. A battered sign in faded gothic letters hung above the door of the poky little shop, huddled between two shining glass and steel buildings. It was an anachronism, a tiny island of the past.

Katya peered in the dark dusty window, crammed with a jumble of old furniture and junk. "No one seems to be here," she said.

Roo rang the bell insistently several times, and they heard movements from deep inside and shouts in Russian. A light flicked on, and the door opened a crack. "Who are you? What do you want?" It was a woman's voice, very low with a slight accent.

"Police." Roo handed in his ID, and the door opened to an elderly woman wearing an expensive black dress accentuated with a large choker of pearls. She was tall and aristocratic looking. Her angular features were made more distinctive by a light hook in her delicate pointed nose. Her gray hair was pulled back in a chignon, and her large dark heavy-lidded eyes resembled Maxi's.

"Countess Suvorova-Turbatov?" Roo said.

She nodded. "What is it? Has something happened?"

"I'm here about your son, Maxi."

Her eyes grew into huge pools of distress, and she stepped back to let them in.

The room, an extension of the front window, was crowded with the detritus of a lost world, as though every Russian who fled the revolution had left their possessions with the Turbatovs. Balalaikas, samovars, swords, dueling pistols, sets of china, old toys and books were scattered in dusty confusion around the room.

"Please sit down." The countess moved some boxes off two chairs.

"And who, young lady, are you?" She turned to Katya, who sat with her knees against a table filled with photographs in silver frames.

"I'm Katya Marston. Abigail Townsend was my guardian. I own the gallery with your son Maxi." Her voice was timid, a little breathless.

The countess frowned. "Ah yes, that Katya. My Maxi spoke of you. You have a Russian name. Why is that?" She leaned forward as though accusing her of some crime.

Katya just nodded, not knowing the answer herself.

"Tell me what has happened," she said, turning to Roo.

A man's voice called to her from the back of the shop. She answered in sharp Russian. "My husband, Sergei. Now please." She gestured toward the back of the store. "He asks that you have morning tea with us."

The back room was surprisingly elegant, well furnished, with a round mahogany antique table and French Empire chairs. One wall was covered in old icons in gleaming gold. The remainder of the room was devoted to family photographs, some of Maxi as a child dressed in Russian military uniform.

She introduced Sergei Turbatov, white haired frail looking in smoking jacket and slippers. "Excuse my attire. I have not been well," he said, puffing on a long ornate cigarette holder.

"Please sit down," the countess urged and calmly served each of them a cup of tea. They sat for a moment in silence, and then Roo cleared his throat and said, "When was the last time you saw your son?"

"Something terrible has happened," the countess said, standing up from the table.

"Your son has disappeared. He could have been kidnapped. Last night there was a break-in at the Little Swan Gallery. He was seen being escorted by five men out of the building and into a car. We have been trying to trace the car and to identify the men, but so far there are no leads. It is early yet."

"Oh no," The countess cried out. She moved her head back and forth, as if to deny it, and sank into her chair.

"Can you tell us anything that might help to find him?" Roo said.

"I knew he was in trouble. I am not surprised. His personality changed when he began working for that Townsend woman. I tried to keep him away from her and those criminal Russians. Both were unsavory. Her scandalous behavior was reported in those newspaper articles after her murder. I knew it would lead to no good," she said in a choked voice. Her husband nodded in agreement, puffing delicate traces of smoke into the air.

Katya was furious. "Abigail was not unsavory. She was wonderful. She gave Maxi his chance, and now he is part owner of the gallery."

Roo interrupted her. They had come to get information, not save Abigail's reputation. "I found some strange items in your son's room at Kutuzov's apartment."

"You searched his room? Did you have a legal right?" Sergei Turbatov said.

"What did Kutusov tell you?" the countess asked. The couple seemed frightened.

"I found a computer printout with a heading 'The Ark' and a swastika drawn underneath."

"I was hoping it wasn't true." The countess raised her arms dramatically. "I suppose Kutusov told you the swastika was once the sign of the Brotherhood, but that is a long story. I don't think it is necessary to go into it now," she said.

"Yes, I think we need to hear this," Roo said, although he was anxious to get out of New York. He walked to the shop window and surveyed the street, deserted in the falling snow. The countess turned off the shop lights, put out the closed sign, and returned to the back room.

Wisps of smoke curling around his head, Turbatov stared at the samovar as though it mirrored his thoughts, and spoke in a heavily accented voice. "Even after Lenin and his Bolsheviks took over Russia, and the Tsar and his family were executed, the Brotherhood continued to exist into the 1980's. Many of its members believed that some of the Tsar's children had been saved. Maxi's father was among those believers who foolishly plotted against the Soviet government. Now his organization is degraded, revived by criminals, using the name and prestige of Maxi and our family to make it legitimate."

"Who are they? Do you have names? It might save his life," Roo said.

"We don't know," the countess said, "Maxi tried to convince me some of these people were dedicated to the monarchist cause back in fashion in the new Russia. I didn't believe him."

"Maxi came here two days ago with an incredible story. He said an archive exists with a powerful secret that could restore our family's lost fortune. He asked me if either his poor deceased Papa or I knew anything about this hidden archive. I knew nothing. He said it would be very bad for him if he did not find it. He acted crazy, frightened."

"I pleaded with him to end his association with this false Brotherhood group. But he said he was unable to; he was in too deep with them, and now they have killed him, I am sure." Her voice ended in a sob.

"Now Marina, that may not be the case." Turbatov patted her with his frail hand, but she shrugged him off.

"They promised my poor son he could return to Russia and retrieve our lost lands and his title. It was almost as though he had been hypnotized to believe such an absurdity."

Roo looked at his watch. The countess had gone off on a tangent. She wept into the white lace handkerchief, then continued in a hoarse savage voice. "The past has returned to haunt us. Maxi claimed his father and grandfather had kept a dangerous secret. I have remained ignorant of this, but there could be something hidden in the family papers." She leaned forward whispering. "I am the only one who has access to papers my late husband left in the safe. Maxi came here two days ago asking about this archive. He pleaded with me to give him the documents, but I refused. It is too dangerous. Now I am giving up."

She got up abruptly and left the room. Turbatov excused himself and limped along behind her, shouting, "No, no Marina, Don't do this." There was a long argument in Russian before she returned holding a large folder.

"My husband believes this material is dangerous. He wants to sell it, to offer it to the FSB. I think they will kill us. In the past they have murdered anyone associated with these secret papers. Just recently one of the last of the old Brotherhood, Prince Androvsky was found dead at the Russian Embassy in London. He supposedly fell from a high balcony."

Turbatov who had returned to his seat, interrupted in a low voice. "There is an old secret police saying. 'Anyone can commit murder, but it takes an artist to commit suicide.'"

Katya felt dizzy as though she might faint. The full realization that she was in danger had hit her. That evening at the embassy she had waited for the prince who had information about Abigail. He didn't show. They killed him. They knew about her. Would kill her.

"The police said accident; I say murder, but who can prove it?" The countess shrugged her shoulders. "Just so you are warned that something in these papers might be fatal. I only have tried to protect my son."

She handed Roo the folder. Inside were several documents and a photograph, dated 1921. It was labeled *Headquarters of Baron von Ungern-Sternberg.*

"Who is this baron?" Roo said.

The Countess drew up in revulsion. "The stories about him are terrifying. Our families were escaping the Bolsheviks, hoping to get to Harbin or Shanghai. They attempted to cross Mongolia, led by a Buddhist monk from Muren Kure the great Buddhist monastery and, unfortunately, fell into the baron's clutches. The men in the party were forced to join his army. I, of course, wasn't born then, but I can identify Maxi's grandparents, and my husband, who was only five." She pointed to the figures in the photograph. "This may have been taken when they were preparing to leave the madman's camp. They were desperate to escape my mother-in-law, Natalya Suvorova, Maxi's grandmother was murdered."

Her hands shook as she refilled the teacups.

"It was a great mystery that the baron permitted the family to leave. It was most unusual. No one ever escaped him. He murdered those who tried to flee in a most brutal way, skinning people alive." Her thin face constricted in fear.

"My father-in-law, Count Suvorov seemed ashamed, would never talk of the escape. Even in his late years, he blamed himself for what he called the failed mission. He said it was a dreadful tragedy. I know only what I have told you, nothing else. Take them. Maybe something will help find my poor misguided Maxi."

"Couldn't you translate these papers for us?" Katya said.

"No, that would not help my Maxi. I don't want to be involved. I no longer want to have anything to do with this. They will kill us."

Roo put the photograph back in the folder. "We'll take the risk." He remembered Kutusov's claim that Turbatov was an informer for the FSB. "I am heading upstate on a tip that your son may have been taken to a place near the Tolstoy Foundation. I'll be in touch if there is any news of him."

At the door, Roo said, "I think you should go directly to the police. I can give you a number."

"No, no, it will do no good." The countess vehemently shook her head. "They can't protect us. Please help Maxi."

Chapter 32

Mikhail
St. Paul de Vence, France: February 2002

KATYA MARSTON WAS gone. The report, which he had reviewed several times since returning to the South of France, stated
that she had escaped his men at the department store and was last
seen in an unmarked police car with an unknown law officer. His
men picked up the trail and followed the 1999 Chevy Impala to
Bensonhurst in Brooklyn, but lost them. Their excuse for failure was
a blinding snow storm. That was no excuse. He ordered them to
continue searching the area.

She had vanished while under his men's experienced surveillance. There could be only one conclusion. Whoever had taken the
girl had inside knowledge of his plans. One of his agents had double-
crossed him. He smashed his fist into his antique desk, splintering a
side panel. Agitated he ran his hands over his head repeatedly to quell
the uncontrollable anger coursing through him. He must keep his
focus even though enemies surrounded him.

He reviewed his list of known enemies, untrustworthy agents,
bodyguards and supposedly loyal men inside the compound and

ordered security checks. Only Stavrogin would remain loyal, but his agent had been out of contact for several days.

When the traitors had been identified, he would personally finish them. He had not forgotten the many ways to kill, the techniques of *chernaya robata,* the black work he had learned in the KGB.

He ordered Bebe to close the second security perimeter gate at the entrance to the road leading to the house. The slight whirr of the gates coming down told him it was done. He was locked down, safe inside.

A tremor of emotion crossed his face as he wistfully recalled his glory days as a powerful oligarch residing in his restored palace in Moscow. Then too, he had bodyguards, but had never felt under threat until he lost favor. The memories came back to him; walking down the long halls of the Kremlin to Yeltsin's office, knowing that the president would never move without his advice; the halt of traffic to clear the highway while his cars sped to his dacha outside Moscow set in hundreds of acres, within a forest of birch trees. He had felt alive, all-powerful. Nothing could touch him. It had all ended when Putin became president and General Letinov, his enemy, someone Mikhail once had taken great pleasure in humiliating, had usurped his place of power.

He stared at the grilled windows facing the quaint cobbled street where he could never idly stroll, and his vision returned to the grand receptions in the Kremlin. He was one of the important guests, the oligarch who had the ear of the president. He had belonged to the exclusive clubs, attended the glittering dinner parties with beautiful women at his beck and call, and until recently, celebrated Russian Christmas in Courchevel, skiing in the Millionaires Cup. The contrast this past Christmas at the ski resort had been painful. Powerful acquaintances, unwilling to risk government disapproval, had avoided him, knowing he had been targeted for his opposition to the Putin government. He was holed up like a rat no matter where he lived, his movements restricted, in prison.

Bebe knocked, creeping in on ludicrous tiny feet that seemed incapable of bearing the weight of his enormous body, and meekly handed him another communiqué. He grasped it eagerly, reading it before the door closed. This new information collected since Katya Marston's disappearance did not offer much hope. The Chevy Impala had been abandoned on the street in Bensonhurst. The girl and her escort were heading toward upstate New York, but the type of car and the license plates were unknown. His experience told him this was a false trail.

Bebe returned and reported that he had begun security reviews on his most trusted men here and in Little Odessa. The pimps, Vlach and Nika, wouldn't hesitate to take him out. And he had never trusted General Mirov, the old White Russian, a puppet of Letinov. Then there was Marousia, the girl they provided. Could it be Marousia? An unreasoning fear of her betrayal brought him to his feet.

He locked his study and walked quickly down the hallway to Marousia's bedroom. She was tumbled among the sheets, sleeping. He took off his clothes and slid in beside her. Thinking how easy it would be to kill her, he caressed her silken body, moving his hands over her breasts and down between her legs. She woke and turned toward him smiling. Could she betray him? He crushed her to him, his anger turning to urgency and need, and she let out a small sigh, and moved her legs apart, taking hold of him, coaxing him inside her. He shuddered as the waves of release swept over him, blanking out everything for several blessed moments.

He stayed beside her, his heart thumping, feeling her brilliant green eyes on him. "Have you had contact with Nika or Vlach since we met? Do you see them?"

Bewildered, she answered slowly trying to discover the danger in his question. "No, Mr. Borisov, not since the night of the party."

"Are you sure?" He reached for her and roughly fondled her neck so delicate, so easy to snap. "It takes only a little time to check you know." His voice was dull, expressionless.

She flinched, sudden terror in her eyes.

"Tell me, do you know anything about Vlach's activities?"

"Only when Vlach came for me, he hired some of the men from the *kolkhoz* to work for his boss. They were former soldiers." A small bruise was already growing on her soft neck.

"Where?" he asked, gripping her arm.

"I don't know. I heard somewhere near the Mongolian border. But I would never want to contact them. They are bad men. I am so happy here with you. This is like a wonderful dream, a paradise." Her voice was shaking.

He believed her. It must have dazzled the girl to be plucked out of a desolate kolkhoz and installed in his luxurious homes. She seemed even to have accepted his sudden fits of anger and brutality.

To ease his conscience, he indulged her by sending her with Shamil, his bodyguard with fashion taste, to shop in Nice, giving her carte blanche at Chanel, Hermes, and other luxury shops. He paid for treatments at the most exclusive beauty spa. She was impeccably groomed to his standards. In the past two weeks, she had become more voluptuous, in spite of her natural slimness.

She looked the part, an oligarch's pampered mistress with flashy clothes, but still radiated a curious innocence. Once, after he had cornered her in the hallway and roughly taken her, she said that he was so good to her. It was strange, how nothing really changed for Russians. The Raven had once told him that after the 1917 Revolution, many middle class and aristocratic women became prostitutes or mistresses of powerful men in the Cheka to survive. He recalled a photograph of the old Bolshevik at a party wearing a black leather coat with a young woman, one of his many mistresses, Princess Baranova close at his side.

Mikhail relaxed but did not loosen his grip on Marousia's arm, pulling her roughly on top of him, and then changing his mind, let her slide off. "Are you an orphan?" He knew very little about her and wasn't interested, but felt obligated to ask.

She drew the sheets around her body and curled up her legs. "No, my mother died of tuberculosis, and Guri, my brother, a soldier, was killed in Chechnya. It's only dear papa who is alive, but he is very ill. He lives alone. The doctor thinks he has cancer. I didn't want to leave him, but he insisted."

It was the same old tragic Russian tale. Mikhail supposed that her father was his age or younger and unlucky, like most of the population. She was innocent, and he felt low for being suspicious of her, and relieved that he didn't have to kill her. He should do something nice for her.

"Would you like to call your papa? Talk to him as long as you want. Does he have a phone?"

"We use the one at the co-op store."

"I'll set him up with a cell so you can call anytime."

"Oh thank you. You are so good." She flung her arms around him, happy that he was no longer angry.

Watching him while he dressed, her green eyes filled with tears. "What happened? Who hurt you?" She was staring at his scarred back and arms.

"It was a long time ago." His voice was harsh with anger. He had revealed this private ugliness to her. He was getting old, vulnerable. There had been only other time in his life that he let down his guard before a woman. For years he wore a shirt when he took someone to bed.

She seemed to shrink like a tiny animal at the threat in his voice. "I'm sorry," she said.

A few minutes later he stood alone, naked in his large marble bathroom, the lights in the double mirrors illuminating the deep scars snaking down his powerful back and over his shoulders and arms to his wrists. His disgrace could never be known; he never would speak of it to anyone.

His dark past like a vial of poison was buried deep within him, but now against his will, it began to slowly leak memory.

He was back in the Zona, a *maloletki*, juvenile criminal. He had escaped the orphanage, gone back on the street, and had been picked up by police. With Sasha dead, he was forced to rely on himself. After he knifed the leader Pick who had stolen his food, they had invented a special punishment for him in the *maloletki* barracks. It was a hellish place. The guards were terrified of the juveniles and never dared enter.

The first excruciating lick of pain from the hot wires mingles with waves of laughter, then nothing. The juveniles throw him outside the barracks and the guards, not believing he would live, push him into a corner of the infirmary.

He wakes up to the burning pain conscious for a few moments of the world around him. He is lying on his back, his hand curled in toward his face. Through the haze of pain his eyes focus on a strange mark on his wrist. Horror fills him at this sign, a swastika, and he wonders who did this while he was unconscious; making him a Nazi, butt of a dangerous joke. The Raven is beside his bed, but he says nothing about this mark of the enemy from the last war.

He is not sent back to prison and begins his instruction when he is well. Even though he is called Mikhail Borisov, inside he is *Noch*, not human, out of control.

He turned away from the scars in the mirror, and stepped into the shower, cold water pouring over him to quell the burning. The Raven had trained him well. Once he remarked with satisfaction, "You are the complete finished product."

He dressed and went back to his office hoping for some news of Katya Marston. Unlocking the 18th century desk, which once belonged to Grand Duke Sergei, he took out his private computer and clicked it on. He jumped back, recoiling in shock.

Noch. The email, like his memories, called to him. *Give up the girl. Tell what you know.* Two mug shots of him, Mikhail Borisov, young, wild-eyed, head shaven, appeared on the screen. Terror in a white streak of light blinded him for moment. The message was signed *the Shaman.*

Chapter 33

Mikhail
St. Paul de Vence, France

SHARP DAGGERS OF light struck the terrace of the stone house, like the questions assailing Mikhail. Who could know *Noch*, his name from the past? Who could have his mug shots? He had believed the Raven destroyed his past records. The blinding white light pierced his head, the pain driving him back into his study. In a moment of sheer panic, he pounded his fists on the desk, and threw his Sevres teacup and saucer into the fireplace. It took some moments for the pain to recede. He stumbled to his desk and fell to the chair, rubbing his hands over his head, struggling to breathe, to control and order his mind.

His fist landed on the button ringing Anya. She was there in a moment. Bebe was behind her. They stood rigid with fear. "Are you hurt boss?" Anya said.

Before he answered she was picking up the pieces of china.

"Stop," he ordered, "Pack everything now. We are leaving for the yacht. It's no longer safe here."

Bebe moved toward him, his face like a burst balloon, his mouth stretched open like a small cavern. Still breathing hard, Mikhail held up his hand and stopped him from coming closer, not wanting him to see the mug shots on the screen.

"Find out everything on a man called the Shaman. Use Interpol, every source we have." Bebe crept out, and he heard the frantic patter of his feet crossing the hall to the communications room.

In spite of his fear, his mind began to work in his usual cold rational manner. This was the unknown enemy he sensed had been waiting for him over the years. In the native Evenk language shaman meant 'one who knows'. Did this crazy know everything about him? He went to the small oak cabinet, poured a whisky into a Baccarat crystal glass and gulped it down, then read the message again.

The Shaman's demand that he give up the girl indicated he was still on the hunt for her. Breathing hard, Mikhail forced his eyes down below the message to his old prison mug shots; the two poses side and front, along with his name and registration number, were displayed clearly on the screen.

"*Noch*," he whispered, and for a moment he was a boy again. Curiously he looked much the same as he did now. The battered face staring out at him was adult, hard and embittered even though he was twelve or thirteen when the photographs were taken. The bumps and bruises hinted at his story. They beat him to force him in front of the camera..

He frowned and shrugged off his churning feelings, going back to the most important question. Did this shaman have only these mug shots or his entire prison record? If his life before he became an agent were ever known, he would be dead to the respectable world. Even if he possessed the *ukase*, it would be impossible for him to return home.

He had been innocent of crime, a victim of the Politburo law that children of political enemies could be imprisoned at the age of twelve. But Russians did not want to be reminded of this sordid part of their history. They would never accept a leader who had been a lost street kid or a juvenile criminal. The prospect of his entire record held by an enemy terrified him. He jumped up, spilled his second glass of whiskey, shouted at Anya to mop up, and then went down to the communications room.

The cameras and computer screens blinked ominously. His two technicians on headphones shot to their feet. He nodded, indicating they should sit down, then stood beside them and watched his message go out to his agents in the States. One million dollars would be added to the pay packet of the agent who found Katya Marston and brought her to him. He would make the bitch scream until she told him everything.

The Interpol information on the Shaman showing up on the screen was disappointing. There was no biography, no revealing photograph. Most disturbing was the report of his military force of ex-soldiers located on a base in a remote area of Mongolia. Anonymous sources claimed that the mysterious man was secretly allied with General Letinov and others in the government, and that he would control the next Russian president.

Mikhail stirred uneasily. It was reported that the Shaman practiced the healing arts and headed a religious cult. Rumors of orgies and ritual murder in the camp continued to circulate, but there had been no move on the part of the government to investigate. The last agent from Interpol to penetrate the Shaman's territory had been shot, and his body dumped on the outskirts of Irkutsk.

He would not answer the messages. Interaction could only bring harm. Then he walked back to his terrace, his footsteps sounding lonely along the hall, his mind returning to his mug shots he believed were erased from his file.

The Raven claimed that he had created a new identity and background for Mikhail, that it was a clean start and that all of his past records had been destroyed. All lies. After many frustrating hours of searching through the old Bolshevik's Siberian files, he understood that his controller hoarded documents, even pieces of waste paper. He became suspicious when he had not found a scrap of information on his childhood and past. This total absence could mean that the cruel old bastard had removed and hidden his entire personal file. But where? *See French Files.* The Raven's written command flashed through his head. Boris, the former KGB archivist possessed these files. He sent a message to Boris that he was ready to make a deal. It was urgent that he retrieve these records.

He passed his office, filled with boxes. Anya was directing two men packing up the last load of books. He had ordered that the files from the secret room remain, with the exception of the important ones he personally carried. An air of emptiness pervaded the charming stone house with its polished floors, its terrace overlooking the valley. He felt a sense of loss, knowing he might never see it again.

He had hired Little Lev to meet Boris the archivist in Albania to negotiate for the first section of the French Files and waited on the terrace for his call. If Lev were successful, the rendezvous would take place tomorrow. Once Mikhail checked that the files were complete, he would hand over five million dollars. After Boris received this first payment, there would be another meeting to collect the remainder of the files and hand over an additional five million. While he waited on one of the elegant wicker chairs, he turned on his computer. Fear sliced through his stomach as the Shaman's words appeared.

How happy I was when I discovered you again, Noch. And you had climbed so high, became a part of our noble secret service, feeding off the state. It is a pity you refuse to engage in any dialogue with me. You must realize that it is very dangerous not to agree to my demand. Hand over Katya Marston. This demand is not unreasonable.

Staring out over the valley, he puzzled over the last part of the crazy message.

*It has been prophesied. The one designated by blood shall rule Russia
again. I am that chosen one. You must give up the search for the
ukase. It belongs to me.*

Lev's call came, and at the risk of being ambushed, he set off to
meet him at the Lyon stop. He had no choice but to go himself. He
could not trust anyone. His convoy of three armor-plated Humvees,
two as escorts, moved swiftly along the Autoroute du Soleil. Mikhail,
panic somewhat diminished, rode in the middle van surrounded by
armed guards. He reasoned that the Shaman did not have the girl and
felt confident his men would find her first. Boris had guaranteed with
his life that he had not sold duplicates of this section of the French
Files. Boris had blown his cover to make the sale and knew that
Mikhail would find him if he tried a double-cross.

Racing toward Lyon, he went back to the files' strange history,
which intertwined with his and the Raven's past. The French Files
belonged to the Deuxieme Bureau, French Intelligence, and contained documents from the early 20th century to 1940. When the
Nazis invaded Paris in 1940, they moved the material to Berlin. After
the fall of Berlin in 1945, the victorious Red Army took the files to
Moscow and they remained under the Raven's control until his death.

Russia began returning the documents to the French in 1992,
but stopped in 1994 when the Russian Parliament criticized Yeltsin
for bowing to the French. Although the Russians denied it, the
French claimed that more than 10,000 boxes of secret service files
were missing. He now understood that these missing documents
were not held by the Russian Government, but had been stolen by
Boris who planned to sell them to interested parties.

The Raven must have assumed the French Files, then under his
control, would never leave Russia. Mikhail figured that the old
Bolshevik had kept his most sensitive personal information hidden

among the French intelligence documents, believing that they were safe from government scrutiny and would be easy for him to access.

Little Lev was waiting in the car park near Lyon when Mikhail arrived. The meeting was hurried. There was no time for the usual vodka ritual. Lev was shaking as Mikhail examined the file numbers to make sure they weren't forgeries. He did not speak to Lev, just nodded that all was correct and handed him the open suitcase with the cash. Looking frail and worn, his mouth drooping to the side like a scar, Lev counted the packets. There were no goodbyes.

The Humvee sped through the night. It was over and he was safe, but he could not rest. This first shipment, in a large metal trunk, filled the seat behind him. He knew it would take some time to go through the documents, but couldn't resist opening the container. Flicking on the light from above, he turned in his seat and struggled with the heavy hinge.

He felt oddly suspended in time as he lifted the lid. The first folder was sealed and marked:

Personal, to be opened only after my death. The Raven

Taking a huge breath, he broke the seal. He saw first a sepia photograph dated 1921 of a pretty young aristocratic woman, dressed in a traveling costume, standing beside a Mongolian man. His robes and entourage suggest he is Mongolian nobility. The woman is slim and graceful, her light hair piled in a chignon. She holds a hat and stands some distance from a group of Tsarist officers. She seems to be saying farewell and has a sad wistful look.

An enormous Buddhist Temple carved out of rock rises in the background. Mikhail was sure it was Mongolia. He remembered a second group photograph in the same year he had found in the *Ukase* file. It had a similar background with the same party of Russians who seemed to be preparing for an expedition. He believed both pictures were taken the same day. And in each it was the same young woman, gazing wistfully at the camera.

His mind drifted back to another photograph he had found in the Raven's documents from the hiding place near Perm. He searched in his wallet and brought it to the light. The date is 1946. The young woman with elaborately braided hair, in quaint ceremonial robes looks straight at him. He placed the photographs side by side and a slight chill passed through him. Even though the young women were separated in age by over thirty years, the faces were the same.

Chapter 34

Katya
Interstate 80

IT WAS STILL early morning when Roo and Katya left Imperial
Treasures, moving fast out of New York City in the blizzard. The
truck chains clunked softly as Roo swerved around snow ploughs,
laboring to keep one lane open.

Katya said, "Sheriff Yoder, you said you found a photograph of
me in Maxi's room." She was thinking of last night's break in, and his
accusations against Maxi.

"Yeah, you're posing at the top of a mountain in ski clothes.
Look in my bag in the first folder."

She fumbled through the documents and found her photograph,
hardly recognizing the happy carefree woman posing at the top of the
mountain.

"I remember this. Abigail took several pictures of me in
Courchevel, in the last two years before she died." Her voice quavered. "Of course, she must have given one of them to Maxi."

She gasped, clutching the door handle; the wheels slid on the ice
spinning the truck in a circle, the sky revolving around her. Roo

swiftly turned the steering wheel into the spin, and the truck flew back on the road. He went on as though nothing had happened.

Still gripping the handle, she remembered Maxi's remark that he hadn't known she existed until Abigail's death then realized he must have found the photograph after she arrived from London. They had passed the outskirts of Manhattan and turned onto Route 9. Through sheets of snow, Katya glimpsed a sign to New Jersey: they were travelling south.

"We're not going upstate," she said.

"No, but I wanted it to get around that we were headed that way. Kutusov claimed Maxi's stepfather was an FSB informant."

"You can't mean that Maxi's mother and stepfather would tell the killers about us." She was shocked.

He didn't answer her question. "The countess and her husband were leaving town. Maybe the killers caught up with them."

"Oh God, that's terrible," she said. "Where are we going then?" She tried to keep the fright out of her voice.

"Tecumseh County."

"What? You can't." Her voice rose, and she gripped the truck door, as though this would halt this crazy journey. "But that's where you're from. Where you found the body. But why? It's so far from New York." She had never dreamed he could be taking her there.

He watched the road. "I know the country and the killers don't. It will be easier to hide you. You'll be safer there. I can protect you."

His words reminded her that she was a fugitive. The truck moved inexorably on, and she wanted to scream and fight but knew nothing would stop him.

"But we could have gone anywhere, at least closer to New York." She protested in panic. She had the wild urge to jump out and return to the gallery no matter how unsafe it was. She opened the door, and the snow pelted her as she took a deep breath and prepared to jump.

He pulled her back roughly, and caught hold of the swinging door, slamming it, "Christ, you're going to kill yourself." He held her with one arm, while he slowed down, alarm on his face, his voice urgent. "Listen to me. There is another reason for going to Tecumseh Country. The archive could be hidden near the cabin where Christina was murdered." He let her go and drove on slowly.

"The circumstantial evidence points to both women being murdered for their knowledge of the archive. Abigail left a clue that it's hidden in Tecumseh's Forest." He reasoned. "Her friend Christina disappeared in 1970 and resurfaced in Tecumseh County in 2000 where the killers caught up with her. I have a hunch that Christina was hiding out all these years because she knew where this archive was hidden."

"I guess that means we have to go to the middle of nowhere, if your hunch is right." She brushed off the snow, shivering from fright and cold.

He went on as if he hadn't heard her. "It gives us a head start to finding the Blood Archive. That is if you want to."

"Of course, I want to. It was Abigail's last wish," she said, moving back on the seat. "But won't the killers trace us?"

"Eventually, yes."

"I'm like bait. You told me there was nothing in the cabin where Christina Gartner had been living."

"That's right, but I wouldn't expect the archive to be in such an obvious place. And we don't know what's in the documents Abigail left with her note. We might find out more when we get them translated." His argument left her exhausted, without protest, as the truck ploughed through the path ever farther away from New York.

None of this seemed real to Katya. How was it possible these two friends, part of the New York social scene, became involved in something so dangerous that Russian killers would stalk them? And now she was hiding from the same murderers even though she knew nothing.

"I don't understand why Abigail didn't just tell me where the archive is in her note, instead of leaving this strange clue about Tecumseh's Forest."

"She was afraid it would be intercepted." He leaned forward wiping the fogged up windshield.

Abigail meant those words on the envelope, 'Trust no one'. She flashed him a glance. His mouth was firm, drawn tight across his face. He seemed an insurmountable block of determination.

"Maybe poor Abigail gave them a hint of the location when they ..." She stopped, choked with tears.

"Don't think so." He drove intently, staring in the rear view mirror, but the road was empty. Katya huddled miserably in her ski jacket, watching the landscape shrouded in white slowly transform from used car lots, fast food restaurants, DIY stores, and garden centers to open fields smooth with snow, then to blanketed mountains, solitary, devoid of human life. The sky was steeped in baleful clouds, throwing down snow. She was trapped.

She stole frightened glances at him. Each time he turned back to scan the road, the dim light picked out the scar on his forehead. His explanation for going to Tecumseh County seemed contrived. Her thoughts ran on in an ominous rhythm with the windshield wipers. He was driving in the opposite direction from where Maxi might be held, away from helping him, away from anyone who knew her. Her mind raced on in panic. No one knew where she was. She even had a momentary crazy feeling he could be the killer, taking her to the woods to die.

She had been stupid for trusting a complete stranger, for speeding across the country to an unknown place. What was to stop her from calling the local police and going directly back to London?

She reached down in her handbag for her cell and saw the recorded message; her body flooded with relief. Sometime last night there had been a call from Maxi. He must be safe. At least he was alive. Maybe they wanted ransom. Or he might be released and would come for her. She clicked on her phone. "Katya, I'm worried. If you get this message, tell me where you are. I'll come for you."

The sheriff's large powerful hand clamped down on hers.

"What are you doing?"

"I'm answering Maxi. He called last night." She tried to keep her poise even as she struggled to get away.

"No. It's not safe." He gripped her hand like a vice and veered off the road, skidding to a stop. He wrenched the phone from her.

"You're a bastard," she screamed, striking his arms and chest.

A bear-like growl came from him. He gripped her shoulders, holding her like a rag doll.

"Listen to me."

She stopped screaming, her body limp, overwhelmed by his sudden physical force.

"You're being stupid. The killers have Devlin's car. They're hunting for us and could trace us through your phone." His eyes were like shards of steel. He held her tightly for a few moments longer, and then pushed her back against the seat. He got out of the car, smashed the phone with his boot, and threw it into the adjoining field.

She sat back limp in the seat, cowed by his frightening anger, breathing in short gasps, trying not to cry, as he started the car. Without her cell, there was no way to contact Maxi or anyone who could help her.

He drove several miles in silence, then said, "I heard his message. You know he's all right. You can't tell anyone where you are, even Suvorov."

She burst out, "Why is it just you? If it's so dangerous, why aren't the regular police handling this?"

He frowned, gazing at the road, and said shortly, "It would be harder to protect you. It would call attention to you. No one except Devlin knows where we're going, and then even he doesn't know the exact location."

She caught her breath, exhausted from her outburst, still feeling the strong beat of his heart, his solid warmth lingering on her body. It was disconcerting and lessened her anger, but confused her. Everything had gone wrong. She didn't have control of her emotions, control of anything.

He turned off the road into a truck stop, American Diner, appropriately lit with red, white, and blue neon. "While my phone is secure, I need to make some calls," he said, driving past the parking lot full of semi trucks, their drivers waiting out the storm.

They passed a darkened building next to the diner, with a sign *Topless Dancers*. She wondered if details of her embarrassing antics in London clubs had been in the police file. Roo got out and surveyed the area before driving to the pumps.

Katya opened the door to the diner and was assaulted by the loud shouts and laughter of noisy truckers in jeans and ski jackets. The room suddenly went silent and they watched her with hostile interest as she hurried through clouds of cigarette smoke to a booth. She shivered at the room's rawness, at the lino floor stained with mud, and the grease covered windows and walls. The hoarse twang of a country and western song filled the room with melancholy.

A tall lean man with bloodshot eyes and a lined face like eroded soil came to take the order. She recoiled. For a panicked moment his apron looked splattered with blood, but it was only stained with baked beans and barbecue sauce. Unable to think about food with the men watching her, she ordered a hamburger and coffee. It was late afternoon, but the snow and heavy clouds forced the owner to turn on lights. Just beyond the pumps, a dark shadow flitted by and disappeared into the snow. It had to be her imagination. The killers couldn't have followed them.

Turning away from the staring eyes, she huddled in the booth studying the knife cuts and initials carved into its sides. The image of Abigail struggling to leave a last warning message rose before her. Blood Archive? What could it mean? She was ashamed at wanting to abandon Abigail's request to find the archive, to return to her old life as if nothing had happened. It would be deserting the person who cared for her and had done everything to make her life perfect. Before her guardian's murder, she had been a spoiled brat, given anything she wanted and most of all, protected from any danger.

Aware of the growing boldness of the stares and the inaudible remarks she guessed were about her, she worried over what she would do if one of them approached. Her legs felt weak and she was so tired she wouldn't be able to run. There was no refuge out there, only the forest.

Then Yoder came in, his cheeks flushed from the cold and slid in the booth across from her, and the diner again filled with conversation. She couldn't figure him out. It would have been easier for him to send her off to the police and not be involved. "But why are you doing this? What do you get out of it?" she said.

"This is my first important case. My main objective is to find the killers and this 'Blood Archive' seems connected."

"Then what happens?"

"I'll go after the killers, and you can go home to Maxi." He looked at her cautiously, expecting another outburst.

She forced out the words. "I'm sorry. I just lost it." A song about divorce wailed across the room.

"Don't worry," he said, not looking directly at her. "It's ok. I lost it too. Sorry that I was so rough. I hope I didn't hurt you."

"I'm ok," she said, still smarting from the rough way he had treated her.

She grimaced when the man slapped down the order.

"You're not eating?" He chomped down on his hamburger.

She frowned. "I don't feel hungry."

"I'll try to find a better place for our next stop," he said, finishing his hamburger and eating hers as well.

Back in the truck, she tried again. "Please, can we contact Maxi to make sure he's all right."

"It's not safe. I told you."

"You know, you are totally wrong about him. He couldn't be involved in anything so brutal."

"Interpol came up with a photograph of your boyfriend with Kayakov and an unidentified figure dressed in a monk's habit, his face hidden in the hood," he said in a maddeningly reasonable tone that made her grit her teeth.

"Kayakov," she said aloud, seeing the odd Russian in his long priestly robe, staring at her with cold insect eyes while he expounded on his true religion.

"Kayakov has a long prison record, and while inside, became a leader of convicts. They call him *A Thief Professing the Code*. He controlled large parts of the prison. Now he operates this security firm, with the convicts who were behind bars with him." Roo was intent on incriminating Maxi even if by association.

"Then, as I explained to Countess Suvorova, I found your photograph, the letterhead inscribed with an Ark and a swastika sign in your boyfriend's room." He gestured toward the back. "It's inside the same folder." She reluctantly took it, holding it gingerly as though it were a dangerous weapon, and gazed forlornly at the strange letterhead.

"I just can't believe you found this in Maxi's room. Couldn't it belong to his friend, Kutusov?"

"Yes, it's possible," Roo admitted. "The old émigré is a strange character, a little shifty. He could be lying about everything." He lifted one hand from the steering wheel and pointed to the photograph she now held. "Interpol investigators believe the guy in the monk's robe is the power behind Kayakov. There isn't much information on him. He calls himself the Shaman. The photograph was taken at the Shaman's compound, somewhere in Siberia." A car passed, throwing up water and snow on the windshield. Roo slowed for a few moments.

"A shaman. What's that?" She shivered at the sinister sounding word.

"Devlin filled me in last night after I reported to him. In short, a shaman is a healer and spiritual leader who uses his magic powers and goes into trances, to intercede in the spirit world. These priests have existed for 8000 years in the tribal societies in Tibet, Mongolia and isolated places in Siberia."

"They couldn't really exist today. It's too creepy," she said.

"Devlin said many of them were killed during communist rule, and some went underground. Since the fall of the Soviet government, strange cults and shamanistic healers have cropped up all over Russia. But my guess is that this guy is not a genuine shaman. I bet more of a killer than a healer."

She stared at the photograph of Maxi, Kayakov and the shadowy figure in the monk's cowl.

"I can't believe this. It's so out of character. And no matter what his mother thinks, Maxi never could be connected to this strange sect. He's a Harvard grad." She noticed his ironic smile, and realized her statement was ridiculous.

"Let's talk more about your Harvard boyfriend. I think it's interesting that before he disappeared …"

"Kidnapped," she cut in, "and escaped. I'm sure he was trying to prevent the robbery."

He slowed down while a truck roared past, slapping water across the windshield.

"Ok." He didn't want to argue. "We know sometime before your boyfriend left, he begged his mother, the countess to give him his grandfather's papers, believing their contents might lead to the lost archive. You have to wonder how he discovered the archive existed."

"I wish you would stop calling him my boyfriend. It's so sarcastic." She turned away to the window, looking out at deep shadows collecting between the trees, strangely humiliated and furious at his nasal drawl of 'boyfriend'. It sounded cheap.

The snow had spent itself, and only a few tired flakes drifted to the ground. The temperature had risen, melting the drifts to mush on the road. Wanting to go as far as he could before dark, he drove faster, the chains on the tires clanking against the hard surface.

The highway wound slowly out like a white ribbon tying up the Appalachian Mountains. They crossed the Delaware Water Gap. Even in her distress, she admired the wild beauty. The range of stark majestic trees, their branches draped with white epaulets of snow, paraded down the mountain, breaking ranks at the gap over the river.

Roo turned to her, his face disappearing into the twilight. "The pioneers trekked through the gap going west into the wilderness."

"It still looks like a wilderness. I'm going into nowhere, so far away from London and New York." Her voice was mournful. He stirred uncomfortably and silence overcame both of them.

To her, this country was strange and unfamiliar compared to the gentle English countryside with its cozy stone villages. The snow covered land spread out before her, savage and lonely. A few scattered shacks, abandoned tractors, and trucks nibbled at the wilderness.

They stopped again at a service station at the end of the storm. While Katya bought coffee, he removed the snow chains. There were only a few cars and trucks on the highway. It would be easy to spot someone following them.

Roo said, "We can relax for now. They can't know where we are."

Back on the highway, as darkness fell, silence again lay like stone between them. She felt herself losing heart, giving in to him for the moment, knowing she had to be civil. And if all he said was true, she might be safer with him.

"I know it's my 'legacy' and all that, but really, what could possibly be in this archive?" Her voice caught in her throat.

"Maybe it is not what the archive contains, but what these killers can make of it," Roo said. "I'm hoping we'll have more information after the Suvorov papers are translated. We know it's important enough to kill for."

"It's just so hard to believe this could have anything to do with Russians," she said.

He paused for a moment, then said, "There is something else I didn't tell you that supports the Russian theory. Last night Devlin told me something he remembered reading when he was studying the Bolshevik terror and the techniques of their secret police. It's an old superstition. Many of the Cheka murderers believed the victim's eyes reflected the image of the killer."

"So, before they killed …" She felt suddenly unbearably cold.

He finished the sentence. "The killer slashed out the victims' eyeballs."

Chapter 35

Katya-Roo
Interstate 80

KATYA WATCHED THE road unfolding, leading her into something dangerous, horrifying. She flinched as headlights from an oncoming car stared like huge disembodied eyeballs. She thought of Abigail, who had tried to protect her, tortured and murdered.

Thinking back to all the warning signs that led her to be trapped in this truck, she said, "I had the sense that someone was following me before I left England, but thought it was probably my imagination. The first time was in Courchevel. I was vacationing with my fiancée."

"Oh yes, your fiancée." He frowned slightly, the scar on his forehead deepening.

She had ceased even having a thought of Philip until this moment. Her relationship with him seemed to belong to a Neolithic past, but the wounds from his abusive insults remained, bringing her down.

"I think I told you before it didn't work out with Philip," she snapped. She was an idiot to bring up any bit of her personal life, which certainly would confirm his opinion that she was a slut. She hated it that this complete stranger knew she was having an affair with Maxi. He had to think she was cold hearted, taking Abigail's lover. She searched his expression for contempt, expecting it, but instead noted his brief look of puzzlement.

Changing the subject she related the incident at the teashop in Courchevel, omitting the thug's most offensive comment, and the accident two days later on the ski slope. Realizing how it all came together, she mentioned again her strange invitation to the Russian embassy. "I thought it was a strange coincidence that Prince Androvsky was found dead early the next morning, but believed the police report that his fall was an accident until Maxi's mother said it might be murder."

"I don't think we can trust the countess. We received a report from London. The inquest ruled an open verdict which means there is not enough evidence to conclude whether the prince jumped or was thrown from the balcony."

Staring out at the road, unwinding ahead taking them into the night, she was certain he had been murdered. "The prince was trying to warn me." A truck passed, throwing up waves of water.

Roo's eyes narrowed in concentration. "You didn't tell me about the incidents in Courchevel when I interviewed you."

"I just didn't connect it all. How could anyone imagine all of this?" She vowed that no matter what he asked her she would keep that disgraceful hazy night at the Russian nightclub a secret, even if it was a major clue.

Darkness had fallen like a hood over the land, and Katya thought how easy it would be to disappear forever into this blackness. The only sign of life was traffic in both directions. The seat was hard; the bones in her bottom clattered each time they hit a small bump. The smell of manure was much stronger with the heat turned on high.

She longed to be safe in her flat in London or at the sanctuary at Skeffington's enjoying Claire's soothing massages and beauty treatments, or back in New York at the Little Swan Gallery, anywhere but in this truck heading for some terrible unknown destination. She had left her world behind with her Prada suit and fur coat in that Brooklyn closet and might never return.

In a last attempt to persuade him to turn back, she said, "Just how will we ever find someone in Tecumseh Country to translate these documents? Wouldn't it be easier to find a translator in New York?"

"It's been taken care of. Maybe you should try to get some sleep."

She curled up in the seat, away from him, and closed her eyes against her pale reflection flying by in the window.

As they hurtled through the night, Roo could feel her anger and fear, like another presence in the truck. For a while she had seemed on the verge of hysteria, and he wouldn't have known what to do. But then to his amazement, she had drifted off to sleep just as she had last night at Devlin's.

He mulled over Suvorov's call. What did it mean? Was he part of the robbery or did he, as Katya believed, escape? She stirred and moved against him, resting her head against his arm.

The truck labored on, eating up the road, its motor grumbling. Roo kept glancing out the back window, but only an occasional semi passed.

He reviewed his calls made at the gas station. He couldn't buy another Sim card at the truck stop, so took the risk that no one had tapped the line. The secretary at the OSU Slavic Languages Department in Columbus seemed to be waiting for his call and gave him the telephone number of the translator. "Her name is Eugenia Scott. She is the best, but I wouldn't get your hopes up. She has always been difficult, and resigned some years ago after a political disagreement with her colleagues. Since then she's be a recluse. If she turns down the job, call me back."

Eugenia Scott had answered her phone. "Who is this? Who are you?" She sounded cranky, suspicious.

"Tecumseh County Deputy Sheriff Yoder."

"I don't like police," she quavered. "How did you find me?"

"Wait. Please don't hang up. Gloria Davis at the OSU Slavic Department gave me your number. She said you might help us. We need several Russian documents translated. We're on our way to Columbus now."

There was a long silence as though she'd gone away from the phone, then she said, "Gloria is a very nice person. She has always been a friend. What is this about?"

He briefly described the documents left to Katya.

"Katya," her suspicion returned. "Is she Russian?"

"No, I don't think so. Her last name is Marston."

"Right, I'll meet you in Columbus at the Sunflower Market, 9th Avenue and High Street at 10 a.m. tomorrow. I am assuming I will be paid well. I am only doing this for money. How will I know you?"

"We're both in our early thirties with light hair. I'll be wearing a plaid lumber jacket."

"I'll find you," she said, abruptly hanging up.

He made one last call to Ben Tyler, explaining as much as he could over the phone and asked for his help. He wanted to keep Stumpy ignorant of his presence back in Tecumseh to protect him. Besides, the Sheriff's office had always been the center of leaks and town gossip, and he was worried Stumpy and Miss Gracie Logan wouldn't be able to keep their mouths shut if he turned up with someone like Katya.

In the long emails they had exchanged, Devlin had approved his plan, but Roo was uneasy. His last message had been returned unanswered. He tried several times to reach him on the secure number, desperate to give his boss their exact location and to find out if they had picked up Maxi. The line was dead.

He was on his own. Even though he had made a tentative arrangement with the translator, he had not decided exactly where in Tecumseh County he was taking Katya until the minute he had turned on the highway, heading home.

He wondered if his intuitive flash that both women had been murdered for hiding the archive was merely an illusion. He could be in deep shit if he was wrong. Katya believed his motives were suspect, and in the worst imaginable scenario, she could even charge him with abduction.

He was exhausted, but didn't doze off. He was jumpy, and wanted to turn on a CD, but was afraid he might not hear something on the road. And then it would wake her.

She was sleeping close to him. Her wonderful smell of citrus trees overcame that of the manure. Her hair spilled out on his shoulder like pale corn silk, and he thought with a certain self-disgust, that he could have driven on forever. He admitted that he desired her, yet wasn't sure he even liked her. She was exasperating, difficult, with a mind of her own. He felt a sudden anger that she had made him forget Janey, the true object of his devotion. She was in love with that slime ball Suvorov. How could she sleep with her dead guardian's lover?

She was beautiful, well-educated, cultured, used to luxury and privilege. His only job had been deputy sheriff in the middle of nowhere, and he would be classified in any survey as a redneck, one of the rural poor. In ordinary circumstances, he would never have the chance to meet someone like her.

But, he argued with himself, even though she appeared shallow and spoiled there was some evidence she was kind. She had hugged Geoffrey in his embarrassing drag costume. And she truly did mourn

Abigail. As if dreaming his thoughts, she let out a sigh, moved closer, and he could feel her soft breast heavy against him. He sheltered her with his arm, and the truck moved smoothly, like an animal that knew it was going home. Back in the diner she had asked him what he got out of doing this for her; he hadn't told her the entire truth. It was true that he wanted to solve his first important case and that her archive was connected to the murders. But it was also he could not help himself, felt protective of her, worried about her. And he didn't want her to go home to Maxi as he suggested. It was insane since he hardly knew her.

The clouds had pulled back like a curtain, revealing brilliant sparks of stars, and words from Shakespeare's sonnet flowed over him.

Love is not love / which alters when it alteration finds, / Or bends with the remover to remove. / Oh no, it is an ever-fixed mark, / that takes on tempests and is never shaken. / It is the star to every wandering bark.

To him the guiding star was loyalty in love, the only belief you could hang onto in life. Yet he knew from bitter experience that almost everyone betrayed those they loved best.

Chapter 36

Katya-Roo
Columbus, Ohio

IT WAS BARELY light when they arrived at the outskirts of Columbus, a flat sprawl of low built houses, car lots and fast food chains. Gray remnants of clouds hovered overhead like dishwater scum. Katya woke, embarrassed to discover she had been curled up against the sheriff the entire night. She quickly moved over against her door.

They drove into a Wendy's Restaurant with wide windows overlooking the street. Katya went to the restroom, brushed her teeth, washed her face, and pulled her hair back in a band. Staring into the mirror, she realized her once familiar image had faded, replaced by a white faced hunted woman. Dabbing on some moisturizer, she noticed the beginnings of tiny wrinkles around her eyes. Wrinkles were the least of her worries.

The deputy sheriff waited for her at one of the gray Formica tables designed for hygiene and easy cleaning. The restaurant had few customers this early. A middle-aged couple sat at a table in the far corner, and across from them a man in a ball cap feasted on a burger and coffee.

"What would you like?" Roo asked. His face was pale with fatigue, and he needed a shave. He had pulled over during the night for a few hours to try to sleep, but had been too worked up to rest, and returned to the road again.

"Just coffee thanks."

As he carried two cups of coffee and plastic spoons to the bare table, Katya longed for breakfast in her cozy London flat. Aware of her mood, he concentrated on the map, finding 9th Avenue and High Street, where they were to meet with Eugenia. He asked the sleepy girl behind the counter for directions to the nearest Kinko's copiers.

They waited in silence until Kinko's opened and quickly made copies of all the documents. Back in the car, Roo said, "I think we should ask for Abigail's letter to be translated first. The material from Countess Suvorova-Turbatov seems less urgent to the case."

She agreed. "The countess claimed the Suvorov documents were important, but her story about the family doesn't seem to have anything to do with the archive. Maybe she was making it up." The Turbatovs could be guilty of *vranye*, the creative lying Maxi had described.

They drove along High Street to the edge of the OSU campus, and easily found the orange and yellow tiled Sunflower Market. Huge sunflowers painted on the windows made it hard to miss.

Roo parked the car on 9th Avenue, lined with run down rooming houses. He scanned the area for a few moments, but only students carrying book bags hurried along the street in the cold. The organic health food store and its small café were crowded with customers buying takeaway lunches and shopping for produce and vitamins. It seemed an unlikely place for killers to hide. After he had checked all the aisles, they sat at one of the tables near the entrance, ordered tea, and waited.

After a half hour Katya said, "Shouldn't she be here? I think we should go."

He surveyed the room again. "Let's wait a few minutes longer, I think we're safe. Come with me."

They walked past the coffee bar to the far end of the café. Roo pushed open the door of the produce cooler, a huge glass and stainless steel room stacked with vegetables. It was arctic because of the outside temperature. A woman crouched down behind a huge pile of cauliflower, intently peering through the window out to High Street. She would have been comical if there was not a palpable air of fear surrounding her like the cloud of steam from her breath. She didn't hear the door open and jumped away in panic when they approached her.

"Wait, are you Eugenia Scott? I'm Deputy Sheriff Yoder. I spoke to you by telephone yesterday."

"I could be that woman." She glanced out the window toward the street, before turning again and staring at them. "Show me your identification."

Roo gave her both his badges. Katya scrambled around in her large handbag for her passport.

The translator, a small woman in her late fifties, very thin and slightly hunched, examined the documents. She was scholarly, her wrinkled face obscured by large steel-rimmed glasses, fogged in the cold.

Her frowsy gray hair, fastened back with a rubber band resembled a bunch of tangled electrical wires. She wore clumsy looking snow boots and a gray worn coat two sizes too large. Abruptly raising her head from the documents, she frowned over her glasses, and then bent down, continuing to study them. It was freezing in the cooler, and they exhaled small clouds of moisture each time they took a breath. The temperature, the sliding door, and the stainless steel reminded Roo of the morgue. He was jumpy, thinking he might find a corpse lying among the squash.

"One can't be too careful," Eugenia Scott said, "I must be sure of your identity. I have been hunted for years and never know when they will find me." They stood, teeth chattering, while she continued to pore over the IDs.

"Miss Scott, I think you're safe. Why don't we get out of here? You must be freezing." He couldn't understand why she was so afraid. Who were they he wondered.

She started to protest, but seemed to think better of it and followed them back to the small cafe fronting the street.

"Please sit down," Katya said.

Eugenia sat two seats away from them, staring out the window.

"Can I get you something?" Roo said.

"Black coffee, thank you." She was brisk and businesslike.

When he returned with the coffee, she picked up the cup in both hands, blew on the liquid to cool it, and chugged it down. "Now, what this is about? I assume from your ID that it is some sort of criminal case. Believe me, I am only doing this for the money." Her accent was Midwestern, but there was a hint of something indefinably foreign and scholarly about her, as though she had grown up in a library or language lab.

Roo again explained that Katya's documents were a legacy from her guardian, and they urgently needed them translated. He started to give her more detail, but she raised her hand. "Enough. That is all I need to know for now."

"Let me inform you as to how this will work." She glanced in quick birdlike movements at the market door as a group of noisy students entered. "If you change my plan one iota, you will never see me or your papers again. But, of course, I assume you have copies."

She took the papers and quickly leafed through them, sternly wrinkling her brow. "You've made these copies at Kinko's, I would guess. If the contents interest me, I will translate. When I return the finished material, I will spend exactly one half hour with you for explanation, and then I must leave. You will pay me in cash then. Each time before departing, I will give you the next meeting time and place." She peered around again, suspicious of the obese checkout girl reading a magazine.

"Now we discuss my fee. I will want two hundred dollars in cash for each document, on the dot."

Katya said, "That's fine. I have cash with me."

Eugenia noted Roo's look of shock. "Yes, I'm expensive, but I need the money. Pushkin and I must get away from here. We want to retire, perhaps to a dacha in Florida, although I've never been."

Roo wondered vaguely who this Pushkin was. Maybe this odd little woman's husband was named after a Russian poet, but she didn't seem the type to be married. He was disappointed at this transaction, but they agreed immediately to all her conditions, even though he was reluctant to return to Columbus.

It would have been safer to have the papers translated all at once. This woman was so paranoid that this could take days, and they needed the information now. Gripping the papers in her tiny crooked hands, she shoved them in her plastic shopping bag, and leaning toward them, whispered, "North Market at Short North tomorrow at 1 p.m., when it is most crowded. I will work tonight. Maybe I will have something finished for you."

As they drove out of town, Katya hunched down in the seat, miserable and exhausted. "We know nothing about this strange person. How can we trust her?"

"We have no choice. It's the only way to find the archive."

They pulled onto I-71 and stalled in traffic for ten minutes, but then to Roo's relief, it thinned out. As they drove south, a large black Mercedes followed them out of the traffic, and kept pace a short distance.

He watched nervously out the rear view mirror until the car turned off at the last city exit. "Don't worry," he said, "I think we're ok. Ben Tyler, a friend, is meeting us to switch the truck for a car, in case the killers have spotted us."

She eyed him suspiciously, a note of doubt evident in her voice. "What about Detective Devlin? Will he help us?"

"I wasn't able to reach him, and it's too late now to try to contact him." He didn't tell her the secure phone number and e-mail were defunct. He had to keep trying and take the chance that they still weren't on anyone's radar, as Stumpy would say.

Ben was waiting for them at one of the crossroads. Katya stood back, intimidated, as they whooped and pounded each other on the back, in her mind a strange greeting. Ben looked fearsome, like a giant bear with his long bushy hair in a ponytail and his shaggy beard. He was dressed like the deputy sheriff in jeans, boots and plaid jacket, what she assumed must be local custom.

"Everything ok?" Ben said.

"Yeah, so far. This is Katya Marston. Ben Tyler."

He reached out and grabbed her hand. It disappeared within his giant paw. "Nice to meet you. Heard all about you." His dark eyes were lit with admiration. She tried not to shrink back, wondering what he had heard.

They quickly switched the luggage to an old green Chevy, more comfortable and without the manure smell. After the luggage was loaded, Ben picked up the book he had been reading from the front seat.

"You're reading *War and Peace?*" Roo said, surprised, trying to mask his amusement.

"Yeah, Fiona and I are reading it together most evenings," Ben said.

"Things are good?" Roo said.

"Yeah." He broke into a smile. "The registration's in the glove compartment. You stopping at Henny's for groceries?"

Roo nodded.

"I checked out your place, and put in some basic provisions, like salt, and cooking oil, but nothing fresh. You'll be safe stopping in at Henny's." Ben said.

"That's what I planned. Thanks."

"I won't call. We'll meet as planned. Come to my place if there's trouble," he said, clambering into the truck and driving off.

Ben's casual mention of Roo's place, of getting in provisions filled Katya with apprehension. Where was he taking her?

Chapter 37

Katya-Roo
Tecumseh County

THEY LEFT BEN and drove south for miles on the main highway, a straight strip through flat limitless farmland, dotted with lonely grain silos like spires of cathedrals. The landscape changed when they turned northeast onto a small secondary road and were suddenly plunged into a 19th century world. Flanked by rolling hills, large white frame farmhouses perched neatly on stilted porches, surrounded by snowy fields stitched together by fences, like the Grandma Moses painting in the gallery.

Katya was astonished when men, like patriarchs from a distant time, appeared on the landscape. Wearing black trousers, coats, and wide-brimmed hats, they were feeding large square blocks of hay to cows in the fields near the white barns. More bearded men in black hats and coats, driving horses hitched to small black carriages, passed them on the highway. The women inside wore bonnets that reminded her of Queen Victoria's mourning clothes.

"Where are we? Who are these people?" She at least had a right to know their destination. Trying to curb her panic, she stared out the window at fog rolling in from the distant hills.

"They're Amish. A religious community. They're strict, don't believe in violence or machines or modern dress, and live pretty much as they did when their ancestors settled here in the early 1800's. They're good people, and they know me. We can buy food here. They would never tell strangers about us." He was abrupt, and shifted nervously in his seat as they started up the hill.

"That's where we're stopping, The Crossroads, Heinrich Muller's store." He pointed to a small cluster of buildings consisting of Muller's cheese and sausage factory and the general store, selling hardware, grains, dry goods, and groceries.

"Henny lives a few miles from here with his parents and family. When we were small, we used to meet up in the forest with other boys and play army games, forbidden by the Amish." Roo parked near the fuel pumps.

They stepped inside the long low building, dark in spite of the large windows, facing the parking lot and fields. Two Amish men leaving the store glanced at them with mild curiosity. Bewildered, feeling as though she'd entered a time warp, Katya stumbled over sacks of feed and grain piled near the large wooden counter. Iron pots, pans, rope, scissors, and a mélange of household objects from a time before electricity hung from hooks above the counter. Two days ago she had been shopping for face cream in Saks Fifth Avenue and now she was in Heinrich Muller's General Store in the middle of nowhere hiding from killers.

Muller was a short stocky man wearing large bib overalls. His pale ginger beard covered the lower half of a very round face and emphasized sensuous red lips, a bulbous nose, and button blue eyes covered by coke bottle rimless glasses. He shook Roo's hand, nodding when he introduced Katya. "So you're back at the farm." His hard acquisitive blue eyes magnified by the glasses, examined Katya as he spoke.

"New car?" He jerked his head toward the Chevy outside.

"Yeah," Roo said, putting off any questions.

"You want groceries?"

Roo nodded and pointed to cans of beans stacked on a shelf behind the counter and to sausages hanging in a ring from the ceiling slightly to the left of the pans.

Katya searched around the dry goods and sewing materials for a telephone, thinking she might be able to quickly phone the gallery, but her hopes sank. There was none. She wondered what they did in an emergency.

"How long you staying?" Heinrich began packing in brown bags as Roo picked out things he wanted.

"Only a few days. I'm on a case and would appreciate it if you didn't tell anyone. I mean no one. It could be dangerous if it got around I was back."

"Sure," he said, still staring at Katya. She thought he was rude, even if he did help carry the groceries to the car. As they shut the trunk, he said something to Roo she didn't understand and let out a low whinny of laughter.

"Was that German?" she asked as they pulled out on the road.

"A dialect. I know a little."

"What did he say?"

Roo's face flushed. "Nothing much, only that we'd better hurry. The fog is coming in."

She guessed it had been a sexual comment. So much for his being religious. "How do you know that this Heinrich won't tell anyone about us?"

He looked straight ahead, "He's my friend and loyal to me. My Dad was born in this community."

Surprised, she sneaked a glance at him. She tried to imagine him in a beard and one of those hats, pushing a horse drawn plough or driving a buggy.

He blushed, reading her thoughts. "I was never part of the community, although I know most of them well. Dad left them before I was born and never thought of returning after he married and after Nam, because the Amish don't believe in killing their fellow men. They're very religious. If Henny gives his word, he means it. Don't worry about him."

She did worry about that odd man and everything else. She had never felt so alone, so lost from her own world. The fog was creeping in fast, growing thick, and partially obscuring the general store and the farms beyond. He turned on the headlights, and she caught glimpses in the window of sweeps of empty land and forest. "Where are we going?" she asked again.

"To the farm where I grew up. Now that my parents are dead, it's mine but I haven't lived in it for a long time. Everyone around here thinks it's empty."

"How far is it from the place where you found Christina?" Her question conjured up her own worst fears.

"About ten miles. It's mostly forest in between." A huge tear in the shroud of fog revealed rolling hills, still covered with snow, and a large forest of dark bare trees, brittle in the cold.

She cringed at the sight. "Someone could be hiding there."

"Yes," he said, giving her no comfort. He made an obvious attempt to change the subject. "We had a dairy farm, but my Dad liked the woods and kept acres of trees rather than cultivate. People thought he was crazy, but he said the forest reminded him of when the Indians lived here. When I was small he told me the old stories of the pioneers and Indians. Before he ..." Roo stopped, and made the turn onto a lane. The Chevy jerked back and forth on ruts and crawled slowly up the hill toward a farmhouse framed by two giant oak trees. It seemed to rise out of the fog like a hostile apparition, waiting for them.

"Are we staying here?" She was shivering violently.

"Yes, it will be safe." His voice was firm.

They stopped in front of the house, and the fog began slowly closing around them. The old wooden farmhouse was in a state of decay, its white paint scaling off like dead skin. A sagging porch trailed across the front. Its windows, bare of all but one shutter hanging precariously, glared at her, hostile, unblinking. A large branch of the oak tree by the drive held the remains of a swing. It moved slowly back and forth, as though a phantom child had just jumped off.

"Leave everything. Come with me." He took out his gun, and pushing her behind him, walked around the house, past the empty cornfields bordering the front and the right side of the lane. He took big strides, sniffing the air for smoke, his sharp eyes gazing into the clouded distance and then sweeping over the ground near him, looking for tracks.

Her insides thumping in a dreadful cadence, Katya stared into his broad back and stumbled along close behind him, exhausted and cold, trying to think of nothing, to make her mind blank.

Behind the house two empty barns and a grain silo, worn and scabbed, leaned together supporting each other like derelicts. Beyond them lay a small strip of field and then the forest. Shadows from the veil of fog flew at her when she lifted her eyes from his back. She heard whispers. Ghosts of the dead, she thought.

When they had covered all the ground thoroughly, he said, "I think it's ok."

She waited at the front of the house, while he drove the car into a barn and pulled shut the door. He carried their bags and the groceries to the sagging front porch.

She saw his face go white as he unlocked and pushed against the door, its hinges shrieking, as though something unspeakable hid inside. Torn cobwebs flew at them. The house seemed malevolent, as though it stored horrifying memories and did not want to be disturbed. It was very cold. The wooden floor creaked in protest as they climbed the stairs to the second floor.

They followed the same routine inside, mice scurrying at their feet. With Katya at his back, Roo went through the house. Off the small landing there were four rooms and a crudely installed bathroom. Three of the rooms were closed off with large boards nailed across the entrances. Back downstairs, he swept through the dining room, the old fashioned kitchen, and the living room.

"It's safe. No one's here," he said to reassure her. She noticed that the Formica table and chairs in the kitchen looked as though they were purchased in the 1960's. A wooden table stood alone in the dining room. The walls covered with faded flowered wallpaper were bare of pictures. Only a tattered calendar from 1988 hung crookedly above the kitchen counter.

Roo opened a door off the kitchen to steps leading down to the cellar and Katya backed away, stumbling over a chair. "Stay here, while I check," he said

Stiff with dread she listened to his steps below going into each corner. "Nothing. Just cobwebs and rats," he said, coming up.

"Rats! Oh my god," she said, again on the verge of tears. "Why are those rooms boarded off upstairs? Could someone be hiding in there?"

"No way, my dad closed off the rooms to save on heating bills."

He drew the limp faded curtains and turned on the central heating, installed when the farm had a prosperous year. Afternoon light filtered in ghostly patterns through the fog, slowly closing them off from the outside world.

He picked up her bags and motioned her into the downstairs bedroom. "This is my room. You'd better sleep here."

She sat on the bed, unable to move, listening to him opening cupboards. He returned with thin faded sheets and towels and threw them on the bed. "These are clean. I wrapped them in plastic bags."

"Thanks," she said, avoiding his eyes.

After he left, she pushed back the curtain a few inches and peeked out the window past the barns directly into the black of trees and thick gray nothingness. She quickly drew it shut, her skin crawling with pricks of fear. Fright moved her to action. She made up the bed, and unpacked the toiletries retrieved from her ransacked apartment. She placed them on the large chest alongside several photographs of a younger Roo and some trophies, one of which was engraved with the words *State Champions 1988 Paint Creek High School.* Another shaped like a football was inscribed *Reuben Yoder State Player of the Year 1988.*

In the Paint Creek High School team photograph, she picked out Roo and Ben, without his beard.

A framed newspaper article with a picture of Roo in football uniform announced that he had won a scholarship to Ohio University. So he was an athlete, which accounted for his strength. He was handsome in the photograph and looked happy in contrast to his usual serious expression. It seemed he had been destined for success.

Heat had begun flowing through the house, and she took off her jacket and went into the kitchen.

"Can I help?" She felt inhibited, shy.

His face had changed since they had come here. It was drawn and thin, his light eyes had grown dark with some obscure pain, and she found herself feeling sorry for him, not knowing why.

His smile was a slight grimace, "Well, I'm opening a can of baked beans and frying some sausages. I know it's probably not what you're used to, but it's quick. It'll soon be dark, and we can't have lights. No need to advertise our presence. Anyway, we have an early start tomorrow, and I have to get some sleep. If you want to shower, there's time before dinner."

"That would be great." She grabbed her cosmetic bag and followed him upstairs, recoiling at the drain odor when he opened the bathroom door. He pulled down the stained blind, showed her how to adjust the antiquated shower, and closed the door.

She undressed quickly, tiptoed over the cracked lino floor and into the shower cubicle, trying not to notice the mildew growing like fur on the tile. As hot water coursed down her body, she pictured him showering as a young boy after coming in from the fields. He was puzzling, rather cultured, in spite of his flat toneless voice. Growing up here in the country next to people who didn't believe in using electricity, she could hardly expect him to even be able to read. She left the bathroom, darting past the boarded up rooms. For one horrifying second, she thought she heard a faint noise behind one of the doors and fled down the stairs. Not wanting to be alone, she hurried into the kitchen.

"What can I do?" she said.

"You can set the table." He pointed to a drawer. She nervously searched for knives and forks in the mess of cutlery and cooking utensils, reminded in the awkward silence that he was a complete stranger. A faint melancholy howl from somewhere in the forest reverberated through the kitchen and she jerked, dropping a knife that clattered loudly to the floor. She started at the noise and quickly picked it up.

"Welcome to the Ritz," he joked, putting the pan with beans and sausages on the table. "We even have napkins, although they're paper. And I must add, the sausages are organic, cured by Henny himself."

He appeared to be joking but she burned at his mocking tone, and guessed he must have been offended by some of her comments.

"Help yourself." He handed her a large fork.

She forced a bright smile and to be polite, took more than she wanted, cutting a small bite of sausage. "Sheriff Yoder, I hope you don't mind, but I noticed your trophies and photographs. You were quite a star."

He lowered his gaze to his plate. "That was a past life. I'd forgotten that stuff was there."

"Was it lonely growing up out here?"

"You mean no shops, restaurants, or nightclubs?" That was a direct shot at her. "I mostly worked on the farm. We had a huge crop of corn and a big herd of dairy cows then. The rest of the time I spent in the woods with Ben and my other friends, tracking, hunting, and daydreaming. I read a lot in the evenings when I didn't have football practice or 4H and Grange meetings. My dad didn't like the time I spent reading. He said it didn't do any good if you were going to be a farmer."

"You were famous here. And a scholarship? Is that how you became a law enforcer?" She sounded false, overly friendly.

"No, it's a long story."

She remembered his Wordsworth quote and tried again, "Did you study literature at college? You must have." Her English accent seemed absurd in this kitchen.

His gray eyes leveled straight at her. "I didn't go to college."

Abruptly, he left the table, mumbling, "I just want to check." He took his gun and flashlight and went outside. She could see the light, frail and wandering in the fog, circling the house.

She cleared the table and washed the dishes, noticing that her manicure was chipping and thinking how little it mattered, how really inconsequential and shallow her life had been before Abigail's death.

He came back, looking relieved.

"Will they come at night? You think they'll find us here?" She had finished the dishes and stood by the bedroom door.

"I've been thinking," she said. "What if I give up this Blood Archive? Somehow tell these killers they can have it. It would be reasonable. Or we just quit searching for it. I am sure under the circumstances Abigail would understand. She wouldn't want me to be in danger. Then we can go back to our lives."

"They'll kill both of us anyway, for just knowing about it."

Her lip trembled uncontrollably.

"Let's see what Eugenia has for us tomorrow. This could be over soon. I think we should try to get some sleep."

"I hate to take your bed. Will you sleep upstairs?" Her voice quavered.

"No, here on the couch. It will be easier to keep watch."

She brushed her teeth, staring into the mirror. She looked faint, ghostly as though she was fading away. She might deteriorate out here in the hinterlands. She could disappear, and no one would know.

She rushed downstairs and found he was waiting in the hall. "Here, in case you didn't have time to pick up pajamas." He handed her one of his sweatshirts. "It's extra large and clean."

"Thank you," she said, giving up her attempt to charm him. She didn't care anymore.

She lay rigid in bed trapped in darkness, listening to the house come alive with faint whispers, and footsteps. It didn't help that this sheriff, who was supposed to protect her, disliked her, even hated her and thought she was a shallow, ridiculous tart.

Not entirely pleased with his behavior, Roo went upstairs to the bathroom. He supposed he had been surly but she deserved it. Why the fuck did he feel the need to explain to her, apologize for everything? He didn't know why he had to emphasize that the sheets and his sweatshirt were clean, like he was some untouchable.

He showered quickly, thinking that when they had first hit the country roads, he had been happy, back in his territory, but had underestimated his feelings about the farm. Coming out of the bathroom, he found a blanket in the hall closet and then was facing his parent's bedroom, their angry voices echoing inside. He hesitated, then pushed open the door and was smothered with memory.

It was the end of harvest, all the corn in. He had returned home from a date with Janey. They had made love in the back seat of his

Ford, and it was the happiest he had ever been. He stopped on the porch to look out at the moon and graceful silhouettes of the trees dark against the sky. Gunshots fractured the night. There was a splintering noise, screaming and then, silence. He ran to the house and threw open the bedroom door. His mother slumped in the chair, motionless, the gun on her lap. She was bleeding from a cut on her lip. Bruises like purple flowers blossomed on her face and neck.

For a moment he did not see his father's body crumpled in the corner, legs sprawled lifeless like a puppet, blood pouring from his chest. Then he was calm and moved as though sleepwalking. He checked his father's pulse and knew he was dead. He worked in a daze, taking the shotgun from his mother who had passed out, wiped off her prints, and clutched it as though he had pulled the trigger.

He remembered calling Stumpy and the ambulance. They took his mother to the hospital, and his father's body to the morgue. He was locked in jail.

Now standing in the dark hallway looking at the bedroom, the old sadness crept back, catching him unawares. The aftermath was even worse. His lawyer proved that his father was drunk and had attacked first his mother and then him. The verdict was self-defense, and he was set free. He had felt a terrible hurt. His mother had not protected him, had looked out for herself, and let him take the blame. He would have done so anyway, but there was no protest from her. It was so unnatural if you think of how wild animals defend their young. He figured that something must be wrong with him. After that, his mother, the daughter of a banker from a distinguished pioneer family, became a drunk and slept around. It was as though the residue of years living with his father had entered her body like osmosis.

Janey too deserted him, and he never discovered if her abandonment was because he had changed or the scandal was too much for her. Unable to bear Janey's betrayal, he descended into a state of near madness: blankness like an incomplete poem, fell upon him. Stumpy had saved him, forced him back to life by offering him the job. His old friend had said, "You know, you must always try to find a saving grace in your parents."

He slammed the bedroom door shut and clattered down the steps.

Katya was standing at the bottom, her eyes wide in fear.

"I heard noises. Were you talking to someone?" Her voice rose. "Is that why you're running? You saw them?"

She put her hands over her face. He grabbed her to him and held her.

"No, it's nothing."

"I can't bear it." She was incoherent. "Will you stay with me, sleep by me. You don't like it here, I can tell. Why can't we leave?"

"You're right. I hate the house. It holds bad memories for me, but it's the best place to hide from them. I know."

Looking slightly comic in his oversized sweatshirt, her hair askew, and at the same time beautiful, she still clung to him when he led her back to his bedroom.

He lifted her up and tucked her in, pulling the blanket over her long smooth legs. He felt himself grow hard, and his mind veered off crazily into images of kissing her, undressing her, running his hands over her. She interrupted his fantasy.

"Thank you," she said, her breath coming in shudders. "Tell me something, anything, to help me sleep."

He sat up in the chair next to her and began the story of Spybuck, a legendary Shawnee, who refused to leave the land where his ancestors were buried, and took a defiant last stand, holding out for weeks against the settlers. As he went on, he heard his father's voice echoing in his own. Halfway into it he realized it wasn't a good story to tell someone who was frightened. But before he arrived at the part where the settlers had cornered Spybuck, and he disappeared into thin air and became a ghost haunting the woods, she was asleep.

He checked again around the house and then returned to the warmth of the bedroom, and settled in the chair, his gun by his side, a blanket covering him. He was too worked up to sleep. Tomorrow Eugenia Scott would have the translated document that could lead them to the archive.

Chapter 38

Katya-Roo
Columbus

THEY TURNED OFF I-71 onto High Street in heavy traffic through downtown Columbus. The skyscrapers rose out of the flat land like modern grain silos climbing out of the fields, dwarfing the small low houses. The cars steamed like cattle in the cold as they passed the Arena Crossing Apartments near the new hockey stadium and parked at Spruce Street next to the North Market, a cavernous renovated Quonset hut crammed with small specialty shops. They were early for their meeting with Eugenia. Roo nervously looked over the area, passing Best of the Wurst, specializing in sausages, Black Creek Farm Produce, and Benevolent Bakery.

He hurried Katya to the huge elevator, up to the second floor gallery with a view of the parking lot, street and the entrance and shops below.

Katya waited at one of the tables, placed around the edge of the gallery and watched the deputy sheriff go downstairs, checking every aisle for danger. She thought of the past two terrible days, grateful to be away from that house and in a normal place. Despite his kindness last night, it seemed odd that he didn't try to find out what had happened to Maxi after his phone call. The real reason she supposed was that he didn't care. They might locate the archive today, and she would be returning immediately to New York so Maxi's phone message didn't seem to matter.

He placed muffins and tea on the table.

"Thank you," she said. There was coolness in her voice.

Thinking of last night, an uncontrollable anger at her aloofness swept over him. "When are you going to start using my first name instead of Sheriff Yoder? It should be Deputy Sheriff Yoder anyway."

She slammed down her cup, spilling the tea, her eyes lit with golden sparks of anger, "When you stop using boyfriend to describe Maxi."

"Isn't he your boyfriend? Aren't you sleeping with him?" He scowled, had wanted to say fucking him, but restrained himself.

She stabbed at the pool of tea on the table with a napkin, and turned away from him watching a mother with two little boys at the next table.

He took a savage bite of muffin, wondering how he could be having this conversation when a hit man could be somewhere in the busy market waiting to strike. It was funny how you got used to danger; how it didn't seem real and other things still mattered, like did she really love that pompous fuck, Maxi. He didn't ask. Eugenia Scott was creeping through the entrance below. He ran down the stairs to get her and led her to a chair beside Katya and asked if she would like something.

In a vain attempt at disguise, the translator wore a flowered headscarf that drooped over her strained wrinkled little face. She nodded, pointing to the muffins. "I'll have the same." She did not remove her coat and clutched her plastic bag to her chest, only slightly relaxing her grip when Roo brought her bran muffins and hot tea. Her eyes were wide, surprisingly beautiful, a soft pale blue behind the steel-rimmed glasses.

Still on the edge of her chair Miss Scott pulled off her scarf letting her hair escape, but did not remove her woolly gloves with the fingers cut to the knuckle like a market vendor. Biting with relish into her muffin with tiny white sharp teeth, she finished it quickly, nervously dabbing her napkin around her mouth. In a birdlike movement, she slightly inclined her head, ready to begin.

"Some of the material is written in Old Russian. The author was quite a scholar. Even I, who have worked on some of the most esoteric Russian documents, struggled. At first I could not believe what I was reading. It is so outlandish. Through the night I checked the text many times to ensure the words were correct."

She took a sip of tea, then dug into the plastic bag and brought out the paper. "It is a very odd document, and to say the truth, I have been thinking it over since coming to this market. I do not wish to continue. This could be a KGB trap." She darted quick glances at them, while rummaging in her bag for the remaining papers, placing them neatly on the table.

"I dislike intensely the contents of this document and have concluded that the author, although a scholar, is unbalanced. And of course, even if the translation is accurate, it may not be true. If you pay what you owe me, I shall go now."

"Please," Katya said, impulsively reaching out and touching her hand. "Please help us, we need you. We must know what is in all the papers."

Roo said, "Don't worry. It concerns only a legacy left in someone's will. It has nothing to do with you." He tried to curb his impatience. "We're leaving Columbus as soon as the translations are finished."

Eugenia hesitated. Thinking it over, her face transformed with a lovely wide smile. "You're right. It does concern the past, and I am only the translator. I will take a chance, mainly because I like you."

She patted Katya's hand. "It is very lonely being a translator. But I must ask for an increase in my payments."

Katya opened her handbag and brought out a wad of bills. Roo was shocked that she carried so much cash.

"Thank you." Eugenia beamed, leaning forward and counting the bills in her lap. "Five hundred is very good. Pushkin and I need it to get away." She expertly rolled the bills into a tight wad, put a rubber band around it, and placed it inside the plastic bag. "No one will know anything of value is in there," she said to reassure herself. She drained her cup and then settled in.

"Now we can continue. What I abhorred from the beginning was the document's title 'Krov Arkhiv'. Just seeing it written on the paper brought on an attack of nerves, and I needed to take my calming pills."

"How does that translate?" Katya asked.

"In English, 'blood archive'. But I am not sure if the meaning in this case is blood by murdering or blood that is family descent. But you will see."

Eugenia stopped abruptly and gaped in horror at the next table occupied by the mother and her children. The two boys were standing on chairs throwing food at each other, hitting the wall behind them. Both of them had straws sticking out of their nostrils and their blond hair was dotted with chocolate cake.

Their mother, clumps sticking in her long golden hair, was making vain efforts to stop them.

Eugenia muttered, "They have turned into monsters in front of my eyes. Just like the Bolsheviks." Her hands fluttering in agitation, she placed her neatly typed translation on the table beside the original text.

The Blood Archive.

The words seemed to leap from the page.

If this document is translated, I am gone, murdered by the unscrupulous beasts willing to commit any atrocity to grasp the way to power.

The Blood Archive, Krov Arkhiv I, holds the Tsar's Last Ukase, an official edict issued in secret in 1918 by Russia's last Tsar Nicholas II before his death at the hands of his Bolshevik captors. This edict, the law of the land, is so powerful that whoever finally possesses it will have the means to rule Russia. For over thirty years, I have hidden the ukase from murderers who want to use this powerful tool for their own evil purpose.

The page ended, and Eugenia wordlessly pointed to the next one.

The Archive includes official documents, which validate the authenticity of the Tsar's Ukase. It also contains a detailed account of my involvement with this dangerous edict.

"This could be Abigail," Katya whispered.

After my years of extensive research to create the archive, I have drawn the conclusion that the Tsar issued this last order in the hope that one or more of his heirs might be rescued. This final edict would provide the means for any descendant of the Tsar's family who might have survived the massacre to reclaim the Russian throne.

Christina Gartner, Archivist.

Chapter 39

Katya-Roo
Columbus

THE MURDERED WOMAN'S words, unreal in the bustling
atmosphere, hung in the air. Roo and Katya froze, stunned by the
message, oblivious to Eugenia's distress at the two boys rampaging
around their table. Abigail had said her legacy held a secret from the
past, but Katya had not dreamed it would be something so powerful
and deadly. For a moment, the market noise faded. Downstairs, people were buying food, browsing, but they seemed to be moving in
another time and place. Whatever was happening to her was not attached to the normal everyday world. It was as though the archive
was pulling her back to the past.

Eugenia shrieked when one of the boys came close and tugged at
her chair.

Roo, recovering from the initial shock said, "What do you think
of this *ukase* story? Could it be true or just a hoax?"

Eugenia, distracted by her terror of the two children, who were
now circling tables on the other side of the room, straightened her
glasses, and finally answered, "This description of a *ukase* is out of the

ordinary, but possible. Documents from the past are always coming to light. But what exactly could this unusual edict be? I have no idea."

"You didn't find out more about where the archive might be hidden?" Roo asked.

The boys had been shepherded out by their mother, and Eugenia sighing with relief, quickly regained her composure. She drew herself up in a huff. "No, there was not one syllable concerning the archive's location in the document in front of you. Do you question my expertise or my honesty?"

"Oh no," Katya said, "It's just that we were expecting to find out where it is hidden. We thought the document would be more ordinary."

"I understand that." She was mollified. "I also was surprised as I was led to believe this was a mundane translating job."

"Is it really possible that a direct heir to the Tsar could be alive?" Katya said.

Eugenia paused, thinking. She seemed hesitant. "Yes, it is possible. Any heir would, of course, be third generation. Indeed, I have a great deal of knowledge of the Romanov family. For many years, I worked as a researcher for the great historian Anatoly Sergeievich Serov who specialized in the Russian Revolution and the Romanovs' downfall. And then my own Papa also had a great interest in the subject."

"Please, tell us what you think," Katya said.

Eugenia drew her tiny self up importantly as though delivering a university lecture. "There are many different accounts of the family's imprisonment and murder. It is very complicated because of the political situation in Russia in 1918. The country was fighting WWI during the revolution, and the Germans, the enemy in the war, defeated and occupied much of Russia. Then a civil war for control of the country raged between the Bolsheviks and the Whites." She stopped for a moment and looked suspiciously around the room before continuing.

"I am sure Lenin and most of the Bolsheviks planned to kill all the Romanov family to make a clean break with the past. They didn't want a figure to unite their opponents. The Bolsheviks, still a minority, used terror to hold power. They were ruthless, torturing, and killing." Roo nodded. He had read about this in Devlin's books.

The translator looked off into the distance, into the past. "Lenin would have planned to save some of the Romanovs, only if he were holding them to bargain with the Germans, the Allies or private persons, relatives of the family. We also know the Bolsheviks were short of money, and the Germans helped finance their way to power.

"But when World War I was over, and the Bolsheviks took control of Russia, Lenin would have had no use for any of the Romanov family, and then would have eliminated them." She made a sharp cutting movement across her throat.

"Do you think that's what happened?" Katya said.

Eugenia sighed, "I can only give my learned opinion which differs radically from the generally accepted theory. I believe Lenin's plan to kill all the family went wrong, and one or more of his royal hostages escaped his clutches. Any survivors would, of course, have been forced to hide from the Bolsheviks for the rest of their lives."

Roo stirred, restlessly wanting to go, thinking this was irrelevant. "I don't understand why their deaths or survival can't be proven one way or the other."

"You must try to imagine those times," Eugenia said. "In 1918 Civil War was raging. The Bolsheviks had begun the systematic killing of anyone who was of the nobility or middle class. The Tsar and his family were imprisoned in Ipatiev House, in Ekaterinburg, Siberia. Toward the end of their miserable existence, the guards had become more radical and hostile. It was very hot that Siberian summer, and the family was cramped together in the house. They were not permitted to open windows, which had been painted over to block any view of the street, and were allowed outside for only a few minutes of the day." Her low rasping voice carried them back to that house of terror.

The bustle of the room faded, and Katya pictured them suffering in the heat, knowing that death waited.

"In the early hours of July 17, 1918, the family and servants were awakened, ordered to dress, and taken to the cellar. They were lined up as though for a photograph and shot by the Cheka, the Russian secret police. In spite of rumors that some of the family survived, it is generally accepted that all were murdered that night."

Hunched toward them in her chair, she was oblivious to the clatter around her. "Two days later, the White Army entered Ekaterinburg and drove out the Bolsheviks. White officers immediately went to Ipatiev house to look for the Romanovs. There were bullet holes and bloodstains in the cellar, but the family had vanished.

"There were many investigations into their fate, two by the White Army, some independent, others funded by the Romanov relatives. But most émigrés and even the Soviets have accepted the findings of the White investigator Sokolov. His report, published in France after he fled Russia, concluded that all the family and servants in Ipatiev House were executed and buried near the Four Brothers Mine on the outskirts of Ekaterinburg near the village of Koptyaki.

"Sokolov's report contained a list and photographs of many of the family's possessions found in one of the mineshafts. The photographs of the murder room walls marked with bullet holes and stained with blood supported Sokolov's theory, but the family's fate remained a mystery. Investigators dug up the mine and the area nearby, finding remnants of clothing, teeth and even a severed finger, but no bodies." She raised her hands as if to emphasize this point.

"Then, the Bolshevik's deliberate refusal to explain what had happened to the Romanovs created more confusion. Rumors that some family members were alive swept across Siberia. I have read eyewitness reports that the Empress and the Grand Duchesses were seen in Perm after the reported executions. There were sightings of one Grand Duchess trying to escape on a railroad car. No one knows the truth. Six years after the family's disappearance, the Bolshevik government formally announced that all had been killed, but rumors persisted that some of the family survived and they continue to circulate today, fueled by Russian claimants." She sank back in her chair, exhausted by her speech.

"But didn't they find the bodies of the Romanovs?" Roo said. "I read it in the paper."

Eugenia nodded her head. "The mystery appeared to be solved in 1989. Several newspapers reported that the bones of the Romanovs had been found in the woods near Ekaterinburg. After much controversy, samples of the bones were sent to the Forensic Science Service at Aldermaston England in 1992 for DNA tests, which confirmed that they were those of the royal family. This conclusion is generally accepted, but I do not believe this." Her eyes snapped with indignation. "I am convinced that finding the bones was all a ruse on the part of the government and the KGB. People who live in the West are too naïve. One has to be aware how that brutal organization distorts facts. Believe me I know from experience."

Roo wanted to ask her about her experience, but she went on. "In 1998, the day after Yeltsin's inauguration as President, the bones were buried in St Petersburg's Cathedral of SS Peter and Paul at a service which most of the Romanov family and even Yeltsin attended. This burial settled the entire question for the public."

She frowned and leaned over the table. "You must realize. One can never believe what is said officially in that country. The Bolsheviks and those who followed them always made it a virtue to lie to their enemies. It is enough to say that the KGB handled the investigation. No matter that they changed their name to FSB, they are still the same killers. It was in their interest to find the bodies and solve the case. There were questions concerning the validity of the DNA tests and accusations that the tested bones were taken from graves of other Romanovs. Some claimed that the evidence was contaminated. I believe all these claims to be true."

"It also was reported the remains of two Romanovs were missing. One of them was the Tsarevich, the other, one of the Grand Duchesses. Experts are still debating which Grand Duchess."

Her face grew red, hot with indignation. "I have been expecting for some time that the Russian authorities will miraculously find two more bodies, and using the same fraudulent methods, attempt to prove that they have found the remains of the Tsarevich Alexei and the Grand Duchess. Frauds, they are frauds." She raised her voice, causing two women who had just sat down with their food, to stare at them. "They are liars. Never, never believe them."

"But why would they do something like that? Who would this benefit?" Katya said, taking a sip of tea and realizing she had let it grow cold.

"The Russian government would look competent, responsible and most important, human, to the world. But inevitably there would be money involved. Hah!" she said in disgust.

"But doesn't that leave the way open for anyone to possess and use the document if they could find it?" Roo said, "Even claim to be the rightful heir? Some crooked politician could announce this to the world in a PR coup."

"You are absolutely correct," she said. "And this is why I am afraid," she lowered her voice to a whisper. "To do so would mean that everyone who even knew about the Tsar's order would be eliminated. They are *Besy*, bestial monsters, lying in wait out there."

"But it was so long ago. And even if one of the Tsar's children survived, it surely couldn't be relevant today?" Katya said, trying to be rational.

"Ah my dear," Eugenia said, tilting her head. "The past never goes away. It is a sly creature always lying in wait to capture one."

"I don't know how important the *ukase* is now. But anything is possible since the end of communism." She shrugged her shoulders. "Every day I read all information on the internet about the New Russia, and surprising as it may seem, there are several movements or parties in the country who would like to capitalize on the old Romanov connection."

She looked at her watch. "But I have gone over the thirty minute limit. Next time, you come to me. I have been upset since I discovered the dangerous material in the translation. But I sense that you mean no harm and have begun to feel trust in you. You must have guessed by now that I am Russian, although I was very young when I came here." She smiled shyly.

"I would like that, to learn more. You are so knowledgeable about Russia," Katya said.

"My house is not far from here. Here is my address. We will have a genuine Russian tea. Give me another day to work on the remainder of the material. Come at 10:30." Then she leaned down to them and whispered, "My Papa spoke so often about the Grand Duchesses that they became my imaginary sisters. It was unspeakable what the guards did to them during those last days in prison. The poor girls were not even permitted to use the toilet without one of the beasts accompanying them. One can only imagine." There was fear in her eyes as though she had been there to witness their agony. "There was no one to defend them from the guards. They were all alone."

Chapter 40

Roo-Katya
Columbus

ON THE WAY to the car, Katya burst out, "I don't understand this. Why would Abigail be involved in something like this? She was always so practical. And what does this have to do with me? Why would this archive be my legacy? Christina Gartner doesn't explain how she acquired the *ukase* or how Abigail became involved. She doesn't even mention Abigail."

Roo started the engine and said, "At least we have a motive for both murders, no matter how crazy. When we find the archive we'll have the answer."

"Eugenia warned us that anyone who knows about this could be murdered."

Would anyone believe this? He could hear the mocking sound of New York cops laughing at his report. It wouldn't be great for his reputation. This hokey story had seemed preposterous until Eugenia echoed Kutusov and the countess claimed that there were important Russians with a serious interest in reviving the monarchy.

And then Stumpy had once remarked, gently patting his comb over, "Politicians will promise or do most anything to get elected. Even me."

He looked over at Katya, mentally tracing her slender nose, the delicate curve of her cheek. Her eyes were closed, and a frown furrowed her brow. The letter and Eugenia's story of the Romanov deaths had shaken her. He was jittery too, disappointed that the letter hadn't revealed the archive's location, and irritated that Eugenia refused to translate all the documents at once. It grew more dangerous for them every time they met with her.

Tiny white specks of snow began hitting the windshield like bb pellets and he put on the wipers. As they approached the small crossroads off I-71 he welcomed the sight of Ben's dark bulk waiting beside the car. He would run the story past Ben. His buddy was full of common sense.

Katya opened her eyes, surprised at the stop.

"Come on, we're changing cars again," Roo said.

Ben had been waiting and brushed the snow crystals out of his dark hair and beard.

"You guys all right? You look like you've seen a ghost."

"We're ok. I want to talk to you. Get your opinion. Let's go to the Oaks." He hurried Katya into the gray Ford Escort, and Ben followed them in the Chevy. They drove for a few miles on a country road until they reached the edge of the highway, roaring with traffic, and stopped at the Oaks Restaurant, a square plain brick building with red checked curtains at the windows and a large sign at the entrance advertising homemade country cooking.

"It's all right. We're safe." He reassured Katya as they got out if the car. "We can talk to Ben and eat an early dinner."

The Oaks was spare, very clean, furnished with plain wooden tables and high booths. It smelled of roast chicken and coffee. They sat in the back in a wooden booth, away from the large front window,

Roo and Katya on one side, Ben on the other. The highway buzzed in the background. A group of women who looked like schoolteachers occupied a booth in the front, and two salesmen drinking coffee sat at another table. Katya gawked at the waitress, a pleasant looking elderly woman, dressed in a long cotton lavender dress and apron, her gray hair drawn back in a bun and covered with a white net cap.

Roo whispered, "She's Mennonite. Not as strict as Amish."

She placed paper mats in front of them, then brought over the coffee pot from behind the counter and poured before taking their order. Roo and Ben had chicken and mashed potatoes with a side of slaw. When Katya ordered only a salad, the woman smiled, creasing her plump cheeks and said, "My dear, you are going to waste away."

They went over what they had learned that day from Eugenia, and Ben listened, astonishment on his face. Roo waited for him to say 'total bullshit'. Instead he stared off into space, took another mouthful of potatoes, and said, "If I didn't know the background I would say it's all complete horseshit, but important secrets from the past have been hidden before. It's not totally out of the question. You know it has to be about money."

Katya picked at her salad, then put down her fork and said, "Eugenia's a nice person, but a little unbalanced. Do you think she's telling the truth, that she actually translated what was in the paper?"

"You can always get another translator to check," Ben said.

"It's too late for that. Besides, there was no reason for her to change what was in the document, however crazy she seems," Roo said.

Ben efficiently cut into his chicken and ate it with more mashed potatoes, ruminating, then said, "And so, thirty years ago, these two young women, with no connection to Russia, somehow became mixed up in this."

"Yes, we believe they became friends when Christina married Lawrence Digby and moved to New York. Abigail Townsend and

Lawrence's family traveled in the same crowd, and Abigail was a Harvard classmate of Digby's." Roo dug out a photograph of the two women at a party at Andy Warhol's Factory. Ben put down his fork and studied the picture.

Roo said, "After 1970 there is no record of Christina's existence until she comes out of hiding in 2000, posing as Adelaide Safford, buys the farm and then is murdered on the property. The last trace of her after the divorce is her move to 82nd Street in Manhattan, next to a Russian woman named Mme. Feodosia Antonova. It is strange that both disappeared from their apartments in April of that year. According to the landlord's records, Christina's apartment was burgled just before she vanished."

"There is something else I found in police records. Mme. Antonova was on the missing person's sheet. Christina reported her missing." A savage gust of wind hit the front window, threatening to blow it out.

"Russians again," Katya said, her face tense and pale. "You didn't tell me that."

The waitress cleared the plates. "The special dessert is home-made apple pie." Both men ordered it with mounds of ice cream.

Roo said, "We can only speculate that Christina came into possession of the *ukase* during that short time after her divorce and before her disappearance. We can assume that she was hiding from her killers then and created her archive. I believe she asked Abigail for help."

"Where do you think she could have hidden this archive?" Ben said, tackling the pie.

Roo sighed, "Almost anywhere in the United States. We found a Jeep Cherokee under a tarp at the side of the cabin, registered to her alias, Adelaide Safford. It's possible that the archive was large, and she used the jeep to haul the documents."

"But she could have hidden them long before she arrived at the cabin." Katya said, despairing. "We'll never find it."

"I know. That's just one possibility. The only other clues we have, not counting the Russian documents, are Abigail's letter, two keys labeled Number 10, and a crumpled piece of paper," Roo said.

"And since you think both women were murdered by the same man, I guess you have to look at all the suspects for Abigail's murder." To Roo's surprise, Ben didn't dismiss the weird story and had become intrigued with the mystery.

"Yes," he said, "Petrosian, an Armenian émigré, tried to buy into the gallery and was angry that Abigail refused his offer. He runs a car wrecking business and had the means to dump Abigail's body in the Trade Center ruins. Ranulph von Burkhardt is also under police surveillance."

"You're kidding," Ben said, grinning at the name.

"No. He's also Russian, of Baltic descent and runs the Volk gallery. He had a falling out with Abigail." Roo described their visit to von Burkhardt's apartment. "He certainly has an inclination for torture."

Katya sank down in her seat, in disgust, reminded of her night at RUS. The bite marks had faded, but not her sense of humiliation.

"Then there's Kayakov, another Russian in business with Suvorov, part owner with Katya of the gallery. He's head of a protection business called the Brotherhood. Interpol says he works for some crazy in Russia called the Shaman who runs a religious cult and maintains a military force somewhere in Siberia. I have no real evidence against him, but just have a feeling." Roo showed him the photograph.

Ben whistled in amazement. "You couldn't make this up. Could they be working for someone else or in partnership?"

"Either, but we have nothing concrete on any of them. The killer could be someone entirely different, unknown to us."

He stopped short of mentioning Suvorov as a suspect, knowing it would upset Katya. He was hoping Devlin had found the scumbag and brought him in for questioning, but he was worried about his boss. Why hadn't he contacted him? Why had he cut him loose?

He put down his fork, leaving some of the ice cream and reflected aloud what had nagged at him since he found Christina's bones. "There is something else that really puzzles me. In the cabin, there were two crystal goblets and a bottle of champagne, opened just before her death. It seems like she was welcoming someone, maybe someone she loved. And yet, she had a shotgun and didn't hesitate to use it. Either a stranger arrived or the man she knew was both her lover and killer." A loud warning horn from a truck on the highway blared through the restaurant, and Katya jumped at its sudden alarm. Roo could see how she hated talking about this, how it frightened her, bringing back Abigail's terrible death.

Roo slid out of the booth. "Time to go. We want to be back before dark."

Before they left, Ben jumped out of his car, walked over, and motioned him to lower the window.

"I went by earlier today to check on your place. Everything seemed normal." He frowned, his black brows beetling together. "I did find a footprint in the back yard between the old milking barn and the house, but figured it was yours."

"Probably mine," Roo said. "I just forgot to rub it out." He was puzzled. He did walk there every night patrolling the place, but always took care to cover his tracks.

"You seem extra jumpy," Ben said.

"No real reason except for what you just told me."

"I'll check back through the woods." Ben took his twelve-bore shotgun from the Ford's back seat.

"Sorry, forgot. Chains are in the trunk. It's going to be a heavy snow tonight."

"Thanks for everything Ben."

Katya was distraught. "It still doesn't all make sense. I can see how Abigail could have helped a friend, but how do I fit in?"

"You are part of the mystery," he said, half joking but knowing it was true.

They stopped at the general store to fill up the gas tank. While they were inside paying, Henny stared out the window at the Ford Escort, obviously curious about the change in cars, but Roo offered no explanation.

He was edgy, driving slowly on the back roads, already coated with a layer of snow. He'd put on the chains in the barn in the morning. He went over everything in his mind. The killers could have found them.

Chapter 41

Mikhail
South of France

MIKHAIL SANK BACK in the Humvee, his hand resting lightly on the last section of the French Files on the seat beside him. Relief overcame him; he had secured the only copy of the record of his life.

When the Humvee slid back onto the highway, he smiled grimly at the high shriek trailing off as they gathered speed. His men were sending the little cunt Lev into a deep final sleep. In the next few hours while the Humvee rolled toward the South of France, they would complete the black work inside Bradford's Removals, burying pieces of Lev in different isolated wooded spots, and abandoning his Jag. As reward they would keep the suitcase with Boris' payment that Mikhail had handed over to Lev.

After Lev's call, he had dispatched a squad to Albania, to take out Boris, the archivist holed up in Tirana's best hotel. Two more hit men made a quick trip to Paris, and with three bullets ended Mirov's career.

Now that Boris was eliminated, Mikhail possessed all documents relating to his past.

Revived by these reflections, he switched on the light, and turned to the folders in *Section B* marked classified, sealed in 1978. He broke the seal and opened file *R103. Dossier: Mikhail Borisov.*

Suddenly dizzy, his spine tingling, he eagerly leafed through the thick file; it contained his entire life history. He would spend time later, going over it carefully.

Attached to the front of his dossier were three additional documents stamped *S540-1.* He blinked in amazement. These were Stalin's personal papers, stolen years ago by the Raven, from Central Party Archives and still classified material even today. He pressed a button and growled an order for Shamil to slow down, so he could read carefully. The first was a typed report to Stalin.

February 8, 1924.

He stopped for a moment to consider the date. This would have been shortly after Lenin's death, when Stalin was scheming for complete power.

We have reports of subversive communities of religious sects hiding in isolated areas of Siberia. Some members of these sects are followers of Rasputin and the Khlysts, and other radical religious groups. Living among them are class enemies of the revolution, some nobility who fled St. Petersburg, and White Guards who disbanded after the Red Army's glorious victory over Kolchak's Siberian army in the civil war. We are immediately beginning another campaign to find and destroy these wreckers, enemies of the people.

Mikhail opened the window, staring up at the clear night sky, feeling the cool air cross his face, puzzling over why this report to Stalin was included in his personal records. He continued reading.

Regarding this subject, I recently contacted Vladimir Bonch-Bruevich whom you know well as Lenin's former personal assistant and a loyal party member. Bonch-Bruevich, a distinguished scholar, compiled and edited two volumes of materials and documents on the history of Russian Sects, among them the Khlysts, Dukobhors, and Old Believers.

During our meeting we *discussed his books, published in 1907, which I have read.* He *mentioned that in the course of his research on sects, he had interviewed Rasputin. The report follows.*

Your most loyal comrade, Felix

Felix could only be Felix Dzerzhinsky, fanatical head of the Cheka. His forbidding statue in front of the Lubyanka had been torn down after the fall of the Soviet Union.

Khlyst Sect

Khlyst, which means, whip, is the name given to the Khlysty by out-siders because of their forms of self-punishment, which include flagella-tion. The sect calls its members True Believers. Outlawed by the church and state before the revolution, the Khlyst sects exist mainly in isolated areas of Russia, particularly Siberia. They live in communities called Arks, led by a man and woman they believe are the Mother of God and Christ. The sect believes that first they must sin, and then repent and when forgiven, they possess the Holy Spirit within them. Members are forbidden to have sexual relations except on 'rejoicing days'.

During these religious celebrations, they whip themselves into orgiastic frenzies, dancing and whirling, and ending with promiscuous sex.

Children born after this rejoicing period are thought to have the Holy Spirit within them.

It is widely rumored that Rasputin adopted many of his beliefs from this group, a rationale perhaps for his immoral sexual behavior. It was said that there was a Khlyst underground place of worship in his cellar in his village of Prokovskoe in Siberia.

Mikhail stirred, rustling the papers. The face of Dzerzhinsky, thin ascetic, crazy eyes of a fanatic appeared like a shadow in the window. When Mikhail joined the KGB agents still called himself Chekisty, and believed the first chief's rule; Chekists must be pure and free of corruption. It was only later he realized that Dzerzhinsky's use of *Chistka*, 'cleansing', meant killing.

He hurried on to another report from Dzerzhinsky to Stalin, eight days later.

February 16, 1924

Dear Comrade Stalin,
As requested, I have directed the Cheka to search in isolated areas of Siberia for one specific group of Khlysty led by a reactionary, a White sympathizer called the Elder, aka Pavel Navikov. He left St. Petersburg for Mongolia in 1918 while we were arresting all enemies of the people. We believe he may have traveled with one of the escaped subjects, the most wanted of all the outlaws, a focus of the resistance movement.

He stopped, took some water from the refrigerator, and drank it down, wondering why the escaped subject had not been named. Who was this subject described as the most wanted?

*We must find this subject in order to destroy the resistance movement
and to ensure the revolution succeeds. We know that Navikov met
with Baron von Ungern-Sternberg in Mongolia and left shortly after
the baron was captured by the Red Army and hanged. We have heard
rumors that Navikov, the Elder, is now living with the Khlyst group
in a remote village somewhere in Siberia. The man is known as a great
healer, a Blood Stiller, who learned his art of healing from Rasputin.
Navikov is a dangerous enemy of the people, capable of fomenting resistance. It is my conviction that his fame as a healer will lead us to his
sect, and he will be eliminated.*
Your most loyal comrade, Felix

Mikhail's hands shook when he put the file back. He was faced
again with the mystery of his shadowy past. Was the Ark, described
by Dzerzhinsky, the same community where Kosloff had taken him
and Sasha? Could the Elder be the same man who had welcomed
them that day in the forest clearing; the man who had named him
Noch?

It was possible that Navikov hid from the Cheka from the revolution to the 1950's.

Another document, *B1040*, had been lifted from records of the
former all-powerful head of Russia's security services, Lavrenty Beria.
Dated March 1953, after Stalin's death when Beria was in control of
the government for a short period, it was a Politburo directive calling
for amnesty to over a million prisoners in the Gulag. It also stated
that armed prisoners at the Dalstroi complex rebelled at being denied
pardons and escaped.

Mikhail took deep breaths; the sudden memory returned of the
stick men who came to the Ark and killed the True Believers. They
had been escaped prisoners. He did not know why the Raven had
included this information, but it could be a warning. He saw them,
their brutal faces, tattooed bodies, arms and legs like dry kindling.

Could one of the stick men still be alive and remember him when he was *Noch*?

Emotionally exhausted, he slept as a defense against the past, keeping his file close to him, while the van moved smoothly on the highway. By early morning they were in the South of France, driving through the Old Port of Nice to the harbor and his yacht.

When they pulled up to the dock, the acrid smell of burning wires filled the air, illustrated by a curious small plume of black smoke. Grabbing his assault rifle, he rushed onto the deck with his men, cursing himself that he had moved to the yacht before adequate security had been installed. The usual sounds of the crew working on deck were absent and there was that singular unearthly silence that accompanied death; a silence he often experienced in the past after completing a job. He motioned the men to search below and heard their feet pounding underneath him. His eyes followed a streak of blood, a trail that dripped off the edge of the yacht into the water.

He waited on deck for a few moments while his men examined the engine room, and the communications center, both trashed, his expensive weaponry stripped. They reported that most of the yacht had been reduced to an empty shell, and the crew was gone. Dead, he knew.

He ordered his men to the remaining staterooms and hurried down to his own quarters. His only thought was of Marousia. She had begged him to let her move early to the yacht, saying how much fun it would be, and foolishly he had given his permission. He cursed again out of fright, and his steps slowed as he entered his bedroom. He put his gun to his side and stopped transfixed with horror. Even though he was inured to violence and had committed acts of unspeakable brutality, he choked at the sight and vomited. He supported himself against the wall, trying to comprehend. It was as thought he had passed some boundary and was dealing with more than a killer, a kind of madness incarnate. Propped alone on the pillows, still warm, slender and beautiful, sheathed in a red net stocking held by a lace garter was Marousia's severed leg.

Chapter 42

Mikhail
Courchevel, France

Noch, you have been foolish. You sinned when you refused to answer me. Punishment followed. Shame about your beautiful whore. I left you a small piece of her as a keepsake, a reminder of my power over you. I am the one who knows all. I know where the woman Katya Marston is and will soon have her. You have no chance now. The ukase belongs to me. You must obey me. You must give up the search. Soon I will come for you.

The Shaman

Mikhail crouched, waiting for the nausea to pass. He had suspected at first that the brutal attack on the yacht had been the work of one of General Letinov's hit squads, but with this message he knew he was facing a creature more deadly than an ordinary hit man. There must be something in his own dossier, some connection that would lead him to the identity of this Shaman.

He wiped his face with his handkerchief, averting his eyes from the computer screen to the large window of his chalet and the untouchable mountains, the purity of the deep snow. He must hunt this creature down and destroy him. It would be difficult. His only information on his adversary had come from Interpol. Despite using all his old contacts in intelligence he had come up with nothing new on this threat.

After the yacht murders, he realized the house in St. Paul de Vence was under surveillance, and had retreated to his chalet in Courchevel, easier to defend because of the mountains and his arsenal of lethal weapons. Bébé had taken care of everything, closed the yacht, and bribed the authorities. Workmen took several days to install reinforced steel doors and infrared laser monitors. He also had demanded extra electronic fencing and a bombproof room. Wires and cameras were concealed in every room of his charming Alpine chalet. Still he did not feel safe.

Taking up his pistol, he went downstairs to communications, next to his security room down the hall from his large gym and swimming pool. Although not as sophisticated as his set up in St. Paul de Vence, it was adequate.

It was ironic that he had become the prey. His eyes grew darker, more reflective, as he tried to control the rampaging panic, and restore his mind to some semblance of cold logic. He reasoned that the Shaman had first located Katya Marston early in January, but had lost track of her and now perhaps knew less than he did about her location. And then he had the advantage; he possessed the French File. Even though his mug shots had appeared on his computer screen, the Shaman did not have his records or he would have used them without going to the desperate measures of killing Marousia and his crew.

He had hired two more men from Little Odessa in New York to find the girl. Both Lato and Stepan had been tracking specialists for Spetznaz before signing on as his private hit men.

Downstairs, he nodded to the two technicians on duty and watched the blinking screen.

They had first picked up a cell phone signal on a highway going west from New York, and then had tracked Katya Marston and her escort, a minor law officer, to a market in Columbus, Ohio. Arrangements had been made to pick them up and bring them here.

Satisfied with the results, he went upstairs to the kitchen and made a cup of tea from the samovar placed there, and gazed out over the mountains. He noticed the tiny dark tracks of a marmot that had passed near the chalet. He walked across the hall to his office, picked up a key from the desk drawer, opened the secret compartment in an old mountain chest, and took out the metal box containing the French Section B files which he had not read. Lifting the lid, he found himself staring at an old folder labeled *Romanov: Classified*. Curious, he broke the seal on the folder and leafed through the yellowed papers.

He was brought up short by a handwritten order from Lenin to the Raven.

1918 Moscow.

Confidential: Keep the subjects alive. They are needed as pawns to deal with the Germans who are eager to rescue them. Rumors have come to me that before his death, the bloody Tsar Nicholas II issued a secret ukase hidden by his followers. It would be beneficial to have the criminal Tsar's last order in party hands.

Take care of your health. The party needs you. Ilyich

Lenin's use of Ilyich, his less formal name, indicated the Raven was an intimate of the leader. Mikhail paused, forgetting his own danger for a moment. He was amazed that Lenin too had searched for this document realizing its importance. He went to the next report to Lenin, recognizing the Raven's elegant scrawl on the expensive paper.

1921, Harbin, China.
After July 1918, subjects were under house arrest in old headquarters near Perm. With your authorization they were removed, and the story circulated that they escaped, aided by White Guards. One was disguised as a boy. Re: your request, I found no trace of the Tsar's last ukase. I left Mongolia soon after, and am now in Harbin. Have learned from reliable sources that the subject has vanished, believed to be dead.
The Raven

He was astounded that his controller, a colleague of Lenin's, had been involved with the Romanov family after their imprisonment. It seemed unlikely that the Bolshevik spy would hide any of the Romanovs from Lenin or later Stalin. He believed the Raven initially had hidden these documents to protect himself.

Mikhail rose from the chair and put the file away. Then he ordered Anya to bring him tea and bread. Sudden tears came to his eyes as he chewed the dark bread thoroughly, slowly, as comfort. When he was a child that one piece of precious bread had to last. He paced back and forth, knowing he could no longer put off a thorough examination of his personal file, no matter how painful.

He picked up his dossier, his life drawn out on a map like a perilous journey. As he read he hunted desperately for some mention, some clue about his parents. He looked impatiently through official prison files to his last release, his examinations and entry papers to the KGB. There were records of his brief posting in Vietnam when he had stolen the identity of Jack Reilly who had been killed along with his entire platoon, and then, the details of his failed mission to find the *ukase*.

The letters moved erratically across the page as he read the graphic description of his forced return to the Lubyanka and the interrogators and then his tour to Afghanistan. Recorded conversations included those during his brief affairs while he was making love. He was overcome with melancholy at the sterile record, no home, no family or relatives. "Nothing but a specimen under a microscope," he said aloud, shifting through the papers until he came to the appendix labeled 'Early Childhood' with two attached documents. The letter, handwritten on thick bond paper, was dated 1951 but there was no location.

My Dear Kosloff,

I know I am your hated enemy, but think of the Brotherhood and do this for your cause. I have located the all-important subjects at Kolyma, Prison 45 Kilometre. The chief administrator of the prison notified me. It will be a great sacrifice, but I ask you to rescue them. I will arrange that you cross the border without trouble and take passage on a boat from Magadan to Vladivostok, where an army truck will be waiting for you. I cannot be associated with this rescue. If you are caught I cannot help you. The future depends on this. We must act before Stalin, our great leader hears of it.

Mikhail's heart drummed in fearful anticipation. This was about him. He was one of the all-important subjects.

I must warn you that Stalin, whose paranoia has grown to epic proportions, received a letter from a woman named Vera Tolmatov, a prisoner in Camp 45 Magadan since 1946, notifying him of the existence of the subject. I know you are aware that I am acting out of self-interest, but surely it does not matter if you are able to save the subjects. Full details to follow if you agree to the mission. The Raven

He jumped up and paced the room, hardly able to believe it. "Kosloff," he said aloud, reviving the memory of the block of a man with a flat eastern face who took him and Sasha from the Zona to the village. For a moment, he is a child soaking up Kosloff's warmth, watching him driving the truck. He sat down hurriedly, picking up the next document.

Order 50, issued 1954.

It directed local police in Irkutsk to search for two boys who had disappeared from a religious community called the Ark. They were reported to be living among the *besprizornye, the lost ones* in the railroad station. Mikhail suddenly realized that the Raven had ordered the raid on the homeless children in the station to find him. That day haunted him. He had been one of the lost ones lying in wait to attack the well-dressed man who got off the train. Feral, grunting, the pack swarmed over the man, ripping at his clothes, clawing at him searching for money and food until his terrified squirming ended in death. Gunshots rang out, scattering the pack. Some were caught and beaten with clubs. Sasha lay on the ground by the truck, all life gone. Mikhail's anguish and heartbreak haunted him.

Most shocking to him was the letter he found addressed to Andropov, head of the KGB and then head of Russia's government. This was the man he had called 'the professor', who took part in his interrogation in the Lubyanka. His interrogation and confession were attached.

April 10, 1978
My dear comrade Yuri Vladimirovich,
I believe we now have the understanding that the subject known as Mikhail Borisov, real identity unknown, will be rehabilitated and re-instated in the KGB, perhaps appointed to a province where he will not

be noticed by my enemies, or better still, to an undercover assignment in Afghanistan. I am in complete understanding with you that this will not save me, but am sure he will prove useful in transferring some of my personal network.
Your comrade and friend, the Raven

Mikhail's head was spinning. Putting himself at risk, he unlocked the glass door and stepped outside onto the terrace, startling two chamois with huge antlers crashing through the trees. "Is this true?" he shouted to the frightened animals, to himself, to the world. He stood motionless, a small dark figure against the sky, inhaling the cold clean air, watching birds soar and land safely on the trees. It was clear that the Raven, his controller whom he had hated and feared all these years, had saved him from death. The old Bolshevik had removed him from the Gulag, rescued him from prison and then placed him in the KGB, hiding him among the enemy.

It was as though he had been lost in a wilderness and finally discovered the open trail, the secret to the old Bolshevik's true feelings. The words of the proverb the Raven had written on the file came back to him.

The soul of another is like a dark forest.

Chapter 43

Katya
Tecumseh County

THE SNOW WAS falling in thick wet gobs when they reached the farmhouse lane. Katya stared out the window; dark shadows of her own fear moved past in the whiteness and in the sinister sticks of trees cracking in the wind. She reluctantly went inside while he patrolled the area with great care.

He came in as she was going up to the bathroom and said, "I found no footprints, but the snow could have covered them." Katya looked with growing panic into the bathroom mirror. Part of her face had disappeared into the stark glare of the bare overhead light bulb. She was fading, like overexposed film, a mere shadow of herself.

Eugenia had said something scary about the past, lurking, waiting to catch you. She believed it. Her thoughts returned to the Romanovs shut up in that house waiting to die. Maybe it was the translator's suggestion, but again she sensed that some threatening past was invading her, crowding out her present existence.

She heard movement outside, and crept over to the window, pulling the blind to one side to look out. The wolf stood a few feet from the house, its ears pointed, its light gray eyes looking up at her.

The twilight cast an orange glow on his thick, snow covered ruff. Then she caught a glimpse of a shadow looming near the edge of the barn and quickly dropped the blind. Her heart clattering around in her chest, she ran down the stairs, knowing she had to tell him even though they hated each other.

The sheriff was in the kitchen and turned toward her, scowling. "What is it?"

"I heard a noise, saw a shadow by the barn, but it could be nothing." Her voice was high and breathless. She realized it would be her fault if they were found.

"Get ready to run," he said, taking his shotgun and creeping out the kitchen door. She grabbed her jacket and bag and sat rigid in a kitchen chair, studying the cracks in the lino, and the picture of the forest in autumn on the old calendar for what seemed an eternity, until the door opened.

"There was nothing out there." He scraped the snow from his boots and put his gun down on the kitchen table.

Without a word, she went to the bedroom, closed the door, and lay down on the bed, not bothering to undress. After an unbearably long tense period, exhaustion crept over her, and she was drawn slowly into a strange dreamlike state, as though going into a past memory.

She is walking in the upstairs hallway of the farmhouse. Whispers and movement emanate from behind one of the boarded rooms. Then she is inside the room. It is very hot and stuffy. She is surprised that the windows have been painted over, and she can no longer see into the forest.

In the semi-darkness, she becomes aware of shadowy figures moving restlessly, and straining her eyes, makes out three girls and a boy in strange old-fashioned costumes. She looks down and finds to her amazement, that she is dressed in similar clothes; leather boots, a long skirt, and a white long sleeved high-necked blouse. The phantom figures in the room are strangers to her, but they seem to know her. They wrap their wraithlike arms around her, and whisper to her but she doesn't understand. There are distant sounds of laughter and boots stomping.

"The guards are next door. You can hear them." The girls' whispers become clearer to her. With growing horror, Katya realizes they are all prisoners.

The door flies open, and a girl is thrown into the room. She has a wild harried look, her hair is undone, her fine linen blouse is open and her skirt is ripped. Clots of blood drop out from under her skirt onto the floor. They all cry soundlessly, shaking with grief and fear. The girl points to the room next door.

"They do not care. I heard them. Soon they will take us to the cellar and kill us."

There is a knock. They huddle together watching the guards, smelling of alcohol and sweat, crowd in at the door. Their strange unformed slabs of faces with insect eyes stare at the prisoners; they are drunk and violent, smashing bottles on the floor, laughing and cursing at them. Katya sees the men's eyes on her body, knowing something bad has happened to all of them. But what is it? Thick arms reach out and grab the smallest girl, dragging her out of the room.

One of the girls wraps her arms around her and whispers, "Be brave. Soon they will come and knock for you." For a moment Katya sees her clearly. She is blond, with almond shaped eyes in an oval, beautiful face. Katya reaches out to her but she fades like the others into nothing.

"But what is it?" She begs the shadows in the corner of the room.

"What is it?" she woke up screaming, stiff with fear, traces of the phantoms still before her.

"It's all right."

She was looking into the face of the deputy sheriff.

Chapter 44

Roo
Tecumseh County

THE RISING SUN came like a knife slit through the torn curtain, and Roo woke with a start, stiff from sleeping in the chair, still
worried about the footprint Ben had seen even though he had found
no trace of it. He put on his jacket and boots and again walked the
entire area in the half-light, but discovered only the wolf's prints in
the heavy snow, which had fallen overnight. He passed the milk barn
and heard a faint banging noise. He stopped still for a moment; the
killers could have traced them here. Then he realized it was an echo
of memory of his Dad dropping the milking cans and cursing after a
long night of drinking. He had to keep calm, think like a professional
even though nothing in his life had prepared him to dodge hit
squads.

As he made his way back to the house, he supposed Katya did
love Maxi and was worried about him. He supposed she had let him
hold her out of fear after her nightmare. It suddenly occurred to him
that he had not thought of Janey except to remember that he hadn't
thought of her for days. Maybe those years of living with memories

of Janey had kept him safe from getting involved with anyone else. He shrugged. That's exactly what Ben claimed.

His mind clear from the fresh air, he opened the kitchen door, wiped the snow off his boots and went into the warmth. He looked in the bedroom. She was sleeping peacefully so he closed the door softly and went into the kitchen and made coffee. His thoughts returned to the archive. He took out Abigail's letter, the keys, and the crumpled paper from his bag and placed them on the table next to his shotgun, then read the letter again. The one clue, Tecumseh's Forest, seemed obvious, but it did not mean the archive was hidden in Tecumseh County. The great Shawnee leader had roamed over large areas of the territory in his efforts to unite his people, so his forest could be anywhere in at least four states, if that was what Abigail meant. He sighed, discouraged.

The painting of Tecumseh, captured by the artist in all his majesty, had stirred him. He felt a kind of mystical kinship to the famous chief, a true noble savage. He closed his eyes, recalling the background with the small figure stepping into the vast impenetrable forest and wondered if that was a clue or there was something else in the painting he had missed.

"Too late," he muttered, picking up the wrinkled paper. It was jagged on the edges and looked old, almost like parchment. He smoothed it out on the kitchen table, and opened the curtain. Bright sunlight streamed through the window, illuminating it and Roo noticed for the first time, very faint markings, straight geometric lines on its surface.

He quickly took the paper outside to the front porch for better light. A thump caused him to reach for his gun and crouch down, but it was only a branch felled by heavy snow. He rose and brushed the snow from his knees, still holding the paper in one hand and saw, in the distance, the wolf standing at the edge of the forest. He nodded; acknowledging the bond between them, then took the paper in both hands, examining it carefully in the bright sunlight. There was another mark that resembled a faint circle. He studied it for some time. Then he rushed in to wake Katya.

He sat down beside her on the bed and showed her the fragment again. Her golden hair was down around her shoulders, and he couldn't help being dazzled by her beauty. He remembered caressing her forehead the previous night and stifled his urge to crush her to him.

Instead he said, "I am almost sure this is part of an old map. I discovered some faint lines like markings of territory."

His excitement at the discovery was dimmed by her reaction. She appeared dazed, as if still trying to erase her nightmare.

She finally said, "They could have discovered we're hiding here. How do you know the footprint Ben found was yours? Shouldn't we leave and check into a hotel?"

But Roo wasn't listening. "I don't know for sure, but I think the circle at the bottom might be a compass."

"But how will we possibly find out if it really is a map and then a map of what? It could take years," she said in despair, pulling the covers up around her.

"We'll try the State Library map section." He knew it was a risk to keep going into Columbus. He had wanted to meet with Eugenia today but she had insisted on more time.

In the car, she touched him on the shoulder. "You saved me from going mad last night. Thanks." There was warmth in her eyes, and she smiled "Can I call you Roo?"

"Yeah, that's fine." He didn't take his eyes from the road.

"I would like it if you called me Katya." He had avoided using her first name and felt color rising to his cheeks. For the first time he believed they were in this together. He would never let anything happen to her.

Chapter 45

Roo-Katya
Columbus

ON THE WAY to the library, Roo went back over Christina's bizarre letter, wondering how she had become involved in a conspiracy so dangerous that her life was threatened. He pictured her hiding out, growing old alone, head bent in front of the computer, obsessively constructing the archive. Checking in the rear view mirror, he saw a black car turning onto the road, following them at a leisurely pace toward downtown Columbus.

"Someone's tailing us. Get down," he said, taking out his gun and placing it in easy reach on his lap. Katya quickly crouched down below the window.

The Mercedes was weaving toward the pavement. Roo pulled over into the library driveway, and waited as the car slowly meandered past. He managed to glance in the window, and let out his breath. "It's nothing," he said, smiling, feeling stupid.

The driver was a tiny elderly woman, barely able to see out the window. Her head was visible only when the car hit a small bump. He had been spooked by Eugenia's nervousness and her stories. It still seemed unlikely anyone could have traced them, even someone following them from New York. Katya raised her head. She had stopped wearing any makeup, and looked even more beautiful, her skin luminous in the morning light.

They parked in the underground lot and ran up the stairs to the main library, a grand restored federal style building. It was Monday morning, and the place was empty except for a homeless man, who slept stretched out on two chairs in the main reading room. Momentarily conscious, he rose up in alarm when he saw them, shielding his face, then sank back into his stupor.

A small dapper man with tiny squeezed features, like an apple crushed in a cider press, stood behind the enquiry desk. A nametag penned to his navy blazer identified him as Cyril Cutler.

"Hi folks. Can I help?" he said, pressing together his soft hands, destined from birth to leaf through books.

Roo explained that they wanted to look at old pioneer maps from 1760 to 1800.

"That's a very unusual request." Cutler gave them an enquiring glance as he led them to an area with long map drawers and asked them to wait. He returned a few minutes later, shaking his head, his face even more compressed in disappointment.

Patting his dyed blond hair into place, he said, "Sorry folks, but we don't have anything from the period you want. Can I ask exactly what you have in mind? If I knew I could maybe be more help."

"Isn't there another library that might have old maps?" Katya said quietly, sounding very English. Cutler stared, openly curious.

"What about the OSU Library or the State Historical Library?" Roo said.

The librarian frowned, his features disappearing into tight little creases. "They may have something, but you might have more success if you try Len Bowers, a friend of mine who deals in old maps and documents. He's an expert. His shop is in the Short North Area, not far from the market." Cutler wrote down the address. "Len's a great guy. He also deals in guns, just to let you know. You won't find him at the shop today. He'll be getting ready to go to Carl's Bar on South High. He goes about six or so. It's kind of rough there. Carl Schmidt's a Vietnam Vet, a former Marine and a lot of those guys hang out at the bar. Many of them haven't adjusted. Lots of fights there."

Several hours later, after failing to find anything remotely resembling the old paper in map collections at the University and State Historical Libraries, they decided Len Bowers might be the best bet. In an attempt at safety, they drove through Clintonville, a peaceful tree lined suburban neighborhood. Dark angry clouds blew across the sky like the breath of a ferocious beast, threatening to swallow up the small charming bungalows. Katya watched two women walking dogs, and a man and woman, dwarfed by the vast clouds, resembling miniature toys, cleaning snow from their drive. Near the curb, children had built a snowman, complete with hat and cane. Its melting face seemed to glower malevolently at her, a grim reminder that she existed somewhere outside the safety of this suburb, in a limbo of fear.

Forced to wait until they could meet Bowers, they stopped in late afternoon for lunch at a neighborhood restaurant. The North Star was a cheery modern spot furnished with long wooden tables, and benches, and an entire wall with racks of magazines. The menu suited Katya, and she ordered a Buddha Bowl, with vegetables and tofu, and herbal tea. Roo had a flat bread pizza with fruit juice. They found one of the smaller tables in an alcove, past two women in sweat suits sitting on stools in front of the restaurant reading magazines. Just across from them, three men worked on computers. Katya took a long breath, relaxing in the peaceful atmosphere. It appeared so safe, so commonplace that it seemed an illusion that Russian hit men could be lurking in these suburban streets.

She sipped her tea and said, "This will take years, not hours. It could be that it isn't even a map, but just an old piece of paper

Abigail put in to throw the killers off." She stared out the window at the grey darkening sky and flinched as passing traffic threw up black vile looking slush.

Roo kept his eye on the street. He fidgeted, taking out the fragment. "It's these very faint markings I didn't notice before that make me think it is a map. It looks very old." He mused aloud, "This is about as far as you could get from anything Russian and probably the reason Abigail used it as a clue. The killers wouldn't have any idea who Tecumseh was."

He absently finished his apple juice. "Maybe Len Bowers can help us."

"Isn't there some way for you to get in touch with Devlin?"

He reached across the table and grasped her hand. "I didn't want to scare you, but I haven't been able to contact him. The phone and email have been shut down."

She gasped and tried to take her hand away. For an instant, the cars on the road outside blurred into threatening unformed beasts. "I am so scared. Couldn't we try to reach him through the gallery or Maxi? They could get help."

Roo shook his head, and tightened his grip on her hand. "I just don't trust anyone right now. We'll wait until we find the archive."

"Then what happens?"

"I'll go after the killer, and you can go home to Maxi."

She turned to watch an attractive woman about her age, wearing a sweat suit, fill up her coffee cup and pick up another magazine from the rack. So safe.

"I know you want Maxi to come get you, but it is too dangerous. You really love him, don't you?" It was more of a statement than a question.

"I don't know." She seemed to be telling the truth. He had caught her off guard. "I think the only person I have ever really loved was Abigail."

Surprised at her answer, he felt a rush of happiness. She must have mixed feelings about that slime ball.

His question about Maxi had made her bold. "You have everything about me on your files. But what about you? It doesn't seem fair that I know nothing about your life. Have you ever loved someone?"

He looked out the window again at the passing traffic, the headlights reflecting on the greasy street, and then down at his plate.

"I loved this person, but it's been over, at least for her, for years." He was still holding her hand. They sat, not speaking for a long time. A clatter beside them broke the mood as the waiter cleaned up the table where the men with computers had been sitting.

Then guessing what was on his mind, she said, "What will we tell this Mr. Bowers?"

"Nothing about the archive. Only that we're trying to find out if the paper is part of a map."

"And this bar? Mr. Cutler made it sound dangerous."

"You'll be safe with me." He squeezed her hand before he released it and looked at his watch. "Let's go."

They waited until 6 p.m. in the parking lot next to Carl's Bar. Katya knew he was protecting her only because this was his first important case. He had said his main objective was to find the killers and the Blood Archive was connected. Although it didn't make sense, she felt hurt and disappointed that his motives had very little to do with her. She studied him in the half-light. He was wearing his plaid lumber jacket and jeans, and she admitted almost grudgingly that he was attractive. There was something endearing about his football injuries, the bump on his nose, and the scar on his forehead. He was more forthright, she thought and maybe more masculine, less polished than the sensuous Maxi. It was absurd, but she felt a momentary regret that she had not met him at a different time in her life.

Her feelings were unreasonable, she knew. She was involved with Maxi, cared about him, but at this moment longed for Roo to take her in his arms and hold her. The bad things he had read in her file made this scenario impossible, and she sensed he just felt sorry for her.

Carl's Bar, a low structure of soiled brick, leaned like a forlorn vagrant into the growing darkness, at the edge of a glossy chic urban renewal area. Its large front window, cracked down the middle, was encrusted with several decades of dirt. The temperature had dipped and shafts of freezing wind coughed up papers, beer cans, and trash along South High Street. The curb was lined with shiny pick-up trucks.

"Do we have to go in there?" Katya said, hanging back.

"Yes," Roo said, opening the door to Shania Twain singing *Love Gets Me* and the sound of boots stomping in rhythm. The music was coming from a CD player on the edge of the long bar. In the middle of the room, clouded with cigarette smoke, men and women in western dress were moving across the floor like a chorus line, led by a tall man swathed in white from cowboy hat to boots.

"How odd," Katya said wrinkling her nose at the strong smells of beer, cigarette smoke and sweat. It was like stepping into a Wild West movie. The threat of unpredictable violence seemed to hover in the clouds of smoke.

"Line dancing," Roo said, "It's very popular here." They went to the battered dark wooden bar, which ran the length of one side of the room and sat on the high stools. There was a stir as two men gazed at Katya, making comments just out of earshot. The bartender, a large stout man, had lost his left arm to his bicep, and a series of safety pins held his shirt around his stump. He manned the bar efficiently with his right arm, tucking glasses under his left armpit, serving with his right.

"What'll you have?" His mean black eyes were suspicious. A scowl spread like muddy water across his round doughy face topped with a grizzled crew cut. Roo turned to ask Katya, his voice lost in the song. *That love gets me, My heart changed my mind.*

But the bartender interrupted, "And what about you, pretty thing?"

"A mineral water please." Katya said.

He leered at her. "Don't carry that, just pop."

Roo translated, "That means a soft drink."

"I'll have a coke," she said. Roo ordered a Bud, his head crowded with the music. *Must've been the way he walked. (gone and done it) Or his sweet sweet talk, (gone and done it.)*

Two men sitting next to them, eyes on Katya, insisted on introducing themselves. Hank was tall and powerful, his hair slicked back from his forehead emphasized his dark bony features. Don, whose build and demeanor were similar to Carl's, was bald, and had a nasty smile on his thick lips holding a cigarette. He said, "Pleased to meet you," all the while undressing her with his eyes. Katya tried not to recoil, and nodded hello.

"Are you Carl?" Roo asked when the bartender slammed down the drinks.

"Yah, so what? Who are you?" Carl scowled and picked up his cigarette resting on the edge of the bar. Katya noticed large rings of sweat circling his shirt at the armpits and cringed under his gaze that lingered in coarse admiration.

"I'm Deputy Sheriff Yoder. This is Miss Marston." He held out his badge.

"Yah, so how can I help?" Carl drew on his cigarette and blew out the smoke through his nose.

"We're looking for Len Bowers."

"That's him over there. Queen in white. He thinks he's fuckin' Roy Rogers."

The music ended with extra stomps, shouts and clapping and Len came to the bar and took a long draw on his beer.

Roo and Katya walked over. Roo said, "Mr. Bowers?"

"Yep. That's me." He was a large hard muscled man with eyes that squinted as though scanning a prairie for rustlers. The diamante decorating the hat and cowboy shirt sparkled. A holster belt with a huge shiny buckle completed his outfit.

"Deputy Sheriff Yoder and Miss Marston," Roo said.

"How'd ya do? Lord, you're a pretty missy." He tipped his white hat to Katya, ignoring Roo. "Have you come to dance? The next one's good for beginners. Thirty-two counts. You just line up with the rest of the ladies, across from me. I'll show you the Grapevine." He flashed a smile. "I'd sure like to give you a twirl."

Roo stepped in front of Katya. "Mr. Cyril Cutler at the library said he was a friend of yours. Said you were an expert on old maps and you might be able to help us."

Len's smile faded. His eyes narrowed and his mouth became stern.

"What ya got?" His dark eyes were sharp with interest.

"It's a torn piece of paper that we think might be part of an old map, but we don't know for sure," Roo said.

"Let's go over there." The room had been cleared of tables for the dancing. Len led them across the floor; a field sprouting old cigarette butts, to a forgotten table in the far corner away from the bar. Even in the dim fluorescent light, Katya recoiled at strange gobs of yellow and red stains stuck on the walls, a vivid record of past fights.

"You comin', Len?" A thin woman dressed in a fringed pink cowgirl skirt and shirt and matching boots, dark fifties spit curls surrounding her brightly painted corn doll face, pleaded for the group lined up and waiting for their star.

"You go on, Candy. I'll join in next time." Toby Keith's, *A Little Less Talk, A Lot More Action* rang out across the room.

Len turned to them. "You got it here?"

Katya took the paper from the folder and handed it to him. "Could this be a map?" she said above the stomping.

Len smoothed the fragment on the table with long tanned hands and studied it with interest. The door opened and slammed shut and two men dressed in black suits came in, ordered drinks and sat at the bar. Roo knew they were strangers and as Stumpy would say, stood out like sore thumbs.

"All of this looks like someone's just made squiggles," Katya said, "How will we ever know?" She looked up, watching the dancers advance across the room.

"No pretty missy, not squiggles. This is a map all right, and it's no fake." He held it up to the light. "Primitive. Yes." He shouted above the music. "Even in this light, I can tell by the paper that it's probably 18th century but can't see much else. Could be valuable. That's all I can do tonight. Come by my shop tomorrow, say around noon. Did Cutler give you my address?"

Roo nodded, thinking finally they might be on to something. He watched one of the men in a suit come out from the toilet and go toward the bar, bumping hard against Hank as he passed.

"We have an appointment in the morning, but can be there by noon," Roo said. A crash and screams of pain from the bar drowned out the music. Hank and Don had kicked the strangers' bar stools out from under them, and they writhed on the floor like fishing worms on the hook.

The dancers tripped around the victims, Candy making a last twirl as they dodged the men on the floor and came to a stop. The music died to the sucking sounds of collapsing flesh as Hank and Don's boots pounded the screaming men. There was a brief silence from the dancers before a noisy hubbub began, and the two regulars left the bar.

Len said, "Christ, he shouldn't have messed with those two. They're as mean as shit when they're drunk."

"See you tomorrow," Roo said, hurrying Katya toward the door. As they stepped over the two prostrate bodies, he looked down, frozen for a moment. One of the victims had a gun tucked into the waistband of his trousers. A rush of adrenalin dizzied him before he pushed open the door and ran with Katya down the street. It was a Makarov, a Russian pistol.

Chapter 46

Mikhail
Courchevel, France

MIKHAIL SAT AT his desk oblivious to the view from his window and studied the ordinance maps. Circles were drawn around sites in Columbus, Ohio where Katya Marston and her companion, identified as a deputy sheriff, had been seen. On the Tecumseh County map, he traced the larger circle in the extensive forest, the area within a hundred mile radius where she was believed to be hiding. He threw the map down in disgust and stared at the flames gobbling up the logs in the stone fireplace. The maps were no guarantee. Her capture could still go wrong. The Shaman's men may have found the hideout; or she and the deputy sheriff could escape again.

He turned on his computer, knowing an email from the Shaman would be waiting for him. The message, crackling with energy, coursed through him like a lightning strike.

Noch, I still remember your face just as you turned and went away, leaving me bleeding and dying. You were my brother and abandoned me to die even though I begged you to stay with me. They took me away and tried to kill me over and over. I survived because I have the power,

the inner light. Noch, you must yield to me. You must understand the
extent of my great power. Den is coming for you.

Sasha's pale face, his wide eyes a fathomless white, passed before him, on that hot dusty Siberian summer day when he had left him in the truck. He paused. The high jagged mountain peaks seemed to loom closer, advancing ominously toward him, dwarfing his men on watch. The message beckoned.

You must give me the archive to fulfill The Elder's prophecy. You be-
lieved we were brothers, but I used you as my tool, a strong body with-
out a soul, to do my bidding. Now you must again obey.

Mikhail jumped away from the desk and stood as though in a seizure. The fear flowed deep in his veins, in the pumping of his heart. He had not connected the messages, the use of his old name. He had not thought it possible Sasha could be alive. He had seen him motionless, a tiny figure, lying with the dead on the ground in front of the truck. The Raven had told him he was dead. How could he explain, after all his brother's suffering, that he had gone for help?

Tears stung his eyes. A hurt like no other gripped him. He did not want to believe Sasha had murdered innocent Marousia and was coming for him. Yet the rational part of his mind knew the man was his enemy, controlling an army of convicts, mercenaries, willing to commit any atrocity to come to power.

Where had Sasha been? Shut up in prison, back in the Zona all these years? Did torture and deprivation turn him into this insane killer? They had been lost boys and had become monsters, created by the system. Mikhail knew he too was soulless. It was true.

Fumbling through his book collection, he picked up *Tales of the Heroes.* He desperately needed to revive the cloudy happiness of living at the Ark. Removing the book's protective cover, his racing heart slowed; the pages would take him back to the safety of those years.

Before opening the book, he stopped for a moment, remembering the information in the Raven's files on the Elder who had fled the Baron's camp in Mongolia and hid in the remote Siberian village. The Elder, real name Navikov, had been a devotee of Rasputin, part of the Romanov inner circle before garnering his own following, and could have been aware of the possible survival of a Romanov heir. A sudden revelation came to him. The Elder had believed Sasha was that designated one.

For all these years, Mikhail had never been able to recall exactly what had happened at the Ark. The dim impression of happiness he experienced there had been an illusion, something he wanted to be true. He had faced every kind of imaginable death in Afghanistan, but now quaked with fear. His hands trembled as he slowly opened the book to face his true memories.

Idyllic scenes passed in front of him: the deep blue of the sky, the birch trees, the beautiful golden domes covered in snow, the elders in colorful dress. Memories, once a vague blur like slowly developing film, rushed back, assaulting him. Then he is *Noch* again, the outsider.

Taking deep breaths, he turned the page, forced into the picture. Frightening scenes in black and white passed before him. They carry Sasha into the village square to be worshipped. In the center of the circle, his frail limbs writhing, he cries out the prophecies. They listen to his strange speaking in tongues when he sees the light, the Rapture. He rises up from his trance, pointing with his tiny hand, accusing one of the terrified adults in the circle. Then the beatings of the guilty begin.

He tried to blot out these memories by quickly turning the pages. There is Sasha, the favorite of the Elder, using his power to heal, stopping the flow of blood from a man's dismembered arm. The followers believe in his power, believe he is the chosen one.

The time of the Rejoicing frightens him, and he hides during the wild dancing. Sasha stands in the middle of the forest, surrounded by the men and women. He cries out, "It is the Rapture." Frenzied, tearing off their clothes, the naked men and women fall upon one another.

Mikhail closed the book, but the terrifying images remained. The stickmen with the strange marking on their bodies emerge like goblins from the trees. Even though he is a child, he knows that they are without pity when they overrun the village. Sasha, so small and frail, sits in a circle, drinking with the men.

After the killings, he and Sasha run away into the forest. The last picture he remembers is Sasha bent over the Mother of Christ, the kind woman who took care of them. He wields a large hunting knife in his tiny hands.

Chapter 47

Roo
Columbus

THE KILLERS WERE here. The foreign thugs beaten up last
night in the bar had been trailing them. Hank and Don, the barflies,
had unwittingly saved their lives. Menace drooped in the clouds, in
the black crusts of dead snow marking the highway. The landscape
passed in a gray blur as they sped up I71 toward Columbus and
Eugenia's house. The Ford Escort coughed like a consumptive even
though Ben claimed he'd overhauled the engine.

Katya had withdrawn into frightened silence and he tried to
think of something to comfort her. Last night, after they left Carl's
Bar, a cold fear like the sharp wind had cut through him. A killer
could be outside waiting for them, and he had driven wildly in the
darkness. The car slid over snowy back roads he'd never been on
before.

While he skidded on the icy roads and tried to keep from crashing into a ditch, Katya became hysterical, begging him not to go back
to the farmhouse. He had tried to reason with her, saying that it was
the safest place to hide. She was quiet after that, but he could hear

her rapid breathing as they came to the lane and approached the farmhouse, the bare trees surrounding it like grasping claws.

She would not tell him about her nightmare, only that it was like a strange terrible memory pervading the house. He could see the abject fear in her eyes when she had retreated to the bedroom

He didn't try to explain again. She wouldn't believe him anyway; she was emotional and not a little delusional, and she hadn't seen the Makarov pistol on the thug last night. He had let her think it was just a bar fight.

It was past 2 a.m. when he had finished his patrol around the farm, and then tried to sleep in the chair in the bedroom, listening to her soft breathing. He woke the next morning to find that she was dressed and ready to leave, sitting stiffly in a chair, politely refusing breakfast

He attempted to initiate conversation as they reached the outskirts of the city. "The Suvorov documents could have information on the *ukase* since the family were friends of the Tsar. The countess seemed to believe it. Otherwise, why would Maxi ask for the papers? After we pick up the translation from Eugenia we'll go directly to Len Bower's place." She nodded and seemed to have recovered.

Roo looked at his watch, wanting to be on time. They were meeting at the translator's house at 10:30. He was frustrated and irritated with Miss Scott. She was stalling over the translations, undoubtedly for more money, while they were risking their lives. In his more paranoid moments, he suspected she was working for the killers. This had to be their last trip to Columbus and their last connection with her.

Turning from South High onto Indianola Avenue, he drove slowly until they found the house, number 1109, a small wooden boxlike structure like many on the street, it's only decorative feature a tiny porch with cookie cutter trim. In need of a coat of paint, the translator's home seemed faded, slightly removed from the rest of the street, like an old blurred photograph receding into the past.

The small front lawn, still patched with snow, was neat in comparison to that of the neighboring house, where three motorcycles were parked in the drive. Heavy metal music blared from an open window on the second floor, and the melting snow exposed the litter of beer cans, fast food cartons and used condoms. As they got out of the car, a tall lanky skinhead, with a short red crew cut, an eagle tattoo on the side of his face and a skull imprint on his leather jacket, rushed out of the house, jumped on his Harley and took off, passing them as they walked up the sidewalk.

Eugenia opened the door before they could ring. She wore a long black dress. A black and pink flowered shawl was draped around her shoulders. Her iron gray hair was tamed back in a bun, and emphasized the watchful anxiety in her large pale eyes. "Welcome. I greet you *a la Russe*."

She threw her arms wide, and then kissed both of them, left, right, left. Music floated out from the small sitting room. "For you, I put on my favorite Prokofiev, *Peter and the Wolf*. It was my happiest time as a little girl listening to it. Please come in, come in." She urged them into her living room.

"You know, I still love the happy ending, when Peter catches the wolf and takes him to the Zoo." She sighed. "Nothing ends so happily in the real world."

The house was neat and sparse, a time warp of the fifties with an indefinable foreign air. A couch, cheaply upholstered in a green flowered print, occupied the middle of the room. Faded curtains in a complimentary pattern hung on the two windows. A plain square desk in the corner held her computer and stacks of papers, next to pine shelves, overflowing with books in Russian.

Eugenia noticed Katya looking at a balalaika on the coffee table and said, "I played long ago for my Papa. Maybe, if I survive, I will play for you."

Roo suppressed a snort of indignation. He was sick of this melodrama. There was something not quite right about the woman, something deceitful, dragging out the time needed for the translation, pretending she didn't want to do it, and then accepting more money. Katya, hopelessly naïve, seemed unaware of her phoniness. Eugenia led them to the kitchen, past her bedroom and Roo glimpsed two icons of saints hanging next to her bed. Their large heavy eyes followed him, chastising him for his uncharitable thoughts.

"I am so happy you came. We will have tea. We must discuss. Please, sit down at my humble table."

The small table, covered with a white cloth, groaned under the weight of a battered steel samovar and glass cups. Small plates were stacked with black bread and butter and jars of jam and honey.

"Please, take," she said, pouring the tea. Roo now accustomed to this ritual, stirred a spoonful of jam into his cup. His mood had lightened now that he was sitting down to breakfast. The black bread spread with butter and jam was delicious and even Katya, who never had an appetite, seemed to be enjoying it.

There was a jingle of a bell and a thump as an enormous black cat with white markings on its paws jumped on the window ledge. It pressed its nose against the glass, and opened its mouth in a comic howl.

"Oh, it's dear Pushkin," Eugenia rose and opened the window. "I must introduce you. He never misses tea. He is very artistic, very temperamental," she said proudly as though the cat were an eccentric but accomplished relative. "You know he is named after Russia's most famous poet." Roo was surprised and amused that Pushkin would be Eugenia's traveling companion to Florida.

The cat jumped down from the window, hissing at them, showing sharp teeth, and curled up in Eugenia's lap, obscuring everything but her head that peeked over his luxuriant brown fur. "He is very independent and spends much time with the neighbors, but always comes for tea. He is all I have.

"I was born in Russia, and after my mother died, we emigrated. I lived for many years here with Papa, now also dead." Her face seemed to crumble with melancholy. She patted Pushkin, her little hand disappearing into his thick fur, and coaxed him onto the floor in front of a saucer of tuna.

"Papa was everything to me, a great man. He taught me all I know." She reached over and picked up a silver framed photograph from the kitchen counter.

"Here is dear Papa."

Eugenia's papa had a large square fleshy face with tiny eyes. His hair was cut short in military style, and he wore a uniform with several medals pinned on the front. His shoulders loomed out of the photograph. Roo guessed the unsmiling Communist official had posed for the camera sometime in the late forties or early fifties.

"Your father was in the military?" Roo said.

"Yes, a very distinguished man." She abruptly rose and carefully placed the photograph back on the counter. "He was stationed in Siberia until we left the Soviet Union. When we arrived we changed our name to Scott. It was more convenient."

Then with the air of a child showing her toys, she opened a small cupboard near the kitchen door and pulled out two leather bound albums embossed on each cover with a double eagle.

"I thought you might be interested in these. They are photograph albums dating back to the early 1900's."

Roo sighed, thinking he was going to have to spend time they couldn't afford looking at her relatives and would never learn what was in the Suvorov papers.

She opened the first album.

"If you notice," she said, slowly turning the pages. "These are extremely rare, featuring Tsar Nicholas and his family and members of the court, including Rasputin."

Katya shivered at the photograph of the strange man with long straggling hair and wispy moustache, dressed like a peasant. His hypnotic eyes seemed to stare directly at her, impelling her to succumb to his wishes. The mad monk was sitting on a bed with a small boy, surrounded by four lovely girls. She wondered if these children had been victims of his power, evident even in a photograph.

"That picture of him with the Romanov children is the only known one in existence. Rasputin wielded enormous influence over the Tsarina and the court because he could stop the bleeding of the Tsarevich, a hemophiliac. It was mysterious. No one has ever explained how he did this, but he claimed to speak with God." Eugenia shook her head as though to dispel the supernatural air that hung over the table. "He was a controversial figure, very religious, but a débauché, who seduced many of his aristocratic followers in the name of religion. Such power could not be tolerated. As you know, Rasputin was murdered by members of the royal family and their right wing entourage, and everything was lost."

The translator's eyes shone with pride at these faded, sepia pictures. "Papa collected. He told me that many of the photographs were actually taken by the Tsar's family while they were imprisoned in Tobolsk and Ekaterinburg." She turned the page to four smiling young girls, sitting on a rooftop taking the air.

"This is on the roof of the house in Tobolsk, their first jail in Siberia. They were still allowed out in the sunshine then."

Eugenia said, "And I have this. It is very precious to me." She pointed to a photograph, similar to the one Countess Suvorova had shown them. "It belonged to my dear Papa. Much of the other material as well was given to him in Siberia by an old friend, one of the

Romanovs' guards at Ipatiev House in Ekaterinburg. Papa also told me many personal anecdotes about the family, which he learned from this friend. But Papa kept this guard's name secret. During Soviet times, it was very dangerous to have any connection to the Tsar. People were sent to prison and executed for less than that." Her voice was barely audible, so filled with fear that they could have been sitting in a Soviet kitchen during the days of Stalin waiting for the secret police to knock.

Small precise handwriting identified each of the subjects in the rare photograph from 1916. Eugenia pointed to the photograph and explained as though she were an intimate friend or relative.

"Tsar Nicholas II, 48, sits among his daughters, and Tsarina Alexandra, 44, stands directly behind him. Next to the Tsar are the Grand Duchesses Olga, 20; Maria, 17; and Tatiana, 19. Anastasia, 15, has her arm around her brother, the Tsarevich, Alexei, who is 12. Papa said they were a harmless, charming family and didn't deserve their fate. *Besy*, they are beasts," she hissed. Startled, Pushkin leapt up. She opened the window and he jumped out.

"Dear Papa was obsessed with the family and would look at this photo often, although it was forbidden to own such things."

The young women wear white linen dresses; their luxuriant hair piled up except for the youngest whose hair falls to her shoulders. Their eyes seem to sparkle; they are smiling. Katya closed her eyes and suddenly felt the brush of a white blouse, the soft arms around her fading to nothing.

Sensing Roo's impatience, Eugenia quickly collected the albums and returned them to the small cupboard. Then she poured them more tea, stacked the plates onto the counter and turned down the music on the tape recorder. "I know you are in a rush. Pardon a lonely old woman's indulgence, but I wanted to share those precious belongings of my Papa's with someone before it was too late. Now for the business in hand."

She retrieved the papers from her desk and placed them on the table along with her translation. "These are curious historical documents, written as reports to an unidentified person. Notice the paper is thick, of high quality. Look at the dates." She tapped her tiny index finger on the papers. "The last was written after the defeat of the White Army in the Civil War. The Bolsheviks had taken control of the country, although their hold was still precarious. But read for yourselves."

She waved them toward the papers.

Harbin August 10, 1921

We have failed in our mission. Entrusted with the safety of the subject, we traveled by train from Perm to Chita and then by horseback arriving at Urga, the Mongolian capital on April 10, 1921. As planned we met the White Tsarist, Baron von Ungern-Sternberg who rules Mongolia. He took us to the Bogd Khan, who resides in a great palace overlooking the city. He is the great Lama, spiritual leader of the Mongolian Buddhists who call him the All-knowing God. He lost political power when the Chinese conquered the city and imprisoned him. The Baron drove out the Chinese and released the Bogd Khan and now has influence and power over him. The All-knowing One smiled enigmatically from his throne in the great room and welcomed us.

I was encouraged by this benevolent welcome until the Baron, in a loud agitated voice, stated he was not interested in our mission and refused to aid us in moving the subject overland.

"Wait, wait," Katya said, "Maxi told me that when his family fled they carried something for the Tsar. It was a person, not an object." They eagerly read on.

I had hoped that the unsavory rumors concerning the Baron's behavior were untrue, but his rule of the city and territory is cruel and unpredictable. Urga is a place of terror and death. Soon after our audience with the Bogd Khan, our party was taken captive and the men coerced into the Baron's army. Our terrified women were forced to work in the laundry and kitchen and very often beaten and violated to amuse the brutalized troops. Because of my high ranking and reputation among Tsarist sympathizers, I convinced the Baron, who is mad, that if our party were permitted to leave, I would, upon reaching Harbin, recruit a division of White troops to fight with his army. I tried to fulfill the mission: taking the subject to safety.

The Baron gave us permission to leave, but only on the condition the subject remain in Urga in his custody. Horrified at this turn of events, I pleaded with him to let our poor charge go with us, but he refused and threatened to kill all of us. He has learned of the importance of the subject. My dear wife requested an audience with the Bogd Khan to ask him to persuade the beast to relent. She did not return to us and was never seen again. A monk from the great palace told us that she suffered a horrible beating at the Baron's orders and died the next day. I searched for her body in the Place of the Dead, outside the walls of the city where the black dogs eat the flesh of the departed, but there was no trace of my beloved. It was a terrible price to pay. My heart is broken. I will never recover from this monstrous deed.

Even as I pleaded the Baron told me that he had great plans for the subject and claimed he was being merciful to our party, noting that deserters from his army were hunted down and met a terrible death. He looked at me, his hair flying; his eyes deranged, and said with a strange giggle, 'Burning alive, that's what we do to traitors.'

To my utter dismay and sorrow, the Baron announced before we departed that he intended to marry the important subject in our charge to the Mongol Prince, Bayer Gun, commander of his Chahar Division and a descendant of Genghis Khan. This marriage has become part of his crazed plan to conquer Russia and establish a great Asiatic empire.

Katya said, "The person he calls the subject, the one they are trying to rescue, is a young woman."

"And a very important person since her identity was disguised," Eugenia said.

Roo looked at the last page. Count Maximilian Alexandrovich Suvorov, Maxi's grandfather, signed the report.

"The Countess Suvorova, Maxi's mother claimed she didn't know how her family managed to escape the Baron, that it was a mystery. No wonder Maxi's grandfather was ashamed. He made a deal to save his life and deserted this poor girl," Roo said, going back to the report.

It was difficult to take leave of the subject who was being prepared for her wedding. She was in a state of trauma and grief from the horrifying past incidents of her life and unhappy to be separated from us, but was very brave and resigned to her fate. She urged us to leave as soon as possible before the Baron changed his mind.

We were entrusted with the safety of the subject, and are ignoble in our desertion of our charge, but had to consider our family's welfare. Our mission has failed.

Most important: I take comfort and am hopeful that she may survive because she possesses no identity card nor knows anything about the

Tsar's edict, which has disappeared. I have heard it was smuggled out of the country earlier this year.

They picked up the second page with yellow dust clinging to it, as though it had been in the desert.

We must warn you that the Cheka is aware of our mission. This places the subject in more danger. One of our original party, a Russian aristocrat who organized the subject's escape from Perm, was discovered to be a double *agent. His mission was to hand over the subject and the ukase to the Bolsheviks, but he was exposed as an enemy by one of the monks. He escaped and I have heard from sources that he has been seen in Harbin. His nom de revolution is the Raven, aka Peter von Krantz.*

"Even then there were Bolsheviks and Whites searching for the *ukase*," Katya said.

Eugenia had been watching them and listening carefully as they read the translation and tensed up in fear when Roo left the table and looked out the windows at the street and side yard.

"We have to leave as soon as we finish," he said, sitting down again at the table. They continued, reading quickly.

Harbin March 9, 1922

I have learned from one of our agents still operating in Bolshevik held territory, that during the last months when the Red Army was closing in, the Baron in a fit of uncontrollable rage murdered the subject's husband, Prince Bayer Gun, ordering him to be buried alive. The grief stricken subject was hidden by the monks at Urga and later smuggled out of the city. She died in childbirth hiding in a nomad tent in the Mongolian mountains. The fate of the child is unknown. We must make every effort to save the child.

I remain a dedicated servant to the monarchist cause and believe we will prevail.

Katya scrutinized the page closely and noticed a small swastika next to Suvorov's name.

"The Brotherhood sign," she said, "Count Suvorov was reporting to members of his group who wanted to rescue the Tsar and his family."

She took Eugenia's hand. "Thank you for all your help and for the lovely tea." Then she opened her handbag and brought out the five hundred dollars.

"Oh, you are so generous," Eugenia said, nervously rolling the money into a wad and placing it in her high heeled shoe.

As Roo opened the folder to put in the papers, a photograph slipped out on the table.

"It must be connected to these reports," Katya said.

"You have a photograph?" Eugenia said in a shaky voice. She hurried to her desk and brought back a magnifying glass. Bending over the old faded picture, they were drawn into the landscape of bare hills, with a temple in the background. The glass dwelled for a moment on the pale eccentric looking figure dressed in a Chinese robe, open to reveal his chest covered in medallions. Even from the distance of the old photograph, his eyes bear the look of insanity, as though he cannot control the demons inside his head.

"That's the Baron. I think it's the day the count and his group left his camp. And that must be the Bolshevik spy, the Raven," Katya exclaimed in excitement. They focused on the only member of the party who seems aware of the camera. Dressed like the other men in high boots and a military tunic, the Raven is young and strikingly handsome, but his angelic blond perfect features are shadowed by his dark sinister expression.

The glass moved to the edge of the photo near the temple where three Buddhist monks stand with a tall Asiatic man wearing a Russian officer's uniform. "He must be the prince," Katya said. Looking up at him is a slim young woman, dressed in an elegant riding outfit. She has light hair and large dark intelligent eyes. Her features would be classical except for her mouth, slightly too wide. A sad wistful expression pervades her lovely oval face.

Katya's voice lowered to a whisper, "I am sure she is the one called the subject, the person left behind." And she was suddenly staring into a past where victims, at the mercy of brutal leaders, were lost or murdered without anyone caring or knowing, without any recourse. The only proof this young woman existed was this photograph and the reports written by Suvorov. She could understand Eugenia living in fear. There were still monsters out there.

"But that doesn't really explain anything," Roo said, bringing her back to the present. He thought the papers were disappointing, and contradictory to the claims of the countess, worthless and unimportant to finding the archive.

"Even though these documents have nothing to do with me, I sense I am in danger." Eugenia said. "I have been frightened all my life, but after translating these documents, I am positive the secret police will finally catch up with me. Pushkin knows. He has been behaving differently as though to warn me. You have to believe that I am not crazy."

Katya said, "We do not think you're crazy. We believe you."

"Émigrés are never really safe. They never escape *dlinnaya ruka Muskvy,* the long arm of Moscow," Eugenia said, her voice cracking in despair. "The KGB, the Organs, never let you alone. I have been hiding for years."

"But that was forty years ago. The Communist government is gone. Surely you're safe now," Katya said, to comfort her.

"I don't believe it," she said stubbornly. "Pushkin and I will be off tomorrow." She trembled. Her hair had begun to come loose, short-circuiting around her head. "I feel you are my friends. I trust you. If something happens to me, please find my dearest Pushkin. He will be able to tell you what to do. I want you to have the albums.

"But also," she whispered, "there is something else I have in my possession. Some material I thought perhaps I could sell. It was the only reason I didn't destroy it, but I have a premonition it is too late for me. I have suspected all along that you were investigating a death, but I don't want to know. I know too much as it is." She lowered her shaking head and muttered something under her breath.

"What is it?" Katya said.

She looked up at Katya, an expression of terror passing over her face. "There is an old Russian proverb that haunts me, *He who remembers the past, let him lose his eyes.*" She moved slowly, almost painfully to show them to the door.

Katya suddenly remembered, "I have been wondering about a Russian word I heard some time ago. I looked up the word *mochit*, which means literally to wet. Could there be any other meaning for it?"

Eugenia's face looked drawn and white. "The verb does mean to wet, but it became over the years a KGB term for killing. Blood, of course. Blood is wet."

For an instant, Katya caught, like a flash from a camera, a glimpse of the shadow girl from her nightmare, thrust back into the prison room, her clothes ripped, blood dripping from under her skirt onto the floor.

Chapter 48

Roo
Columbus

"WHERE DID YOU hear that word *mochit?*" Roo asked. He was taking a circuitous route to Len Bower's shop through part of the city called German Village, bumping through tiny alleyways, past picturesque shuttered old brick houses from the 1800s. But, they were moving in a more dangerous world, outside the prosaic charm of the neighborhood.

"When I had my ski accident and lay half conscious, I heard someone say it. And then," her voice faltered, "I overheard Maxi use it on the telephone."

Roo parked in the middle of the North Market lot, already filled with cars, and they walked through the market to the door fronting High Street, then two blocks to the old brick shop tucked between a Greek restaurant and an art gallery.

Bower's Old Time Memorabilia, printed in old-fashioned letters, hung above the entrance. It seemed redundant, but maybe Bowers just wanted to make a point. A chime tinkled out a few bars of *Home on the Range* announcing their presence.

"Hi ya," Len was standing near the door as though he had been waiting for them. Less flamboyantly dressed today, he sported a tan cowboy hat, and matching boots. He twinkled a smile at Katya, and Roo realized the guy, who was about the same age as Stumpy, fancied himself a ladies' man.

"Can you wait a minute? I have to make a call." He loped behind the counter into a back office.

The front of the shop was jammed with books, maps, posters, and old flags. Gold-framed plaques with Len Bowers' credentials hung along the walls. Antique Dealer's Association was framed prominently, along with old certificates of membership in The Minute Men, John Birch Society, National Rifle Association, and State Historical Society.

"Do you really think we'll find anything here? I don't trust him," Katya whispered.

Roo said, "He might be a crook and an old lecher, but I think he's knowledgeable about maps."

There was another framed photograph of Len as a soldier with his buddies. Roo should have guessed that he was a Vietnam veteran.

Len came out of the back room.

"What a drag out fight last night. I thought you would arrest them." He examined Roo suspiciously. "Guess it wouldn't be your jurisdiction," he said, although Roo knew he didn't believe it.

"We wanted to get an ambulance, but those guys refused even though they got the shit kicked out of them. Excuse my language," he said to Katya.

"Were they regulars?" Roo said.

"Nope, foreign. Told Carl they were Serbs visiting relatives in Steubenville and wanted some action. They got that all right."

"So they didn't go to the hospital?"

"Not as far as I know. They limped off in a hurry as soon as they came to. Didn't want the cops either."

Roo didn't like it. But still, in that battered condition there was no way that the gunmen could have followed them back to the farmhouse. There might be other goons who had picked up their trail.

"Now, let's have a look at that map." Len rubbed his long hands together, and then gently carried the fragment to the counter and turned on a large magnifying light. He removed his cowboy hat, revealing black dyed slicked down hair, and bent his head, scanning the paper carefully.

"Ha! Just as I thought," he looked up, grinning. "Though the light at Carl's was bad last night. It's primitive, about 1790, probably drawn on the spot by a trader or hunter." He went back to the map, engrossed.

"Could it be a map of a place called Tecumseh's Forest?" Roo tried not to show his growing excitement.

"Tecumseh's Forest, now that's a good one. I never heard of that, and I know my history. It could be around here but also could be in a lot of places in the Midwest. The chief got around." He scratched his head. "I take it you young folks mean the Shawnee Chief Tecumseh, Shooting Star."

"Yeah," Roo said, "We were hoping it was a map of his hunting ground."

Len popped on his hat and strode over to the shop door, flipping over the closed sign. "Don't want anyone bothering me for guns right now."

Then he brought out three folding chairs from behind the counter. "Sit down here and let me tell you about Tecumseh. The great Shawnee leader is believed to have been born at Old Piqua on the Mad River in 1768, that's near Xenia, Ohio. After his father Pucksinwah was killed during the Battle of Point Pleasant in 1774, his mother Methoataske moved farther west, but Tecumseh remained in this part of the country."

"He was raised by his sister Tecumpease and older brother Chiksika, who trained him up to be a great warrior. Some historians claim he spent his childhood and young adulthood roaming the Ohio territory with his brother. You have to realize that in 1790, most of this area was still a wilderness, populated by explorers, Indians, trappers and traders." He tilted his cowboy hat to the side and leaned back precariously on his chair. "By the way, where'd you get this?"

"It was left to me among a group of papers," Katya said coolly.

"I'm thinking that there could be a copy of this entire map somewhere. We should search for maps from Tecumseh's early childhood up to 1803 when he was grown and tried to unite all the tribes against the settlers. By then he had moved his base to territory in Indiana. Let's go back to my computer."

They carried the folding chairs back to the office, lined with locked cases of assorted weapons. Len claimed his computer listed map collections from 1400 to the present from dealers and museums across the country and abroad. Roo and Katya sat at the large oak desk while he went over the list of maps from that period. First they looked for those drawn between 1768 and 1790, and when they found nothing that resembled the fragment, expanded their search to 1803.

It was past one, and they had found nothing to match. "Whew, damned hard," Len muttered. There was a kick at the door, followed by shouting, then several more kicks. He jumped up as though he'd been stabbed by an electric cattle prod. "It's Marge with my lunch." He rushed to open the door to a petite woman in her early thirties, wearing a short fur coat and leopard skin tights. She tottered precariously in her spike-heeled cowboy boots, juggling a huge basket in tiny arms. Marge had shiny blonde hair cut in a straight bob, and a thin pretty, but hard looking face. Her large blue eyes, edged with black liner, were screwed up in anger.

"What the fuck you doing locking the door? I nearly dropped this cordon bleu crap on my pussy." Reaching only the middle of Len's chest, she glared fiercely up at him.

He jumped to attention. Taking the basket, he placed it on the counter. "Sorry Honey Bear. I'm trying to identify a map for these folks. This is Reuben Yoder, deputy sheriff and Katya Marston. Marge Weaver."

Marge looked at Roo through slit eyes, "Hmm, Yoder. You're Amish?" Her voice was loud and precise, like a sergeant's call to attention. Len seemed to wilt under her assault, losing at least two inches in height.

"Well, my dad was, but I'm not," He was intimidated by her accusing tone.

"Good," she said, placing her hands on her tiny hips. "There's enough food for everyone here. Could you help me hon?" she said to Katya.

Marge opened a drawer in the counter and brought out white Limoges china plates, silver cutlery, pale blue linen placemats, and napkins. Len put up a card table, and Roo, feeling a desperate sense of urgency, carried the folding chairs from the back, wondering what the fuck they were doing, how they had got into this. They had no time for a set down lunch. Katya arranged the table setting. Marge, her amazingly long rhinestone studded nails clicking on the plates, dished up a ragout and mashed celeriac. There was also a fresh green salad. A delicious aroma filled the shop.

"Marge is a cordon bleu cook, spent a lot of time in Paris," Len explained meekly as they sat down to eat.

"Then I had to come back to this mediocrity to take care of my Mom."

"Ah Marge, it's not so bad here." Len seemed embarrassed that they would think he was the mediocrity.

"I guess you're right. I was exaggerating," she said, uncharacteristically mollified, but actually concentrating on the wine.

"I uncorked this earlier," she said bringing out a Baccarat crystal carafe of red wine and pouring it into crystal goblets. "It's a fucking good bottle, Grand Cru Les Musigny. Fifteen years old, Burgundy, Cote de Nuit."

"This is absolutely delicious," Katya said.

Marge beamed. "You must be one of those English. People there are really nice and civilized, but the cuisine there is terrible, consistency of cow poop, although I admit I've never tasted that delicacy. How'd you end up here?"

"Actually, I am not sure. I'm only staying a few days before returning to London," she said, wishing it were true.

They ate in silence, relishing the food for a few moments, and then Len explained about the piece of map. Marge squinted her eyes again, and said, "Have you cross-referenced with maps of tribal settlements drawn in that period? Maybe Tecumseh drew the map."

"Good thinking, Honey Bear. Now that would be a very valuable find." Len said, turning to them. "Isn't she great?"

"Let's have coffee and crème caramel." Marge smiled at the compliment, fluttering her absurdly long false eyelashes like a schoolgirl while she picked up the plates and slapped down smaller ones.

Katya had dined in Paris Michelin starred restaurants, but Marge's food seemed more delicious, maybe because she had been eating at fast food places and at the farmhouse. She was impressed and strangely reassured by Marge's profane but strong friendly presence. After they were finished, she helped clean up, stacking the dirty dishes in the basket.

"Gotta go," Marge said, effortlessly picking up the basket. "Nice meeting you. Come to my place any time for a meal."

Len helped her with her coat, and gave her a peck on the lips. "Thanks Honey Bear. It was outstanding as usual."

"Listen, you prick. Get your ass home as soon as you close up. You're taking me to the Women's Club for a cooking session." She rushed out the door, banging it behind her.

They watched her leave like people recovering from a storm. "Marge does have bad language," Len said apologetically, "but you always know where you stand with her. She grew up in the country. Her Daddy, Boss Weaver, owned a big chunk of land in three counties. And she always packs two 45's. She's a great shot in spite of those tweeny arms. Met her at a horse race in Kentucky. She's a deal younger than me, but we've been together now for 5 years. She's a good woman, but you don't want to get on the wrong side of her." He seemed terrified of her and in awe of her tough independence. Roo guessed it probably didn't fit his generation's idea of how a woman should behave. Women's Lib seemed to have passed him by.

They hurried back to the computer and tried Marge's suggestion to cross-reference early maps with tribal villages and examined ten maps in that category. One labeled 'Northwest Territory' caught their attention. Dated circa 1790, it was described as being drawn by an anonymous trader.

"Well, I'll be," Len said, bringing it into better focus. At the right of the map in a crookedly drawn box was the key, which enabled them to trace the Scioto and Olentangy Rivers; then the Mad River, the tribal villages and Piqua, Tecumseh's birthplace. The map's description of territory in central Ohio led them to believe the forest was somewhere in this vicinity. There was a faint mark near the edge where their fragment seemed to fit.

Katya drew in her breath, hardly able to speak. It seemed to be a match. She peered through the magnifying glass and saw some faint markings at the end of the key. "It's the letter 'T'," she said, catching her breath. Beside the T, barely discernible, faintly written in archaic

English, were the words, Tecumseh's Forest. Roo and Katya looked at each other, hardly believing it, not wanting to show excitement in front of Bowers.

After they had copied and enlarged the map, Roo thought of something. "Is it possible that Abigail had a map collection?"

Len looked at them, puzzled. "Who is Abigail?"

Katya said, "My guardian, who left me the map." Then she turned to Roo. "She had a few framed in the conference room, but I just didn't think."

Len clicked on the site again and found more information. 'Early Trader's Map. Northwest Territory 1790 Townsend Collection, Little Swan Gallery, 9 Mercer Street, New York City.'

Katya was stunned. This was no coincidence. Abigail's desperation and terror seemed to rush into Bower's shop.

"She ripped this valuable map. How could she ever believe I would find it?" she said. Abigail had known her so well that she had taken the chance Katya would somehow find the map. Suddenly her actions the day she was murdered became clear. She saw Abigail, her mind working like lightning, in terror of the killers, racing to the lawyers to get the envelope, returning to the flat, tearing off the section of map and hiding everything behind the Ansel Adam's photograph.

"Is it possible to see what's in that area of Columbus now?" Roo said.

"Sure, easy." Len was alert, watching them as he went over to a shelf and picked out a Franklin Country Ordinance map. He unfolded it and placed the copy of the old map beside it, tracing the location of both the Olentangy and Scioto Rivers. Roo found the modern area first. Adrenalin coursed through his veins.

"A shopping mall? That can't be." Katya did not believe it. All three checked the site again, but came to the same conclusion.

"Hot dog, we found it," Len yelled. "Yeah, it's big and real nice, a great place to go for dinner."

It was hard to imagine, but Easton Town Center, the shopping mall, was built on the site of the young Tecumseh's hunting ground.

Len studied them with a strange expression, which Roo read as sly. "You folks looking for something special?"

"No, we just wanted to make sure it was a map. We thought maybe we could sell it." He didn't sound convincing.

Katya was silent, studying the shopping mall with disbelief.

"If you are, maybe I can help." His folksy voice held an undertone of menace. "I can sell this piece for a good price if you're so inclined."

Roo quickly took the map and put it back in the folder. "We'll think about it. Thanks. Thanks for everything. By the way, what do you charge for spending so much time with us, giving an expert opinion?"

"Nothing for that, just a cut if there's anything goin'," he said. "Where are you staying so I can reach you? I could have a buyer by tomorrow."

"Holiday Inn in Worthington. We're heading off there now," Roo said. Katya gave him a quick incredulous look. It was the opposite direction from where they were going.

The door kicked open and Marge came rushing in. "Your car parked out front?"

"No," Roo said, "I'm two streets down. Will I get a ticket?"

"No, you're ok. I noticed a black Humvee, like the pimps use, just down the street, sitting there motor running. I thought it might be waiting to pick you up. When I looked inside and saw the two guys, decided they were planning something like a break in. I knocked on their window and told them to fuck off or I'd call the police."

Roo drew in his breath, thinking she could have been killed except that they weren't interested in Marge. "Did you get a look at them?"

"The one in the driver's seat had pulled down a hat so I didn't see his face. The one beside him was leaning over. They drove off. By the way, I just wondered if you folks found out anything interesting."

"Thanks to you and Len, we did discover that the fragment is part of a map," Katya said in a smooth voice. Outside, the clouds had grown darker, closing in over the shop, giving it a dingy film noir look.

Marge looked less friendly, even menacing. Her small frame blocked the door, and one of her 45's was visible under her coat. Roo worried about the guys in the car but suspected she could be lying, trying to find out where they were parked. "I can go along with you if you're in trouble. I'm packin," she said, caressing the handle of the gun.

"Yeah, she'll do it." Len nodded in agreement, his eyes hard and mean.

For a few tense moments they seemed to be trapped by this strange couple in the middle of a peaceful shopping district.

"I think we'll be fine. I was worried about a ticket," Roo said as though it had nothing to do with the men in the Humvee.

He swallowed hard, felt his gun under his jacket, and was poised, ready when Marge stepped back to let them out. They said a quick goodbye and walked to the end of the street.

Then Roo raced around the corner, dragging Katya by the arm, going away from the parking lot, ducking between alleys with sheds, bicycles, and trash cans. From the alleyway they had a last glimpse of Marge on High Street, looking both ways for them, then he collided with a trash bin, sending it rolling. "Shit," he yelled, hopping and holding his leg, but continued to run.

"Are you hurt?" Katya asked, trying to keep up.

"I'm ok," he said, limping as they reached the still crowded parking lot. There was no sign of the Humvee, so he didn't think they had spotted his car.

They drove off slowly to avoid attention, and Katya said, "I didn't like the way they behaved toward the end. They were scary."

"That's right," he said, rubbing his leg, which hurt like hell. "Did you notice Marge stopped swearing? That must be when she's really dangerous."

"So we're not really going to the Holiday Inn," she said.

"No, I'm hoping we're out of town before they check there."

"I just can't believe those two are killers."

"Me either," Roo said, "but I don't trust them. They knew something was up and wanted in on it. He's probably a fence."

"I hope no one is following us." She nervously looked out the back window.

He hadn't handled Bowers that well. He could have concocted a better explanation to make Len less suspicious of them. They had risked a lot to find Tecumseh's Forest, and the large shopping center seemed a dead end.

Katya interrupted his thoughts. "What about the men Marge saw in the Humvee?"

"I think she was making that up, but we still have to be careful."

She turned and continued to watch out the back window.

"The archive could be large if Christina didn't put it all on computer discs or memory sticks," he said, musing aloud as he maneuvered through heavy traffic.

"She could have buried it somewhere, or she might have taken the material to a storage place," Katya said.

"Storage place," they said in unison. He pulled into a gas station and asked the attendant with a long sleepy face behind the counter for a phonebook. He leafed through the yellow pages while standing.

"Can't take it away," the attendant said. Roo showed his badge and took it to the car. Katya sat close to him as they searched through the list of storage companies.

"There," he said. "Drake's Self Storage. Security guaranteed. The address is at Easton Town Center, just off Worth Avenue near the parking garage."

"Could it be? Have we found it? It could be all over soon." Katya gave him a hug and then pulled back, aware of what she'd done.

He nodded. "We'll go tonight. The hours are 8 a.m. to 10 p.m. We may need Ben's help."

Their triumph was marred by the thought of Abigail's terror and her desperate attempts to keep the archive from Katya's enemies.

As they left the station, Katya said, "You know, I'm very worried about Eugenia. She seemed so frightened. She had something else important to tell us, do you think?" Her face was soft with worry.

Roo looked at his watch. He was reluctant, knew it was dangerous, and didn't want to keep Ben waiting. He had a sudden picture of the eccentric little woman as she said goodbye. Her upper lip with its little moustache quivered, drawing up over her sharp teeth, reminding him of a small hunted animal. He had heard her frantically throw the locks on the door.

"Yeah, sure. We'll just drop by. It'll make her feel better."

It was late afternoon, and the temperature had dropped below zero when they arrived at Eugenia's. *Peter and the Wolf* blared out from the house, as they made their way cautiously toward the front door. Roo noticed that the bikers' house next door was quiet, even though one of the windows was open, and a ragged curtain billowed out like a warning flash.

The front door was ajar. He took out his gun, and pushed it open. Katya stayed close behind him. She started to call out for Eugenia, but he stopped her. They crept through the house, his arm outstretched, holding the gun. Intruders had trashed the place, throwing everything from closets and drawers into piles on the floor.

The small kitchen cupboard was open. The precious albums were gone. Her father's photograph lay smashed and torn along with other family pictures.

The music went on, incongruous in the dark ravaged house. Roo surveyed the living room, before they moved out the back door to the small porch and searched over the fences bordering the back gardens, their plots deserted. Back in the living room, the computer was gone and the desk had been hacked to pieces. Roo figured they had used an axe. He turned off the old fashioned tape recorder, leaving a terrible silence.

They paused at the bedroom door. He reeled back in shock. His memory of that moment was of Katya's high-pitched screams. She fell back into the living room, still crying out. He picked her up and carried her out to the car. Her body was limp, and he wondered if she was suffering from shock. He propped her on the seat and she stayed, silent and stiff like a mannequin.

"Lock the door. Stay here. I'll be back," he said, choking on his words. He ran in a crouched position to the front door, and walked through the house again. Everything passed by him in slow motion, as he approached the threshold of the bedroom and stood for a moment. He ran to the back door to get away, gagging, everything in front of him going into black spots. Still gripping his gun, he collapsed in a heap on the back porch, his knees juddering, taking in gulps of fresh cold air.

He caught a glimpse of fur and sat up. Pushkin was hiding underneath the back step. The cat began to howl in a strange almost human way. He was sure the animal had witnessed the murder. He checked the back yards again, but everything was still and silent except for the screeching cat. Eugenia's words came to him over the racket, 'Pushkin will tell you'.

He placed his gun down on the porch and grabbed at Pushkin, slowly dragging him out from underneath the step. The cat was heavy, over forty pounds and fought hard, scratching and biting, but finally stopped in exhaustion. Roo sat holding the animal's huge trembling body, stilling him. Through the thick cloud of terror which enveloped him, the thought penetrated that this was ridiculous; a woman dead inside, possible murderer still around, and he was clutching an enormous cat.

Pushkin clawed him again when he tried to look at his collar. Printed on the underside was PO Box 45, University Branch, 234 W. 18th St. Cols. 43210. Key, the word came through his scrambled horror. There had to be a key. The cat was scratching, struggling to escape and the small bell on his collar clattered, like a loud alarm. Wrestling with the bundle of animal fury, he managed to turn over the bell and found a small key attached to the clapper. He was viciously raked across the hands, streaming with blood, but managed to unhook the key. The cat shot away from him and fled into the neighbor's yard.

Roo remembered with shock where he was and taking his gun, hid behind the steps. Sharp pain from the scratches gripped him, and he wiped his bleeding hands on his shirt. The noise might have brought back the killer, but the adjoining gardens still were empty. He removed his jacket, vest and shirt, trembling in the cold, before putting on his jacket again. Using his shirt and vest he frantically wiped his prints and blood off everything while he retraced his steps, stumbling back into the house. He knew it wasn't professional, but numb with horror, he could not look again at poor Eugenia. The words, 'same killers', like a neon sign flashed over and over in his mind.

Katya was lying in the car seat in a fetal position. She looked up when he opened the door, her eyes holding the same wild fear as Pushkin's. "Are you all right?" she said, strangling a sob.

"Yes," he said, "The cat scratched the hell out of me, but they're only surface wounds." He threw the shirt in the back seat and struggled to tear the vest into strips.

"How awful," she said, her voice hoarse. She sat up and took the vest, tearing it into bandages and gently wrapped them around his hands. He winced with pain, and to his surprise, she reached up, and softly stroked his face.

"Are they out there?" she asked.

"No, I'm sure they're gone."

Her face crumpled in grief, and she cried over and over, "Why would they do something so terrible?" The question hung in the air.

His hands, bleeding through the bandages, shook violently as he started the car and raced toward the post office. They went through a section of the university, past unreal scenes of laughing students walking to class, while the grisly picture rose before him. Eugenia was tied to a chair, wearing red fishnet hose and garters like a stripper or hooker. Her hair stuck straight out from electric shocks, her arms and legs twisted like a Raggedy Anne doll. He gasped, taking deep breaths, trying to control the urge to vomit. He had forced himself to closely examine Eugenia's body and even now, he reeled back in the seat as though hit by a club. Her eyeballs, hollowed out from the sockets, left weeping holes in her face. They floated in a pool of thick blood on the floor in front of her chair.

He wanted to stop and throw up, but had to keep going. "She left us a key on Pushkin's collar. We have to get to the post office before it closes," he said, conscious of her sobs. He parked and left her inside, locking the car. The place was empty. A clerk bent over his counter, not bothering to look up. He opened Box 45 and with trembling bloody hands took out the envelope. On the front was Eugenia's small neat handwriting; she had mailed the package to herself.

When he returned, Katya was still weeping. "I think I'm going to be sick," she said.

He opened her side of the car and helped her to the back of the building.

"Thanks," she said, waving him away. When she returned, her face red and blotched, she said, "But shouldn't we do something?" Her voice was full of tears. "Please, let's go to the police."

"There is nothing we can do for her now. We can't get involved."

"So the killers know we are here," she said in a dull voice, finally believing it. "They wanted to find out where we are staying and thought Eugenia knew."

"Yes, but she couldn't tell them anything. They didn't locate our car or they would have searched it. Since we left Len's no one's been following us." Roo knew that the time had come that he dreaded. He would have to face the killers. He was the best marksman in the county, but he had not even shot as much a rabbit in years.

"Oh my God, what will we do?" She leaned over in the seat in a sudden fit of panic.

"They would need military radar to find the farmhouse. I'm taking the chance they don't have it. We won't meet Ben at the usual spot in case they're watching him. We'll drive to the farm, pack up and wait until it's dark to go after the archive."

She wiped her eyes and looked straight ahead. "Eugenia seemed to know she was going to be killed. I was beginning to feel attached to her."

In that instant, Roo understood Katya. Like him, she was alone in the world. He took the envelope from his jacket and tossed it on her lap.

Chapter 49

Mikhail
Courchevel, France

SASHA WAS THE Shaman and had become his implacable enemy. He repeated this alarming fact aloud to the mountains, his heart pounding with dread. The knowledge, like a bad disease would not go away, but Mikhail forced himself to remain steady while he waited these last few days to get his hands on the girl.

Before he knew the identity of his enemy, he had decided not to answer the Shaman, to engage with a lunatic. Now he couldn't bring himself to answer out of fear. Avoiding the venomous commands he would find on his computer he exercised for longer hours in the gym, took walks, and skied off piste with bodyguards in attendance. He wanted this to end, to have a normal life and knew this longing could be his downfall. At night, the Raven crowded his sleep, mocking him for failing the mission.

Attempting to escape from his luxurious cage, to recapture his wild nights in Moscow, he had risked going to a nightclub. Bebe and Shamil had watched nervously while he ordered bottles of Cristal champagne for the girls surrounding him. He was escorting a girl who reminded him of Marousia to his car when he saw one of

Vlach's minders and didn't dare bring her back to the chalet. After that reckless night, Vlach had requested a meeting. He had not answered. The pimp knew that Mikhail's security had been breached and that poor Marousia was dead. He sensed that Vlach was working for Sasha and had been involved in the murders on his yacht.

This morning, after two hours of strenuous exercise, he went to the communications room. His mood reverted to despair as he read the latest report. Two days ago his men had tailed Katya Marston to a bar, but had been attacked by locals and lost the trail. But they now had located the girl's position in that same isolated forest within a fifty mile radius and were combing the area. Soon they would find the hideout. She was without protection except for the cop, who would be a minor irritant for the ex-Spetznaz killers. Imminent success did nothing to relieve his growing fear, a weed rooted deep inside him. He wandered slowly back up to his study, gazing out over the trees, hiding all but the jagged mountain peaks, wanting this to end, wondering how it would end. He did not know how long he sat at his desk, but it was twilight when he clicked on his computer, knowing Sasha's words would be there.

But this time something curious appeared on the screen. It seemed to be an official document, a birth certificate. Confused, he took his reading glasses from his shirt pocket and carefully scrutinized it. Dizziness overwhelmed him for a moment as his mind raced back to the part of his past linked to this document. He remembered it all now, as clearly as though it had happened a few hours ago.

It was 1970 when the Raven had assigned him to search for the *ukase* in the United States. This had come after Vietnam when he had infiltrated a group of American prisoners. His legend and cover was Jack Reilly.

Carrying his computer, he moved into his living room, rang for Anya, and asked her to bring him a bottle of vodka, which he rarely drank. Shivering with cold in spite of the roaring fire, he wrapped up in a throw near his chair. Anya brought the vodka with some bread and cheese and looked at him, imploring, "Please, you must eat."

But he waved it away, and poured out a glass, drained it and poured another with shaking hands. He clasped them together to still them as her beautiful open face with the large brown eyes, the cloud of blond hair rose before him. She had said with hatred in her eyes that she knew that he was one of the enemies. How could she think that he was her enemy after the nights they had spent together? He took another shot of vodka and whispered her name still remembering how he had loved her even though it was futile.

He stared at the screen. The document which had so shocked him could be a forgery. Before he had time to deal with its significance, another message came.

My power reaches everywhere. Stavrogin betrayed you long ago and works for me. I know where she is. If you do not cooperate and give up your information on the archive, my new agent will hunt down and kill Katya Marston before you can reach her. I have sent Stavrogin to put her and her companion into the final deep sleep.

He took a long drink, this time from the bottle. Sasha's power was overwhelming. Stavrogin, his own agent he had trusted to follow his orders, had been working for his enemy. He could see Stavrogin, creeping through the forest in Tecumseh County, closing in on Katya Marston, planning her death.

Moving quickly from his chair, he sprang into action, and spent the next hours issuing orders to his men to protect the girl and the cop from Sasha's agents. Energized by his decisions, his next move was to take care of Stavrogin. His eyes turned a dead black color when he placed the call to a secure number in New York, and spoke to the Priest, someone he had regarded as a friend since he had been undercover in Vietnam. The ruthless assassin was part of Mikhail's network, but remained a sleeper. He had not been called upon since the end of the Vietnam War. He was the only man who could stop Stavrogin from killing the girl.

The Priest was a loyal man who wouldn't forget Mikhail had once saved his life. The quiet gentle voice answered, and went silent while Mikhail explained. Before he ended the call, Mikhail said, "Deal with Stavrogin before he can harm the girl. I will send you the exact location. He will be near her in the Tecumseh County forest."

Chapter 50

Katya-Roo
Tecumseh County

THE WOLF STOOD on the front porch, his pale eyes regarding them as though he had come to warn them. He raised his head to the sky, and his mournful howl brought her to tears. Then he trotted slowly past them into the forest.

Katya waited while Roo followed the wolf's path back to the barns. He felt a stab of terror as he stared at the partial heel print barely visible in the falling snow. The killers had followed them here, had found them.

He ran back, pushing her inside the house. "They found us. We're going as soon as it's dark. Leave everything but the documents."

She was silent, shocked as they packed the files and their passports and documents in his backpack. When they finished, Katya unwrapped the rags from his hands, which had stopped bleeding and found some disinfectant and large bandages in the medicine cabinet. He forgot everything for a moment as she gently cleaned the scratches, already healing, and dressed them.

Then he pointed to Eugenia's envelope. "Let's open it," he said. "We have to know what's in it now."

She nodded, a tremor going through her body. "Yes, I know."

They sat at the kitchen table waiting for the dark. She opened the envelope and began reading the neat script in a soft timid voice.

To my young friends, Roo and Katya,
When you came with the documents, you were like messengers of death.
I knew my life would be over, that somehow after all my years of hiding, I would be found out.

Katya stopped, her tears dripping onto the paper. "It's my fault she's dead." She waited for a moment, collecting herself before she could go on.

My real name is Eugenia Gregorieva Suslova. I was born in Siberia.
My father Gregori Petrovich Suslov defected from the Soviet Union in 1951 bringing me with him. We have spent our lives in hiding from the KGB. After they discovered our hiding places in New York and Chicago, we again changed our name to Scott and moved to Columbus in 1959, believing that the monsters would never think of looking for us here.

Papa always said that the KGB wanted him dead because of the secret documents he found in prison files and because of something he had done to offend Stalin.

"Eugenia Scott was Eugenia Suslova," she said in a stunned voice. "And her father was not a harmless émigré, but a defector running from the secret police. No wonder she was frightened."

I kept my father's papers along with the albums of the Tsar and his
family in the hope that I could sell the information, but it is too late.
These documents are from prison files. I leave them to you.

"The albums are gone," Katya said. "The murderers took them."

He picked up his gun and walked to the living room and back to the kitchen, checking out the windows in the fading light while Katya frantically leafed through three translated documents that Eugenia claimed had been copied and sent to Stalin.

She waited anxiously until he returned. "It's ok," he said.

It had grown dark, and Roo clicked on a small flashlight. Katy said, "This document, dated 1947, is a death certificate for a young woman who had arrived at Magadan prison complex in 1946. Her name was unknown, but those who arrived with her called her the Princess. She died on the same evening she arrived." Katya shivered, thinking of the poor woman.

Then she picked up four small grubby pieces of paper, covered with miniscule untidy handwriting. "It's a letter, written on what looks like old cigarette wrappers," she said. "It seems to be from a woman prisoner." She read Eugenia's translation.

Dear Comrade Stalin,
In 1946, I assisted at the birth of a male child in Camp 45. I am
sure the mother was of aristocratic birth. She was called The Princess.
It was very unusual that she spoke in English. I was the only one who
understood. When the child was born she called him the 'one designated
by blood'. She died a few moments later. I do not know the fate of the
baby. I thought it was important to report this to you, our great leader.
As a loyal member of the Communist party, I want to appeal to you
dear Comrade Stalin. I was imprisoned by mistake. I have proved my
loyalty to you by reporting this incident of counter revolutionary

behavior. There are still enemies of the people hiding among us in all disguises and we must be diligent. I beg you to review my case.

Comrade Vera Tolmatov.

There was an attached typed official note.

Attempts to question prisoner Tolmatov failed as she died soon after.

Katya stopped and held her head for a moment. Roo reached out and put his arm around her. "Go on," he said, intrigued, wondering where this was leading.

She picked up two official looking cards and their translations. "These are registration cards for two children, male, age approximately five years, of mixed blood, identity not known. They were released from the prison orphanage to a Petr Kosloff in January 1951. The releases were signed by Eugenia's father. This is so very strange." She drew close to Roo, feeling his solid warmth in the surrounding darkness as they read the last part of Eugenia's letter.

My father held the position of prison administrator in Magadan, part of the Gulag, the Dalstroi prison complex. In 1951 he aided in the escape of two small boys from the prison orphanage. He never explained to me the reason for his action. I suspect it was for money or advancement.

Although there was no trace of the child born in 1946 in the prison to the woman called the Princess, or of the small boys who escaped, Stalin was ruthless, wanting all evidence of their existence destroyed. That destruction included persons like my father who had seen the records and had released the two children. It is my belief that these papers were

connected to information that Stalin already possessed. In fear of his
life, father defected with the papers. I swear this is the truth.

Eugenia Gregorieva Suslova

"Oh look," Katya cried, holding up a photograph of two small children side by side in cribs their tiny faces squeezed and thin, their heads shaven. "Why would they kill poor Eugenia? Her papers had nothing to do with finding the archive. Were we the cause of her death?"

"Maybe they thought she knew where we were hiding. But how were we to know she was the daughter of a defector?"

"I just don't see how this has any relevance to the archive."

"Only if there really is someone alive who claims to be the Tsar's heir," Roo said.

"Do you really think Eugenia's killers are the same as those who murdered Ab and are after us?" She moved closer to him, to shelter in his warmth and strength.

"The method points that way," he said.

"What's that?" Katya froze at the faint sound coming from outside the house.

"Let's go." Roo stuffed the papers in his bag, and then stopped, listening. They heard sounds of movement in the field in front of the house.

"Wait by the cellar door," he whispered. He moved through the rooms, flicking on lights, and turning the old tape recorder on high volume. Willy Nelson's voice leisurely flowed out onto the porch.

Then he opened the door to the cellar.

"No," Katya said, in a furious whisper, the worst fear of her life upon her.

"You have to," he said. "Follow me now." The footsteps outside were heavier, crunching through the show, coming past the drive toward the porch. Moving down through the darkness, Katya seemed for a moment to have descended into a terrifying place from her nightmares. She is looking through sheets of blood, scrambling for cover in the echoes of gunshots.

Holding her breath in terror, she became accustomed to the darkness and saw the faint light from the cellar door. As they passed the boiler, a rat jumped against her leg. Roo smothered her shriek. Heavy footsteps climbed the porch steps. The front door crashed open, and they could hear the stamp of boots going through the house. She hung on to his jacket as they moved around old machinery and cold storage boxes with aged rotten apples until they made it to the cellar door, recessed like a window. The door had not been used for years, and the hinges stuck. Crashes and shouts from upstairs were moving toward the cellar door. His muscles straining, Roo pushed at the door. Its rusty hinges creaked and it opened, with a clatter drowned in the noise above. They climbed out at the side of the house.

As they crept toward the forest, Katya glanced over her shoulder and saw three dark figures carrying weapons on the front porch. Guttural Russian voices echoed through the night.

They plunged into the forest. It was snowing hard. They had no snowshoes, but still moved quickly in places underneath trees not yet deep in snow. Roo carried only his pistol, which would not be a match for a semi-automatic, or for more than one killer. 'How many?' he wondered. There had been men inside the farmhouse and three on the porch.

Katya saw into the forest for the first time as they stumbled along as though on phantom ground. Shouts from the house drew nearer, and branches cracked as the killers entered the trees. She followed close behind him, bumping into his rucksack, stumbling over branches, trying not to cry out. She wondered if Roo knew where he was going. If the killers didn't find them, they could get lost and die

of cold. Suddenly he pulled her through the trees, and they emerged
on a summit. The valley of the Amish rested below. Their dark farms
gave off smoke from chimneys like strange slumbering animals. The
forest was silent now except for their heavy breathing. They had lost
them for the moment.

She dimly remembered Roo saying they had to get to Ben's, fifteen miles on the road. Her feet and legs were numb with cold. She
didn't think she could make it. They struggled on through driving
snow, tripping over branches and roots of trees, passing another
farmhouse. They saw a lantern in one of the windows, the light a
sharp dagger in the dark. Inside, Moses Gottlieb bent over a table
mending a harness while his wife moved through the kitchen. Roo
shuddered, thinking how they didn't believe in violence and of the
killers coming upon their innocence. He was sorry that he had to en-
danger them.

He knocked at the door and Moses answered, his pale blue eyes
surprised and frightened behind his thick glasses, until he saw Roo.

"Come on in," he said.

The kitchen was warm and smelled of wet clothes, meat cooking
and faint cow manure. A huge fire burned in the stone fireplace, and
there were baskets filled with dried herbs on top of a cupboard. Two
blond children, small replicas of their parents, the boy with a bowl
cut and little girl with braids, stood at the door of the kitchen,
watching them with eyes excited at this novelty. Hannah was a pleasant looking well-built woman with thick glasses and fair rosy skin.
Katya felt as though she were hallucinating. The family seemed unreal
as though they had stepped out of a woodcarving or some ancient
German fairy tale.

"Please, have a seat," Hannah said.

Wet and cold and still shaking with terror, Katya collapsed at the
table while Hannah warmed some milk on the top of the stove and
gave it to her. Katya drank it quickly, gasping and shuddering.

"Turn out your lamp," Roo said, standing by the fire. "Someone dangerous is out there. When we leave, lock up, and don't let anyone in. We have to get as far as Henny's tonight, rest there and then make it the rest of the way on foot. I wonder if you could help us."

He spoke to Moses in a low voice in the Amish dialect, and Moses nodded as he answered. Roo clapped him on the back, and he and Katya followed him to the barn. Moses hitched the large brown horse to the family's black buggy and lanterns were placed on hooks in back and front of the carriage.

"I think you will be all right," he said. "Old Pete knows the way. Just stable him at Henny's, and I'll go by and get him tomorrow."

Roo tried to pay him for his trouble, but he refused. "Your Grandpa was an honorable man in our community. We always help friends. There aren't many cars or trucks on the road at night, but be careful. Remember stay as far over as you can from the middle of the road."

"Here Reuben." Grinning, he gave Roo a wide brimmed black hat. "They will think you are one of us."

The falling snow was damp, and the cold crept in through the cloth of the buggy. Katya's stomach churned as they turned down the dark lane and onto the road, which wound and curved up and down over the hills like a rural rollercoaster. The carriage skidded in the snow, but the horse seemed imperturbable and moved slowly, keeping the buggy off to the side of the road. In the distance a car, its lights on high beams, was creeping up on them. Katya waited, holding herself stiff with terror. As the car passed sharply, bathing them in blinding light, the buggy tottered to the side. Suddenly it was dark again, and they moved on.

Katya glanced at Roo's silhouette in the strange hat. His muscles were straining as he struggled with the horse, which seemed to know better. It was clear he had never driven one of these carriages. When the semi passed she screamed in the enormous rush of high beams, air and noise. They were forced off the road, and teetered precariously for a moment on the edge of the carriage wheels, until the horse surged forward, pulling them upright.

Her mind rushed on at this strange horror. They were in the 21st century, clopping along in a horse and buggy, fleeing from killers who were either on bikes or in cars with hi-tech weapons. It would be easy to rip through the side of this carriage with a knife, or to come upon them with a truck and crush them. She had thought the wagons were charming, but now they seemed deadly. After the truck, the night was quiet, but Katya still clutched the side and drew close to Roo.

The horse clipped along, tossing his head in the snow, and in the distance they saw a light at Heinrich Muller's store.

"He must be doing inventory," Roo said. "We're lucky. I wasn't sure he would be here this late." When they reached the store, he stopped and looked around the parking area. Then they took the horse back to the stables, quickly rubbed him down, threw a blanket around him, and tied him in an empty stall, which had water and hay.

Roo pushed through the door, thinking they could stay here for the night sleeping on the feed sacks and his friend would drive them to Ben's in his carriage in the morning. Only one kerosene lamp lit the room, and it seemed strange that Henny wasn't at his table working at his accounts. He heard a dripping noise and something fluttered in his chest when he saw the crushed eyeglasses and blood running down the side of the counter. In the half darkness he made out what was in front of him. Henny's head, eyes still wide open in terror, rested on the counter. Katya let out a hoarse wild cry.

He carried her away, fumbling with the back door, running in terror into the darkness. The killers could be hidden somewhere in the store, watching them. A stream of sorrow and horror ran through him. Christ, his friend. The killers had tortured him to find out where they were hiding. He gently put Katya on her feet.

Then they were moving back into the forest. Roo struggled on with heavy backpack figuring that the killer had not expected them to show up here. The loud burst of gunfire from the semi-automatic shocked him.

"Get behind me," he said, pressing her between his body and a large tree. He could feel her shaking uncontrollably. A dark shadow appeared through the snow in front of him. Even though visibility wasn't good, Roo shot several times, but the figure vanished into white.

"Stay here," he whispered and crawled along for several feet. He heard a distant crack of branches, then nothing. He crept back, expecting to be fired on again and pulled Katya along, going toward the direction of the shots, taking cover behind each tree. A thin trickle of blood appeared in the snow, which grew larger as they advanced, ending in puddles. The smell of blood pervaded the clear air.

A man's body lay in the snow, his snowshoes sticking in the air. His white camouflage suit and balaclava were soaked with blood. A pistol was clipped to his belt and the Uzi he had fired at them rested beside him.

From the distance, Roo couldn't see if he was still breathing. "Can you cover me?" he said. She nodded and he handed her the pistol.

As he drew closer, Roo realized that he had not killed the man. He had been hit in the head from behind by an assault rifle. He checked the man's pulse but there was nothing. Roo jerked back when he saw the large hunting knife attached to the dead man's belt. Clipped to his jacket was a field phone, used in the military for long distance communication. He ripped the phone from its case and motioned Katya forward. She was shaking, still pointing the gun at the lifeless figure.

"Don't worry," Roo took the gun from her. "He's dead."

Katya's eyes fell on the tortoise shell lorgnette lying in the snow, its golden chain broken. Roo remembered the chain link he had found near Christina's body. Everything was still for a long moment. Then he ripped off the blood soaked balaclava.

Chapter 51

Roo-Katya
Tecumseh's Forest

ROO CHANGED DIRECTION, dragging Katya back into the woods, branches clawing at them, and tearing their clothes. Knee deep in some places in snow, he tried to keep underneath trees where it wasn't as deep. He heard heavy boots behind them; all the while his mind ran on. Poor Henny dead; Maxi Suvorov shot by an assault weapon. The killers were roaming the forest. They skirted the edge of fields passing dark farms, where he could hear the muffled noises of cows in their sleep.

Snow dropped like a curtain and combined with only a slit of moonlight through the clouds, made it impossible to see more than a few steps ahead, but he knew where he was going. It was imprinted from the past on his mind.

He was on the old Shawnee trail he had discovered as a young boy. He had heard his dad say of him, one of his rare compliments, that he was a natural tracker, a woodsman. He remembered long ago tracking a deer on one of the trail's branches all the way to Ben's farm. Instinct guiding him, he began to run ahead, but Katya had not followed him. He struggled back and found her covered with snow, leaning against a large oak tree. He wanted to shout at her but that would have broken their cover. He half carried, half pulled her through a tangle of trees and bushes. Exhausted, he stopped, trying to silence his heavy breathing. The footsteps crashed through the underbrush, nearly upon them.

Moving instinctively, he pushed her far underneath an elderberry bush, then heaped snow over her, leaving a small space for her to breathe. He laid some branches he found nearby on top of the bush, hoping they wouldn't see his marks in the falling snow. Then he crawled back into another set of bushes and waited, with his gun, his heart pounding. They came, their heavy boots crushing the twigs. The smell of tobacco bruised the clear air as they passed, speaking in low harsh merciless voices. He was sure they were cursing in Russian. To contain his fear, he tried to count them, but couldn't see. There would be no chance to reason with them, to explain. Devlin's utterances came back to him. '*Chistka,* cleansing, purging.' The Cheka word for extermination echoed with the sound of their boots.

But who were they? Who had sent them? They passed close by her hiding place. "Don't move, don't move," he pleaded under his breath, willing her.

He waited for long moments, the ground swaying underneath him, until their footsteps, and voices grew faint and died in the distance. He ran to the bush and like a madman uncovered Katya. Her hood had dropped, and she was soaking wet, frozen, her teeth chattering. He carried her back into the forest, and was forced to stop for a moment, bent over wheezing, then continued on the trail for what seemed like hours, only hoping his instinct, a memory of the past, was true and he was going in the right direction.

They reached the trail's end suddenly, emerging from the trees at the edge of a field. A distant light filtered through the snow, showing the back of a small farmhouse a half-mile away. He strained his eyes, not sure where he was, knowing he was unable to go on. Scrambling and snarling, erupting from a barn near the house, a pack of hunting dogs attacked them. The dogs surrounded them, leaping at them, their teeth bared. Katya let out a sharp cry and clung to him.

"Don't move," Roo said. "Don't make a sound." Barking savagely the dogs circled them, threatening, barring the pathway to the house. In the distance, a bulk of a man hurried toward them. He was aiming a shotgun.

It was Ben, calling off the dogs with a sharp whistle. They went whimpering, and howling in disappointment back to the barn. "Man, what's happened? I didn't know what to think when you didn't turn up at the meeting place. Where the hell were you?"

Roo picked up Katya, who had fallen in the snow, and carried her to the house. Ben followed. "Man, what's going on? You scared the shit out of me."

"The killers came after us at the farmhouse. They're out there, not far away," Roo gasped, drawing his breath.

They entered the house and he gently placed Katya on a bench by the door; wincing he pulled off his gloves. Ben stared at his hands. "What the hell happened to you?"

"A disagreement with a cat. They're almost healed," Roo said, ripping off the bandages.

They thawed out in Ben's kitchen, a square white room furnished with an ancient refrigerator, stove, wood table, and chairs. It faintly smelled of dogs and baked beans. After he'd given Roo clothes and Katya his robe, he put their wet clothes in his dryer in the outdoor room next to the kitchen. Roo wrapped Katya in a wool blanket and gently rubbed her feet to get her circulation moving. Ben opened a cupboard, took out a bottle of Jim Beam, poured three shots of whiskey in water glasses, and they all three quickly drank it down. Katya continued to shake until the whiskey took effect, and seemed to slide away into a trance while Roo sat with his head down breathing hard and told Ben about the murders.

"Jesus," Ben whispered, his face pained, taking a swig from the bottle. "And this poor woman turned out to be the daughter of a Russian defector, hiding from the Russian secret police for years."

"Yeah." Roo poured another drink. "Her real name was Eugenia Suslova. She left us a bunch of papers her father had hidden from the Russian secret police. But I'm sure she was murdered by someone tailing us."

Ben sat for a moment, with his head in his hands. "She probably told them all she knew about where you were going. But that doesn't explain how they discovered you stopped for supplies at the general store. Henny was forced to tell them you were at the farm."

Roo's body jerked with revulsion. "Maybe the murders could have been avoided, if we had just come to Miss Scott's, I mean Eugenia's, sooner. If I hadn't been such a dumb fuck." He was worried about Moses and his family and filled with guilt that he had involved them.

Ben was adamant. "No way, these bastards mean business. They know how to find people. Who are they anyway?"

"Russians. Heavily armed mercenaries. They could be Petrosian's men, or Russian secret service, although I doubt that. Or men associated with Kayakov." Roo took out Maxi's phone and they both examined it. There were coded numbers for New York, Siberia, and France. Recent calls from France were to a code name, Stavrogin.

"You know, I'm surprised that Suvorov was in on this," Ben said. Katya raised her head. Her face looked small, like a little girl's.

"Maxi could have been coming to help us," she said in a faint voice as though she didn't really believe it.

"I don't think so," Roo said softly. "He was shooting at us when he was hit from behind. I still can't figure out how we managed to escape." He thought of Suvorov's knife. "Maxi could have murdered Henny."

Katya let out a sob and put her head down on the table.

He still hadn't taken it all in or fully realized what Maxi Suvorov's death meant. Even as much as he disliked him, he was surprised that the man who posed as a dandy had the alias Stavrogin and had committed those brutal perverted acts, like dressing up women before he tortured them. The picture of Eugenia tied in her chair overwhelmed him.

"Excuse me," he said. He was hot, his stomach lurching. He ran down the hall to the bathroom and threw up. He flushed the toilet and washed his face with cold water, staring into the mirror, his face white with shock. Suvorov was a sicko, twisted, chasing Katya to kill her. But how could someone so sophisticated believe the primitive superstition that the killer was reflected in the victim's eyes? The countess claimed Maxi had been brainwashed. Scary, weird, but it might be true. He was taking orders from someone. Roo went back to the kitchen hoping Ben hadn't heard his gagging.

"So you don't know how many Russian killers are out there?" Ben said, taking his shotgun and going to the window and peering out at the forest.

"More than six, but I couldn't count them. The snow was blinding. Anyway, we have to move. The storage place is only open until ten."

Katya sat numb, inured finally to any horror. Even if they found the archive inside this storage place, it never would be worth all the deaths.

Ben looked out the front window of the farmhouse toward the lane. "How did they find you?"

"Not sure. They may have first traced our direction on the highway from a phone signal." Roo didn't look at Katya. "Or maybe they saw us the first day we exchanged cars. And then they had someone in Columbus, watching us." He was thinking of Len and Marge.

"Your clothes should be dry," Ben said. "We can make it if we go now. I'll take the van. It'll do better on the road in the snow." He locked up and hurried out to the line of garages near the house.

The country roads were choked with snow, but Ben drove expertly through the storm. After they were on the road for a while and there was no sign of the killers, he put the headlights on high beam. Avoiding Paint Creek, he ploughed through two back roads to Mt. Sterling and then turned onto Route 56 and finally I71. They passed the Digby Downs exit, once the homestead of the Digby's, now torn down for a housing development. Katya thought of Christina, the archivist whose life ended near here. The snow had stopped, and the roads were clear when they reached Route 670 and followed the signs to Easton Town Center. They traveled in silence, the car echoing with anguished cries of the dead.

Katya's hair had fallen loose in a tangle, but she didn't bother to fix it. She was struggling to keep back the horrifying images of Eugenia and Henny. But what shocked her most was Maxi lying there in the snow, his handsome face, the face she had kissed, covered in blood. She had given up her belief that he had come to rescue her. He had completely fooled her and Abigail, deliberately seducing them both for the archive. And then he had turned into a creature indescribably evil. It was real to her now.

Choking tears, she tried to fix her mind on some middle point away from this horror to concentrate on finding the archive. But when she looked out the window into the darkness flashing by, she was overcome with hideous scenes of his hands caressing her body, torturing Abigail, murdering Christina, slashing out their eyes, the hunting knife for skinning animals tucked in his belt.

The bite mark still burned; the emotional scar would never go away. She had believed her attacker at RUS had been von Burkhardt. But it was Maxi who drugged her, deliberately frightened and humiliated her, so that he could control her. When she thought he loved her, he was planning her torture and death.

The shopping center seemed unreal, as though they had dropped out of a nightmarish fairy tale into ordinary life. Built in neo-colonial style with slanted roofs and shutters, its lights glittered invitingly. Ben passed through one of the main streets crowded with late night shoppers walking about in the snow. Katya hunched down in the back seat, watched well-dressed people shopping, having normal lives, wondering if she would ever have dinner in a restaurant and or go to a movie or do anything normal again. Then she thought of Abigail, and knew her guardian would have urged her to go on, in defiance of the killers.

She studied Roo's rugged profile, thinking how mistaken she had been about him; how she had not believed or trusted him.

Roo looked at the map as they headed toward Drake's Storage. An extraneous thought came to him, and for a moment he saw the land as thick, impenetrable forest. But the trees were gone and Tecumseh's hunting ground had been covered over with housing developments, fast food restaurants, fancy shops, car lots, and supermarkets. For an instant, he pictured the two noble savages, Tecumseh and his brother, out of time, lost ghosts wandering past the stores.

They drove away from the main shopping area and skirted to the east out of the traffic. Drake's Storage, a huge boxlike structure, loomed straight ahead. Ben circled the brightly lit parking lot, going past two cars parked under the lights, and then pulled up next to the building's entrance. Braced to get out of the car, Roo no longer had to convince himself that this was real, that it was happening in the middle of Ohio, a flyover state; that he was on the dangerous trail of some ancient secret.

Ben checked behind the building while Roo and Katya rushed inside. They presented the key to the night watchman, a bored guard with a very round face, half-closed bulbous eyes and two chins, sitting at the front desk watching CSI on his small television. Irritated that he had been called away from his program, he said, "We close in an hour. Come back tomorrow."

In a rush of anger, Roo showed his badge and pushed him against the wall.

"Listen you fat fuck, you'll stay open as long as we want. Turn off the lights and lock the door. Don't let anyone else in." Katya stood back in shock at his outburst.

"Ok, ok." The watchman held out his hands, smiling weakly. He lumbered, his beer belly bouncing through the winding long halls to locker number ten.

Ben joined them, and they waited in tense silence in the dim light as Roo put the key in the lock and the door swung open.

"Geez," Ben breathed.

"The Blood Archive," Katya said, in awe.

They faced a large room stacked high with scores of metal filing boxes.

They listened for the ominous clatter of boots in the hall, overwhelmed by the number of boxes.

"How will we ever find the *ukase* before they catch up with us?" Katya said what they were all thinking.

"We're screwed. They're probably all written in Russian," Ben said.

Roo looked at the nearest stack, "You're right. We're screwed. The boxes are numbered, so we have to search all of them."

Katya turned to Roo, "Do you remember? Christina hinted that there was one important file called 'Krov Arkhiv I'."

A tense half hour passed as they searched, scrambling through the files until Katya spotted it high in the middle of the first stack.

Roo stood on some boxes and brought it down.

"I know what we need is in here," she said. "But some of the others could be important."

"I'll come back and load these up later. We can keep them in my garage. No one will know," Ben said.

"It'll be too dangerous for you to return," Roo said, "We have to take them now."

They struggled to move the metal boxes quickly while Katya kept watch by the van, gingerly holding Roo's pistol, feeling faint just looking at it. They finished the last of the files while Katya signed the papers, and the watchman, still avoiding Roo, locked the door.

They were exhausted, but a collective excitement filled the van as Ben drove out of the shopping center and onto the highway. The night sky was clear. Its moonlight made them visible. Roo felt his skin prick with danger. Instinct told him that someone was following them, but no car was in sight as they plunged back onto the country roads.

The file, Krov Arkhiv I, was placed on the floor in Ben's living room. They sat like supplicants, urgency filling them, on the one leather couch, the only furniture in the room other than a giant television that filled the opposite wall. They pulled the blinds, shutting out the outside. The dogs had erupted when they drove in but became quiet as soon as Ben got out of the car. "No one will ever come in here," he said. "If anyone comes around, the dogs will let us know."

Katya knew that they were waiting, impatient for her to open the file, but she hesitated. Abigail had called it her legacy. It had been left to her, but it could be some terrible hoax. She fumbled at the latch and lifted the lid.

"Is that it?" Ben said, his voice registering disgust and disappointment.

A memory stick fell on the floor. Roo remembered thinking the box had been very light. He turned it upside down, and shook it and a scrap of paper floated out. Curious, he picked it up and gave it Katya.

"It's the torn half of an old photograph. What could this mean?" Katya said.

"We need a computer," Roo said, putting the torn photo in his pocket. "Where can we get access this time of night?"

"I'll call Fiona," Ben said. "I don't think my phone has been tapped. We'll take the risk. She has a good computer and her book club should be finished by now."

Chapter 52

Roo-Katya
Tecumseh County

ALTHOUGH THEY BELIEVED they were safe for the moment, they left by Ben's kitchen door, creeping along the side of the house to the barn and the line of garages. Ben's old Range Rover clanked rhythmically as they drove to Paint Creek.

It was 1 a.m., and the town lights had been turned off. Roo felt like a phantom as scenes of his ordinary life before he found Christina's bones, before the archive, drifted before him. Nelson's Diner with its dim night lights, looked melancholy, like a Hopper painting he had once seen in the Columbus museum. He was reminded of Stumpy, a rotund figure, eating dinner there alone.

The town square glistened with crystals of snow, and its old buildings, the library, courthouse, elementary school, frosted with slabs of white, looked like a page torn from a book of fairy tales. But out there beyond the town's innocence the dark men waited. Eugenia had called them, '*Besy*, bestial monsters, not human.'

He could feel Katya trembling, hear her rapid breathing as she hunched down beside him. He stayed as close as he could to her, hoping he wasn't overstepping, realizing that he wanted her desperately, amazed that he could have these thoughts when any moment they could be killed. The fear in her eyes was like that of the fox he and Ben had once cornered. He had looked at the huddled animal and refused to let Ben shoot it. Ben had been mad as hell at him for days afterward.

They passed the turn to the Sheriff's office, and he worried that someone in Paint would spot them and tell Stumpy, or that the police would discover the murder victims and he and Katya would be embroiled in the investigation and vulnerable to the killers. He jerked, startled at the dark shadows lurking on the road and grabbed his gun, but as the car passed, saw they were only trees blowing in the wind.

He struggled to organize his thoughts but it was hard while he was holding a gun. Maxi had tried to kill them, but who else was hunting them down? There had to be at least two groups from the farmhouse and then the men in the forest. Questions about Devlin bubbled up as though from a deep well in his mind. Was he out there somewhere? Why couldn't he contact him?

Fiona Lindsay's large turn of the century house, with ornate gingerbread trimming, perched on the edge of the town before the fields and forest took over.

"It's her parents' house," Ben said. "They moved to Florida." He drove down the long drive, parking at the back, and they ran up the path to the back porch guided by the light from a small globe lantern. Fiona was waiting for them and quickly opened the kitchen door. She was tall and willowy, dressed in black tights and top. Her pretty face, with a small slender nose and broad forehead was framed by very curly red hair. Her smile faded and her eyes widened behind her horn rims when she saw the guns.

"Come in," she said, slamming the door shut in the hall and rushing them into an old fashioned kitchen with oak wood cabinets and large mahogany table and chairs. A pot of chicken noodle soup was simmering on the stove, its appetizing smell pervading the room.

Ben quickly introduced Katya, and Fiona partly recovered from her fright, managed to smile at her. "Pleased to meet you. I hope I can help out."

Moving gracefully like a dancer, she ushered them into a book lined room with a roaring fire and square couches surrounding the fireplace. Grandma Moses prints decorated the walls. A copy of *War and Peace* with extensive notes rested on the coffee table.

"Did you hear any news?" Ben asked, looking out the windows as he pulled the curtains.

"No, I haven't. I turned on the TV after book club, but there was nothing. I've made coffee and thought you might like some soup. Please sit down, make yourselves at home," Fiona said, going into the kitchen.

Ben followed her, speaking to her in a low voice. Roo saw them in a passionate embrace and felt an unreasonable twinge of jealousy. They brought back mugs of chicken noodle soup and thick whole grain bread and butter. Fiona smiled at Katya again, handing her a mug. "I made it this morning. You probably need some food."

"Thank you, you're very kind," Katya said. She liked Fiona immediately, noting her warmth and generosity, qualities she believed were Midwestern. In other circumstances they might be friends.

Roo took the memory stick from his bag and handed it to Fiona. While they sat on the couches and ate, she studied it and said it would work. Ben shut off all the lights except for one above the desk, giving the room a strange ghostly glow. They crowded around the computer in expectant silence, while Fiona plugged in the memory stick and clicked on the file.

Blood Archive: Ukase
Archivist, Christina Gartner.

A faded photograph floated on the screen. They stared in surprise. Katya recoiled in horror. It was a group photo of the Romanovs and their servants. The Tsar and his son, Alexei sit on chairs in the middle of the room. The Tsarina in the left corner of the room sits in front of three of the Grand Duchesses. The fourth girl is standing by a woman servant clutching a pillow. The slightly blurred faces stare at them in unsmiling innocence, safe forever in the moment of the photograph. Katya closed her eyes. Then she is in the room, hearing the murmur of their voices, standing beside the girl with golden hair and blue eyes. The girl leans close to Katya and whispers, 'It is all right. They just want to take our photograph.'

Katya knew that in the next few seconds, the peace of the room would be shattered. The girl in the picture is unaware that in that short time she will be screaming, running futilely around the small room, filled with smoke and shouts from the killers, to escape the crack of gunshots and the dull stabs of bayonets.

She cried, "Stop!"

They looked up from the computer, startled.

"Katya, What's wrong?" Roo said.

"It's the Tsar and his family. Look at the date and time."

Ipatiev House, 2:15 a.m., July 17, 1918 was written on the photograph. "This was taken just before they were murdered," she said, her voice shaking.

Screams and gunshots seemed to hover over the eerie picture. They all sat in silence realizing they were looking at the family from the same position as their killers.

"Look at this." Fiona pointed to the screen.

Three subjects in the photograph have black circles drawn around their heads.

Fiona clicked to the next page. Three mug shots, the faces snapped front, right, and left appeared on the screen. Looking closer they saw that the subjects are not convicts but three of the Romanov children. Christina's note underneath explains that in October 1917, the Bolshevik commissar ordered the family to pose like convicts for identity cards.

The Tsarevich Alexei stares out at them with dull hopeless eyes as though knowing what awaits him. He is identified as Citizen Alexei Nikolaievich Romanov registered with the Cheka with the number 29-34-08. The next number, 29-34-09, belonged to one of his sisters, Grand Duchess Anastasia Nikolaievna Romanova, who smiles into the camera. The third card, noted as added later, with the number 29-34-10 was that of another sister, Grand Duchess Maria Nikolaievna Romanova. The camera reveals a sad bewildered face.

This third identity card for the Grand Duchess Maria was crushed, perhaps meant to be destroyed. Dark stains partially obscured the writing at the top.

Found in Perm, Siberia, 1921.

"These are the same three persons circled on the group photograph," Fiona said, clicking back to compare them. Roo thought of Christina and the strange events that brought him here looking at her archive. He remembered his dreams of her in the forest, crying out incoherently to him. Was this what she had been trying to tell him? He wondered how these strange photos had come into her hands.

"What is all this? Where is the *ukase?*" Ben said, getting up and checking outside.

Fiona looked up at him and said, "Let's take a break." They went to the kitchen and brought back a tray with coffee.

"I don't see what the woman's getting at," Ben said, handing Katya a steaming cup.

"You're right. It's not clear," Katya said, cradling the cup. She had recovered from seeing the photo, and her voice was quiet and steady. "But we haven't finished with the file. Christina must be leading us to something with those photographs. It's just a theory, but I wonder if all the information about the *ukase* was photographed in 1918 to keep it safe, and Christina stored it in the remainder of the archive which we haven't yet seen. No one would suspect that rolls of old film would hold the secrets."

Fiona shivered in disgust. "What a terrible thing to do, take a photograph, like a souvenir, of those poor people just before they were murdered. They look so innocent of what's going to happen to them."

Ben finished his coffee and said, "Fi, can you go through the next stuff fast? We don't want to stay and put you in danger."

Fiona waved her long delicate hands for a moment as though directing imaginary traffic then sat down and quickly clicked to the next page.

A receipt came up on the screen. Dated November 1916, it recorded that gold bullion worth two hundred million dollars was held in the Swiss Bank, Pictet & Cie in Geneva. It was noted that the original receipt was in a deposit box in the same bank. They sat stunned.

Roo broke the silence. "This is what the killers are after."

Ben let out a low whistle. "What do you think the bullion's worth today?"

"It could be billions," Roo said, his voice filled with awe.

"Do you think this is a hoax or could the fortune still be in the bank?" Ben said.

No one knew the answer. Gripped by the discovery, they read on. Christina had anticipated their questions.

The new owner of the ukase must be aware that a vast fortune with power to ignite a revolution waits in that vault in Geneva.

"Goodness gracious," Fiona said to the room.

The last picture, snapped by a modern camera, was of the torn half of the photograph found in the archive file.

"But what does this all mean?" Ben said.

"I think Christina was telling us that the photographs are the key to the fortune. We have to get to Geneva," Roo said.

Later that evening, Katya was just stepping out of the shower and planned to try to sleep, when Fiona knocked. "Katya, put on my robe and come. I've found something more, another file hidden on the memory stick. I think it's for you." Katya dressed quickly and ran to the computer.

They waited in suspense as she opened the file. "It's a letter addressed to me." Katya said, her voice sounded faint faraway.

Roo stood over her shoulder while she read aloud.

My Dear Katya,

It may be years after my death when you read this letter. The Blood Archive is yours. You must save it from falling into the hands of those who would use it for evil.

As I write this last letter, I am looking at a photograph of you that Abigail sent me. You are dressed in a ski suit and standing in front of a giant icy peak in some ski resort. You are so beautiful. I am very proud that you are my daughter and am heartbroken that I was not able to ever see you or to know you.

The Blood Archive also tells the story of why I had to abandon you. My dearest friend Abigail who took care of you will lead you to the archive when she believes you are ready. The story of my past is all there for you to judge …

Chapter 53

Katya
Tecumseh County

THEY LEFT FOR Cincinnati Airport at sunrise, Ben driving Fiona's blue Fiesta. Roo climbed in back with Katya, his gun resting between them, and scanned the horizon.

"You know they'll be out there somewhere. They're never going to give up the fortune," he said.

They took the alley behind Fiona's house, past garages, rabbit hutches, gardening sheds, and scarecrows in old jackets, waiting to be put out in spring. The alley led to a road that had served a strip mine, abandoned years ago. Katya shivered in the harsh light. The snow sticking in small bare trees failed to cover the scars cut in the land.

She was exhausted and seemed to have lost all feeling about the victims and the fatalities that followed in her wake. Now that they had found the archive, it seemed that certain death awaited all of them.

"It's fresh, no tracks," Ben said, his large shoulders filled the front seat as he maneuvered through the snow. As the car rattled over ruts and bumps on the deserted road, she returned to the one shocking fact. Christina Gartner, the archivist who was murdered in the cabin, was her mother. It seemed like some terrible joke, but she knew it was true.

She had not slept, tormented by the face of Christina Gartner floating in front of her. She could not grieve for this stranger as she did for Abigail, and could only feel regret and sorrow that she had never known her.

That morning while Fiona packed a bag for her, Katya had read the last part of Christina's letter with a horrified fascination, and began to understand how the strange past events fit together. Her photograph, posing for Abigail at Courchevel, had been in Christina's pocket, and she had looked at it the day she wrote the letter, just before she was murdered. Maxi had killed Christina, taken the photograph, copied it for the killers and then had begun his search for her.

For a moment, Maxi was in front of her at the airport looking at her not with admiration as she had thought, but because he recognized her from the photograph and even then was planning her torture and death. She forced herself to keep still, afraid that her body would begin quaking and never stop. Katya saw her mother, collecting the last of the archive, writing this letter. Phrases of the letter jumped out at her, as the car raced through the scrub.

I became involved, accidentally. Dangerous to have any knowledge of the ukase. Everyone who knew of this was murdered. I had a brief affair with the man who was your father. It was only to protect you that I was forced to abandon you, gave the care of you to Abigail. I hope you are not alone.

Now she understood Abigail's unreasonable demand that she stay away from New York. She had feared the killers would discover Katya's identity. Alone, she thought bitterly, glancing at Roo holding his gun out staring out the window. Maybe that was her fate.

The road wove around small hills, past abandoned barns and rusty machinery used in the mine. Her thoughts were like this same twisting road, turning and winding and always leading her back into the past, into something even more terrifying than she already had faced. They passed a clump of green pine trees, an oasis in the grim landscape and then drove for a while beside a creek.

Ben broke in, "Let's see if there's any news." He clicked on the radio. Everything was driven from her mind by the cheerful matter of fact words of the broadcaster.

She heard Roo say, "My God, they killed the bikers in the house next to Eugenia's."

Ben swerved off the road and they careened on its edge until he could stop the car.

"Fuck," he said, his normally placid face distorted in panic.

She heard snatches from the newsreader. 'Brutal murders on Indianola at the edge of the OSU campus. The bodies of five men, one a student were found beheaded. Miss Eugenia Scott, the woman living next door, a recluse, also murdered after being tortured. Police state that it is the work of a serial killer. Worst on record. No other details have been released. Press banned from taking photos. Police have not issued an official statement, but believe that the killings were drug related, and Miss Scott may have been an innocent witness.'

"It was a Russian death squad. They never leave witnesses alive. The guys next door were dead when we discovered Eugenia's body," Roo stammered in shock, remembering the strange quiet of the house next door.

The pleasant, neutral voice went on. "In an unrelated, but equally brutal incident, a night watchman at Drake Storage near Easton Town Center was found dead this morning at the business entrance. Police have not yet revealed his identity."

Roo said, "They could have trailed us to Fiona's."

Ben said, "My God, Fiona. I've got to call Fiona. She said she was going to see her girlfriend Lucy." His voice was rough, like he'd been eating gravel. They waited, hardly able to breathe, until they saw the look of relief on his face. "She's all right. She's with friends at the diner."

They said nothing more as they raced over the small road toward the entrance to the main highway. The flat bare facts of the deaths lay before them like the fields they passed.

When Ben said goodbye at the airport, Roo handed over his gun, "Thanks, I'll get in touch as soon as I can."

"I'll handle everything," Ben said. Katya reached up and kissed him, which startled and pleased him. "Remember," he said, sticking his head out the window as he drove off. "There's no way those fuckers won't kill for the money."

Chapter 54

Mikhail.
Courchevel, France

THE SOFT VOICE said "done" and Mikhail's phone went dead. The traitor Stavrogin had been eliminated. The girl and the law officer had found the archive, and his men were trailing them. They appeared to be heading for the airport in Cincinnati, final destination unknown.

Mikhail was in his favorite chair in the large reception room that overlooked the mountains. It was a brilliant morning, the sky fathomless blue, almost sinister in its depth. He was gazing out intently, blind to the beauty of nature, watching for sudden movement, then an attack. One of his men on patrol passed the window. He gave him a thumbs up.

His triumph at finding the archive was tempered by terrible anxiety that ran through him like prison wire. He had managed only to cage the panic, to be able to think. He rose from the chair and paced back and forth past the window, his mind working feverishly. He believed the document that had so astonished him was a forgery, a devious attempt by the Shaman to control him. Forgeries of official certificates were common among his companions. But in spite of this, he wanted to see the young woman in person. Then he would decide how to end her life.

He stopped pacing and made another call to Little Odessa. He frowned, listening to the nervous voice on the other end. The group had encountered another hit squad in the Tecumseh County forest, but could not identify any of the gunmen, who spoke Russian. The Shaman's men. He hung up, thinking it was like fucking Afghanistan in the middle of the U.S. He let out a short harsh bark of laughter at his joke. There had been a number of casualties, inevitable in this kind of operation. He shrugged his shoulders. Taking life, what was so hard?

Still in his bathrobe, he picked at a hangnail, realizing that he was becoming slovenly and unkempt since Sasha's deadly messages had come to him. He wearily pulled the robe tighter. A strange fatigue had come over him. Simple, childlike questions rose in his mind. Would he still be able to use the *ukase* to destroy Sasha? Would he be able to go home? That was all he wanted.

Sasha, the Shaman. He pictured the tiny pale face, eyes closed in death, the last time he saw him. Mikhail was awestruck that he had survived. Where had the police taken him that day in Irkutsk? When none of his contacts or Interpol had come up with anything on Sasha's past, Mikhail had sent Shamil into the prison underworld to trace him. Before being hired as a bodyguard, Shamil had been released from prison shortly after the fall of the Soviet Union and had lived with other gang members in the enormous Rossiya Hotel in Moscow.

Late last night he had returned from his brief sojourn with his gangster friends and was waiting to see him. Mikhail went over to the table by the couch and rang a service bell. There was a knock and Shamil stood before him, resplendent in a new Armani suit. His recent haircut, short around the edges, stood up from his forehead, giving him a startled look. He reeked of expensive cologne, and his nails were buffed, immaculate. Mikhail, self-conscious, pulled his robe tighter and asked if he had spent the entire time shopping and having beauty treatments.

"Well, yes, that's what my contacts are doing. Profits are good," Shamil said, posing like a magazine model.

Mikhail motioned him to a chair. Shamil sat, carefully pulling up his trouser legs to protect the creases. He spoke in a surprisingly literate Russian peppered with American slang he had picked up from TV programs and gangster movies. His large dark intelligent eyes lit up and his voice was low and pleasant.

"The first anyone knows of the Shaman is in Vorkuta prison when he was in his early teens. No one I spoke to had any idea where he had come from. At that time he was known as *Solnyshko,* Little Sun. My source tells me he was tattooed with a large yellow sun on his chest. Little Sun was installed as the wife of the most powerful mafia leader in the prison, the Chechen, Ruslan Nuchaev." Shamil laughed uncomfortably. "You know what that means."

Mikhail nodded. This had to be Sasha. Suddenly the scenes of copulation, of violation in the middle of the barracks returned. The prison odor of the slop buckets filled his nostrils, making him nauseous. He motioned Shamil to go on.

"Those wives were always separated from the others and held in contempt. But Little Sun was different. Soon after he became the favorite, Ruslan was found dead one morning, stabbed with a kitchen knife as he slept. At this time Little Sun changed his name to the Shaman and unusual as it seems, became the new power in the prison. You know, life and death over everyone." Shamil extended his slender arms jingling with diamond bracelets to indicate the power.

"The man was feared by everyone and still is. My source remains anonymous. There were rumors that he performed miracles, had some sort of mystical power and controlled even the camp officers. I heard he killed *zeks* in strange ceremonies." Shamil looked like a frightened deer facing a shotgun.

"He was released in the early 90's along with many of his followers and disappeared." He shrugged his shoulders. "That's all anyone knew."

Mikhail said almost to himself, "And now he has an armed camp in Siberia and is allied with General Letinov and other likeminded in the Kremlin who want to destroy me."

He rose from the chair and shook Shamil's hand. "Good work. I commend you."

Shamil nodded, and Mikhail watched his elegant figure saunter from the room thinking that after he secured the archive, he would call a meeting with General Letinov and try to make a deal. He believed the general and Sasha had been connected for years and were plotting a coup from that fortified kingdom in Siberia. It was time for him to strike, to begin Sasha's destruction. He opened his computer and typed his message.

Den, I know the document is a forgery. But even if it were genuine, it would never have changed my mind. Katya Marston and the law officer, Reuben Yoder are dead, lying in the forest in Ohio. I have control of the archive and the ukase. I think we can make an arrangement to accommodate us both. I will meet you if you agree. Time and place?

Noch

He rose from the desk. Still, still, even after the emails, the murder of Marousia, the revelation that he had been used, it was hard to erase the fond memories of his friend, his brother, memories he'd carried with him to survive. Sasha had done things he found revolting to keep him alive.

He went to the chest and took out the last section of the French File.

He would read the last and then burn them all, so no one could make use of them. His eyes lit like a magnet on a photograph of the Raven, perhaps in his early fifties in military uniform. He has his arm around a beautiful young woman wearing an embroidered robe. It was the same woman in the snapshot found in the old Siberian files.

Mongolia, 1945 was written at the bottom. This intrigued Mikhail. He knew that the Raven had been in Mongolia on a mission during the civil war, but this young woman would have been a baby then or perhaps not yet born.

He picked up a report dated March 10, 1946, written in a bold hand on thick expensive paper.

The attempt to smuggle the subject across the border into China failed. It was an accident of fate that border troops stumbled upon my men and the subject. She was mistaken for a spy and disappeared into the gulag. It is believed she is dead. She was pregnant. I managed to keep these papers from Stalin by bribing Beria with a young girl.

With a shock he recognized the Raven's handwriting.

Mikhail recalled Stalin's order to Beria and the subsequent trial and execution of Dorji and the Mongolian unit, the blood stains remaining on the papers.

His heart racing, he stared down at faded photocopies. A document signed by Suslov, an administrator in the Gulag recorded the birth of a male child in March 1946 in Camp 45, the day the unidentified woman arrived in the prison. Suslov noted that the mother died that day, but the baby survived and was placed in the nursery along with another child born at the same time.

"Suslov," he said aloud, remembering that the prison administrator had defected to the United States. He must have stolen the records from the Gulag after Stalin had ordered elimination of all those with any knowledge of this information.

The second photograph was slightly blurred. He could not see if the two small boys standing in front of a U.S. army issued truck are smiling. They look so tiny, fragile, like miniature toys. A massive birch forest rises behind them. He remembered Kosloff pointing to the box, explaining that it was a camera. He was one of the boys in the picture. Sasha was the other. Tears stung his eyes. He rolled up his sleeve and stared at the small tattoo on his arm.

But it was after he read the last report in the file, describing the Raven's visit to Mongolia in 1945 that everything came crashing down on him. He, who prided himself on his control, let out an enormous cry of anguish, like a tortured animal, wanting to be free. It could not be true.

He felt his fear escaping, scratching at the cage. He rushed to the bathroom and stared in the mirror at the face of a *zek*, a convict with blood shot eyes, the putrid taste of *balanda*, prison soup, on his tongue.

"Who are you?" His words were quiet, inquiring as he peered into the black eyes of an anonymous killer.

He was lying in the dark of his bedroom when his phone rang.

Bebe said, "They are on their way to Geneva now."

Chapter 55

Roo-Katya
Geneva, Switzerland

ROO SAT BACK with relief as the plane took off for Paris. The wheels went up and they floated above the blinking lights of Cincinnati. Stretching beyond the city was the darkness of the forest where the killers hunted them. His heart raced, thinking of the murders left in their wake and of those frantic moments before Ben telephoned Fiona and they knew she was all right.

"Did you see any of them getting on the plane?" Katya said, turning to him but not meeting his eyes.

"No," he said. "I checked when we boarded. We're safe until we land in Paris and change to the Geneva flight." Only a married couple and two single women were behind them in the First Class Cabin. In the short time at Fiona's, Katya had arranged the tickets on her credit card, and there had been no trouble getting through security. Everything had been easy except for the long tense wait in the lounge.

Katya lapsed into silence. Roo watched her warily, waiting for her to go to pieces. In spite of the terror and the shocks they had suffered, she still looked beautiful, although her usual delicate color was gone. She was wearing a blue sweater of Fiona's and jeans. He had borrowed Ben's leather jacket.

The plane reached cruising altitude and the stewardess poured them each a glass of champagne. "Here, drink this," he said.

She dutifully took a small sip. He drained his glass, studiously avoiding looking at her, pretending to read the menu.

She took another drink, and said in her very proper English voice, "You must know, I owe you an apology. They might never have murdered anyone, if I hadn't tried to phone Maxi. It was stupid, but I just didn't believe he would …"

"It wasn't stupid," he said. The stewardess, a pretty brunette poured him another glass. "How would you know Maxi was a killer? He was a skillful operator. They would have found us anyway."

Katya closed her eyes for a moment then looked at him. "Now that you've solved your case, you don't have to go on with me. It's not fair to you. You can take a plane to New York from Paris." Her voice was expressionless, alarming.

He stared past her out the window. They were above the clouds now and the sky was shot with stars. He blurted out, almost in a panic. "What do you mean? I would never leave you." Embarrassed, he backtracked. "You couldn't know. And Maxi was working for someone who completely controlled him."

Then he reached over and impulsively put his arm around her. She pressed close to him, and for a moment he ceased to worry about what could be waiting at the end of the flight.

As though reminding him, she said, "What will we do after we find the contents of the ukase. I'm not brave like Abigail or Christina."

She hesitated, as if getting used to the idea. "My mother. I'm so scared. I just don't want them to torture me."

His lips grazed the top of her head. "I'm not sure, but think I have a plan. We'll just try to get to the bank first. Don't worry. I'll work it out." He wondered what they would find there. It had been such a long time, that even if it wasn't a hoax, the chances of anything still being in the safe deposit box seemed slim.

Sleep, come quickly, Katya silently begged, finishing the rest of her drink, and lying back. There were two Katya's now; the controlled English woman, poised and calm, and the other woman, hidden deep inside her, who could not stop screaming. She could keep the horror away if she behaved in a cool controlled manner, wrapping that screaming person in layer after layer of sheets, over the terror, until she could no longer hear her.

A silence descended on her, drowning out the sound of the airplane motor. She struggled to escape the picture slowly developing at the edge of her sight. She fought hard to keep it away, but, inexorably, it slid in front of her. Sheets of blood rained down. In the shower of red, Eugenia's face floats, tilted up in agony, as though trying to see, her little mouth open in a silent scream; then Henny's eyes, still reflecting the surprise of terror, face her. She used all her will to force the picture away. When it faded she was so tired and slipped into an exhausted sleep.

Roo saw that she was sleeping and covered her with a blanket, his hand on her, watching her until her breath was even and slow. The poetry stored in his head had deserted him in these past weeks. He knew no poems about murder, but looking at her he murmured some lines. *Still, still to hear her tender taken breath / And so live forever—or else swoon to death.*

He supposed the lines were what Katya would call in her cool English voice 'Over the top', but it was true. That's what he felt about her. Keats, a true genius, was dying of TB when he wrote *Bright Star* and Roo thought the lines didn't fit with someone like him enjoying a full meal on his first transatlantic flight. He had been hungry and stoked up for what might await them tomorrow. The stewardess removed his empty tray, and he glanced at Katya. It was a complete mystery to him that she could survive on what she ate. He would never leave her unless she asked him to.

The series of events since finding the archive were dizzying; it seemed unreal that he was on a plane with Katya, heading for Geneva, in the hunt for billions of dollars. More danger awaited them when they changed planes in Paris. If they were lucky, the killers might not know their destination.

He had been tempted to report in to Devlin's office, but it was too risky. He wondered why there had been no contact or attempt to help him. If something happened to them, Ben had the entire fantastic story, and he only hoped he would be believed.

In spite of exhaustion, Roo couldn't sleep. He tried to plan their next move. If they made it to the bank and the safe deposit box held the treasure, he would try to contact Devlin, the police in Switzerland and the press.

He worried that the treasure might not be there or that the photograph would not give them entry. His mind worked on, droning like the engine, trying to fit the pieces of the puzzle together.

Even before his downfall, the Tsar had a contingency plan to save his children. After the Revolution when the Romanov family was imprisoned, the Tsar issued his last powerful edict, hiding the treasure from his enemies. For a moment he envisioned Tsar Nicholas II, a small handsome man, mild mannered in spite of his military posture, sitting at his desk in Tobolsk, a prisoner, about to be taken away to some unknown place, to death. The Tsar must have known that he was a dead man, but believed that some of his children might survive, rescued by the Brotherhood, and would use the treasure to regain the throne.

He was haunted by the ghostly photograph of the doomed Romanovs and servants, picturing the killers aiming their guns at the victims, deciding which one of the family each was going to take out. He thought about the circles around the heads of the three children and the matching identity cards, and sat up in the reclined seat, his mind racing in the darkness of the plane. The stewardess came by, asking if he wanted anything. He asked for a glass of water, and absently thanked her when she brought it.

It occurred to him that this last photograph of the Tsar and his family might not have been taken by a sadist, but by someone planted with the killers to rescue them. Perhaps the rescuer wanted to indicate something about these children, maybe that they survived that day. Was this what Christine was trying to tell them; that some of the family survived?

Weird disparate thoughts entered his mind as the seatbelt sign lit up and the plane hit turbulence, disturbing him. He had the sense that these thoughts were connected, but didn't know how. He was thinking now of the Suvorov papers and the photograph of the Suvorov party taken in Mongolia with the young woman they called the subject, forced by the crazy baron to stay behind. He saw nothing that fit together. Kayakov, Eugenia's father, Maxi, characters alive and dead floated in front of him.

He went back to the enormous fortune and what it would mean if one of these crazies got their hands on it. He turned on his light and fumbled in his bag. He checked first that he had the torn photograph and the other photos from the archive file he believed would open the bank deposit box. He remembered Kutusov, his eyes wild under snaking eyebrows, describing the swastika as the sign of the Brotherhood. But even in his wildest speculation, Roo never would have imagined that a photograph ripped in two in 1918 with this sign from the past would release the enormous treasure.

An even more outlandish thought occurred to him as the turbulence died, and the plane floated on smooth air. He sat upright, knocking over his water glass. What if someone out there was the real heir, someone directly descended from one of the Tsar's children?

The killers were waiting for them outside Geneva airport. It was spring ski season and the airport was crowded with groups of snow seekers, businessmen and UN bureaucrats. Skiers in designer jackets and expensive luggage filed through passport control and customs. Roo and Katya tried to stay in the crowd, hoping they wouldn't be noticed.

They were in the hall looking for a cab, when a stocky man approached. It was the thug Roo had tripped in Saks. His scars from the broken glass still hadn't healed. He was Eastern European, maybe Russian, certainly not American. He gave them a threatening look and signaled with his arm. No one in the crowd noticed the two hoods blocking their way.

A well-dressed, slim man took Katya's arm while the other thug, very large with a face that belonged in a lab jar, held Roo's. He felt the knife pressing against his back and saw the other man doing the same to Katya.

"Come with us," one said in heavily accented English. "Do not shout for help." There was no way to resist. Their blank neutral eyes lacked even a spark of humanity. They escorted them out the door to a huge armored Humvee.

"In the car," the big man ordered in a rough voice, relieving Roo of his bag and Katya of her handbag, while the other one took the wheel. The locks on the car clicked with an ominous finality.

The two hoods spoke only rudimentary English, only enough to give orders. The one with the strange undeveloped face seemed to be in charge.

Looking for some way to escape, he saw that the men carried pistols and kept assault rifles on the seats beside them. He glanced over at Katya, who was terrified and about to scream for help, but he shook his head. Her hand, cold, trembling touched his. He gripped it hard.

As the Humvee picked up speed, Roo stared out of the darkened windows and tried to memorize what he could of the landscape. Shortly after, they passed Swiss customs without stopping and entered France.

The killers now had the *ukase*, so there was no need to keep them alive. If the thugs stopped in some deserted place to kill them, he would attack and tell her to run. The worst scenario, rising in front of him, was Katya being tortured. Roo had not dreamed of this. He felt out of his element, as the Humvee climbed higher into a plateau beneath the high snow covered peaks of the Alps. His thoughts scattered like the birds soaring overhead. He hoped that Devlin had sent out an alert for them.

It would be suicide to go after these men now. He would wait for some chance to contact police, maybe if they made a stop. Katya stayed close to him, sheltered by his arm.

Katya glanced up at Roo, studying the men and the windows trying to find a way to escape from the car. She wondered if he was afraid of anything. She had been so unfair to him, not trusting or believing in anything he said, rude and stupid when he tried to be kind and protective of her. She had lousy judgment. She could not see the driver but her attention was caught by the big man with the rubber mask of a face in the passenger seat. His large hands wiggled constantly, the fingers struggling and wringing as though they were crushing a neck.

Her mind became very clear. She had never loved Philip or Maxi. She was attracted yes, but it was not love, more of a way to have someone protect her. Now they both seemed like total strangers to her. Roo, despite all their differences, had captured her heart. She believed she had loved him the first day she saw him standing in the gallery admiring the Rublev. She had never had this feeling before, and all she could do was rest her hand in his as they were driven to some terrible death.

She could hardly believe it when they reached Moutier, a small town at the bottom of the mountains, and watched the scenery pass by in the darkened window as they wound up the mountain road.

To her amazement, they were on the road to the ski resort of Courchevel, climbing past Le Praz then the resorts of 1500, 1650, and finally driving through La Porte de Courchevel 1850, where she and Abigail always stayed.

It was late morning and through the prison of the darkened windows Katya watched skiers taking coffee breaks, meeting for lunch, browsing and shopping. Chic, well dressed in furs and giant sunglasses without rims, they paraded by, unaware of her distressed stare. She tried to control her panic, to keep from pounding on the window and shouting out for someone to help them.

They quickly passed the Altiport, where she always met Abigail arriving by plane, and then they were beyond the Annapurna Hotel, passing the last of the luxurious chalets, reaching an isolated area and a set of high gates. In the distance a vast snowfield extended to stands of trees and towering mountains, part of the National Forest. The driver spoke into his radio, and the gates swung open. Guards in military uniforms with assault rifles, holding giant dogs on leads, waved them on. They drove through another gate manned by more guards until they reached a grand chalet built like a huge fortress within the trees.

Chapter 56

Roo-Katya-Mikhail
Courchevel, France

THEY WERE PUSHED through a front hall to a massive living room, one side glass, overlooking the mountains. A large fit man in his late fifties waited for them in front of the crackling fire. He had close-cropped light brown hair turning gray and swarthy skin. His straight features were marred by a strange indentation above his left jaw. But it was his dark eyes that Roo found disturbing. They were killer's eyes, cold, calculating, missing nothing.

The man bowed slightly in a formal manner. "Welcome, you've had a long journey. Let me introduce myself. I am Mikhail Borisov. And you are, I believe, Katya Marston and Reuben Yoder. We have been following you for some time." He spoke good English and sounded like a New Yorker.

He took Roo's bag from the bodyguard. "Thank you Bebe," he said, clutching it to his chest, and turned to them. "I assume that the contents will be all I need."

Before Roo could stop her, Katya said, "Go ahead, you murderer. You might as well shoot us now. You have what you want." She became more and more hysterical, releasing all of the fear and heartbreak. Roo tried to calm her, but she jerked away from him. Borisov watched impassively.

"I don't intend to harm you," he said and gestured to Roo who led her sobbing to the huge couch. Although Borisov spoke to him, his eyes were on Katya, studying her closely. "You must not be afraid. I ordered one of my old colleagues, the Priest, to save you. He killed Stavrogin, known as Suvorov on my orders." Roo pictured Maxi lying in the snow in the forest.

Roo said, "What do you want then? Why are you holding us?"

"Believe me. I want to help you. I am an old friend of Katya's father."

Katya was still trembling from her outburst, and started at him in surprise and hostility. "Oh so you know him. So he is Russian, this man who abandoned my mother and me. It's even possible he murdered my mother. I find it hard to believe you want to help me."

"You must believe me. That is not true. He did not kill your mother." He walked over and stood above her, still holding Roo's bag.

"I do not know why you have come to Geneva, but I assume it is connected to this material." He gripped the bag even tighter. "I have been searching for this for a long time. It became necessary for my men to follow you, to protect you and bring you here." His smile was bleak. "Now I must study the documents you have brought me. Anya will take you to rooms. I am sure you need rest after your long journey. We will meet again later," he said, closing the door behind him.

Roo wondered if that meant in front of a firing squad. An old woman dressed in black, her round face and gray hair covered with a headscarf, led them to a luxurious suite of rooms. A table was set in front of a crackling fire. The woman left and returned with a tureen. "Tschi. soup," she said. A tray of assorted cheeses, black bread, and fruit accompanied the liquid. She gestured for them to sit down. She spoke very little English, but her eyes were kind.

Roo ate quickly. He needed strength and didn't know what to expect. He had read that Borisov was an oligarch who had been thrown out of Russia. The man lived in luxury, yet Roo sensed from the hard hungry look in his eyes and the terrible dent in his face that his past life had been one of deprivation. Obviously, the man feared for his life. This place was like an army camp. Katya, still standing by the fire, said in a choked voice, "How can you eat at a time like this?"

"I have to," he said. Spurred by his example, she sat down and tried to eat some of the soup. When they finished, Roo walked around the room, looking out at the mountains wrapped in shadows. He crept over to the window and tried to open it and jerked back. He had looked straight into the frightening rubber face of Bebe grinning like a Halloween mask. He quickly dropped the idea of trying to escape.

He turned to Katya, still sitting at the table. "Listen. I think it's ok. I know this guy is bad, but I think he would have killed us right away, after he got what he wanted." He didn't know if this was true, but sensed, the way Borisov looked at Katya, that he was not going to kill them.

Mikhail hurried to his study, thinking over his plan. If he killed and buried them here, only Sasha would know of the Tsar's order, and he also would soon be gone.

He tore open the bag and at last, possessed the key to the treasure, what he had been seeking for years.

As he eagerly read the material, it seemed he finally knew all of the Raven's secrets. He was brought up short by the poignant last photograph of the Tsar and his family, knowing who had taken the picture. It was all there, everything he expected. The Tsar's deeds and titles would make him legitimate, and the fortune would take him back home, to power. He moved to ring for Bebe. It was time to get rid of the girl and her escort, time to prepare for his return to Moscow. Then he read the notes in the archive written by Christina.

He stopped, his heart thumping painfully. He imagined the Raven's hand on his shoulder, pulling him back from ordering the murders of the two, guiding him back to the haunting revelations in the French Files. Opening the file box, he read the startling documents once more as if somehow the words would determine his decision. But it was Christina's letters; they diminished his desire to possess the *ukase*. When he reached her last words, the desire ceased to exist.

He had wanted this archive desperately, had killed for this, but it no longer mattered to him. Undermined by a sudden unexplained exhaustion, he began to sob as though his body would break. He knew he would never go home.

He thought of Katya and a huge weight like a heavy stone moved in his chest. The treasure belonged to her. He wanted these last minutes with her; he must try to save her. The man with her was very protective, but he was a novice, no match for Sasha's thugs. He gazed at the documents once more, and then placed them in an old worn leather folder.

Borisov appeared in their room almost furtively. His face had aged dramatically, the powerful haughty expression replaced with sorrow and vulnerability. They both stood up, expecting to be ordered out in the wilderness to be shot.

"Please sit down." He poured them a glass of wine, which Katya grudgingly took from him. "I must tell you this story from long ago. Twenty-five years after the Russian Revolution when Stalin was dictator and ruined so many lives, two boys were born in one of his prison camps. Their mothers died in childbirth."

Borisov paced the floor in front of the fire. "The boys were removed from the prison orphanage when they were five. They had only each other. I was one of those children who became a lost boy." Katya was astounded, remembering Eugenia's photograph of the babies with shaved heads in their cribs.

"The other child, who spent most of his life in prison, became a healer and a mystic. He believes he is reincarnated and calls himself the Shaman. He has the strange gift of prophecy and healing which I have witnessed." His voice had taken on urgency, and he paced in front of the fireplace.

"He believes he is the heir to the last Tsar. He was once my brother but has become my enemy and is in league with important people in the government to take control of Russia. To achieve this, he needs the Tsar's last *ukase*. I, too, have been searching for years for this document, but I have come to the decision that neither of us must have this power. You must go to Geneva and take possession of the treasure. The Shaman is here, hiding somewhere in the mountains. His men have been seen in the village. I will meet him soon."

"The Shaman is here, hunting us." Katya's voice choked with fear.

He ignored her exclamation. "I have told him you both were murdered in the forest in Ohio. It will not be easy for you to escape. The Shaman has men everywhere. We must wait until just before sunrise tomorrow, but I will not be able to protect you for long. They are closing in." He gazed for a long moment at Katya and left.

Borisov summoned Roo later that night. He was sitting in the chair by the large glass window, cradling an assault rifle as though it were a baby. Outside the mountains hunched like fierce beasts. The fire had died into little coals, giving way to the dark. The Russian had been working on papers and now placed the last of them in a leather folder.

"Take this." Borisov returned Roo's bag. "Everything is there." Then he handed him a Makarov pistol. "In case they ambush you, it might give you a chance. If they capture you, I suggest you use it on you and the girl." He gave Roo the old leather folder. "This is for her if you escape. But do not give it to her until she is safe. We can hope

I have deceived the Shaman, and he still believes you both are lying dead in the forest."

When Roo returned to his room, Katya was standing by the door naked, her clothes dropped on the floor. Embarrassed, he turned to go.

She said, "I was waiting for you." He thought she had totally flipped out, but was not going to argue.

She pulled him down to her softness, whispering, "We have until tomorrow to live." He made passionate love to her, as though he were a scout moving in the wilderness, exploring her. He had the dream of walking through the forest, searching and find his home.

Chapter 57

Roo-Katya
Courchevel, France

EARLY THE NEXT morning, in the dark, a man wearing a military uniform and a balaclava led them to the edge of the mountain. He did not speak as he opened the high metal fence and motioned them out, hurrying them along down a steep path cut through deep snow near a high cliff, until they came to the curving trail to the village. The snow had been cleared from the trail, but in the below zero temperature, they slid, nearly falling, not knowing where he was leading them, expecting gunshots to ring out any moment. Katya was running, out of breath, the word *mochit*, like a sharp siren, ran through her brain. They were here. The men who had tried to kill her that day on the slope were hunting her again.

Now they were down in the center of the resort, sliding down the snowy path, passing the chic shops and restaurants. Everything was still and frozen in the sunrise. The resort slept, pampered under the soft blanket of snow, too quiet for Roo's comfort, and he gripped the gun Borisov had given him. Only the few who swept the sidewalks and manned the shops were out on the street. They followed their escort to Rue des Tovets where some vendors at the market were setting up their stalls. The market people, who drove their small vans through the mountains to all the ski resorts in the area, came to Courchevel on Wednesday and Thursday. Their stalls spilled out at the edge of the street, selling ski clothes, honey, candies, sunglasses, sausages and cheese. Katya had always browsed through the market after skiing, so it was familiar, and yet very strange in the first light of day.

Their escort led them to a man waiting in front of a honey stall. "This is Fredric. He will take," their guard said in broken English and then left. Fredric, a tall dour man who had not shaved for a few days, nodded gravely. Even though the sun had just risen, he already had stacked his jars of honey, soap, and candy on red checked cloths next to a stall with knit wear and sun glasses.

He motioned for them to get in the back of a small white van parked behind the stall and then jumped in the driver's seat. They crouched inside, waiting and watching out of the tiny back window while a black Range Rover with darkened windows cruised slowly past. It seemed like forever.

"The Shaman must know we're here," Katya whispered.

Roo gripped her arm to stop her trembling as the car returned and again drove slowly past the street. Through the van's tiny back window, he glimpsed a shadowed face and a glint of metal. The car continued on, creeping up, past the Croissette, toward the ski lifts.

Fredric immediately spun the van around before speeding out of the resort and down the mountain taking the curves at breath taking speed. A rush of silver light and snow swept by them. Roo steadied Katya as they bumped around in the back of the van. Fredric drove like a maniac, passing near the edge of deep chasms. Only a few inches kept them from plunging down the mountain. As they flew through the lower resort, 1650, an SUV waited by the hotel on the turn but made no move to come after them. Roo let out his breath when they left the resort area and continued more slowly down the mountain toward La Praz.

Now that they were safely out of Courchevel, Katya began to think of Mikhail and felt some sympathy for her mysterious father's friend. Even though she knew he was a thug, he had helped them get away.

As they swerved around the road, she said, "Why would he do this? Why give up the archive and help us escape?"

"I don't know. I didn't tell you, but I thought he was going to kill us when we first arrived. He didn't seem like a man who would worry about anyone else. He probably didn't plan it this way."

He remembered the oligarch's dead eyes, like being in the nothingness of the darkest mine when Borisov shuffled over to him like an old man and gave him the leather folder and the gun. Roo struggled with his words. "But in the end he seemed tired, maybe just like someone who wanted to go home, wherever that is."

Mikhail sent his last message to the Shaman. *Meet me in the National Forest.*

The reply came instantly. *Yes, Noch, I am coming for you. I know where you are.*

There was a chill in Mikhail's stomach, and he experienced the drop into that strange dark void in his mind when it was time to kill.

"The girl in the photograph," he murmured. He looked at Katya's picture once more and smiled grimly. He had been willing to torture and murder her for the *ukase* and its power. Now, his quest seemed empty and futile. He was tired of running and hiding, living like a convict. He only wanted to save her. The sun was streaming in, and if all had gone well, Katya had made it down the mountain.

Maybe he could stop Sasha and reason with him without killing him. They were brothers once. Mikhail was mystified at how he had survived and become the Shaman, of what he must have suffered and overcome. Yet Sasha had always believed that he held immense power within him. Mikhail too believed in him and had been his instrument at times of his potency.

Before he joined his men, he took a last look out at the trees, picked up a volume of children's poetry and began reading a verse by Daniil Karms, a Russian poet who had been tormented by the secret police.

Even as he grouped his men in formation to destroy the Shaman, Mikhail wished that they could be brothers again. But they were lost, all lost. Lines from Karms' poem raced through his head.

He kept going straight and ahead, and kept looking ahead.
He didn't sleep, he didn't drink, he didn't drink,
He didn't sleep, he didn't sleep, drink or eat.
And then one day at sunset he entered a dark forest,
And since then, since then, since then he has vanished.

Below in the resort, skiers gathered in the morning sun for their first run while Mikhail moved out into the National Forest with his Spetznaz ski patrol, his troops following in snowmobiles. Equipped with assault rifles, hand rocket launchers, and grenades from his weapons storeroom, they traveled past the chalet beyond the first line of trees, ready to attack.

But Sasha's men were there, behind the trees. His crack unit of over 50 men had been waiting for them all night. Mikhail was surprised by the numbers. It was an ambush; they were surrounded. Two of Mikhail's men were immediately hit. The others found cover or fought in hand-to-hand combat. Mikhail tried to defend his chalet, but then ran through the battle toward the attackers trying to find Sasha, to stop this. They were brothers. In his haste, he did not see the two men invading the chalet. Mikhail was bewildered, stunned by men dying around him. Where was he? Where was he? He saw flashes of the Gulag, Afghanistan, and the stickmen attacking the Ark.

Just ahead of him, Sasha appeared in a long white robe like a vision from an icon. Mikhail stumbled and fell in the deep snow, and struggled to his feet in front of the Christ like figure. He could see that he still did resemble the Sasha he knew even after all these years. He was frail, had not grown near to Mikhail's height. His hair and beard were long and gray. Mikhail reached out to him, but was rebuffed. He tried to reason, but his words sounded strangely out of place as though he was speaking a different language.

He shouted, "Who is the powerful friend in the Kremlin? Maybe we can make a deal. Can we stop this and talk?"

Sasha put his hand to his lips for silence, just as he had done long ago when they were children. His eyes grew light, almost white, and Mikhail found himself drawn in, held to them like a prisoner.

"*Noch*, you must tell me where the *ukase* is hidden," He demanded in a high voice, over the clamor.

Mikhail said, "I have given it away. It does not belong to either of us."

"You traitor." His face dissolved into hatred. His robe was open, showing the tattoo of sun and rays on his emaciated chest. "I am the one designated by blood. Did you not know this? The Elder anointed me. Can't you see the Rapture? Look at me." He was the last image Mikhail saw. Sasha, his arms wide, stood in the blinding light exploding around them.

Fredric was speeding out of Le Praz, a charming old skiing village. Katya and Roo swayed, hanging onto each other. A giant roar ripped through the air, shaking the earth, and the mountain blasted into a mass of red in the sky.

Chapter 58

Katya
New York: March 2002

KATYA KNEW THIS was all. First, she heard the trickle, then dripping. The picture comes first in black and white; she smells blood. It is dripping, then pouring, gushing in sheets, then clots, filling up, inundating the faces, cascading down. Abigail, Eugenia, sightless behind the screen of blood, Henny in surprise. Then they are gone as blood fills the screen. She waits, eyes closed in terror as the picture loops around like a video, returning again to the trickle. It plays over and over, never ending.

Katya opened her eyes: it was gone. She had been screaming for Roo and felt the touch of a hand. Mercedes, her housekeeper was sitting next to the bed, anxiously watching her.

"It's all right, all right," she said soothing her. "The policeman Roo was here this morning. He has come every day."

Katya sat up. "How long have I been like this?"

"A week. They put you in the hospital for two days, but then decided it might be best for you to be here, and for me to take care of you," she said.

"Thank you Mercedes. You're so kind," she said, nervously waiting for the nightmare to return. Later in the shower, she remembered the explosion and the car going into the ditch at the side of the road, and then she was flying in the air. She could hear echoes of sirens, and smell burning steel and flesh.

When she came out of the bathroom, she asked, "Did anyone call?"

"Yes, Reuben Yoder called while you were in the shower. I'm sorry I wanted to get you, but he said no, that if you were all right, it wasn't necessary to speak with you." Mercedes was apologetic.

Katya tried to hide her disappointment and hurt.

"I am sure he will call again soon," Mercedes said, but Katya wasn't sure. In fact she thought he might never call again. Why should he?

As she drank the tea her housekeeper brought her, the scenes returned. They are back in the van. The driver, his head bleeding, goes on. She must have blacked out. Then they are waiting in a bank office.

Olivier Rognan, a sleek perfumed young man in a St Laurent suit greets them perfunctorily; his moist dark eyes dart like a lizard's over their rumpled clothes. She remembered holding out the account numbers from the mug shots and her own ID. After reading the instructions, he does not blink an eye when she presents her half of the torn photograph. He examines it carefully, looks up, and asks them to please wait. His heels click smartly on the marble floor.

She studies the columns, and the brass fittings on the table which all weave together precariously. The banker returns and from an envelope, produces the other half of the photo. Roo holds her while they watch him match up the jagged edges. Complete, it reveals a picture of a swastika on an arm. But then, did she remember this correctly or was she dreaming it? The room turns in front of her.

Olivier has a sharp intake of breath. Roo has an astonished look on his face.

It is a photograph of the Tsar, a close up of the tattoo on his arm. Olivier leads them to another room with gates protecting safety deposit boxes.

He returns with the safety deposit box, and places it on a large marble table in the middle of the room. "Please ring when you are finished." He points to a button on the table and is gone.

She drops the key on the floor, it clatters, and Roo picks it up. The key sticks in the lock for a moment before it opens.

Everything faded after that to her last memory of the police waiting for them outside the bank. She finished her tea and leaned back on the couch, looking down on Mercer Street. She did not know what had happened to the treasure.

Chapter 59

Roo
New York: March 2002

THE TSAR'S AMAZING treasure, the documents for the billions in gold bullion stored at the bank, the deeds to the vast natural resources of Russia flashed before Roo while he was getting a haircut from Lionel and walking in the crowded streets in New York. As he sat in Devlin's office eating a bagel with cream cheese and staring out at the skyscrapers, events from that day played past him, still astonishing him.

First the roar, like a giant crazed beast, and then enormous pine trees, rocks and earth hung suspended in the blue sky, flames shooting up around them. The driver panicked, flying off the road, throwing them from the van. He could still hear an echo of sirens coming up the mountain. The burning charring smell filled his nostrils as he lay on the ground. Amazed that he was all right, he was terrified, sick until he found Katya lying in a ditch awake but dazed. He picked her up and carried her back to the van. Fredric, a stunned look on his face, blood in his hair from hitting a rock, stood by the van. He motioned for them to get back in the van. They raced down the mountain. Then they were running into the bank.

More pictures came to him. He and Katya, still shaken from the explosion, stood in confusion, not knowing what to do with the treasure until Rognan, the banker suggested they change the account number and leave it in the bank for the time being.

Then he remembered the expression on the banker's face after answering the phone. Armed men were outside. He saw Katya clinging to the table in the safety deposit room and collapsing on the steps of the bank.

Roo recalled the first news announcement he had heard in the Geneva police station, which so far was still all they knew.

CNN reported an explosion in the French Alps, which tore away half the mountainside and destroyed the luxurious residence of the exiled oligarch Mikhail Borisov. There was speculation that it was a war between two Russian gangs. Police believed that a grenade hitting an arsenal of weapons and ammunition, illegally stored by the oligarch, caused the giant explosion. Fire fighters were still struggling to control the blaze, and emergency workers were on the scene.

They found no survivors in the vicinity. Roo still was stunned. Chalet, everything, everyone wiped out like they'd never been. Only a few residing nearest to the chalet had minor injuries from the impact.

Still waiting for more reports from French police, he resumed filling out forms closing the case on Abigail and Christina. There was enough evidence to prove that Maxi Suvorov, alias Stavrogin was their killer. Suvorov, working for both Borisov and the Shaman, had been careless in spite of his training. Crime scene investigators found miniscule specks of blood on his knife that matched the DNA of both women.

Then two days ago Geoffrey Banks, the assistant at the gallery, was cleaning out Suvorov's office and discovered a hidden locked drawer in his desk. Breaking it open, police found a cache of incriminating evidence: maps of the area around the cabin in Tecumseh County, the address of the apartment in Battery Park near the Trade

Center where Abigail had been tortured and murdered, and most important, a receipt from Petrosian for rental of earth moving equipment dated September 12. He figured Maxi and his men had disguised themselves as emergency workers while dumping Abigail's body. Also found in the drawer was a gynecological instrument used to torture Abigail. Roo couldn't even look at it.

He stared glumly out the window at the pigeons, thinking of that day he found the small piece of evidence that placed Maxi at the scene of Christina's death. The link of gold he had discovered near Christina's body was from the chain holding Maxi's lorgnette, broken during her murder and later repaired.

The other murder cases in Ohio, including the night watchman's, remained open. Although Suvorov's method of killing seemed to point to his murder of Eugenia, and the bikers next door, they were still working on that case and on Henny's murder.

Roo looked over at Devlin. "Petrosian has been picked up and charged with accessory to murder. He claims he knew only Maxi and rented the equipment to him. There was a lead to someone in Little Odessa. The place was raided, but it was abandoned. Immigration reports that the four men we wanted to question have returned to Russia." He had the sinking feeling lack of evidence meant the cases would be officially closed. Rage and sorrow over Henny's death made him determined to hunt the killers down.

Devlin said, "I've contacted the Russian government asking for detailed information on Borisov and the Shaman, and for extradition of Kayakov and the other four witnesses. So far, they have refused our requests. We'll just have to hope the State Department can do something."

He wanted to ask his boss any number of questions, but hesitated. Devlin had not explained why he was out of contact. He claimed that he had believed in Roo's expertise and thought if he tried to reach him, he would have blown his cover. He had contacted Ben soon after Roo and Katya boarded the airplane to Paris.

Finally Roo said, "I still can't figure out who was following Suvorov in the forest and actually killed him before he could kill us. Borisov claimed his colleague from Vietnam, someone called The Priest, saved our lives. Maybe it was one of the men back in Russia. I'm just trying to tie things up."

Devlin smiled. "Sounds like nonsense to me. Borisov was not someone you could trust to tell the truth. Anyway, we'll never find out. Their government doesn't release that kind of information."

He quickly changed the subject. "You know, you performed brilliantly. You're a gifted detective. How about sticking around for a while? I could use an assistant." His thin melancholy face looked wistful.

Roo's spirits rose at the praise, but he didn't know what to say. What came out sounded false.

"It's been great working for you. I learned so much. But I don't know. I have to go home first and talk it over with Stumpy. I owe him a lot. He's counting on me." The sheriff was still in shock; his voice had crackled over the phone, asking Roo to get back as soon as he could.

Devlin said, "There's no hurry. Take your time to think it through. See you later. I have a meeting with State Department officials at the Russian Consulate."

Roo waited until the door closed, then took out his phone to call Katya, put it down, picked it up again, his hands sweating. When he thought of her, a great empty chasm opened inside him. It was hopeless. She would reject him. What could he offer someone like her? A shack with a yard filled with Ben's old cars? Now that they were back in place in New York, he could see the great gap between them. He remembered his parents, silent, angry, sitting in the kitchen. His mother, a college graduate, a town girl, wouldn't go near the barns or fields, considering them foreign hostile territory. Yet his parents had more in common, both being from Tecumseh County, than he did with Katya. They must have been in love at one time, thinking it could overcome everything. And it couldn't. So that was it. He would make it easy for her and wouldn't call her before he disappeared back into Tecumseh County. Yet his heart was sore like he'd been punched in the chest. He missed seeing her, missed everything about her. But he admitted to himself that he pursued the case because he wanted success as much as he cared about her.

Finally he weakened and called Geoffrey at the gallery to check on her as he had every day since she recovered.

"Hi, it's Roo. How is she?"

"She hasn't been down yet today." Geoffrey's voice was agitated, going an octave higher. "Look. I have to say this. I think you're being a prick. Maybe you have a chip on your shoulder. She doesn't let on, but I know from the look in her eyes that she's unhappy waiting for you to call. That's it. You won't punch me out will you?"

Roo laughed uncertainly. "No. Maybe you're right."

Chapter 60

Roo-Katya
New York

DEVLIN CAME INTO the office, hung up his dripping rain-coat, creating huge puddles on the floor, and poured a cup of coffee

"Terrible weather," he said, sitting at his desk, removing papers from his briefcase.

Roo nodded in agreement and returned to the report from French authorities that had come in yesterday afternoon. The fire from the explosion was extinguished, and the authorities confirmed that parts of 48 bodies had been found scattered near the house, and the search was continuing. Not all the dead have been identified, but Borisov and a man called the Shaman were among the dead. French police believed many of the men were troops and bodyguards work-ing for the two men. Because it was Borisov's chalet and Russian passports were scattered among the remains, the French government had contacted Russian authorities and were working with them.

The newspapers also were reporting that Borisov, a fugitive from his country, had been wiped out by some paramilitary force from Russia, some suspected the FSB, the Russian intelligence ser-vice. But the Russian government denied any involvement.

Devlin looked over at him, impatience in his dark eyes. "This is turning surreal. We're trying to work with both French and Russian authorities, but have no jurisdiction. The Russians refuse extradition for all the men, including Kayakov."

He lowered his head to read the paper in front of him then said, "General Letinov, official spokesman for the Russian government, has finally made a statement. He claims that the Shaman had no connection to the Russian government and that this was a private gang war. He also says that Mikhail Borisov, a notorious murderer and gangster, was wanted by the Russian government."

Roo said, "It's strange that there was no mention of the *ukase*." The Russians didn't know or didn't ask about the motive behind the blast.

"Yes, if there was someone in the government involved, perhaps they thought it wise not to mention it."

"I think Suvorov was brainwashed by the Shaman. He truly did believe that the man had great spiritual power and would take over the Russian government and Suvorov would be part of it." Roo said. "The only information we have on Kayakov and the Shaman is from Interpol. They knew Kayakov had been in prison and recruited many of his followers there. But this is the weird part. The Russians claim they have no files on the Shaman and no record of Borisov's past before 1970 when he was registered as a KGB operative."

Devlin turned in his chair to look at Roo. "Both the Shaman and Borisov were planning coups. Probably wouldn't have worked, even if they had allies in the Kremlin. Neither one would have adequate support or resources."

"Unless they had the Tsar's document and the treasure." Roo was thinking much more would be clear if only they could question Kayakov. He might be the only witness still alive who had that vital information.

Roo stared down at his computer and jumped in excitement. "Look at this," he said. "Interpol says Russian troops have attacked the Shaman's camp and wiped out everyone. Damn, Kayakov and the other witnesses might have been hiding there."

Over the next week Roo kept busy tying up aspects of his own case, reveling a little in his success, and still avoided calling Katya. He was putting off the brutal truth that she didn't care the least about him.

The day before he planned to return to Tecumseh County, he wanted to see her one last time and used the excuse of delivering the old leather folder Borisov had given him. He also wanted to tell her the oligarch was dead.

They met in the private gallery in front of the Tecumseh painting. She was not dressed up as he had expected, like one of the girls in 'Sex in the City'. Instead she wore a shirt and jeans, and her usual high heeled sandals. Her hair was down on her shoulders, and she looked pale and very fragile, like an angel in a Renaissance painting he once saw in a library book. They both pretended to study the picture.

"Borisov's dead. Killed in the explosion."

"Oh," she said, lowering her head. "I am truly sorry. I thought that might be the case. I know he saved us."

She smiled at him uncertainly. "I imagine you're famous now in the cop world. I want to thank you for saving me and for finding my mother. For everything."

The self-assured coolness had gone out of her voice, but she was still very formal. It was evident to him that she had returned to her world, and had realized she couldn't be involved with someone so far below her.

She said, "It is all so very sad. Abigail and the mother I never knew are gone. I will never get over the deaths of so many innocent people. I feel very lucky to have survived and know you're responsible."

"What will you do with the treasure?" he asked, shifting nervously back and forth. He was light-headed, and tempted, but not brave enough to take her in his arms.

"Do you remember that Mikhail Borisov told us he was an orphan? I keep thinking of the photograph of those two poor little boys."

"Yes," he said, picturing the oligarch standing in front of his fireplace, his dark eyes studying Katya with avid curiosity.

"I have been working with my lawyers and am placing it in a special fund to aid the orphans of Russia. The Tsar's titles to the mines and resources may one day be useful to the children." Roo was not surprised that she was giving away the fortune. He had known what kind of person she was for a long time.

They were silent, holding each other captive with their eyes. He wanted to lie down beside her, make love to her but knew it would never happen again. Their night together was a fluke, an insignificant piece of ancient history that she had forgotten.

He gave her the folder. "Borisov told me this belonged to you and asked me to give it to you when you were safe. I guess that means now."

She took it, running her hands over the worn leather cover with the double eagle. He stared at her lowered head and silently begged her, *Come live with me and be my love*. But Marlowe's lines did not give him the courage to face her rejection. He would go back to Tecumseh County, to the forest and would find the way to tell her what was in his heart.

"You know. It will take me a long time to get over this." She looked up at him, her eyes clouded with tears, and smiled uncertainly.

"You've had some terrible shocks." He swallowed hard. "I'm going back to Tecumseh County tomorrow. The sheriff needs me." He didn't mention that Devlin had offered him a job or that he was still on the case, outside the law, searching for Henny's killers. What was the point?

He thought she looked disappointed, but probably imagined it. "I have some things to do at the office, so I'll say good bye." He made no move to embrace her. They shook hands formally.

When Katya heard the elevator creak to a stop on the ground floor and the door open, something seemed to tear loose inside her. Before she knew what she was doing, she was going down the elevator, begging it to hurry, running past Geoffrey, out the door and down the street, tripping along in her high heels without a coat. People stared as she called to him.

Chapter 61

Katya
New York

KATYA WAS IN the gallery watching Geoffrey direct the hanging for a new show, a retrospective of Abigail's vast collection, dedicated to her memory. It was a final tribute to her guardian, all she could do. Now she was stepping back and was grateful that Geoffrey had agreed to manage the gallery until she made a decision. Her life in London and New York was on hold, and she was uncertain about her future. But she knew she must return to take possession of the Blood Archive, stored in Ben's garage and discover all she could about her mother. Much of her past was still a mystery.

And she did not know if she had any future with Roo, which she desperately wanted. He had not said that he loved her, asked her to marry him or return with him. He was the only one who understood it would take time for her to recover from the trauma; the man she had been sleeping with, had thought she loved, had been a killer.

She had thought the way Roo held her so tight, so close to ward off any danger, seemed to say all that, but why couldn't he tell her? She went back over the day they had spent together, the warmth and delirious lovemaking. The way he looked at her seemed to be of love, but was she interpreting this wrong? She had waited for his words, but there was only silence. She had tried to speak but couldn't. As he left, he said, "I will be back." But he did not say when or why. And she could not ask. She was tormented by the uncertainty. Would he abandon her? Would she be alone all her life like her mother in the cabin? Was she imagining that he loved her?

It had been over a week and she had not heard from him. His silence filled her with grief. So did he mean he might return to visit perhaps in a few years? She could not keep from crying and waved to Geoffrey who was in consultation with the caterer and took the elevator to the apartment. She slowly walked through the rooms, thinking it still was Abigail's not hers. Lonely, strangely removed, she glanced down at Mercer Street filling up with rush hour traffic; it seemed an alien foreign place to her. A snowstorm battered the streets, dimming the afternoon light.

She sat down on one of the couches and picked up the folder left to her by Borisov mulling over his curious behavior. The oligarch had claimed he knew her father, but had told her nothing more.. The room seemed to grow darker as she reluctantly opened the folder with a presentiment that it was connected to her past. It was divided into several sections.

Inside the first was a note.

Dear Katya, This is for you. I hope you will understand. The document concerning you is genuine, not a forgery. I did not know. The heart of another is a dark forest.

Her own heart thumped in fear. What could this mean?

She read the birth certificate slowly, the letters blurring. It recorded a birth on December 15, 1971, at Sisters of Charity New York Foundling Hospital, 590 Avenue of the America's, New York, N.Y. 10011. The baby, a female weighing six pounds, nine ounces, was named Katya Ivanovna. The mother, listed as Miss Christina Gartner, had no fixed address. The address of the father, Jack Reilly was unknown. Feeling the blood rush to her head, she read it again.

Then with shaking hands she turned to the translated attached note.

From the KGB file of Mikhail Borisov. May 12, 1970.
Mikhail Borisov, cover name Jack Reilly, has been sent under guard from New York to Moscow and is now held on my authorization for interrogation at Lubyanka for refusal to follow orders to eliminate Christina Gartner. This woman was a spy deliberately sent to disrupt our mission. The Raven

She dropped the note. Mikhail Borisov was Jack Reilly, her mother's lover, listed as her father on the birth certificate.

She rushed over to the mirror, staring at her reflection and saw Borisov's eyes with the golden sparks in her own. He had been tortured and sent to prison for refusing to kill her mother. She read the document again, and then sat for a long time, stunned, thinking of them, imagining them together. She did not know how long she remained motionless in shock, but felt cold and put the throw on the couch around her before going on.

She next looked at an old photograph of an exotic young woman, posing against barren hills. Her beauty is breathtaking and seems somehow separate from any time or place. Her hair is braided in elaborate circles around her face. She has tawny skin and dark almond shaped eyes and wears elaborately embroidered silk robes and leather boots. Written on the back of the photo is *Mongolia, 1946.* She shivered at the tiny drops of blood near the bottom. A second photograph, snapped in 1945 with a different camera shows the same woman with an older man in uniform who looks slightly familiar. He has strong perfect features, with deep blue eyes and light hair slicked back in the style of the day. His thin lips curve in a slight smile.

She studied the couple for a long time before reading the ornate script written in English on the sheet of expensive paper, torn from a journal.

July 1945: Rumors through my network that a child of the alleged Grand Duchess was alive, led me to return to Mongolia. My first mission in 1921 was to spy on the Suvorovs, the Tsarists who were in charge of a noble young woman staying in the Baron von Ungern-Sternberg's camp. My nom de revolution to my Bolshevik masters was the Raven. I escaped the crazed baron in 1921 shortly after the Suvorov party, and later learned that the alleged Grand Duchess or whoever the young woman was, died in childbirth, hiding from the Bolsheviks.

Years later, standing before me was the object of my search, the unknown noble woman's daughter, Princess Bayer Gun, guarded by the monks and nomads living in private apartments in a hidden Buddhist monastery, near Muren Kure. Even in my private journal, I dare not reveal the location of this monastery, hidden so well in the wilderness that the Soviets had not yet found and destroyed it.

My bitter feelings toward women, a result of my experience with my lover who betrayed me, changed dramatically upon seeing this lovely young woman years younger than I. Her beauty was remarkable, the end result of her royal mother's union with a prince, a direct descendant of Genghis Khan. She looked like an ancient goddess in her dress. Our love was sudden, gripped both of us, a strange ecstasy. She said, 'I've been waiting for you. You have come, just as the Living God prophesied.'

What do I remember? Her smooth dark skin, her exquisite profile in the light of the fire in the Mongol prince's tent; the curve of her body as she lay beside me on the large fur rug. Those passionate nights remain with me and fill me with regret. I could not then take her with me. Her existence as a possible Romanov survivor could not be known. A threat to Stalin's rule. She would have been killed instantly. I vowed to get her out to be with me, and made plans for her escape.

The day I was departing, she went to the temple and sent a thousand prayers to heaven on the prayer wheel. "It is all here," she said. "What we know. All has been prophesied." I felt I never would see her again.

Katya was mystified, sensing this must have some connection to her. Her mouth was dry, and she poured a glass of water from the kitchen and tried to still her beating heart. What did it mean, the question turned over and over in her mind. She returned to the sitting room to continue. The document, on delicate thin parchment was written in English in plain round script, like a schoolgirl's.

March 1946

My mother died when I was born. I never knew her real name or identity but believe she was Russian, of noble birth. My father's people and the monks raised me. I was hidden away from the destroyers, the communists among our own people, who would murder me. I have been lonely even though the monks who shelter me and hide me from the destroyers of monasteries are very kind. Then the day came. I saw a figure trudging toward me through the Mongolian wind and snow. I wanted to shout that at last he has entered my world. My life of seclusion ended, as prophesied. We had little time, but I knew I could love only him. The Raven was not a young man but so vigorous, so loving that I experienced all in those few days. I knew he would be the father of my child. The monks believe it will be a boy, the one designated by blood.

It is months since he has gone, and I am growing large with his child.
He has sent the guardians. Tomorrow we leave, crossing Mongolia into
China and then when I am free, I will meet him again. It is dangerous,
but I am not afraid.

Princess Bayer Gun

Katya was intrigued. The exotic young woman in the photograph had written this. It came to her that all these documents had
come from different sources, and that Borisov had collected and
translated those in Russian for her. She went on to a handwritten
letter addressed to Lavrenty Beria, head of Russia's secret police.

Dear Lavrenty, Please give me any information as to the location of the
party I sent to rescue the girl as agreed with you. I am pleading with
you to find her. Your payment is waiting. The Raven

Just below that was Beria's note of reply, typed on an index card.

My dear comrade, There has been a terrible mistake. I am deeply sorry
to tell you that an army patrol accidentally came upon the Princess and
the rescue party. Before the men were shot, their interrogations revealed
that the Princess was taken to the Gulag. Lavrenty Beria

Next was a letter addressed to Petr Kosloff.

My Dear Kosloff
I am forever grateful to you for rescuing the boy with the help of Suslov
who has now defected. I discovered from Suslov how the boy's mother
died. As you know, the other boy is a foil to protect him. To further
shield the one designated by blood from authorities, he was not given a

name, although he was known as Noch at the Ark. I will give him the
name of Mikhail Petrovich Borisov.

My humble thanks, the Raven

Katya's mind was racing, as she looked at the photo of the two
tiny boys by side by side in the crib. It was the same one Eugenia had
found in her father's papers. Borisov, her father was one of those
boys.

She opened another section of the folder and found three
photographs. The first one was of the Tsar and his family before they
were imprisoned. The second is the Suvorov party and the sad elegant young woman standing near the temple in Mongolia.

The text in English on three different pages appeared to be from
a diary written toward the end of the Russian Civil War, long before
she was born.

Mongolia: 1921
Heartbroken, I said farewell to my friends today and await my fate in
this desolate place. It is my fault that poor Countess Suvorova is dead,
beaten to death because she pleaded for me not to be left behind. The
Baron has ordered that I must stay and marry the Prince. Our issue
will rule his new empire.

I have seen enough horror to no longer care what happens to me. My
family has been scattered to the winds. I do not know if any of them
survived. If they did they will have to hide forever. I have no identity
card and could be anyone.

I will continue to write in English because the Baron, my captor cannot
read it. I am at the mercy of an insane man, and am writing this as
proof that I exist.

I begin when we are imprisoned. I always tried to be as good as my sisters and to this day do not know what we did to inspire such hatred. I suppose it was only for being what we were from birth.

I think first always of being shut away from the outside world, and listening for the knock. When the guards came into the room, they were not human, but changed into beasts. They threw me down, to horrible pain and humiliation. I can still close my eyes and feel the blood flowing from me.

They came for us after the shootings and bundled us into a truck. We waited for one of the Brotherhood outside Perm in an old shack, a meeting place for the Bolsheviks. Then I saw from the window a figure appearing from over the horizon, bundled up trudging toward me. It was the Bogatyr, my hero. He bribed the guards and took my sister and me away. I fell in love with the Bogatyr, during the time he hid us and planned our escape. I do not know what happened to my sister. Another man called the Raven delivered me to the Suvorov's. I loved the Bogatyr but never saw him again. A Bolshevik agent murdered him.

When our party arrived at Urga in Mongolia, the black dogs roaming outside the city walls in the place of the dead terrified me. But I have become accustomed to them. They eat the flesh of the corpses lying outside the city, leaving the ground scattered with hair and belongings. I find Buddhism very comforting because the body is merely a depository for the soul. The Baron says he is a Buddhist, but his beliefs are a mix of shaman's rites, fortune telling, and other superstitions.

The Baron is making forays into Russia, but I believe he will fail. The men fear and despise him. He is very dirty, his hair falls in lank strings around his shoulders, and he wears amulets of every kind, and an open filthy Chinese silk robe. He has made Urga a frightening place; people are murdered if they displease him.

The third page had small watermarks the size of tears.

The baron murdered my husband, Prince Bayer Gun. He was buried alive. The Baron did not touch me, claimed that I was the Mother of Empire. I am about to give birth to the Prince's child and have gone into hiding with the monks because the communists are hunting me. The baron has been defeated by the communists after many of his own men rebelled against his cruelty and is now dead.

In spite of the fact that life is within me, I long for death. It is the picture that I see, that obscures everything, has become all. It begins with a slight sound, a trickle, and I find to my horror that it is blood. It rains blood, flowing down carrying the faces of my family. I bathe my eyes to rid myself of the picture, but it makes no difference. Soon it may cover me, erase all. But I still dream that the Bogatyr, my lover, will appear on the horizon from over the mountain, walking toward me.

Today a dark figure came on the mountain, and my heart leapt. He was coming for me. But as the figure moved closer, I saw that it was a wolf, howling in loneliness.

Frozen in disbelief at these words, Katya stared at the third and last photograph from 1921. It is the phantom girl from her nightmare at the farmhouse, her great grandmother.

Katya had found her family and knew their long sad journey through generations to her. Like the photographs, they travel past her. Her great grandmother and Prince Bayer Gun, standing to the side of the Suvorov group. Her grandmother, the Princess taken to the Gulag, her father Borisov born in the camp, son of the Raven, her grandfather; her own mother Christina murdered because of what she knew. She dropped the photographs but an image remained of her great grandmother, the phantom girl in the white dress who put her arms around her. She had been alone in wild Mongolia, waiting for her lover, who never returned.

Moving slowly in a trance, she closed the folder, and walked toward the window, a shadowy faint feeling coming over her. The snow is blowing hard in the wind over the golden mountains in Mongolia. She is drawing back the flap in the tent and sees a figure on the horizon. A man bundled up against the cold trudges across the mountain through the heavy snow toward her.

A loud blare from a truck horn startled her, and she saw that he was walking down Mercer Street. She heard the elevator to the apartment, then his steps and ran to open the door to fly into his arms.

Important Dates

1914–1918: World War I

1917, February to October: Russian Revolution. Tsarist government toppled. Tsar abdicates and is imprisoned. Civil War begins between the Bolsheviks and those who oppose them.

1917, December 15: Russia exits World War I.

1918, July 17: Murder of the Tsar and his family.

1921, February-March: Baron von Ungern-Sternberg drives the Chinese from Mongolia, brings the Bodg Khan from Manjusri Monastery to Urga and installs him as ruler under his influence. Mongolian Republic declared.

1921, September 15: Baron executed after defeat by the Mongolian and Red Army.

1922: End of Russian Civil War: Lenin and Bolsheviks in power.

1924, January 21: Lenin's death. Stalin begins rise to complete power.

1939–1945: World War II.

1953, March 5: Stalin's death.

1953, March 27: Beria Amnesty releases 1.2 million prisoners from the Gulag, many of them petty criminals. Political prisoners are not released.

1956–1975: American involvement in Vietnam.

1979–1989: Russian War in Afghanistan.

Biographies of Historical Figures

Yuri Andropov (1914–1984)

Leader of the Soviet Union from 1982 to 1984. He was head of the KGB, Russia's State Security Service from 1967 to 1982 and known for his ruthlessness in putting down the Hungarian uprising in 1956, and for the brutality of his agents. He died of ill health in Moscow and was buried in the Kremlin wall.

Lavrenty Beria (1899–1953)

Chief of Soviet Security and Secret Police, NKVD during World War II. Deputy Premier of USSR from 1946 to 1953. During Stalin's purge (1937–38) he and his organization tortured and killed many of the dictator's political enemies. After Stalin's death in March 1953, he made a grab for power but was arrested by a group lead by Khrushchev, Molotov and Malenkov. He was executed, cremated and buried in an unmarked grave in a forest near Moscow.

Bogd Khan (1869–1924)

Theocratic leader of Outer Mongolia in 1911 after the country declared independence from China. Also known as the Bogd Lama, he was the eighth Jebtsundamba Khutuktu, reincarnation of Taranatha, a renowned scholar and writer, and third in importance in Tibetan Buddhism after the Dalai Lama and Panchen Lama. In 1919 Chinese troops invaded the country and placed him under house arrest. He was freed in 1921 by Baron von Ungern-Sternberg, a renegade White Russian officer, and his troops, who drove out the Chinese occupiers.

He was returned to nominal power, but was controlled by the Baron. After the communist takeover later in 1921, the Bogd Khan remained on the throne as a figurehead until his death in 1924.

Leonid Brezhnev (1906–1982)

Leader of the Soviet Union. General Secretary of the Central Committee of the Communist Party of the Soviet Union from 1964 until his death. He succeeded Khrushchev and ruled over a period of economic stagnation. He died of a heart attack and was buried in the Kremlin Wall.

Nikolai Bulganin (1895–1975)

Deputy Premier, member of the Central Committee of the Communist Party and the Politburo. He served under Stalin as deputy Commissar of Defense during World War II. After Stalin's death he became a supporter of Khrushchev who forced him to resign his posts after he joined an attempt to overthrow him in 1957. He was retired on a pension and died in Moscow in 1975.

Khorloogiin Choibalsan (1895–1952)

Communist dictator of the Mongolia People's Republic, known as the Stalin of Mongolia. A great admirer of Stalin, he conducted Soviet style purges in the 1930's against "enemies of the revolution." Over thirty thousand Mongolians, among them many of the Buddhist clergy, were murdered. He continued to prosecute Buddhists and destroy their temples in an attempt to eradicate the religion. In 1949 Choibalsan fell out with Stalin over his refusal to back unification of Mongolia. However, he went to Moscow for treatment of kidney cancer and died there on January 26, 1952.

Felix Dzerzhinsky (1877–1926)

First head of the Cheka, the Bolshevik secret police, established in

1917. He organized the reign of terror to keep the Bolsheviks in power. Known as 'Iron Felix' for the Cheka's merciless torture and mass executions without trial, he died of a heart attack in Moscow and was buried in the Kremlin Wall.

Heinrich Himmler (1900–1945)

Head of the SS and from 1943 onward minister of the interior and head of the Gestapo, German secret police during World War II. At Hitler's direction, Himmler built and oversaw the concentration camps and directed the extermination of six million Jews, and other victims deemed undesirable by the regime. At the end of the war, Himmler tried to hide from the Red Army by disguising his identity, but was discovered and arrested by British forces. He committed suicide on May 23, 1945.

Adolph Hitler (1889–1945)

Dictator of Nazi Germany from 1934–1945. Hitler was responsible for World War II and the Holocaust, which resulted in the deaths of 6 million Jews and millions of others he considered racially inferior. His doctrine of anti-Semitism and lebensraum for the German people resulted in the Nazi occupation of most of Europe and North Africa. On 30 April 1945 when Germany faced defeat, Hitler and Eva Braun, his companion, were married forty hours before they both committed suicide. Their bodies were burned outside Hitler's bunker in Berlin.

Nikita Khrushchev (1894–1971)

Leader of the Soviet Union from 1953 to 1964 during the Cold War. He is known for his denunciation of Stalin's purge in his famous Secret Speech. He supported the early Soviet space program and attempted agricultural reforms. His reign at the height of the Cold War resulted in the erection of the Berlin Wall in 1961 and the Cuban

Missile Crisis in 1962. He was removed from power in 1964 by party colleagues and succeeded by Leonid Brezhnev. He died of a heart attack in Moscow and was denied a state funeral and burial in the Kremlin Wall. He was buried in the Novodevichy Cemetery in Moscow.

Admiral Alexander Kolchak (1874–1920)

Supreme Ruler of The White Siberian Government in Omsk from 1918 to 1920. Previously he was a Polar explorer and Commander of the Black Sea Fleet in 1916. He retreated by train from the Red Army advance to Omsk with his government and followers, including his mistress Mme. Timireva. During the retreat he was arrested by the Czech Legion on the order of General Janin and handed over to the Social Revolutionary government in Irkutsk. He was shot and his body pushed under the ice of the Ushakovka River.

Vladimir Lenin, born Vladimir Ilyich Ulyanov (1870–1924)

Leader of the October Bolshevik Revolution in 1917. He became head of the Bolshevik Russian government from 1922 to 1924. Once in power, he began to confiscate all private property, and ended Russia's involvement in WWI. He founded the Cheka and instituted the Red Terror to eliminate opposition and consolidate power. He died after a third stroke at his estate at Gorki, outside Moscow, was embalmed and placed on exhibition in Lenin's Mausoleum in Moscow on January 27, 1924 where he remains today.

Vladimir Putin (1952)

Current President of Russia. A KGB officer for sixteen years, he became Acting President after Yeltsin's resignation in 1999 and then Prime Minister. He was President from 2000 to 2012. After a change in election laws, he ran for a third term in 2012 and was re-elected President for a six-year term.

Joseph Stalin, born Iosif Dzhugashvili (1878–1953)

All-powerful Dictator of the Soviet Union from 6 May 1941 to 1953. He was General Secretary of the Central Committee from 1922 to 1953 and led the Soviet Union during WWII. He was a member of the Bolshevik party and took part in the Bolshevik revolution of 1917. As General Secretary, he consolidated power after the death of Lenin in 1924 and thereafter ruled by fear. He forced Russia to become an industrialized country and began an agricultural program, which resulted in famine in 1932–1933. During his repressive regime, millions of people were sent to the Gulag. During the Great Purge (1937–38) he eliminated his enemies and old Bolsheviks who were major figures of the revolution on the pretext of rooting out enemies of the government. Thousands were executed. Officially Stalin died four days after a massive stroke, but rumors abound that he might have been murdered by warfarin, a tasteless rat poison possibly added to his wine by Beria or Khrushchev. His body was embalmed and exhibited in Lenin's tomb. On 31 October 1961 it was removed from the mausoleum and buried in the Kremlin Wall.

Tecumseh (1768–1813)

Leader of the Shawnee and a large tribal confederacy that opposed the United States during The Indian Wars and the War of 1812. Tecumseh was born in Ohio in the Northwest Territory and fought against the settlers encroaching on Native American land. He aspired to unite all tribes into an independent Native American nation east of the Mississippi under the protection of the British. In the War of 1812, Tecumseh fought with the British against the Americans and was killed in The Battle of the Thames in October 1813 ending his dream of an independent Native American nation.

Baron Roman Nikolai Maximilian von Ungern-Sternberg (1885–1921)

Tsarist Lieutenant General in the Russian Civil War who became a renegade and with his mercenaries, took control of Outer Mongolia from the Chinese in 1921. He was called the Mad Baron because of his erratic behavior and torture and violent treatment of enemies and his own troops. His beliefs were a confused mixture of Buddhism, mysticism and superstition. The Baron's great ambition was to restore both the Russian monarchy and Genghis Khan's Great Mongol Empire under the rule of the Bogd Khan. He released the Bogd Khan, spiritual and political head of Mongolia, from the Chinese and put him back on the throne. During his short occupation of Outer Mongolia, von Ungern-Sternberg ruled through fear, intimidation, and capricious brutal violence. After a defeat against a combined Red Army Mongolian force in southern Siberia, he was taken prisoner and tried in Novonikolaevsk, found guilty and executed on September 15, 1921.

Boris Yeltsin (1931–2007)

First President of the Russian Federation, from 1991 to 1999 after the resignation of Mikhail Gorbachev and the final dissolution of the Soviet Union on 25 December 1991. He won re-election in 1996 but was unpopular after he introduced privatization of Russia's economy, which brought about a series of economic disasters. Much of the national wealth and resources became the property of a small group of oligarchs. Yeltsin attempted to dissolve parliament in October 1993 when it tried to remove him from office. He was responsible for the military attack on the Russian White House, which resulted in 187 deaths. On December 31, 1999 Yeltsin resigned and appointed Vladimir Putin as his successor. He died of heart failure on April 23, 2007 and was buried in the Novodevichy Cemetery in Moscow.

Read *The Blood Stiller, Book 1, The Russian Trilogy.*

Red Terror in New York.

New York socialite Christina Gartner befriends her White Russian neighbor and stumbles on a dangerous secret from her past linked to the Romanov murders. She is drawn into an émigré conspiracy and a passionate love affair and discovers she is on the kill list of a spy plotting against the Russian Government. This pacey historically accurate thriller weaves intrigue in Revolutionary Russia and contemporary New York into a compelling read.

Available at Amazon.com
The Blood Stiller, Book 1, The Russian Trilogy

Blood and Oil; The Devil's Tears, Book 3, The Russian Trilogy.
The question remains.

Did a Tsar's child survive the Ekaterinburg massacre? Midwestern Deputy Sheriff Roo Yoder hunts for a hundred-year-old treasure and a killer when his high school friend, a successful financier, is murdered. The only clue—a fragment of a share certificate—worth a fortune if the other half is found. Roo's discovery of a link between the missing certificate and his globetrotting uncle's connection to the Romanovs leads him to Baku. Stalked by KGB killers, Roo and an exotic bar dancer risk all to search for the other half of the valuable certificate and prevent an international crisis.

Available at Amazon.com
Blood and Oil; The Devil's Tears, Book 3, And The Russian Trilogy